MANHATTAN
62

MANHATTAN 62

REGGIE NADELSON

CORVUS

First published in hardback in Great Britain in 2014 by Corvus, an imprint of Atlantic Books Ltd.

10 9 8 7 6 5 4 3 2 1

A CIP catalogue record for this book is available from the British Library.

Hardback ISBN: 978 1 84354 839 3
E-book ISBN: 978 1 78239 134 0

Printed in Great Britain by TJ International Ltd, Padstow, Cornwall.

Corvus
An imprint of Atlantic Books Ltd
Ormond House
26–27 Boswell Street
London
WC1N 3JZ

www.corvus-books.co.uk

*For Vladimir Pozner, a Greenwich
Village guy, and true friend, with much
gratitude and affection*

The story of what would later become known as the Cuban missile crisis is replete with accidental figures whose role in history is often overlooked: pilots and submariners, spies and missileers, bureaucrats and propagandists, radar operators and saboteurs.

Michael Dobbs, One Minute to Midnight

The city, for the first time in its long history, is destructible. A single flight of planes no bigger than a wedge of geese can quickly end this island fantasy, burn the towers, crumble the bridges, turn the underground passages into lethal chambers, cremate the millions. The intimation of mortality is part of New York now; in the sounds of jets overhead, in the black headlines of the latest editions.

E. B. White, Here is New York

Before him lay Washington Square. Only eighteen hours in New York and he loved everything, every inch of it. Ah, the square!

Dawn Powell, The Golden Spur

New York City, 2012

WHEN THE SOVIET UNION finally fell apart, in the aftermath, there was a trickle of information, then a stream, then a tidal wave. It was the big story for a while, this tale of the goddamn Cold War, of them and us, politics and war, gulags, massacres, nukes, the KGB and CIA, and of the Cuban Missile Crisis. The truth—some of it—about the main actors and the accidental spies, the betrayals and lies; there was plenty of it, God knows, even here in New York City. But also about ordinary things, the stuff about the Russians—what they felt and secretly thought, ate, desired, the music they loved—that most of us had never been told. Most of us; I already knew some because of Maxim Ostalsky.

Still, in all that flood of information, there was nothing at all about my old friend Max. I did my share of looking. I even thought about going over to Moscow. But he had disappeared into thin air, as if he had never existed, like smoke from those Lucky Strikes he learned to love so much.

Max Ostalsky had been my friend, once. He was the most interesting man I'd ever met, different from anyone else, and there are times I still miss him. If he's alive, wherever he is, I can only hope he's forgiven me.

PART ONE

CHAPTER ONE

October 16, '62

TOMMY PERINO, WHO LIVED upstairs from me on Hudson Street, was twelve and small for his age. A skinny kid with a tuft of dirty blond hair sticking up from his head, he peered out at the world through narrow, wary blue eyes. Tommy didn't give much away. He lived with his father in two rooms, where they had made a life after the mother just took off and left them.

The old man worked the night shift at a cement plant by the river. The Perinos couldn't afford a television set and I had given Tommy a key so he could hang around my place and watch a ball game, maybe raid the refrigerator if he wanted. Some of the time he'd just show up out of the blue and scare the living daylights out of me like he did that Tuesday night in October when I was sweating out a bad dream.

It was the kind I had been having on and off since I came home from Korea, a messed-up kind of dream: somebody punching me in the face over and over, the stink of blood, somebody screaming my name out, in English, or that

Gook language they had, somebody else singing Russian songs, and James Brown moaning, "I lost someone, my love, Someone who's greater than the stars above", the 45 going around and around on my phonograph, "I'm so weak. Don't take my heart away."

I was getting sick, the weather changing, a bad cold making me hack like an old man. Only James Brown seemed real.

I pushed my way to the surface. Tommy was standing over me, his face streaming with blood. He was bloody and scared, and I crawled out of bed and pulled on some clothes.

"What happened? Tommy?" First thing I thought was that his pop got injured; the old man was a scrawny bastard to be lifting cement blocks. "But it wasn't his old man," Tommy said, and I got him into the bathroom, cleaned him up as best I could. It was only a scalp wound, lot of blood; nothing serious, except the kid was howling like a wounded animal. I had never seen him cry.

"What is it?"

"A body on the pier, out by the Hudson, the pier you took me to, Pat," he kept saying. Blurting it, almost incoherent. "I saw him. I wish I didn't see nothing. It didn't have almost no face, like they sliced it off."

"What time is it?" I looked at my watch: 11.27 p.m. "Stay here."

"I'm coming with you."

Jesus, I thought. OK. The kid was scared as hell. I grabbed sweaters for both of us. "Let's go. What the hell were you doing out there?"

"Nothing."

"Tell me."

6

"You told me you did it when you was a kid, you hung out on the piers, maybe find some salvage."

"It's dangerous. The Mob uses those piers for payback, you hear me? How often you been out there?"

He looked down. "Most nights. OK, I heard there's spies coming in on them salvage boats, you know, I heard those guys that look for old metal, chains, anchors, that stuff, and they been running in spies now. Reds. Fucking Commies. Russkis. Cubans. Gonna kill us all."

"Spies, my ass. Come on, Tom, there's no damn spies on the Hudson River. Chrissake, this is New York City, so we're going to take a look, then we'll get you to St Vincent's, get your head looked at."

Truth was, I didn't know anything about damn spies. I was a cop, a homicide detective. But the kid had seen something, and I got my car and we drove out to Pier 46 near the end of Charles Street, between Charles and Christopher, in fact, two minutes by car; three tops. I parked. We ran. Some of the boards on that pier were rotten; you stuck your foot through those soft planks, you broke your ankle. A sharp wind came off the river.

"Take it easy," I said to Tommy. "Where is it, this thing you saw?" Right then, I was more worried about the kid than what he said he had seen. He saw too many movies, always pestering me for some change to go to the pictures. When he was a little kid back when we figured the Russkis were gonna nuke us for sure, every time he heard a plane flying low at night, he'd run down to my place and bang on the door until I woke up and let him in.

"Pat? Over there. Look." Tommy stayed back while I looked at the black body bag. I knelt down next to it.

It had been slung against one of the shacks out near the end of the pier. A single bulb dangling from the shack's metal gutter moved with the wind, the pool of dim light shifting, but enough to catch the body bag. It was damp from the fog that lay on everything—the bag, the pier, my hands and face. The city was only a faint blur of lights, the skyline to the right barely visible.

I looked down. The bag was partway open. Tommy must have done it. I pulled the sides apart.

Inside was a man; what I could see, he looked young. His tongue had been cut out, the mouth forced open and stuffed with a pink rubber Spalding ball. Some skin on the face was gone. Nose sliced off. What was left was soaked in blood, and so was the fringe of black hair. When I scraped some of the blood away, I saw the hole in his forehead, made by a .22.

At first I figured it was Mafia. Like I told Tommy, the Mob used the desolate piers to beat up their enemies, sometimes murder them. Only the Mob did this kind of thing. Luca "Fat Cheeks" Farigno, that fat dwarf of a hoodlum, loved doing it; it proved his manhood; it was his signature. Everyone knew low-level hoods like Cheeks used the piers for payback; break your legs, cut off your ears. Ever since Pasquale Ebola's time, him and Tony Bender Strollo and plenty more that had been and gone. For sure this was a Mob deal; you talked too much, they ripped out your tongue.

Maybe the dead fellow was a homo who got caught in one of the Village queer bars the Mafia ran. The Mayor was getting rid of them, queers and gangsters both; he obsessed with the World's Fair coming in '64. Mayor Wagner didn't take shit from the Mob, he always liked to imply. They didn't like him. Hated him.

"Tommy?" I yelled out, but the kid had receded back into the fog. "Tommy?"

There was a payphone the other side of the shack. I put in a dime and called my precinct. The line was busy.

On a hunch, I got back on my knees, steeled myself, reached inside the bag. Fumbling in the mess of blood and gristle like an incompetent butcher, somehow I yanked out the left arm.

The tattoo was there, inside the elbow. The worm with the words entwined: Cuba Libre. Not again. Christ, not again! Not a second time. I had seen the tattoo before, months earlier, back in July; seen it on a dead girl's arm. Now this. The same goddamn thing.

I felt sick. Sick at the way people took human life like it was garbage and threw it away. Sick because once I saw the tattoo, in my gut I knew somehow Max Ostalsky was connected; or maybe it was what I wanted to believe; he had been my friend, once.

It had been four months earlier, but another life when I first met Ostalsky on a late spring day in Washington Square, the kind of day where girls with long hair lay in the green grass and read poetry, and somebody with a guitar on the rim of the fountain was playing that song about the damn lemon tree.

Next to me on the bench where I was taking some sun sat a young guy, looking at a hotdog guy a few feet away.

Until that day, I never figured buying a hot dog for a complicated operation. Never thought about it until that first time I saw Max Ostalsky, and he was sitting there on the bench next to the statue of Garibaldi, staring at the hot dog man with such a look of confusion, I felt for him.

Or was he standing by the statue? Afterwards, I can't remember if he was already on the bench when I first saw him, or if he sat down after me.

It's June, hot for spring, and he looks miserable in his heavy gray wool suit. He's maybe a few years younger than me, twenty-nine, thirty. Tall and lanky, handsome too, with dark hair that falls over his forehead, but in his glasses and that suit, he resembles a young old man.

He examines the change in his hand. He removes his glasses, then cleans them on the hem of his gray shirt, puts them back on, tucks in his shirt, then ponders the hot dog situation once more, face falling at his sense of failure.

In his hand is a notebook. Overhead the trees are already heavy and green.

Stretching my legs, I lean back on the bench and find a pack of smokes in my pocket, and think: I love this damn place. I love it. The Chesterfield I light up smells really fine. In my other hand is a Coke, the cold green bottle nice and icy in my hand.

Washington Square's only a few miles from where I grew up, but it's like the other side of the moon.

Washington Square!

That arch at the end of Fifth Avenue where Greenwich Village begins always feels like a gateway to all that's fun, free, interesting, sexy, an easy transit to a different world where there's music all the time, where nobody seems to care about making money, and artists and writers hang around the cafés and some of the girls consider a detective like me pretty exotic fare. Maybe seduce me away from my life as a cop into some decadent bohemia.

In my shirt-pocket is a red plastic transistor radio. I brought it for the game, but instead I'm listening to Ray Charles sing, "I Can't Stop Loving You." Ray's the greatest; except for James Brown.

"Got a match?" The girl asking is sitting cross-legged on the grass near me, a blonde in tight black toreador pants and a sleeveless black blouse that's cut in a way you can see plenty of pale skin through the armhole. I snap open my Zippo for her. Raising herself on one long tanned arm to get the light, she says, "Thanks. Cool threads."

It's true. I have on a sharp light-blue knit shirt with navy trim around the collar—it looks pretty damn Italian—that I wear, like they show you in *Esquire*, outside my new brown slacks. My tan leather slip-ons cost me fifteen bucks, but they're worth it.

I spend too much dough on clothes. My ma says I'm a vain bastard. My closet's jammed with sad items I never put on, including last summer's nautical navy blazer, and the white wash and wear pants, an outfit made me look like Joey Brown in *Some Like It Hot*. Not to mention the caramel-colored pinch-front made of some coconut fronds or something I ordered from Henry the Hatter.

The sun is hot on my face.

Then I realize that guy in that heavy gray suit is on his feet, still looking at the hot dogs, and I get the sense that he's foreign and lost. I toss my smoke away. "Can I help you, man?"

He looks at me. He smiles sheepishly. "No, thank you, I'm quite familiar with American customs, but thank you," he says, approaching the cart with conviction, sweat on his forehead. He surveys the hot dogs boiling in water, the relish and ketchup. The food man stares back at him. Who is this clown, the expression on his face says? Who is the hopeless young man, hesitating about the purchase of a hot dog?

Does he feel we're all watching him, me, the hot dog man, even the girl on the grass? His mouth moving, he's like a new convert faced with communion wafers, and thinking: do I chew? Bite? Swallow?

"I will take one of these, please," he says with real determination.

"Whadya want on it, pal?" says the hot dog guy, but the fellow just hands over some money, and hot dog in hand, retreats to the bench. He bites into the naked hot dog in a bun, no relish, no mustard or onions.

I can't stand it any more. "Man, you really do need help. Trust me. You can't eat it like that."

He seems perplexed.

"Come on."

I explain about the ketchup, the relish, the onions, the mustard, and he looks at me, clearly at a loss. "To tell the truth," he says, "I was not quite sure how much it costs for each of these extra items, or if one can have several or all. I did not quite expect this, you see, though I have read many books on New York, and about the United States, but they did not say how to do this hot dog, and I had no idea what is this thick red sauce, and the green sauce, or if I must order both. I have no idea if it is normal to eat it with my hands, and if not, where do I obtain a fork and knife?" He lifts his shoulders to show how hopeless he is, and smiles again.

This fellow has the kind of self-deprecating smile even a cranky hot dog vendor responds to.

"Give him the works," I tell the hot dog man.

My new pal in the suit eats. "Yes, I see, very tasty, really, would you say, delicious? Is this the right word?" he says, after he gobbles the dog, and I wonder what the hell he means "would you say delicious"? Finally, he removes the thick gray wool jacket, folds it neatly, sits back down on the bench. A smear of yellow mustard remains on his upper lip. A little sigh escapes.

"Thank you. Sometimes it is quite difficult to figure out so many choices. Everything is so tasty." His English is good, a little formal, a light accent, but fluent. "Are you also connected with New York University? I am an exchange student." He gestures in the direction of NYU on the east side of the park.

"I'm taking a class this summer."

Rising, the man puts out his hand. "Ostalsky, Maxim," he says.

I shake it. "Pat Wynne. Pleased to meet you, Maxim. Where are you from?"

"The Soviet Union," he says. "Moscow."

"Yeah? No kidding. You're kidding me, right? How long have you been here?"

"It is true, definitely," he says. "I have been here only approximately one week. This means I arrived in time for the summer sessions and I'll stay until next June. I have a Masters Degree in Moscow where I teach English at the university, now I begin my studies for a doctorate. Please call me Max. I am so grateful for your help." He folds himself back onto the bench. "To be honest, I was very hungry."

The Russki is looking around as if he's landed on some foreign planet, although he has solved the hot dog issue.

"I know how tough it is, being in a foreign place, man," I tell him. You could say I'm feeling generous with my time. I have the day off. The weather is good. "Let me tell you, I went over to Europe last summer, visit my relatives in Ireland, then Liverpool, in England, you know? I couldn't make out what the hell any of them were saying, or what to eat, or the money. It drove me crazy. You had to say white coffee if you wanted cream in it, or something, not to mention they drive on the goddamn wrong side of the road. Jesus H. Christ, the money, they got pounds and shillings. I couldn't understand anyone in Liverpool, and they speak English, you know? But what am I talking about, you don't care about my cockamamie cousins."

"Cockamamie?"

I explain. He chuckles, a low laugh that rises and explodes out of him in a way that makes several people turn to look at us. From his pocket, he takes a pack of Lucky Strike and offers it to me.

"Would you like one? I don't know if this is your particular brand, but if you would care to join me?" Beside him on the bench is a book.

"Sure, Max. Pleasure. What's that you're reading?"

"I am reading again short stories by Ernest Hemingway."

"They have American books in Russian?"

"Of course." He tells me that many American authors are popular, especially Ernest Hemingway. "We all like John Steinbeck and Jack London. Many homes have a portrait of Hemingway on the wall."

We light up and I'm, what? Surprised? Astonished?

Never in my life did I imagine I'd meet a real honest to God Russian Commie. Sure, I meet plenty of people in Greenwich Village who are pinkos—Reds, even; people who probably read Marx and do square dancing at Judson Memorial. This is different. This one's from over there, and my first impulse is that he's a spook. Has to be. Aren't they all?

If he is a spy, what the hell is he doing at NYU? Looking to infiltrate the university, or co-opt somebody, a vulnerable soft left-wing girl with sandals from 8th Street, someone he can seduce with all kinds of pie-in-the-sky promises?

Truth is, I'm pretty curious about the Russians. It's like some kind of itch. My time in Korea, son of a bitch little war, didn't make me exactly enamored of the Commies. I got drafted, and spent two miserable years there. Bastards wanted to slaughter you or brainwash you, turn you into some kind of dupe they could manipulate. It was how they got their kicks.

But it gave me this interest in Communism, and the Russians, who are the real goods and run the whole Commie show. So after the war, I got my BA on the GI Bill at Fordham. I studied a little Russian history.

I still read up. There's plenty to read—politics, economics, philosophy, old novels—but almost nothing about real people now, what they think, and feel, or wear or smoke. And now here's one of them, and he seems genial enough, with his smiling, and his compliments on the local food, and his curiosity, and I for sure have never thought of real Commies as sitting around looking to buy a hot dog, or grinning sorrowfully because they can't figure it out, or shaking your hand, seeming like a normal person.

Mostly, people think of them as dark dour men, like on that TV show, *I Led Three Lives*; me and my little sister would watch it on Friday nights, and she'd said, "Do Communists ever smile?" Our ma thinks they're Satan's messengers. Literally. She wrestles with the whole business, and goes to mass every day to pray.

My radio plays Gene Chandler doing "Duke of Earl"—Chandler had even dubbed himself the Duke of Earl—and I'm surprised to see this Ostalsky fellow listening attentively, and tapping his feet, just a little bit.

"These young men have quite such fantastic clothes," Ostalsky says to me, as we sit in the park and watch the passing parade. He doesn't mind seeming dumb about the stuff he asks, and we smoke and I keep up a running commentary as if the fate of nations depends on button-down collars, Madras plaid Bermuda shorts, drainpipe jeans, skinny ties, high-lapel three-button suits.

"What do you say about those shoes?" He's looking hungrily at some spiffy black boots with elastic insets.

I tell him how people in Greenwich Village are different from people uptown who wear suits and go to work in big corporations, the big glass and steel buildings they put up on Sixth Avenue after the War, and I tell him nobody in my whole life ever called it Avenue of the Americas. I give him the lowdown about Beatniks, and jazz, peaceniks and folk music, even rock and roll, people who just live like they want.

Max mulls this over. "But no discipline, I imagine?"

"That's the point, man. It's called freedom."

Does he have anything at all to wear except the heavy suit? Maybe I'll help him get some decent duds. Nosy son of a bitch that I am, I want to know what they wear over there in his dark mysterious evil country.

A cop who passes, glances at us and I can see he thinks we might be queer. I edge away from Ostalsky. It's getting to be late afternoon, and coming from the west side of the park right then is a nun; in her big black and white habit, she resembles a gigantic bird, and she's hurrying a clutch of little kids from St Joseph's towards the playground. A few of the older girls, in their pleated skirts and saddle shoes, set free, run in the other direction like young animals, their skirts blowing up so you can see their still chubby thighs and white underpants. "What is she?" Max asks.

"Who? The nun? She'll be one of the sisters from over at St Joseph's school. My cousin Oona went there."

"Whose sister?"

"You've never seen a nun?"

"No. I've never been inside a church."

"No kidding. Come on, man. I'll show you, if you want." He picks up his jacket, puts his notebook in his pocket.

"You keeping good notes?"

"Yes, definitely. For my classes." Hurriedly, he shoves it into his pocket, and picks up his copy of Hemingway.

I think, I wouldn't mind a look in that notebook, but it's probably just the cop in me, an automatic reflex.

Months later, the way I remembered that day in the park it seemed another life, me eager to talk to Ostalsky, the sun shining. Now I stood on the pier jutting into the Hudson.

The wind whipped the water into waves that spewed over the rotting wood. Hurricane Ella had been rumbling up the coast most of the week, there was a threat of high tides and flooding. Indian summer was gone. Otherwise it was silent except for a radio somewhere, Tony Bennett singing his new hit about San Francisco, and the little cable cars, sweet and incongruous in this stinking sea of death. Seeing the tattoo on the dead man had knocked me for a loop.

"Tommy?" Where the hell was he?

Where was the damn kid? The line to my precinct was still busy. Buzzing at me like an insect in my head. It was two in the morning, I was holding the phone, an eye on the corpse in the black body bag. "Anybody there?"

Nobody answered, not Tommy, or anyone else. Strange because the Port Authority had stepped up security during the Longshoremen's strike. Tonight, the usual guards, the cops who walked this beat, were all gone. Somebody had ordered the shut-down of security. Somebody with power who wanted the dock deserted.

The Longshoremen had gone out up and down the east coast beginning of October. Bad blood between the union guys, the suppliers, the warehouse owners, and the Mob who still had a piece of the action boiled over. Scabs were brought in. Fights broke out, and worse.

The Red Hook strike in '54, I was walking a beat in Brooklyn. People got hurt. Died. One young kid working there got hauled up on one of those big hooks, then dropped on his head on the deck of a ship. Head cracked like a coconut.

When *On the Waterfront* came out, I had to leave the theatre—it was too real; it made me sick. I went back later and saw it three times. That line where Brando says, "I don't like the country, the crickets make me nervous," while he's playing with the girl's glove, Jesus, that was something. Broke my heart. I was in love with Eva Marie Saint for years.

"Tommy? Where the hell are you?"

All I heard was a single dog somewhere, yapping; then it stopped.

Late at night, when business was slow, the warehouse men fought their dogs. I knew an elderly Italian who fed his dogs on hot sausage sandwiches, the dog was always drooling red sauce and his breath stank of pepperoni. Kept them on their toes, he said. Sometimes, they fought them for money. The local hoods came out, juvenile delinquents, too; sometimes the Longshoremen egged them on.

In Korea I'd heard they ate the damn dogs. Life was cheap over there.

"I'm here, Pat." Tommy appeared suddenly and scared the bejesus out of me.

"Listen to me, how did you get beat up?"

"I tripped."

"You telling me the truth?"

"Yeah, OK, a guy pushed me, and I fell on one of them, whadya call it, anchors, big mean iron kind of thing, stuck me right in the head. Cross my heart and fucking hope to die."

"Who was he?" I grabbed his skinny arm.

"I should have told you right away. I found some metal chain around the other side of the shack, figured I could sell it to the salvage guys, and I'm dragging it, I see this guy looking at me out of nowhere, maybe he's gonna take me in for stealing, but he just shoves me over hard. I cut my head. Then he runs."

"One man?"

"Not sure. I couldn't see good."

"What kind of man?"

"I don't know. Tall. With glasses, maybe. Hat pulled down."

"What kind of hat?"

"One of them uptown jobs, like you go to a funeral in, big brim, double dents in the crown sort of. He had a sack."

"What kind of sack."

"Yeah, a book bag, canvas. Pat, I don't feel so good."

"Listen, kid, I need you to do something. You too sick?"

He shook his head.

"Find a phone. There's one on Greenwich Street." I gave him a fistful of nickels and dimes. "Go call my station house, OK? You know the number, right?" Panic was creeping up on me, but I had to stay at the scene, or risk the body might disappear. "Go call it in. Ask for Lieutenant Murphy. If he's not there tell whoever answers you're calling for me, and it's an emergency, tell them where I am, if you can't get through, get a taxi, and go over there, Charles Street, right? Then go home. You can stay at my place. Eat something. Here's a dollar for a taxi. Can you do it?"

Tommy reached into his pants pocket. "I found this. Maybe the man I saw dropped it." In his hand was a silver medal. "You mad I ain't told you earlier, Pat?"

"I'm not mad." I was sure I had seen the medal before. For now, I wrapped it in my handkerchief and shoved it into my pants. "Anything else you gotta tell me?"

"The man, it was sorta like he knew me."

"Go on."

Tommy looked at me. "I seen him before some place. I

swear to God he takes off his hat, and Pat, I see horns. I'm telling you, I know who he was."

"Who was he, Tommy?"

"He was the Devil," Tommy said, crossed himself and ran.

I watched Tommy until he disappeared. I was feeling rotten, sick, exhausted. I sat down on the pier, my back against the warehouse. Out on the water, a few of the big ships lay at anchor, empty. A mile north, maybe less, was the pier where the *Carpathia* brought in passengers who survived the *Titanic*. The *Titanic* would have docked at 59, and never did. The *Lusitania* left 54, and never came back. Ghost ships. Ghosts, too, that lived around here in the dank night.

I had showed Max Ostalsky the piers. I had walked him along the Westside and explained the history of the city, the ships, their stories. It had been me who showed him these damn piers.

Putting my hand into the body bag had made me retch, but I had seen the tattoo, and now, steeling myself, I did it again and found a piece of paper scribbled in Spanish. I took some Spanish in high school, and I made out something about the Cuban Revolution. Somebody wanted Castro dead.

Again I thought about Ostalsky. He loved Castro. Loved the son-of-a-bitch. He told me that the first day we met.

After we leave the park that June day, I show him St Joseph's Church and then we walk up Sixth Avenue where in front of Howard Johnson's there's this raggedy line of high school kids handing out leaflets and calling out how they want "fair play for Cuba."

"I would like very much to visit Cuba," Max says. "I admire this country. I had quite a good friend from Havana in Moscow."

I look at the kids and think, bunch of crazy Reds, but I keep my mouth shut and we move on, me and Max, and I show him the Women's House of Detention.

"Certain times of day, see, Max, the girls in there, they yell out and joke with their pimps on the sidewalk, it's pretty famous, you want to cross over and take a look? Sometimes they hold their babies up so their guys can see."

"Is this permitted?"

"You shocked, man?"

He's looking everywhere, turning around 360 degrees, can't get enough of it, taking it all in, smell of the city, the noise. A man in denim overalls on the corner handing out copies of the *Daily Worker*; a bum panhandling for change; the kid in blue jeans, plucking at a banjo, nobody listening. Carmine DeSapio, in his dark blue dandyish suit, hands out red roses to a clutch of little old Italian ladies. His time as head of the city political machine is fading, Tammany Hall on its last legs. My ma regrets this because her own brother was a big-deal ward-healer and he got a lot of stuff from the party, turkey at Thanksgiving, that kind of thing.

I try explaining to Max about city politics. "Look, the President, when he wants the nomination, his brother, Bobby, goes to sweet-talk the likes of DeSapio. And Frank Costello, who's a gangster, pulls DeSapio's strings. You dig?"

"How does a criminal become so influential in your government? Is that considered proper? Proper, this means correct, I think. Correct is OK?"

"Sure. Correct? Who can say? It's how it is. All governments are corrupt. They're all a bunch of crooks. You know what, Max, it's hot and I'm damn thirsty. How about I buy you a cold brew? Come on, man, we'll head over to the Cedar."

I've been a homicide detective for nine years, and I can't remember when I took a day off for the hell of it. Business is slow. Maybe the weather's too nice for killing. It's not going to last long. But for now, it's making me happy and I take my new pal over to the Cedar on University Place.

"This is kind of you, Pat," Max says, and we climb up on stools. I order a couple of Rheingold and I tell him it's the working man's beer. He likes that. I guess he feels sympathetic to the workers, or something.

"Going, going, gone." On the radio, Mel Allen is calling the game in that sweet singular voice, and briefly I explain to Max about baseball, about Maris and the Mick.

"Do you know that last February, our newspaper reported that baseball is an old Russian game," Max says, tasting his cold beer.

"Gimme a break, man."

"Pat, can I ask you what your work is?"

"I'm a cop. A detective. Homicide. Murder cases. You have those in Moscow?"

"Surely, of course, we also have detectives in Moscow, but there are not so many murders in our society. It is quite orderly."

I don't care about the baseball thing, it's so obviously dumb, but the burst of stupid ideology gets to me.

"I guess it makes sense since people have to toe the line pretty much over there. I mean with the KGB watching you pretty close, right? Nobody's going to get out of line. People can't ever say what they want."

Max ignores the sarcasm. "This beer is delicious, Pat. You know, perhaps one day you would show me something of your work? I would be so interested to visit a, do you say, crime scene?"

"Is this where he drank?" A couple of girls have arrived and are looking around, and yapping. Tourists. This is why I don't go to the Cedar much anymore, too much talk about how it was when the artists were there, too much about Jack this and Jack that, and how Jack pissed in the ashtray, and too many girls wanting to touch the place where he sat, and tourists wanting to see where the famous beatnik writer broke the toilet door.

Used to be girls didn't much come in. Ones that did, the men, those artists and writers, swarmed them. "Like a lamb with a pack of wolves," said my old friend, Tom Doyle, a great sculptor I used to drink with at the Cedar. "One girl was a fantastic looker, and she would only turn up on Tuesdays and moon around until Pollack showed, this was his shrink day, otherwise he was on Long Island." Later on Tom married a great woman—too smart and beautiful to look at me—and moved to the country.

Most of the artists have moved on, some of the time there's a professor from NYU sitting in back in his tweed jacket with elbow patches, writing his novel. Tells me he's writing about the modern condition, anxiety, despair, and I think, give me a good suspense story, like that *Ipcress File*.

"Give us a couple more brews, Kev, will you?"

"Sure. Listen, Pat, you see about how Senator Keating says there's Russian missiles on Cuba? You believe that?"

"I think he wants to rattle the President's cage before mid-term elections. The Republicans hate JFK is what I think. The bastards are out to get him because he's a Catholic."

"For sure."

"My father wants me to put a fallout shelter in his house out in Astoria, says the Reds are gonna nuke us, gonna start in Berlin, or Cuba. Me I'm gonna hole up with a case of good Scotch."

Beside me, Max lights up a Lucky, and I can feel what Kevin is saying is of interest to him.

"They hit us, you don't want to survive."

"Let me pour you a couple," says Kevin, reaching for a bottle of Black & White.

Max picks up his glass. Sips cautiously. "This is very nice," he says. "This is my first drink of Scotch whisky. Of any whisky."

I say I always thought the Russians drink like fish, but he tells me it's mostly working men, and adds, hastily, that it's because they labor hard in the cause of the state.

"Try it like this, first the whisky, then the beer."

After a few, Max gets plastered, but he's a good drunk: voluble, good-natured, a little melancholy. "You said you were not currently married, Pat, but perhaps at one time you were?"

"Yeah, you could say so."

I was young and she was pregnant, and in my neighborhood, you marry the girl. My ma said I had to; no decent man fails in this duty, she said.

"And you?"

"I would take one glass more of beer. Yes, I am married," says Max.

"What's her name?"

"Nina Andreyevna. In our country, everybody has the name of her father. Men also. This is the patronymic. She is a talented teacher of the French language. We have known each other from childhood."

"Do you miss her?"

"Yes, of course," he says.

Turning towards me, his eyes look sad, turned inward. Max puts his elbows on the bar and I can see he wants to say more, but he stops himself as if he's unused to this kind of talk.

If not for the booze, Max Ostalsky would never have confided in me at all, a man he just met. But he's homesick, and feeling the solitude of a new place, and I'm ready to listen. I'm good at it.

"How did you get to come to America?"

"There have been quite a few exchanges the last three years or so, an effort for our countries to know each other better." Max looks at me. "Do you know something funny, Pat? Do you know if it was not for another student, who breaks his leg and cannot take up the fellowship, I may not have been so lucky to come to the United States. It is whispered he fell in love for a Rumanian ski champion. One day, my advisor says to me would you like apply for this Graduate Exchange Fellowship? Would I like to go? Yes, I tell him, yes, of course. May I have another one of those lovely whisky drinks?" he says to Kevin, who obliges.

"Do you know what I wanted to be most of all?" Max adds.

"What's that?"

"A cosmonaut. Yuri Gagarin, do you know what he says,

just as he takes off into the unknown, he says '*Poyekhali!*' I think this translates as 'Let's go.' Let's go. Just like that, no worries. But my cousin, Sasha, he says 'you can't be a cosmonaut, Max, you wear glasses, you're too tall, also you have never even been in an airplane. Perhaps you could be the new space dog, Laika. You shall be Max, the space dog.' Pat, these are good times in my country. We are making so much progress. We feel now, there will be peace and justice and equality for all, and material goods too, and so forth."

Max Ostalsky is a Commie, of course. Every time I get drawn into his story, it comes back to this, all this Commie crap. He's probably a Party member, but I let him talk.

"This trip, it was my first time in an airplane."

"No kidding. How old are you?"

"I am not kidding. I am twenty-nine."

"Do you know about John Glenn," I say, as if somehow to preserve the honor of the USA. Glenn went up in February. Who could forget it, the ticker tape and all, especially coming on the day an American Airlines plane crashed in Queens. "John Glenn circled the globe," I add. "He didn't just go up, he circled the whole damn world."

"Yes. This was excellent news," says Max. "Let us toast to Gagarin and to Glenn, our space heroes."

In the bar that lazy hot afternoon, Max talks and I encourage him. All I know about the Reds is, like the priests say, they live in an atheistic nightmare; that the people are oppressed, and are often sent to prison camps to die; that the system is committed to espionage and sabotage, and a desire to take over the United States and enslave us; also the unavailability of nice clothes and cars. This character is something else.

27

This Max Ostalsky walks and talks like a regular guy. He even glances at one of the tourist girls, the one with the big bust in the very tight sleeveless yellow blouse. He tells me he learned English from the time he was a little boy, with his grandmother, who learned it before the Revolution. "We call her Sunny. She says she does not want to be regarded as an old grandmother with a scarf on her head. My grandfather says the English language is the family business."

"You were fond of them? Are they still alive."

"Sadly, my grandfather died only a few years ago."

"And your grandmother?"

"My grandfather told us wonderful stories of the Revolution," he says, not answering my question about his grandma. "His own father, who was a sugar merchant of Leningrad, had traveled often to America, after your Civil War. He was in New York City and San Francisco, New Orleans, too, and he told me stories about attending lectures by Mark Twain, and listening to music played by Scott Joplin. In summertime, he wore suits like Mr Twain, made of white linen." Max pauses and says something half to himself in Russian.

"Us?"

"Yes, me, my cousin Sasha, who is also his grandson, the son of my mother's sister. My best friend. To me, Sasha says you will have conversations and drink rum cocktails with Papa Hemingway. I tell him Hemingway is in Cuba with the fishermen."

"He's a teacher?"

"Sasha is an engineer."

"And your grandmother?"

"I have been talking too much, Pat," he says, and I get

it that he doesn't want to talk about his grandma; why, I think? Why the hell not?

"Don't worry, man. It's the Scotch. Loosens the tongue. Your secrets are safe with me."

"Secrets? I'm sorry, what secrets?"

By the time we leave the bar, it's evening, a balmy June evening with couples emerging from the Cookery, or the art movie house. Max seems a little tipsy. He tells me some joke about sausages, and laughs to himself. I don't get it. It doesn't matter. I've had plenty to drink. I walk him to 10th Street where he says he has a room.

"Thank you again, Pat. I can now buy a hot dog with some expertise, though I must apologize for my condition. Would you call it sodden?"

"Cheerful. It's nothing, man. You can chalk it up to experience, you know, your first American bender."

"Yes. But thank you for your kindness in showing me around," he says, as we reach the apartment building, the front door covered in a ornamental pattern of wrought-iron leaves. "Good night, Pat," Max adds, as he pulls open the door and disappears inside.

And me, I'm thinking, Jesus, I've been drinking with an honest to God Communist who talks about his pretty wife, and gets drunk, who willingly tries out new kinds of booze, even laughs. Maybe he's not one of them. Maybe he's looking to come over to our side. Maybe I can win him over. But I'm a little bit soused on Scotch, and truth is, I don't think I'll ever see Max Ostalsky again.

At the deli on the opposite corner, I get myself a fresh pack of Chesterfields, then head north on University Place, thinking about looking for a plate of spaghetti. Maybe I'll go up to Gene's. I'm hungry.

You can spot a Fed a mile away, especially in the Village. Across the street, I see him, right then, a young FBI agent, the bad crew-cut hair—his barber must use some garden shears to cut it—yellow and standing up from his head. In his wrinkled tan summer suit, he's standing in front of the Hotel Albert, pretending to read a copy of the *Journal-American*, but looking at the building where Max Ostalsky lives.

This one has to be Ostalsky's tail. All Soviets who come over to America get an FBI tail. Ballet dancers. Students. Diplomats. They're Commies, after all; you have to watch them.

After all, as my pop, ass that he is, says, "Mr Hoover says 'Communism is not a political party, it is a disease.'"

The agent lowers his paper, glances at me, and because I'm plastered, I wave at him and grin. We're on the same side, I think. Right? He looks startled. Behind him, the red neon Eiffel Tower out front of the Albert restaurant blinks on and off.

CHAPTER TWO

October 17, '62

T HE SIRENS TORE UP the cold wet night. From the pier, I could hear them coming closer. Tommy must have phoned the precinct like I told him. Who was the man he had seen? Who was Tommy's devil?

I looked at my watch. Two in the morning. Wednesday already. Cold out. Cold as a witch's tit in a brass bra, like they used to say. Winter coming.

Hurriedly, I zipped the body bag. I didn't want anyone asking why I messed with the crime scene. I shoved the silver medal Tommy had found into my pocket. The sirens screamed louder, and I heaved myself to my feet, tried to light up a cigarette and failed. The wind was whipping me good.

Lights flashed. A dark blue car appeared, bumping over the pier. When it stopped, a pair of detectives got out, and stood waiting while a second car pulled up. I didn't recognize them. They were not from my station house. They wore cheap suits and had the dogged look of men who take orders without question. I went over and told them I was the lead detective, I had found the body, called in the case.

"Where's the kid?" I said.

"What kid?"

"I need the phone in your car," I said and showed my badge.

"We have to ask," said the taller one, indicating the second car.

"Sure, go get permission," I said.

From the second car, two more men, also in plain clothes, got out. I didn't recognize them either. If the guys at my precinct were off duty or on other cases, maybe my boss, or whoever took Tommy's phone call, had contacted other houses for help. Two of them. The older man probably a senior cop from downtown, wore an expensive navy blue topcoat—alpaca, I figured—over his suit. The heavy silver tie gave him the look of a Mafia capo or a corporate vice president. He was pushing fifty. The air of authority went with the big shoulders, the well-fed belly, the black hair; on his left pinky was an engraved gold signet ring. Family crest, perhaps. He had a face that told you nobody got in his way. He made it known right away that he was in charge and worked out of the Commissioner's office. Strode up to me, hand out, though it was a perfunctory gesture.

"Logan," he said. "And you are Detective Wynne."

"I need to make a call."

"Thanks for your help, Detective Wynne. You look done in, like you'd be glad to hit the sack just about now. We're fine here, we have more men on their way, so, let me say thank you again for responding."

I tried not to let Logan rile me. "Will you be working this one, too?" I said.

He stared at me, half irritated, a little amused. "I just came from your station house, Wynne. I have a message from your Lieutenant Murphy."

"What message?"

"You won't be working this case. Murphy said to tell you."

"I think you got that wrong."

"I don't get things wrong. You want to call Murphy? Please. Use my phone. Get Detective Wynne to my car," he said to his driver who hovered near him like a servant waiting for orders. "Let him use the phone all he wants."

Logan towered over me, looking down as if he wanted to punch my face, but was holding himself back.

"Detective, as I said, you won't be working this case, so if you wouldn't mind, please, just get your little car—it's that banged-up little red second-hand Corvette, I believe—and go home. Your boss thinks you need a break. I spoke to him, and he says, Lieutenant Murphy says to me, 'I agree, Wynne could use a break.' Very accommodating your lieutenant, a man who understands how things are done. He said to tell you you're off for the rest of the week. Take some time. Get a little rest. We already know this is a Mob hit. That's how we'll work it. Now, before you go, is there anything you want to tell us about this particular case? Anything you found? Anything you happened to pick up? Any evidence you might be squirreling away? I've seen your record. I know you like to get in on a case first, and sometimes that means keeping certain items to yourself."

"You know all about me."

"Yes, indeed. I know you worked that homicide on the High Line during the summer until it damn well wore you out and you started making mistakes." I felt the bile rise. Logan was the kind of guy who made me want to punch somebody. If I punched Logan, they'd fire me. I'd wait.

"They're connected," I said. "That girl. This man."

"So you say."

"Just who the hell are you?"

"Special squad," said Logan. "Not that it's any of your business. But we take precedence. Call your boss, if you want. Call the chief, if you think it's worth waking him up. Here's my card, Wynne."

I looked at the card. Captain Homer M. Logan.

"What kind of special squad?"

"On a need to know basis. You have no need," he said. "Unless you have something to tell me. Or the kid, Tommy Perino, isn't it? Father's name is Giuseppe. A wop kid, on his way to a record. You don't want to see him in some facility for juvenile deliquents, do you? He lives in your building over on Hudson Street? Maybe he stole something from the scene. I could send somebody by."

"He didn't take anything."

"Well, that's copacetic then, wouldn't you say?" He turned to the young cop who was his driver. "Officer Garrity, take the detective to my car, let him use the radio. You hear me?"

"Yessir."

Cold rain had begun falling. I followed Garrity, the young cop in the brown sack suit, no coat, to the car, and out of earshot of Logan, I said, "I know how it is, man, those bastards ordering you around, what's going on? This your first homicide?"

He nodded. "I was doing regular foot patrol, you know, I been on the job a year, and then Logan needs somebody, and they put me on this, they tell me to buy a suit. I'm supposed to take care of whatever he needs. I don't know why, or what the hell I'm doing."

"You feel like some kind of chauffeur, he has to be thinking you're only good to wipe up after him? Wipe his ass, so to speak?"

"Yeah."

"Don't worry. By the end of tomorrow, you'll be working with me." There was no way I could actually fix this, but I wanted the guy to talk to me. I lied in a tone of voice that conveyed I understood, that we were brothers and that if he played ball with me, he didn't need to take any shit from the brass. I lied. I was good at it.

"You need a smoke?" I asked. "What's your first name?"

"Yeah, thanks. It's James. Jimmy."

I got out my pack and handed it over.

"You want to use the radio?"

"Sure," I said and called my boss who told me I was on leave. Didn't explain, just parroted what Logan had said.

"Thanks," I said, handing the phone back to Jimmy who put it in its cradle in Logan's car. "Anything you want to tell me? You look like a smart cop, and I could sure use some help."

Finally, puffing on the Chesterfield I gave him, he leaned close to me. "I think the Feds are in this. I saw the boss with an agent earlier. I could tell. I heard the word sabotage. National security. I hear them talking about subversive activities. There's long-distance calls coming in from Washington DC and Miami. I'm supposed to stay in the outer office, but people talk. They're keeping the telephone operators on late. FBI agents are coming in, people slamming doors, those hush hush conversations, you know?" Jimmy Garrity gestured to the end of the pier. "Then this homicide comes in a few hours ago, and they're all over it. You think this has to do with Cuba? You think the Russians are going to bomb us? I hear planes at night, I can't sleep." In the dim light, he looked young and scared.

"I think you should do your job, and you'll be fine. OK, Jimmy?"

He hesitated.

"What?"

Garrity lowered his voice further. "Give me your home phone, I'll try to keep you on board."

"Why don't you give me yours?" I said, and he scribbled a number down and tore the page out of his notebook. "Thanks. You don't like Logan, do you?"

"I don't trust him."

"Why's that?"

"In the car, he's always talking about brainwashing, and how we should learn from the Commies, and he reads books about how the Chinese do it, and we should consider using their ways. Told me once torture is a means to an end, and if the end is in our interest, we have every right. He's a mean son-of-a-bitch, I mean, he even makes the girls in the office cry when he yells at them, and I don't hold with that."

"Think hard. Anyone in particular who comes to the office?"

Garrity looked at his boss. A group of men had formed around Logan—the cops who had arrived just before him, two others, Feds, maybe—all of them heads down, all in their dark hats and coats smoking and talking together; like courtiers, they all attended to Logan; there was no way into that closed circle unless you belonged.

"You know, two or three times, I saw a man in an expensive coat, not a cop. I had never seen him, yeah, but he walks right in, doesn't say a word, closes Logan's door behind him."

"What kind of coat?"

"English like. Like in a movie. Belted. Like some spy in a movie. Big head of silver hair. Pompadour. I noticed that. I got an uncle with hair like that."

Tommy had mentioned a man with white hair. "Go on."

"A couple of times lately, I picked up the phone by mistake, and I heard him talking. All I heard was him saying the word 'strike', but when he realized I was on the line, he lost his temper. I'll tell you this, he's obsessed with the Mob. He'll do anything to nail one of them Mob guys, and they're in bed with the Longshoreman, so what can I say?" He was whispering. "Logan nearly socked me. Told me to fucking stay off his phone line."

"Listen to me, Jimmy, you keep me posted. Yeah, and where's the forensics people? There's no one here? No reporters. Brass like Logan usually love getting their pictures in the *Daily News*."

"I heard Logan say to keep the pier clear until he got a good look."

"How come you're so talkative? You're not afraid of Logan?"

Jimmy looked at me. "He saw to it my brother's career came to a sudden end. He mentions the word corruption at

37

his precinct, and he's done. I knew somehow Logan fixed it so he got canned. Bastard."

"That's it?"

Jimmy hesitated.

"What?"

"In the car on the way over, I heard him mention your name to his pal in the back seat."

"Who was he, this pal?"

"I don't know. A uniform. Brass. Logan says, 'This Wynne, I don't want him anywhere near this case. If he gives me trouble, you pay attention,' and the other one says, 'Sure. Be my pleasure, what's the problem?' 'He's a Red,' says Logan. 'He's a goddman Red-lover.'"

"Where is he, the pal in the backseat?"

"Over there, checking out the body."

A hard soaking rain was coming down in sheets. There was no point taking on Logan. He didn't want to hear from me. But I knew it was connected: the dead girl on the High Line last July; the dead man on the pier. Both had the tattoo, the worm and the words 'Cuba Libre'. Two dead. Same tattoo. Both had been too young to die.

I turned my back on the scene, and started towards the street.

"You going home, Wynne?" Logan called out.

"Whatever you say, Logan."

As I left, Logan looked up again from his courtiers in their dark coats and he tipped his hat to me. It was a strange, sarcastic gesture, and it made me feel colder than even the miserable rain.

I didn't go home. I left the pier and went north to the High Line.

I had already spent too many nights on the High Line. I had been up there night after night, July, August. I had to go back one more time. It had been July 4th when they slaughtered the girl, tortured her and left her hanging from the iron railings of the overhead viaduct a few blocks from the pier.

As soon as I get the call—I'm pretty much alone at the station house because it's the 4th, and everybody is at the beach or out partying—I drive like crazy over to Gansevoort Street and leave my Corvette on the corner.

Independence Day, I can hear people on rooftops clapping, watching the fireworks, green, red, gold, white, lighting up the sky and the river. Somewhere through a loudspeaker "America the Beautiful", followed by "Let's Twist Again". Somebody's having a party. All over the city people are partying, celebrating July 4th. Goddamn 4th of July, and I'm on the job.

Where's the cop who called the homicide in? I can't see him. I can't see anyone at all. It's stinking hot, and I'm half blinded by the fireworks that light up the sky.

Thirty feet up, running over Tenth Avenue parallel to the river, the freight line—everyone calls it the High Line—goes from the 32nd Street railyards to the terminal at Spring Street. Use to go all the way downtown. Warehouses stand along the line, their loading docks level with the trains. Some places the line goes through the buildings.

My precinct includes the lower end of the line, which is why the cop on patrol called us earlier. Suddenly, a giant gold flower explodes over the Hudson, and in the light, I see the body.

Is she alive? I'm scared she's alive, afraid she's dead. At first I think, desperately, it's some teenage kid using the place for a game. Some kind of crazy game, like my pop used to say he played as a kid, using the struts of the overhead rail line for a jungle gym. Soon somebody would start a playground chant. The girl would grin, and pull herself up. I glance at my watch. It's midnight. I yell out to her. No response.

Her feet tied to the iron viaduct, she's hanging head down, about twenty-four, twenty-five feet above me, she looks eighteen, twenty. Head seems to bob in the wind coming from the river, or maybe it's some kind of momentum, the weight of her body making her swing, her long black hair whipped around. One arm in a pink and white checked sleeve, a blouse a young girl might wear, flopping like a rag doll's arm. The other arm is gone. Most of the blouse has been ripped away, revealing a plain white bra. It feels obscene to look. Blood everywhere.

Only a piece of the sleeve is left. The arm had been cut off at the shoulder. No chant. No playground games.

Can she be alive? I shout at her. No response. I know she's dead. I know it, but I jump up, trying to reach her. I can't reach her, can't really see her face, she's too high. I can't even grab her arm. This is like some fucking hallucination, but it's real. I can't find the damn cop who called this in.

I can't get to her this way. I'm yelling and running around, looking for some way up to the viaduct. God knows what's up there. I need help.

A block west is the meat-packing market. Warehouses open all night. The first one I get to, three men jump out, and open the back so it fits level with the loading dock. A meat packer, wearing a bloodied white coat, a smoke hanging from his lips, signals for them to start. They shoulder sides of beef off the truck and onto metal hooks, shoving the hooks along the ceiling of the warehouse. Once I worked a case where they found a dead man hanging from one of those hooks. Mob job pure and simple. At night, there's always that dark smell of blood in the air.

I grab for the guy in the white coat. "Where's the phone? Get me a goddamn phone."

"Who the hell are you?"

I show him my badge. Finally, he lets me into the warehouse office, and I call the precinct, and by the time I'm heading back to the crime scene, the sirens are screaming. The meat boss must have heard them too, because he comes running after me, a cleaver in his hand, maybe figuring he could help with some creep out murdering young women.

When I get up the access ladder to the High Line, the place is already swarming, cops, medics, guys setting up portable lights, best they can. Flashlights flicker. The scene is like a movie set, black and white, cops and death.

I get a look at the girl whose feet were fastened with rope, then tied with wire to an iron railing, her body pushed over, head first. Her feet are scarred bad like somebody beat her.

Under the hot light, two hefty cops yank loose the wires, and pull the girl up. They lay her down on the side of the tracks, and the sight of these bulky young men attending so tenderly to this victim, this young girl, even younger than them, is hard to bear, even if you have a soul as calloused as mine.

Detectives arrive. Somebody from the coroner's office is already there. Reporters are crammed onto the narrow track. Flashbulbs go off, all in the ritual dance of death.

"They cut her arm off," somebody yells. "They cut out her tongue," a medic tells me. "Mafia thing, they want to shut you up, want to keep you from writing your confession."

"Was she left-handed?"

"Is that all you feel about it? Jesus, you cops are cold. They did it like she was some animal, but even an animal you would kill first. Those guys at the meat market, they treat a side of beef with more care."

"Thanks, doc." I try to keep from losing it, try to make nice because, you work homicides in this city, you need relationships. Being Irish helps; cops, coroners, city pols, FBI agents, we come from the same place. It's changing, sure, but we still run things, and we help each other out. Cover for your brothers in blue at all times, my boss always says in that sanctimonious way of his.

Reporters who picked up the news on a police radio frequency, they're jockeying for position. A photographer in a stingy brim shuffles around, snaps the body. I could remember when that guy Arthur Fellig was around, taking police shots for the papers. I got hold of one. A long time after, when people decided Weegee—that was what he called himself—was art, I got a good price on it. Now it was only some young dumb photographer from the *Journal-American*.

One of my pals, a detective from my station house looks like he knows what he's doing and I get hold of him. "You OK with this for a couple minutes, man? I want to look around. I'm gonna take a walk," I say, and he nods.

For a few minutes, in the dark, away from the scene, I stumble down the tracks, smoking, watching the orange tip of my cigarette, looking for, what, for something.

"The Wild West was right here in New York City," my pop always said when he brought me over to the High Line. "See, buddy boy, right back to the 1850s, they ran freight down Tenth Avenue, first wagons going to market piled up with potatoes, sides of beef, trolley buses later on, and then the train. That train it ran people down, and they were dying like flies. They called it Death Avenue. These men on horses, the Westside Cowboys, rode in front waving red flags for protection." As a kid, that's what I wanted to be. A Westside Cowboy. Couldn't ride a horse, no place to learn. My old man thought I was nuts. He'd say, "you know, I worked on that line for a while; I was a pretty damn good welder. You shoulda seen them sides of beef, pigs, turkey, all kind of fowl, going right down there. After it was built, I got a job doing repairs for a while. We had it good, even '32, '33, when people was living in Hoovervilles, them shacks by the East River, eating out of garbage scows. You was a little nipper, and we went out on Sundays and had a look. You remember when your Uncle Jack took you for a ride? All you wanted was to drive them trains thirty feet up in the sky."

My pop always loved showing off his knowledge of the city. "Born at home right there on 39th Street, between Ninth and Tenth Avenues, the original Hell's Kitchen, they call it. My own da lived in one of them shantytowns on the river, worked the docks, after he come over during the Famine. We was all Irish then. Good times, building them viaducts."

I can hear his voice, even as, the flashbulbs popping behind me, fireworks spilling a red white and blue finale into the river, I keep walking into the dark. A empty bottle catches my foot, I trip, fall onto my knees on the tracks.

In one of the warehouses is a faint orange glow. Hauling myself up onto the loading platform, I start banging on the door. No answer. Where's the security? On a holiday night like this, you have to figure they'd have security, you didn't know if some thug would be on the prowl. Weeds grow through the cracks of the pavement alongside the tracks. The city is getting shabby.

After the war, the place was always buzzing, there was this feeling we owned the world, everything in everything switched on it in Technicolor—with jazz music for the soundtrack. Then, a couple years ago, white people began leaving. White Flight, they called it.

My cousins eye those Levittown houses on Long Island. You can do OK as a schoolteacher, a cop, a firefighter, and now you could live with your own, my cousin said. It's all they want: the house, the car, the green lawn, the TV and washing machine, the wife who stays home and takes care of things, the kids who keep their mouths shut and desire only what their parents have. No coloreds, either.

My pop, old and bitter now, is always yapping. "If I could, I'd go out there, get away from them coons," he'd tell me. He has a nasty gift for language—still does—that he puts to work dumping shit on other people: Chink, Kike, Nigger. My whole life is running away from him.

But after ten minutes, I'm still clawing at the warehouse door. It doesn't give, I get out my gun and smash a window.

I have a hunch about this, I crawl through into a warehouse space that stinks of dead chickens. Somewhere I hear rats. All I have is my lighter, and I flick it on again and again.

In the far corner is a rusty electric heater, one bar with a faint glow.

Someone's been here recently. Near the heater is a nest of old newspapers in English, in Spanish, the *New York Post*, *La Prensa*, and I scrabble through them like a crazy man, looking at dates. The dates are recent, the papers are from late June, early July, right up to July 2nd. July 2, 1962 says the date on the newspaper. Two days ago. It's the 4th now, the night I find her, find these newspapers. In the pile of papers is a leaflet in Spanish, something about Fidel Castro. A strange, sweet smell comes off it. The girl must have worn flowery cologne, something pretty, lilies of the valley. I light up another smoke. She was here before she died, hiding here, a bed of old newspaper, scared to death.

Did something drive her back out onto the High Line? Did somebody find her huddled, torture her, hang her from the viaduct?

That night, I work the case until dawn, and my mouth tastes like a sewer from all the smokes; I keep on working it day after day, but there's nothing. I start drinking too much.

The case, it runs right through July, my name shows up in a couple of the articles. In the *Mirror*, they even shove my picture in with the story, and some headline about a brave detective, garbage like that. The *Post* picks it up. People around NYU start asking me about it, ghoulish questions about the girl, her death. Why is anyone interested in so much horror; it's not long after I meet Max Ostalsky in the park.

Leaving the High Line now on this miserable October morning, I remembered how Max Ostalsky had asked me about the dead girl. Polite, but insistent.

What did some Russki care about a Manhattan homicide? I had wondered more than once.

Now I knew. He had wanted information on how the cops worked a homicide. Wanted it because he was planning to kill the man on Pier 46. I felt sure about it, but I needed evidence, and I was burning up with fever, sick as a dog, exhausted.

Tommy was asleep on my couch, and I left him there. He could miss school for a day. I washed down three aspirin with a belt of Three Roses—drank it from the bottle I kept in the kitchen— tore off my clothes, fell into bed.

The phone rang. It was my lieutenant. I said I was sick. He said, OK, take some time. Take two weeks. Don't come in, he said. Didn't ask about the case. Don't ask nothing, Pat, he said. Finally, I fell asleep. Dreamed I was running uptown, had to get to the piers, to the High Line, had to save somebody, except the face on the detective who was running wasn't mine. It was Max Ostalsky's.

CHAPTER THREE

October 17, '62

THE DREAM WOKE ME. I couldn't get back to sleep. I drank some more whisky and took more aspirin and I still couldn't sleep. I lay in bed, trying to recall how I fell into the friendship with Max Ostalsky; how I ended up talking too much; how I let him play me.

I had signed up for a course at NYU the summer I was working the High Line. I didn't have much free time, but I went to my class when I could, and it turns out we have classes in the same building, Max and me. Same building; same time. Before class, he always has his nose in a book, checking his work, practicing his English. But afterwards it becomes a habit for us to meet up for a cup of coffee, or a beer.

Around NYU, people like Max Ostalsky. He's good-looking, he laughs, he's interested in everything, and people take notice of it. "He's awfully nice for a Communist," one girl tells me.

Students, professors too, invite him home for dinner. Miss NYU gets her picture taken with Max. Peaceniks inquire solemnly about his views on unilateral disarmament. Sometimes in his old-fashioned brown leather briefcase, he carries little gifts for his new friends—painted boxes with pictures of Russia, wooden dolls that contain smaller and small dollies inside, even Russian chocolate bars.

Max debates anyone who wants to, in class, in the park, he listens politely, and sticks up for his country. But he has a sense of humor, and tells me that for his paper on *Moby-Dick*, he's planning an essay on the whale as the engine of capitalism, and then he chuckles about it.

Does Max know the crew-cut fellow in the wrinkled tan suit I saw opposite his building on University Place is FBI and only pretends he's a grad student? But it's none of my business.

The day in July my name hits the papers Max is waiting for me, as usual, on the steps at NYU, a copy of the *New York Post* in his hand.

"This case must be so difficult, Pat?"

"It's my job."

I can see he wants to talk about it, but I've had it with the story for now. I take the newspaper from him, and lob it into a garbage can. "Enough of that. Enough."

"May I buy you a glass of beer?"

I'm glad for some diversion. It's six, but still light, high summer. The park is full of pretty girls. Everywhere I see girls like the dead girl on the High Line: young, pretty, a whole life ahead of them. I'm not sentimental about the dead, it's my business, but this is different. I could use a drink.

"Sure, a beer sounds good. Why not?"

"That is fine," says Max.

"Nice duds," I say, as we stroll across the park towards MacDougal Street.

"Thank you," says Max who looks pretty good, decent haircut, new tortoiseshell specs; in the chinos and pink button-down shirt, a dark blue jacket over his arm, he looks, what does he look? American. An all-American College Joe and even he way he holds himself, he fits in with the other adult students. A lot of them are in their twenties, even thirties. Most everyone goes to class in a coat and tie, the girls in heels and their mothers' handbags, the ones who are looking for a husband in the dental school at least. "So who's been advising you on your clothes?"

Max glances at the chess players on the north side of the park, eye on a couple of men in hats, one white, one Negro, hard at it.

"You play?"

"Some," he says.

"You any good?"

"It depends who is on the other side of the table."

"Let's get that beer."

"Yes. Sure. It is Mrs Muriel Miller, by the way, my, what would you say, landlady, who helps me with shopping. She is very kind, Pat. I think she considers me like a son, or better to say, a nephew. I believe she is lonely because her own son is married, and on Long Island."

"The clothes?"

"Of course. Last week she accompanies me on top of a Fifth Avenue bus to many stores."

"What did you think?"

"I think she wants to convert me to your system through shopping, and to be honest, the stores are quite amazing,

49

especially this F.A.O. Schwarz. Of course, we have a grand toy store in Moscow, but I am like a ten-year-old boy here. Grown men in suits are admiring the train sets. Perhaps Mrs Miller thinks I will defect for a beautiful Lionel train set."

"How do you feel about that?"

He looks at me, startled, perplexed, concerned suddenly.

"I'm kidding you, man."

"I see." He's uneasy now, just for a moment, fumbling for his cigarettes.

"It was a joke, Max. I'm kidding, I'm fooling around with you, man."

"Of course. Can you believe how time flies, Pat? It's almost a month since we first met. I have been meaning to tell you how grateful I am to you for answering so many of my questions. So many of the graduate students are, would you say, square? I try. I try to sound more, more swinging. Can you say that would be copacetic? Or am I cruisin' for a bruisin'?" He bursts out laughing. He makes me laugh. I say, "Very American, daddy-O."

"I have also become pretty fond of the whisky you introduced me, too. I am down with it. By the way, Mrs Miller asks if you would come for dinner. She is awfully kind, I have my own room, and a bathroom for myself," says Max. "Mrs Miller believes I, a young man, must have my privacy, and I am not sure what this means. We do not have this concept, you see. I feel I have fallen into a magic rabbit hole. What is privacy precisely, Pat? This is not something we understand in my country."

I explain as best I can. Crossing 3rd Street, Max looks around MacDougal like a kid eating cake with both hands, he takes out his notebook and scribbles in it, puts it back.

"What language do you write in?"

"Ah, only English. I promise myself I will only speak in English, I will write in English. If I dream in English, this means I am truly fluent."

"What do you write about?"

"Oh, everything. This is like theater. So many things I have to recall, to write to my family."

Every night the Village throbs with music, music from folk clubs, jazz clubs, bars, cafés, coffee houses. Along MacDougal, kids wait to get into the Gaslight Café and Café Wha and they're crazy with excitement. "Did you hear that new guy, Dylan? You heard him? Is that her, is it Mary?" cries a girl in sandals. "My mother will flip her wig when she hears I've been to the Village."

Suburban kids dressed in black as if for a costume party, return tickets to Long Island in their pockets, throng the street, drunk with the prospect of a night out in Greenwich Village. Italian boys stand around, posturing; like Bobby Darin, or Tony Curtis, they figure, pompadours glistening with Brylcreem, hands jammed in pockets, eyeing tourists with disdain, maybe spoiling for a little action on a hot summer night.

"This is like theater," Max says. "So much." He has out the little notebook, scribbling furiously. Puts it away. Extracts his pack of Lucky Strike. "Where shall we go for our beer?"

"Let's go to Minetta Tavern, it's across the street."

Inside Minetta, Max examines the photos of boxers on the walls and then climbs onto a stool at the bar next to me. He orders Rheingold for us both. I add a double Scotch for myself. Me, I also want some meatballs. I haven't been eating. The food here is good, and it's cheap.

I down the drinks in one gulp and order cheap red wine. I eat a couple of meatballs and order more wine. I feel better. This is what I need, a night off the case I can't solve, and from my nightmares.

"So what's new, Max?"

"I am now familiar with disc jockeys such as Cousin Brucie Morrow, and Murray the K. and his Swinging Soirees for Submarine Watchers, isn't that it, Pat?"

"Max, man, I am proud of you, so easy to fall for the folkie stuff, living down here in the Village, as a reward I am going to take you to a real rock and roll show, maybe even the Brooklyn Fox, or the Apollo." In Max, I can see a potential convert. "The music will send you. The chicks will dig you. You will become Moscow's ambassador of cool, the Messiah of cool even, and some day, I will visit Moscow, and who knows, you will take me to a rock and roll concert over there."

"But cultured people will say it is just noise. I don't think rock and roll can ever have a place in the Soviet Union. But I hope you will come to visit me, of course."

"Wait and see, pal. It's catching on like wild fire. Listen, down here in the Village, the folkies, most of them, think of rock and roll as music for lower orders, peasants you might say, but, man, I took some of my 45s over to Liverpool on vacation last year, and I played them my music, Smokey, and Marvin, and James Brown, of course, and Buddy Holly, and Chuck Berry, and they say, we want you to hear something. I think, Jesus, rock and roll is American. But they drag me into this lousy cellar in the middle of the day to hear these four boys. They are really good. When I go, I leave my cousins a few of the discs, and I got a letter saying the guys in that cellar went on tour with Little Richard who taught one of them, Paul was his name, his hoo holler."

Max thinks Ray Charles is certainly fine so we agree on this and also that it's shame "I Can't Stop Loving you", number one most of the summer, has been topped by Bobby Vinton, who is a drip, singing "Roses are Red". I feel I've done some basic work on Max. "You want to share another bottle of this vino with me?"

"With pleasure. What do you think of my new shoes?" He sticks out his feet to reveal his brand new loafers. "They are called Bass Weejuns, I purchased them at the store, B. Altman, and there is a slot for a penny. I say to myself, Maxim, only in this country could there be shoes with a space for money. It is, as someone said to me, crazy. I call them my Capitalists."

The bartender overhears him and starts to laugh, and it's infectious. Everybody roars with laughter, and Max, too, lets out that infectious chuckle of his, and tells a Soviet joke involving sausages. Soon a guy, still laughing, buys a round of drinks. Max offers to perform a magic trick. I've seen him in the park, entertaining the little kids in the playground, pulling coins from their ears. Look, he says, a Russian coin, twenty kopecks. Max the Magician. Changes his clothes, changes himself. "Can I confide in you, Pat?"

I gulp some wine. "Sure." I'm flattered.

Loose now, Max tells me how he practices English in his room, how he tries to speak less formally, like an American.

"I think this sounding American and looking American go together," he says, and tells me that when he's alone, he stands in front of the mirror in his room, to get the posture right. He understands you have to stand loose, casual, get easy in your joints. Bend your knees, amble around like nothing matters, swing your arms, snap your fingers.

"You see? So in my room, where there is privacy, I rehearse this. What a miraculous piece of language making, a true art form this American slang is, Pat. In the subway I eavesdrop on people, I hear one fellow say to his friend, 'Me and the chick, we are Splitsville.' This is marvelous."

"But you must have slang in Russia."

"Sure, sure, naturally."

Naturally, I think. Sure, they have everything we have, and it pisses me off, a little, this response. "Let me ask you something, Max. Are you a member of the Communist Party?"

"Why do you ask?" He leans forward, and I think for a crazy moment he's going to proposition me, that he thinks maybe I'm a candidate myself. "Yes," says Max. "Of course. It is quite an honor."

"Do they force you?"

"No, Pat, it is something to be desired. Why do some people fear it so much in the United States? They hate us. They say bitter things about Fidel Castro too, and that the Cubans are victims, that all socialists are spies and murderers. I hear them say, better dead than Red. Do they truly believe such a thing?"

"Some. Sure."

"Do you believe this, that it is better to be dead than Red? You know in Russian, red is a beautiful word. It means beautiful."

"I don't want to be dead under any circumstances. No."

"I'm glad."

Better dead than Red. Strange, how it would turn out JFK himself said he'd rather his kids were Red than dead. It didn't come out for fifty years until one of his girlfriends published her trashy little book about him, our handsome young Irishman, our best President; and he would be dead a year and a half after I had that conversation with Max on MacDougal Street.

"In Greenwich Village, many of us feel socialism can be good," says a familiar voice, and Nancy hops up onto a barstool. "Hello, I'm Nancy Rudnick," she says, putting her hand out; she's so beautiful in the soft bar light, it's hard for me to look at her. She's had her dark hair cut very short, thick bangs over her forehead; it shows off her long neck and the round very blue eyes. She focuses on Max as if he's the only person in the bar.

Sliding off his stool and blushing, Max takes her hand, and gives a little bow. "Ostalsky, Maxim. Max."

"I know who you are. Welcome. It's lovely to have you in New York. I hope we are treating you well." She smiles. She's playful. She raises one long slim arm—she has these very long arms, and sometimes I think: the better to make you mine—raises it to adjust a gold hoop earring, and this shows off her figure because in the heat she's wearing only a sheer white Mexican blouse, and a full blue skirt, and red cotton shoes she got in France with ribbons wound around her ankles. She kisses me on the cheek. "Hello, Pat, darling, it's been a while."

I haven't seen Nancy since she let me drive her to Jones Beach in June. Been trying to forget her. "Where have you been?"

"The usual, here and there, but I've missed you, Pat, sweetie," she adds, always in that husky voice that drove me nuts even the first time I see her, hanging on a strap on the A-train, a spring night in '59.

I'm riding the A-train home from 125th Street, been to see James Brown at the Apollo, the first time I've seen him in the flesh. Whatever records of his I can get hold of, I play over and over. Never before tonight have I seen anything like this, it's different from a record or the radio. Clayton Briscoe, a cop works Harlem and who was at the Academy same time as me, one of the few Negro detectives in the city, gets me into the show gratis. I owe Clay. This night changes my life. In return I plan on inviting him down to the Village when Sonny Rollins is on at the Vanguard. He's crazy for Rollins.

So I'm high on it, smoking and whistling tunelessly what sounds to me like a fine rendition of "Night Train", remembering Brown's moves, how he works the stage, like a man with wheels implanted in his feet.

The A-train makes its fantastic run all the way from 125th to 59th, no stops, and I'm hanging on a strap, singing, staring at the Miss Subways poster, and suddenly I'm aware of a girl next to me. "What are you singing?"

"You call it singing? Thanks."

"If it makes you feel good," she says and laughs, a low husky laugh.

"Just something I heard."

"I saw you when I got on," she says.

"You're following me?"

"Maybe, but I'm harmless." She laughs again, and I look at her sideways, this tall girl—almost as tall as me—with long thick shining dark hair held back in a pony tail, the very blue eyes. She's about twenty. She's wearing a straight black skirt, tight black turtleneck sweater, red cinch belt around her little waist. A big brown leather bag hangs over her shoulder, the strap decorated with those peace buttons you see around the Village.

The long legs, the eyes, the voice, the clinging sweater, she is easily the sexiest girl I've ever seen, and she smells like lilies of the valley. I'm glad I'm wearing a new light-blue plaid sports shirt, and slacks I only got a month earlier.

She nods at the Miss Subways poster. "I'm surprised they have Negro girls."

"Does it matter?"

"Yes, it matters. Definitely, it matters when there is any advancement for the Negroes. Don't you believe that?"

"Why? You're not colored."

"Never mind," she says, but I can see she files it, and might hold it against me.

I'm wrong. She comes on to me. I get off at West Fourth, and she follows me. When I ask her if she'd like some espresso coffee, she agrees, and we walk, not speaking, to Bleecker Street where she spots an empty table on the sidewalk at Figaro.

"My name is Nancy Rudnick," she says, and asks me what I do.

I tell her I'm a cop.

"Gosh. Seriously? Do you like it?"

"Yeah, I do, what's wrong with it?"

"I just don't know any policemen," she says.

"I'm a detective."

"I see. Where did you go to school?"

I tell her Fordham. "GI Bill. Korea. Graduated in '55. You?"

Idly, she twirls her hair around a finger, and looks down into her coffee. "Upstate," she says.

"New Paltz? I have a cousin at the state university there. Or Binghamton?"

"Vassar."

But we drink a lot of coffee, and she tells me about how she grew up in Greenwich Village, about her father's house on Charlton Street. She tells me she plans to be a painter and has her own little studio at her father's place and, out of the blue, she invites me over. "Them Village girls are all nymphomaniacs, they believe in free love," my pop would say. Me, I think, if so, good. Great. This girl I just picked up in the subway—or did she pick me up—I'm hooked.

"Do you like music?" she asks when we're at her place, and I nod, and she says, "Crazy", and without waiting for an answer, selects an LP album by Odetta, the folksinger, not my thing, but then Nancy pats the bed that doubles as a couch and is covered with an orange and blue Indian bed-spread, and she's singing along to "Dark as a Dungeon" with so much fervor you might think she comes from a long line of miners. So I fall for her. I fall for it that she loves singing and just like me can't carry a tune. For this girl, I'll listen to anything. I'll listen to her politics. For the legs, and the eyes. "It's kind of not your thing, is it?" says Nancy, and shuffles her albums, puts on *Songs for Swingin' Lovers!*.

"You like Sinatra?"

"Everybody likes Sinatra, what did you think, I only listen to stuff about the workers? Don't be silly. I have almost all his albums."

We smoke a little pot for a while, and giggle, and eat lumpy brownies she baked earlier, maybe with some hash, I can't tell for sure because I'm so high from being around her, and so excited I'm half out of my mind, especially because she tells me straight out that she has a diaphragm and we don't need to worry about her getting pregnant. I'm not used to girls like Nancy.

After that night, I always connect Nancy and James Brown doing his thing at the Apollo, the two great events for me that spring of 1959. Then she's gone, and it's not until the fall of '61 that I see her again, this time in the park, eating a toasted almond Good Humor. Offers me a bite. Says she graduated college, went to Paris to meet some artists, and is now starting grad school at NYU.

I can't take my eyes of her. I'm hooked, and a little desperate; I think of wild stuff I want to do to her, with her, things that I could never tell anyone. We go out on and off, but she's not making any commitments. I'm jealous. I figure if she slept with me when we just met, who are the others?

That year I start signing up for courses at NYU. I follow her around like a dog and sometimes she feeds me scraps, like she was doing at Minetta that night she shows up, when I'm sitting at the bar with Max.

"We don't all believe what Mr Hoover tells us," Nancy is saying to Max. "Some of us even believe that Karl Marx was quite a smart fellow, perhaps Lenin, too. My father believes. My cousin Irma went to a youth festival in Moscow in 1957 and she says there are many wonderful things in the Soviet Union, and everyone was very nice, and all the students danced together."

This makes Max smile. "It is true. I myself was at the festival. It was quite amazing with so many young people debating, declaring friendship, promising to support peace and love, it was such an important event. One young lady taught me to do the Lindy Hop."

"I've been very much wanting to say hello," Nancy says. "I saw you at a party the other night, the artists, over on the Bowery? You know, Maxim, I know my father would like to meet you. He would be so interested," she says. "Please, Maxim, do come to Daddy's house, or we could go listen to some music. Or both. Do you like folk music, or jazz, Maxim?"

"Oh, yes, very much. We like jazz quite a bit in my country, and we have a few good jazz musicians of our own."

"Who do you like?"

"I very much like Stan Getz, Ella Fitzgerald. We like many American musicians. The great Paul Robeson, of course. Pete Seeger. Mr Van Cliburn, of course."

"Do you like Miles Davis?"

"Yes," he says. "But I only know his music from records."

"I have a feeling Pat makes you listen to his stupid rock and roll. We'll go hear Miles one evening," she says. "It's a disgrace how badly Miles Davis was treated as a Negro, even though he's a genius."

Max is all ears, and though he sees it's proper, as he might say, to address himself to me from time to time, all he can think about is Nancy. His face is pink. He's taken his glasses off. He's leaning as close to her as he dares, then he pulls himself up, gulps his beer, and turns to me.

"Pat, do you believe the racism in this country is quite terrible, what would you say?"

"It's not good." I hate putting Americans down in front of a Red, but he's right; the racism is as deep and embedded and hard as the schist underneath the city. "What about Russia?"

"Socialism precludes all racism," says Nancy.

"Yes," says Max. "It's forbidden."

I can't tell if Ostalsky wants to fuck her or make her a commissar.

"Max, you might like to join us on Saturday in front of Woolworth's on 39th Street. We generally picket the store because it refuses to serve Negroes in the south."

Nancy stretches out her long legs, then crosses one over the other, wiggles the foot, making us, making everyone look at her. She sips her wine and sighs a little, with delight perhaps, or just a general sense of owning it all; in Greenwich Village she is a princess, anointed by her father, secure in the strange mix of left-wing politics and fancy schooling.

Max is enchanted.

This is how it begins. It's my doing, I introduce them, and the fact I find myself eating my liver about Nancy and Max is all my fault. At first I tell myself Nancy just takes a fancy to the idea of a real live Commie. At first, I try not to think that maybe she just likes him, but even then, that first time they meet, you'd have to be dead or dead drunk not to feel the electricity between them in that bar.

Never again am I going to date somebody who doesn't like my music. I tell my sisters, "Don't go steady with a boy who has different tastes in music, it will come to nothing." They think I'm nuts.

Nancy looks at her watch. "Oh, God, it's already 9.30. I have a paper to write. Walk me home, Pat darling, would you?" Nancy says suddenly, and on the way to her place on West 4th Street, she puts her hand in mine.

She wants something, she knows how to play me, and she never looks back at Max, standing in the window of the bar, watching us. He's said he'll stay on for another glass of beer, but somehow I get the idea they've arranged to meet later; like two spies they have some secret, something they managed to communicate without me knowing how, or maybe I'm paranoid. Drunk, too. Very tired.

"I guess you're pretty excited meeting a real goddamn Communist, right, Nance? Is that right?"

"Don't be so sarcastic. Why do you do that, Pat? It's a nice night. Please, be sweet."

"And your dad, Saul's gonna jump for joy when you bring him home, right? A Russki, a Red, and educated, too, speaks languages, probably can converse on the finer points of Marx."

She doesn't bite. Instead she squeezes my hand. "Are you OK, sweetheart? I know this case on the High Line must be giving you terrible anxiety."

"I'm fine. Thanks for asking."

"This case, your dead girl, this is the dark side of the human psyche, I believe. Tell me about the girl, Pat."

"Not right now."

"Was she beautiful? Do you think they cut her up before she was dead? It's horrible, and you have to tell me about her. I'm doing a thesis about the psychology of fear and the way people can watch a murder and run the other way? It's a big deal in the world of social psychology."

Nancy never stops, always in motion, always with a paper to write, or a picture she's painting. She has other projects, her job at a community center for poor Negroes, the Women's Strike for Peace, her guitar lessons, her attempts to get a short story published in *Mademoiselle* magazine. She goes at life with enough energy to kill a horse. "I love to eat, you know," she said to me at a place uptown where we were eating ribs once, as she gnawed the meat off the bone, her mouth covered in barbecue sauce.

Once I watched her play the piano over at her father's house on Charlton Street, and she kept her foot on the pedal hard, and played so fast you could barely see her hands. She wasn't good, but she was loud and she had drive. Nancy. Driven. Opinionated, always sure she's right; but when she wants something, she moves in, all smiles and charm, so I know I can't escape, and I'm like a fly drowning in honey, or maybe a sucker swarmed by bees, at least those rare times she lets me stay with her at her place.

At her building on West 4th and Sixth Avenue, after we leave the Minetta Tavern, Nancy kisses me lightly, and leans against the wall. From her large leather bag, she takes a glass flask, the shape of a cigar case. "Look what I got? Bourbon. Isn't that what you like, Pat? Pat darling, you look awfully nice in that new shirt, but your eyeglasses have a crack. Why don't you go see my lovely friend Jorge, who works at the shop, you know, on 8th Street. He's so nice, and he'll give you a break on the price."

"Another one of your boyfriends?"

"Gee whizz, Pat, you've really gone off the deep end. Is it this murder? You're suspicious of everyone, even this hard-working young Cuban. Jorge just sells glasses. Really, he's very nice, he's Cuban, and he works part-time to support himself as a journalist. You should do it. You could get glass in your eye or something."

I tell her I'll go because it's easier than arguing.

"Can you do me a teeny favor, Pat?"

"Honey, I've told you what I know about the High Line case. It's all in the papers. I don't have any more for you."

"Right. But there's another little thing."

"What's that?"

"Really? You're such a peach, Pat."

"Name it."

"Well, I have this party to go to the day after tomorrow, but it's out in Brooklyn, and I don't want to take the subway when I'm dressed up, and I was wondering if you'd drive me. You always say you don't mind giving me a lift."

"You look pretty good to me like that."

"Oh, thanks, but I can't go like this," she gestured dismissively to her sheer white blouse, and the thin cotton skirt. "I plan to wear my new black sheath, with the red cinch belt, you know? And heels, probably, and those long silver earrings Daddy brought me from his trip to Morocco."

"What should I wear?" I don't care for her friends or their parties, but the way I feel right now I wouldn't care if she was attending a party run by Che Guevara.

"Oh, sweets, that's so nice, and you have such terrific clothes, but I didn't mean you have to actually come to it. You'd hate it, Pat. It'll be all writers, and those actors from LaMama trying to get in touch with their emotions and what not, and you always burst out laughing, and also some friends who went to Brandeis, I wish I had gone there, and we'll be planning our next Fair Play for Cuba demonstration, and you'd just get mad." She takes a swig of her drink, and a deep breath, and I look at her, and I want to hurt her. I want to get to her enough so she hurts, but I don't know how. "You'd hate the music, I mean, they'll play Woody Guthrie, and all that folk music that bores you silly."

"Stop it."

"Stop what."

"The lying. There's actors, and music, and politics, you have no idea what the hell you're saying. You have a date, but you want me to give you a ride."

"Be nice."

"Why?"

"Because you love me," she says. "It's like this, Pat, to tell the truth, I do have a date. So you won't mind just dropping me, will you?"

"What's wrong with him? This date?"

"He doesn't have any wheels. And you have your Uncle Jack's lovely red Corvette you bought from him."

"You're really something."

"What? Why?"

"Never mind."

"Honestly, Pat. Sometimes I don't understand you. You like driving me, don't you? You always say you like it. Why don't I come over to Hudson Street one night soon, like we did before, I could meet you over there? I like your place."

"You like slumming it."

The rancid stink of pizza from the place next to Nancy's building gets in my nose. "I have to go. I'll drive you to your party in Brooklyn Heights."

"You are a doll, you really are. Thank you, Pat. I do love

you," she says, and looks at her watch. "Do you want to come up for a little while?"

I have no pride left, and I go with her, and we fight because she tells me she's on the Pill now, and I ask her how come.

She says it's so much easier, and I get mean, and ask if it's easier to pick up guys in the subway. Nancy opens her door, and waits for me to leave. "Don't be such a prude, Pat," she says. "I'd like you to go now."

"Go to hell."

It's a sultry, still night, no air, hard to breathe, Italian families out on the stoop, men in undershirts, women gossiping, swollen feet in backless bedroom slippers.

Outside my building, Tommy is hanging around with some boys who look like creeps from some gang. I tell him it's late, time to go to bed, but he ignores me. Upstairs, I get a pair of ice-cold beers, drag my mattress out onto my fire escape, and settle down. These days, I'm not sleeping. The heat. The case. At least out here, there's a breath to catch.

What time is it? 11:30. As hot as midday. Left Minetta around 9.30, Max still at the window. Left Nancy around 11. I can't get the sight of them, Max, Nancy, out of my head; it eats away at me like a worm in my gut.

CHAPTER FOUR

October 17, '62

ALL DAY WEDNESDAY, COLD seeping under my apartment windows, the murder on the pier too fresh in my head, me hallucinating, feverish, my hands stinking of the dead body, I stayed in bed, trying to sweat it out. When the phone rang, I struggled to get to the kitchen to answer it. I was too slow. Whoever it was had hung up.

In spite of myself, I was hoping it was Nancy. Burning up I lay on my bed, thinking about her.

I wanted Nancy in spite of her and Max being an item almost since they met at Minetta. Me, being a sap, it had taken me a while to figure it out. She was like white phosphorus.

My uncle Jack got hit by the fall-out from a phosphorus bomb in the war. He recovered but his right eye was always screwed up, and it was on his mind a lot, the way those bombs would explode, set things alight, could be used for bombers to find their way. When fragments of white phosphorus hit your skin, they stuck to the flesh, you couldn't get it off, and it burned you bad.

It was like that with Nancy. Whatever it was, it stuck to me. It burned me, I couldn't get it off. She took no notice. Carelessly, she strutted her stuff. Sometimes she let me sleep with her. Sometimes not. She laughed and charmed and sulked, and she got what she wanted. She had the looks and the sex, and I couldn't resist no matter how many times I tried. I knew she was bad for me. I knew she would never love me, or want me the way I wanted her, and it was killing me.

I watched the ceiling of my apartment and listened to the radiator clank, steam hissing. I had to get up. I had to get onto the case, the dead man on Pier 46. I knew it wasn't the Mafia. I felt panicky because I couldn't stand up. My legs were like Jello.

Next door, somebody was typing. Upstairs, somebody was playing opera music. Lot of Italians still around the area, even a few artists who couldn't afford better.

My own pop had said I was going straight to hell for living in Greenwich Village alongside faggots and Commies. But God knows, it was better than the dark, pious, myopic place I came from. I was born on the West side, midtown, what they call Hell's Kitchen. My parents lived in that suffocating apartment where you could smell the cabbage from downstairs, and hear the neighbors yelling, and the sound of my mother saying her beads.

The family, the church, it was all they cared about, maybe baseball for the men, at least until the Giants left town. The women hung up pictures of the President next to the Sacred Heart stuff, and they talked about JFK like he was some kind of saint. Otherwise, they had no vision of life.

My old man hated the Russkis almost as much as he hated

68

the English, and that's saying something. Joe McCarthy was a saint in my house, not to mention J. Edgar Hoover.

"You got to hand it to them, the Russians, they put a man in space, first," I said once because I was obsessed with space, and also to aggravate my pop. He wanted to slug me; I could see it on his thin mean face that was worn down from anger.

But by then I was bigger than him and a cop, and he couldn't do anything about it, or the way I dressed.

"What's with them shoes, Pat? Jesus, faggoty suede boots," he said. "Black turtleneck, what the hell is that?"

After I finished school and the academy, and I was a working cop, I got myself the apartment here on Hudson Street, on the far west fringes of Greenwich Village. The area was still rough, the tenements inhabited by immigrants and dockworkers, who kept chickens in the scruffy backyards. People were hard up. Single men lived alone in rooms with a gas ring. Rolled their own smokes, or picked up pennies from the sidewalk to make the quarter for a pack of Pall Mall.

My place had been a cold-water flat back then, the toilet in the hall, the bathtub in the kitchen, but I got it fixed up, bathroom and all. I could play my music loud as I wanted and I spent summer nights on my fire escape, listening to the stuff coming in on the radio from the south, or WUFO in Buffalo. Didn't have to listen to my father call it "monkey music".

In those days, there were a few other cops who lived around the Village. I used to run into one of them, an Italian called Frank who lived on Perry Street; he had pretty long hair for a cop, but he was sharp as hell, and we would sometimes drink together, or play a little pool.

He had been in Korea, like me. He had the kind of guts I never had. Everyone knew how corrupt the system was, and years later he fought it, and he got shot in the face for his trouble.

Hudson Street wasn't part of the Greenwich Village of cafés, and galleries, cobblestone streets, brownstones and redbrick houses. But at the White Horse, a couple of blocks up, I met writers, and I liked them; I liked the life.

I started drinking there when I moved into my apartment. Sometimes I met girls who asked about that Welsh poet who drank himself to death. Told them I knew him, and I was there that fatal night. It was a great pick-up line.

People fought over politics like it was life and death, and I heard stuff I had never thought about. Sometimes the conversations turned into fights that went on all night. One time this skinny writer, Michael something, tells me about what he calls the other America, whatever the hell that is, but they're pretty happy to have an Irish cop. I know the Irish songs. When I bring Nancy by, Mailer looks her up and down, and Baldwin says she can call him Jimmy. She's impressed, unlike my pa who says to me, "Fucking Dorothy Day, Catholic Workers, my goddamn ass. What kind of Catholic is she? She's a goddamned Red."

Again, the goddamn phone rang; again, I stumbled to the kitchen. It was one of the guys in the office. Voice almost inaudible.

"How come you're whispering?"

"Just listen to me. The coroner, the ghoulish one, you know, with three strands of hair he combs over that bald head? He examined the man from the pier. Said far as he could tell, the wounds matched those from the girl on the High Line. Says it's the same knife. Same everything."

"What else?"

"I have to get off, Pat. That's all I got."

"What's the hurry," I said. "Hello?" But he had hung up. I tried calling back. As soon as he heard my voice, he put the receiver down. I called the station house again; the sergeant said, "Get your rest, Pat."

What the hell was going on? Was it that bastard Logan? Was I no longer welcome in my own precinct?

"What's going on?" I said.

"Just get some damn rest," the sergeant said, and I told him to put me through to my boss. When Murphy picked up the phone, he told me the same thing he had told me the night before: get some rest.

Somebody, and it had to be somebody higher up, didn't want me on the case. Again, I thought about Logan, the bastard on the pier who told me I was off it, that I was not wanted.

I stumbled upstairs to the Perinos' apartment to check on Tommy. He was OK, and his father was home, so I went back to my bed, feeling like death warmed over.

Nancy always told me that I used Tommy Perino. "Use him for what?" I said. "For company," she says, "you make believe he's your son. You ought to get married, and have some kids." She tells me all the time. "What about you?" I say. "Not me," she says. "I don't want to be tied down. Not me."

Tommy was a loner, kept to himself, but he liked a little change jingling in his pockets to make him feel good and right with the other kids. He never took a handout. Not since I met him, first day I move into the building in '57, would he take money for nothing.

So, over the years, I gave him little errands, got him to pick up some smokes, take a package over to the precinct, and I gave him a quarter, and sometimes a buck.

Maybe it's wrong when I ask Tommy to help me on the High Line case. I say, listen, Tom, it's about this arm. We can't find the poor girl's arm. And he says, sure Pat, sure I can help you out. I tell him there's a brand new crisp fiver for him in it, maybe a sawbuck. Tommy's a garbage rat, always diving into the cans, looking for something to sell or salvage. Maybe it's wrong, asking him. But I got nothing else.

It's the end of July, and we're not making any progress. After we fix the victim up some—people react bad when they look at a mutilated girl—we put out a picture of her to the papers; nothing comes back. Jane Doe remains unidentified.

Takes Tommy two days to find the arm. Takes him two days of searching the meat market until he finds the arm in one of the garbage bins. Put his arm right in it, and pulls the thing out. I call it in, and somebody, a couple of cops on that beat, one of the medics, get it and take it away before I see it. Did I ever worry about how it affected Tommy?

Did I notice he wasn't exactly the same kid after that?

"What did it look like, Tom?"

"Like? Like a hunk of old meat, maggots all over it," he says. "It stank. Whadya expect when it's boiling stinking hot in the city," he adds and then goes upstairs to his own apartment.

But this gives us something. The coroner examines the arm. It's a match for the dead girl, he says. The top of the arm matches the wound where they sawed it off, and he explains some process by which he can tell if the flesh, the skin and bone, once belonged to the girl. Also, most important, there's the tattoo; on the inside of her arm, the worm, the words Cuba Libre.

We get the news out that the Jane Doe is probably Cuban. We put the tattoo in the papers. It's only time until we get an ID, and catch the bastard who killed her and hung her from the High Line.

You say the word Cuba, you get a lot of conspiracy theories. In the next few days, after the papers print the story, the phone at the office rings off the hook. People telling me Castro is the actual devil. Castro's spies murdered the girl. No one is sure what the worm means, not at first, but the words Cuba Libre get plenty of reaction.

If the girl is fighting Castro, she is a martyr, people say. The New York Diocese takes up her case, says they will post a reward; anything for someone who fights the Communist evil. One caller informs me that Russians landed on the High Line in a spaceship and did the job.

A lady whose husband was in the 2506 Brigade and died at the Bay of Pigs, says to me, and I'm scribbling it down fast as I can, phone under my chin. "They let us down," she says. "Them Kennedys, they left my husband and his men on that beach to die. The Kennedys killed him, they're killers, they don't care for nobody, and that Bobby Kennedy, he's the worst of all, you ask me they had a hand in this terrible death, poor dead girl." The next caller wants Bobby on the case, he's the Attorney General, he cares for the people of

Cuba, he hates Castro, he's been right in there fighting for freedom.

One man stops into the station house and tells me the girl is Miss *La Prensa*, Gladys Feijoo, the girl Castro kissed when he was in New York in '59. I dig out some clippings from his trip. It's true. A picture in the *Daily News* shows the girl, long dark hair, kissing Fidel on the cheek while he writes in her autograph book. Castro is smoking a cigar. He hired a public relations firm to show him how, and he was a star, charming, talking to everyone, visiting the zoo, visiting Columbia University.

Then I think: maybe Saul Rudnick, Nancy's father, knows something. Rudnick used to teach at Columbia, and I'm guessing he loves Castro like the rest of them. It's a long shot, but I don't have much else, so I call him. Saul says come on over, though he doesn't like me much.

Saul opens the door himself. "Hello, Pat," he says, "Come in."

In baggy brown corduroy pants, and a red sweater, he's a big balding man, about sixty, a lawyer, an ex-football player, long fiercely intelligent face, like a Jewish Abe Lincoln.

In Saul's hand is a copy of the *New York Times*, and I'm hardly in the living room when he says, "Did you see what fucking Bobby Kennedy is doing? What's his business with Cuba? Has his people trying to mine the Havana harbor. Jesus Christ. What can I do for you, Pat. Can I get you a cup of coffee. Sit down, for heaven's sake."

Times I've been in the house, Saul lectured me on the evils of JFK's containment policy, the sadness of the

Dodgers leaving Brooklyn, and why goddamn Rudolph Bing wrecked his favorite operas at the Met. He was also interested in my views; and we had agreed about the rapacity of the damn Yankees. I hated them as much as he did. First few times, when I started dating Nancy, I picked her up at the redbrick house on Charlton Street. Rudnick liked her dates to call for her. I could see he didn't much like me; his idea of a suitor for his princess was not an Irish Catholic cop. But he offered me some of his good malt whisky and made nice. After all, I was his baby's friend.

"Is this about Nancy?" says Saul, leaning against the shining black grand piano. "I didn't know you were still seeing her."

I want him sweet because I need help, so I nod, and, him thinking his baby is safe from me, he sits, gestures to another armchair. I sit, too.

It's a rich handsome room, old Oriental carpets, fine polished wooden floors, good furniture, old sofas, books everywhere. Art, too. Good pictures on the walls. On the piano are clusters of photographs, all in silver frames, many of them of Nancy, of family, even of Saul in his Marine uniform during the war. It's a room with a ripe comfortable feel, and the truth is, deep down, I like it here. I'd like to have this. To belong.

The Rudnicks' Village is a different place from mine, a place of pretty tree-lined streets and redbrick houses that date back to before the Civil War; of nineteenth-century brownstones, where old ladies still live behind lace curtains; of little theatres, and arthouse movies; of prosperous people like her father, and their children.

Last I heard, Saul Rudnick was fighting for a union on behalf of the Mohawk Indians building the Verrazano Bridge. Saul's pretty keen on the working class, except for me. Fordham is not what he has in mind for his daughter; he prefers Columbia boys for his little girl.

Truth is, I like Saul Rudnick. Admire him, too. Sure, he's a Communist, but you have to give it to him, he's a straight arrow. Back during McCarthy, when he's called to testify to the House Un-American Activities Committee, he tells them to shove it, more or less; he says what he believes, tells them he's a Communist straight out; also he never rats out his friends, goes to jail for it. This gives Saul the moral high ground, which he claims with glee. Nancy gets it from him, the sense of always being right.

"Ah, Martha, thank you," Saul says when the colored maid brings coffee on a little silver tray. "Try the ruggelach," he adds. "These are from Greenberg's. Excellent." He stuffs a pastry in his mouth. "Plenty of butter in these babies," he adds. "Now what can I help you with?"

I tell him about Miss *La Prensa* and how somebody identified her as the dead Cuban girl on the High Line.

"Oddly enough, I remember Miss *La Prensa*. I remember that photograph of her and Fidel in the paper. Nice girl, too, if I recall, but nothing in it, not between them. He was a serious revolutionary. By God, he was a handsome man, though. It was April when I met him, what three years back? I was teaching at Columbia in '59, adjunct professor, naturally nobody would hire a Red full time. April 15, 1959," says Saul. "We knew from where the police had deployed their barricades that it would be on that closed-off portion of West 116th Street

"We, students, professors, were not alone. Joining us was a group of local Cuban–American women. Columbia has a tense relationship with the surrounding Harlem community and it is rare for any of these ladies to even consider walking across our campus, but on that day it was their campus as much as ours. Those tiny Latinas sang, and by the time two hours of this cross-cultural camaraderie passed, we have their accent, and we are singing

Wel-cum Fidel Castro, wel-cum ju New York
Wel-cum Fidel Castro, wel-cum ju New York
Wel-cum . . .

"And then his entourage pulls up, preceded by a motorcade of New York City police on motorcycles with lights and sirens blaring. First out of the lead limo was a slight but lithe khaki-clad man wearing a vaguely familiar looking beret. One of the woman whispered, 'Che, it's Che!' How surprised I was that he is only perhaps five feet ten or so, for I have imagined a big man.

"Some of us were not sure at that time who this was, but the little Latina, I thought she was going to faint, so I put my hand on her arm, and held her steady, and we are like that just as the late afternoon sun breaks through, from the car emerges the spectacular backlit Fidel.

"Fidel, who was a man of the people, comes to the barrier, he reaches across to embrace his little ladies, then he strides to us—in his combat boots he is a spectacular strider—and in perfect English, says, 'It's good to be back at Columbia. You know I was once a student here.' He's tall, as tall as me, and I push to the front of the line, and say, 'Dr Castro, welcome,' and he shakes my hand. It was something."

Saul finishes his story, he's been telling it with gusto, but out of the blue he slumps into a chair. His face turns white. I can see the pain.

"Are you all right?"

"It's nothing," Saul says. "I'm fine. My wife will be home soon. There she is. I can hear the door. Ginny?"

"Hello, darling, I'm right here, and I'm going to fix you some Alka-Seltzer. Hello, Pat, so nice to see you." Saul's wife, Virginia, has arrived. She's a tall handsome Negro woman, Nancy's stepmother, and about the nicest person I've met at the house. She kisses Saul, and says to me, "Pat, dear, it's been a while since you've been here, and we miss you, we really do. You're always welcome. Look, why don't you come to our Labor Day Party, like you did last year. OK? Please. Saul, tell Pat he's most welcome."

"Sure."

"You feel bad, dear? I'm going to call the doctor," she says, but Saul waves her away.

"I'm fine. Just indigestion. Let it be, Ginny, please. Nancy is coming later. I'm sorry I can't help you any more, Pat. I remember that girl, the Miss *La Prensa*, but I never got to know her."

"Please, go take a nap, Saul, and you'll feel better when Nancy does get here. Now Pat, let me see you off," she says, and leads me to the front door, shakes my hand, and reminds me about the party.

"Is he OK? Mr Rudnick, I mean?"

"Truthfully, I don't know. He hates the damn doctors, and he never lets me go with him. Goodbye, Pat. We'll see you very soon."

Saul Rudnick's a dead end. I light up on the street, and start for Seventh Avenue. I turn the corner. Coming the other way is Max Ostalsky. He's carrying a bouquet of red roses.

At the corner, I hurry into the coffee shop and sit near the window and watch him as he turns into Charlton Street. Feeling like a spy, or a stalker, I get to the door so I can see Max turn into the Rudnick house. He seems confident, as if he belongs there. It's only a few weeks since we were at Minetta Tavern, him, me, Nancy. Please, Maxim, do come to Daddy's house.

Was that the moment when I knew? When I understood that Nancy had wanted Max, and that she got him? That he had been my friend only until he fell for her? Looking back later, I knew that something in my gut had shifted, something in me had turned bitter and I could taste it. The rest of the summer, through July and August, it began eating me from the inside out.

After I leave Charlton Street, all I want is a drink, but I go back to the station house where there's a note that Gladys—Miss *La Prensa*—called to say she's alive, and fine, and living on East 107th Street with her husband.

On my desk is another message. A woman name of Reyes in Union City; the sergeant scribbled it down, the name, the number. When I call, a woman answers, then, hearing I'm a cop, hangs up. I get hold of the address and drive to New Jersey, to her house, but the door is locked, the lights out. It's probably a mistake, a crank call. The only thing I find in Union City is a flyer pasted to the wall of a shop. A worm and the words Cuba Libre.

A few days later, someone claims the dead girl's body. It's all the information I get; nobody's talking. A man turns up and claims her and they let him have the body, and I can't find out why or who he is. It bugs me all through the summer, the way this Reyes woman leaves a number, then hangs up on me. That her door in Union City is locked, and her lights out.

CHAPTER FIVE

October 18, '62

T HE KID WHO PUMPED gas at the Esso station on my corner was always asking questions. There was a time I had him figured for some kind of agent, FBI, maybe. He had greasy hair and he wore stained overalls, but some kind of feral intelligence was written on his face.

He was there when I filled up Thursday after I crawled out of my sick bed, put on my good gray suit and a blue silk tie, made coffee and got my car. It was cold out. "What's up," said the kid while he pumped my gas. "Nothing much," I said.

"You on a big case, man?"

"Right," I said, and gave him a quarter tip, and drove out to Union City. This time I was going to force the situation. This time I had a second homicide, a second victim with a tattoo of a worm and the words Cuba Libre. I took my gun.

I snapped the radio on, and got Alan Freed, and I listened to Gene Pitney's "The Man Who shot Liberty Valance", which was crap, and then some Roy Orbison. I never liked Orbison, but he was good. There was a difference. You could recognize talent, but if it didn't move you, it didn't matter. Roy Orbison never made me tap my feet, or want to move.

The town looked like somebody picked it up in Cuba and set it down in New Jersey. I had been to Cuba, in '47, me and my uncles, some cousins, a few pals, a bunch of guys looking for a good time. We went down for a long weekend, to gamble, look at girls, or something more because you heard there were plenty of gorgeous babes and we were planning to find out what all the buzz was. Even saw Nat King Cole. Havana was paradise, the girls were stunning, the cocktails had plenty of rum.

One afternoon, while the others were having a snooze, I drove out into the countryside for a couple of hours, looking for a beach where I could take a swim.

I saw the poverty. The fear. The soldiers. Pretty little girls begged for coins, or offered themselves to me, couldn't be more than fourteen. Castro took over, and it looked good for a little while; I understood, I had seen how bad it was. Until later when he threw in with the Russkis and started killing his own if they didn't play ball. After that, I hated the son of a bitch. Max Ostalsky had told me he envied me the trip. He loved Castro. He loved those revolutionaries, or maybe it was just the afterglow, the style, Che Guevara's beret.

In Union City, Alicia Reyes lived above a lace shop where in the window three mannequins draped in creamy veils looked like brides chatting together about their weddings. The time I had been here during the summer, I had knocked on every damn door in Union City and every other Cuban neighborhood. People had shut me out. Now, when I rang the

bell, a small voice replied immediately. "Yes? Can I help you?"
I identified myself.

"I'll be right down," she said, and a minute later she appeared at the door. "I was expecting you."

She looked about fifty. Gray hair tucked into a bun, she was a small woman, skin prematurely criss-crossed with fine lines; she had the tiny sharp features of a little bird.

After she shook my hand, she led me through the shop to a flight of stairs and up to her living room. Pictures of Mary and Jesus and a bunch of saints decorated the walls. I knew them well. My ma had most of them, including the Sacred Heart stuff with Jesus done up like a rock star, all that glowing light and neon-colored spokes coming out of his head.

"Please," said Mrs Reyes, indicating a little sofa with a bright blue shawl tossed over the back, where we sat side by side. Around her shoulders—she wore a plain black dress— was a black lace scarf. I wondered if she was in mourning.

"Your lace is very beautiful."

"Thank you. It is an old Cuban art; for some of us, all we were able to take when we fled was our craft. I should apologize for not seeing you when you came during the summer. Excuse me," she said and disappeared into the kitchen and returned with tiny cups of black coffee and a plate of cookies. "I assume you're here because of the murder on the pier in the Hudson River Tuesday night. Is that right?"

"Yes. I think it's connected to the death of the young woman last summer on the High Line. Her picture was in the papers after he was murdered. Somebody left a phone number for me, but I could never get through. It was you, wasn't it? The two bodies bore the same tattoo."

She felt in her pocket, and produced a drawing. "Like this."

"Yes. How did you know that I was here before?"

"Does it matter?" She lit a cigarette. "Perhaps I saw your name in the newspaper, telephoned, then changed my mind."

"It might matter."

"I'm sorry, then," she said but offered no further explanation.

"Can you help me now? Can you tell me about the tattoo?"

"Yes. You see Castro calls us—those of us who fight against him, whose property he stole, those who want a free country, who desire only to live among our families and friends on our land—he calls us, the real Cuban people, *gusano*. This means worm. You understand?"

I drank my coffee and ate two of the pink cookies. "Yes."

"Somebody quite silly, an American official in Washington DC, one of those, what do you say, gung-ho ex-military men who feels he is a diplomat and understands a country after a few months, and he has indeed been supportive of many of us, he has odd ideas about Cuba. He thinks he can destroy Castro with an exploding cigar. He was involved in the expedition at the Bay of Pigs. He also imagined that it would be good for Cubans to take up the name 'worm' to spread the idea of resistance. Only an American who knows nothing of our country could come up with such an idea, but I believe this is the same man with many impossible ideas when he was in Indochina. I am very fond of the United States, very grateful, Detective, but you are like children, you think you have only to visit a country for a few days, to impose your ideas on it, to know it, to understand. It doesn't matter. People just laughed at him. But a few of our young people, who are fighting against Castro, did take it up. They liked the irony. So they call themselves worms. We've seen this slogan scrawled on walls in Miami and here, as well."

I lit a cigarette to hide my excitement. "You're saying the girl who died on the High Line was on your side? The young man on the pier, too? That you knew them?"

"Yes. They were on the side of good. We believe they were murdered by Castro's spies."

"Fidel Castro has spies in New Jersey?"

She looked at me pityingly. "He has spies everywhere. He will do anything. If necessary he will fight even the United States. Do you know that Comrade Che, as he calls himself, has announced he would drop nuclear weapons on the US, if means the end of the great evil imperialists? Even if it means he takes all his own with him? They are crazy, Detective. But like a fox, you see. They have very good spies, but you Americans don't believe it. Everybody thinks, oh, the Cuban men they are lovers, they sing and dance, they are only good at the art of love, but not the arts of subterfuge and espionage." She laughed bitterly. "There are many right here in the United States, double agents, tough people, who report only to Fidel Castro, and yet Americans, even in the CIA, ignore it, they feel we are idle people, romantic and undisciplined." Inhaling deeply, she squashed the cigarette butt in a silver ashtray. "These people who report to Castro are brutal, so we must have our own. We ask only to go back to our country, to reclaim our houses and our land. Castro and his people know that for us this is a fight to the death.

We will take our island back, or we will die."

"Tell me more about these young people. Please." I was on the edge of the sofa, eating more of those pink cookies—I'd had nothing to eat all day—and smoking, nervous she would change her mind, anxious about how to keep her talking. It was the first decent lead I'd had, but the doorbell rang. "Are you expecting somebody?"

Rising, Mrs Reyes left the room. With her when she returned were three men in suits. They removed their hats. The two young men stood near the door. The third man was older, maybe fifty-five, with a weary face.

Mrs Reyes made more coffee. She produced sandwiches made of Spanish ham and cheese, and there was beer for the men. I gobbled a sandwich. The older man who wore a well-tailored navy blue suit, with a black armband, sat next to me. The conversation was in Spanish, and Mrs Reyes translated.

"Detective Wynne, this gentleman's name is Roberto."

"Roberto what?"

"He believes the young woman you found on the High Line may be his daughter, Susana. She wore this tattoo of the worm, and the words, as protest. God help me, she went into New York to join a demonstration at the United Nations. She was here with us, and she insisted on going into New York, where she was murdered. I let her go." A small sound of intense pain escaped from Mrs Reyes, and she turned away from me briefly to hide her face.

"She lived with you?"

"She lived in Havana, and here."

"Do you have a picture of Susana?"

Reaching behind her to a low table, among the cluster of framed photographs, Mrs Reyes picked one of the girl, the girl I had found dead, hanging from the High Line. With her was a young man but his back was to the camera. They were standing together on a beach somewhere.

I looked at the photograph, and at Mrs Reyes. "She was your daughter."

"Yes."

"But last summer, you didn't say anything."

"I was speechless," she said.

"Somebody claimed the body in August."

"A friend," she said.

"Roberto is Mr Reyes, is that right?"

"Yes. He is my husband."

There was something wrong. Why didn't she introduce him as her husband right away? Why not tell me the girl was her daughter? I got the feeling she was lying, but I didn't know why or about what, unless she was also involved in espionage, in the effort to destroy the Castro regime. There were layers I couldn't dig through, couldn't even guess at; more than ever I felt I was just a city cop, out of my depth, unable to play at these spy games.

"Why didn't he come to us?" I looked at the man named Roberto, whose long face was sunk into his chin. He spoke no English. He murmured in Spanish and Mrs Reyes translated.

"He was afraid. We have made our own investigation," she said while the father, weeping now, excused himself and left the room. A few minutes later, he returned, composed, his face blank with grief.

"I don't understand."

"Some people in your police department wanted money. He was afraid. He was afraid of the police, and also the Mafia."

"I thought the Mafia were on your side. They hate Castro."

"They are on the side of people who pay them. They kill anyone who gets in their way. Perhaps it is somebody who wants it to look like the Mafia."

Mr Reyes turned in order to look me in the face, as if to beseech me. "Please, help us," he said in English and began to weep again. "My daughter."

"What about the young man? I can't see his face in this picture."

"He was her boyfriend. Susana was very young and impressionable, and she had believed wholeheartedly in the Revolution like so many of the young, and left us when she was seventeen to support it. And then more recently, she began to change. She saw what Castro was doing. She fell in with some people who felt the same, and one of them was this young man. He had fought with Castro in the mountains, he had almost given his life, and then something changed him. He saw their system. He learned to hate Castro. I should forgive him because he was a good man, but he pulled my daughter into it. They were to meet in New York. She was a romantic. He and Susana swore to fight against Castro until death. And they did, in the end."

"Have you got a photograph of the young man where I can see his face?"

Mrs Reyes left the living room and returned with a snapshot that showed the two of them, Susana and the dead man from the pier and they were fooling around at a park; they looked like teenagers.

"What was his name?"

"Rica. All he would say was that he was Rica. I assumed

Riccardo was his real name. Thank you. Excuse me, I'll accompany you downstairs, Detective."

On the sidewalk outside the lace shop, Mrs Reyes offered her hand, small as bird bones, so I took hold of it and kept it in mine. "There was more, wasn't there? There was something they told you, wasn't there? Something that can help us find her killer, and that of her friend, of course? Find out why they were killed?"

She nodded, and looked at me hard. "Susana told me that Riccardo had some information. He told her certain things, but he said there was someone else, and he lacked all the pieces of information, but they would meet in New York. He promised me he would not let anyone harm her. I did not like him, to be honest. He was older. He had been close to Castro. I was not sure what he believed. I don't think Susana ever saw him in New York. She telephoned me one last time to say she was waiting for him. That's all I know. They all wore the tattoo. Susana was proud of it when she was here, she would say, 'Mama, look, this is for our country.' But he, he wore a shirt with long sleeves, he covered it up."

"Were they planning something, do you think?"

"You mean an attack? I believe they were going to New York to stop something. Susana kept saying this, even in her sleep. 'We must stop it, Mama,' and then she left. 'Stop.' I would hear her saying over and over. 'Stop.' "

"I'm so sorry for your troubles," I said.

"Riccardo was not a bad man, but he was a zealot," she said. "He felt betrayed by the revolution. He thought of nothing else."

"I'll be in touch."

"Yes, of course."

"One more thing."

"What is it?"

"Why didn't you tell me about your daughter earlier? What's the truth? There must be a reason. I know you were in mourning, terrible grief, of course, but I knocked on doors all summer long, I can't believe you didn't answer just because you worried the cops were on the take."

"I didn't trust you."

"I see. Why?"

"Riccardo, my daughter's friend, he was a peasant, a man of no family, but he spoke perfect English, and several times I heard him on the phone speaking in Russian, and I wondered why. He had been very well educated, and I asked myself, by whom? You have Russian friends, is that not so, Detective?"

"I know a few of them. They're not my friends."

"We knew about your part in the investigation from the newspapers that reported our daughter's murder. But one of our friends also saw an article in what is it called, the *Village Voice*? This past summer? About a Soviet student, a certain Mr Maxim Ostalsky, isn't that right, Detective? It mentioned that you were his friend. Surely this Mr Ostalsky must be a Soviet agent if they allow him to study in the United States. I wondered why a New York etective, perhaps an Irish Catholic from your name, why does he have such a close friend who is a Communist? You saw the article, I imagine, and will forgive my little bit of detective work."

"I saw it, sure," I said. "When it came out."

"Yes," she said and reached into the pocket of her black skirt. "I kept a copy."

"I see."

"Then you understand. I must go upstairs now. You are ill," said Mrs Reyes. "You should go home. It's cold. Winter is coming," she said sadly, as if mourning the season as well as her daughter.

"Let me ask you one more thing."

"What is it?"

"Do you know a Captain Logan? Did he ever contact you?"

Quickly, she shook her head, then walked too quickly back to her door.

CHAPTER SIX

October 18, '62

SOMEBODY HAD BROKEN INTO my place. I usually left a pin in the doorjamb so I could tell if somebody had bust in while I was away. If the pin fell out, someone had been by, and this time, soon as I got home from Jersey, I saw it: the pin was on the floor. I got out my gun and my keys at the same time. I unlocked the door carefully, then shoved it in fast as I could, still holding the weapon.

The apartment was empty. I looked it over. Nothing was missing as far as I could see. Maybe a certain fear, some kind of paranoia was on me, had been since I found the dead man on the pier earlier in the week. Riccardo. His name was Riccardo, according to Mrs Reyes.

After I checked on Tommy, who was at home in his apartment upstairs and confessed he had been into my place looking for a smoke, I went home, sat at the kitchen table, typed out everything Mrs Alicia Reyes had told me that morning and tried to make some sense of it, then I dug out the file I had kept on the High Line case—on the girl who was murdered, who turned out to be Susana Reyes.

But what caught my eye was a copy of the *Village Voice* with Ostalsky's profile.

August 6: it had been August 6 when I first saw the piece about Max Ostalsky in the *Village Voice*. I remembered because it was around the time Marilyn Monroe died. She passed on August 5, and reports of her death appeared in the papers the next day.

How much I loved Marilyn. I'm staring at her picture in the *New York Post* at the office when I knock the ashtray off my desk and it spills butts all over my fresh chinos. "Goddamn it to hell."

"What's with you, Pat?" says the guy sitting at the next desk, a new young detective typing with two fingers, filling out a form.

"Nothing. Leave me be. Do your own damn work."

I'm feeling glum about Marilyn, and pretty much every goddamn thing when my boss calls me in, and says he saw the *Village Voice* and yells at me for palling around with Reds. Murphy sees a Red under every bed, and he considers himself vigilant. Plus, he is not a subtle man.

Lieutenant R. N. Murphy is short with big shoulders and an ugly pug-dog Irish face. His cruddy sour breath stinks of black coffee and the Camels he chain-smokes.

Once he was a star among young detectives, back when he was a favorite of Mayor LaGuardia's. In the war, he fought in the Pacific, he was some kind of Marine hero at Tarawa, which was something, one of the ugliest battles, dead Americans all over the beach. Murphy got a Bronze Star. Makes sure everyone hears it.

"What?"

"Sit yourself down, Wynne," says Murphy. "So what about this Commie pal of yours, man? In that new, what's it called, this rag?"

"The *Village Voice*. And he's not my friend."

"No? Little birdie told me you been meeting him pretty regular for drinks and showing him a welcome to our fair city. You gotta be careful of them son-of-a-bitch Commies, man, you hear me?"

"How do you know?"

The boss laughs his mean pinched laugh. "Gotcha. You told me what I wanted to know. What'd you think, man, that I got spies out watching you?"

"Do you?"

Murphy thinks I'm some kind of bohemian bum, hanging around the Village. To him, I'm a freak, thirty-two with a failed marriage to the girl I got pregnant, the kid I'm never allowed to see, a man who sometimes goes to foreign movies and likes colored music he hates. "Just a friendly warning," he says. "On the other hand, maybe you'll learn something from that Russki. You never know. You find out anything, you come to me, right? Wynne? The FBI would love to hear. Read the piece," says Murphy, leans back in his chair, puts his feet on his desk, and lights up. He wears ugly shit-kickers, big thick black old lace-ups so old the soles are broken. "Just read it."

"I read it."

"Read it again."

"SOVIET GRAD STUDENT DELIGHTS IN GREENWICH VILLAGE" is the headline in the *Village Voice*. The photograph shows Max Ostalsky, smiling, in a new button-down shirt in front of the Washington Square

Arch. In the interview, he says how much he's enjoying his experience in New York, especially Greenwich Village, that everyone is so kind and helpful and his studies interesting, and his particular favorite food is fried clams at Howard Johnsons.

Max even tells a few jokes on himself, he relates how much the hospitality of New Yorkers means to him, and how much their friendship delights him, including the stranger who helped him out, buying a hot dog in the park, a friend he learns is a New York detective name of Pat Wynne. There it is, black and white, me and the Russki. A whisper of something bad hits the back of my neck, raises the hairs. This is no good, this thing about me and the Russian printed in public. The Commies are bad news. There's plenty like my boss still out to get them and the people who make friends with them. I better keep my damn distance, I think, and toss the newspaper into a garbage can.

And then, just my lousy luck, Max—out of the blue, no invitation I can recall—shows up at the station house. These days he looks like everybody—blue button-down short-sleeved summer shirt, chinos—the sergeant hardly takes notice; just calls me to the front door.

"What are you doing here?"

"I'm sorry, Pat, I thought we had arranged to meet. Have I got the wrong day?" He looks apologetic.

"Did we? I don't remember. What did we arrange?"

"I asked if you might take me to see the High Line, and explain about your crime scenes, and you said, come to my office, is that not right? If I am not correct, I'm so sorry."

I'm finished work for the day, more or less, and I want to know what Max Ostalsky has been up to. What's this Commie really want? "Yeah, come on. We'll walk. Maybe catch a breeze off the river. So I see you made the big time, big profile in the *Voice*."

Max doesn't answer, just lights up a cigarette. Outside, on Charles Street, a young guy is smoking a joint. Sees me, tosses it into the gutter.

"You into grass yet, Max?"

"I have my Lucky Strikes."

"How come? You dig the rest of it, the girls, the music, you scared because they showed you some propaganda films about the decadent West at home, and how you do drugs, you'll become addicted like our own people in the ghetto?"

Without answering, ignoring the sarcasm, he says, "I have asked to see the place of the crime, Pat, this is to help me understand the workings of America's Civil Society. If this is not proper, please, tell me."

"Why? You thinking of sticking around, maybe join the police here? Jesus, it is hot. They get heat like this in Moscow?"

"Yes, the summers can be hot," Max says, keeping pace with me.

"You been seeing Nancy a lot?" I keep it casual. We're walking, up Sixth, up Greenwich Avenue, past St Vincent's, and west to the river.

"She has invited me to her father's house for dinner."

"I'll bet you and old Saul hit it off just fine."

"I admire him."

As soon as we get close to the river, I change my mind.

Later, it would come back to me that I should have turned around, and told Ostalsky it wasn't on. Get lost, I should have said.

What do I want with this Russki on my crime scene, pawing over my case, asking questions about the dead girl, pestering me for information, and for what? What's in it for you, Ostalsky, I think, looking at him, at the way he's learned to dress, even learned to walk in that casual way as if he's just out having a ball, smoking his Luckys; occasionally he pulls his little notebook out of his shirt pocket and jots something down.

"What the hell do you keep in there?"

Max stops, replaces his notebook. "Oh, as I have said, notes for my classes. This means words I learn. Books I read. Things I observe in New York. Music. I have been listening to quite a bit of your favorites, to Fat Domino," he says. "He is jolly. I like this Blueberry Hill." He smiles, knows the reference to music might please me; how charming this Russian is, and the more I think about it, too eager to please.

"Fats Domino."

My shirt is wet from the humid air; my eyes burn; I can't remember when I ate last.

"Do you know, Pat, when I was a boy I wanted to be a policeman. There was a murder in our building, this was very rare in Moscow, and I met the homicide policemen, I thought they were very, can I say cool, though cool may not have been quite a word they could understand. I had read quite a few detective stories."

"You had detective novels?"

"Surely. In Moscow, things were possible. My mother adores Agatha Christie. I managed to acquire a few of the

97

Americans, such as Raymond Chandler. Are all of your jobs within Manhattan?"

"Most, yeah."

"What was most difficult?"

"The Mad Bomber, no contest, back in the 50s, you ever hear of him? I worked on that case along with hundreds of other cops. Bastard stashed bombs all over town for years. The worst was Penn Station, it's goddamn easy to hide there, impossible to evacuate."

"I envy you, Pat."

"Yeah? How's that?"

"You do a job where you must see things I know of only in books. You are willing to go to places where you may die. I think they say, you put your life on the line, is that the right expression? All I know is books, I sometimes think. You take care of people. Isn't that so?"

He would be good at my job, I think suddenly. He listens hard. He asks good questions. Put him across the table from a suspect, and they'd pour their guts out.

"Nothing wrong with teachers, pal. And don't underestimate yourself. You could have been a good cop. Or a spy? Are you a spy, Max?"

"Is that what you think?" He looks hurt for a second, then he laughs. "Look at me. I talk too much. I talk to everybody, I behave like a fool, even my nice American clothes are always, would you say, rumpled? When I should be studying, I prefer going to movies all night at the Waverly Theater, listening to jazz until four in the morning, drinking whisky. Do you think I could be a spy? I can't keep secrets. I am hopeless. All my life, I had so many ideas. First I want to be a homicide cop. Then I think I must join the military to support my country, but my eyes are bad, and my feet are flat. I will go to Siberia as an explorer, to track the great Siberian Tiger. I would have loved to be a spy, the kind in a novel of the Great Patriotic War who infiltrated the High German command. But I must settle for teaching English," he says. "I'm talking too much. Tell me a little about how you found the girl here."

We're standing directly under the High Line now; a train rumbles overhead. I point at the viaduct. "There."

"Is it forbidden for you to take me up there?"

Forbidden? It's a word that juices me up. We're New Yorkers. We're cops. We do what we want, nothing's forbidden to us.

"Nothing's forbidden in a free country." I'm bragging, telling him we're so free that a cop can show people anything, which is of course crap. The boss would kill me. Probably call the Feds on me. So naturally I take the Russki up the ladder and along the tracks, to the warehouse. Then inside where the girl hid before she was murdered. It's cold and lonely. I explain a little about the way we process a scene, the procedures, and then, outside, rain comes down suddenly, in soaking sheets. Max Ostalsky is poking around the warehouse, peering into dark corners, turning over crumpled sheets of newspapers, asking questions.

"Leave it. Damnit, Max, leave it, it's evidence. Come on, we're going."

"I'm sorry, yes, Pat, I am so sorry if I have done something wrong."

"Let's go. There's nothing more."

"You seem in a hurry to leave now. Have I in some way offended you? Is anything wrong?" Max asks.

"In my line of work, it always is. Let's go home. It's late. I'm tired. It's raining. I'm going home. You should go home, you hear me? Just stay out of trouble."

"What do you mean?" Max asks. "Am I in trouble?"

A big green taxi with checkerboard stripes passes. I yell for it to stop.

"You want a ride, Max?"

"I think I'll walk."

"It's raining, in case you didn't notice, but do what you want."

Out the rearview window of the cab, I can just see Max as he turns in the other direction, and walks back towards the High Line in the pouring rain on a humid summer night, a wet solitary sorrowful figure. Suddenly, out of nowhere, slipping from the doorway of a warehouse, is his FBI tail. He's under the streetlight and I see him clearly: ragged yellow crew-cut; wrinkled short-sleeved shirt; a tie even in the heat; a copy of his newspaper. He looks around and there's something furtive about him, but then he just puts up an umbrella and disappears back into the dark and out of sight. Right then I know it's time to get rid of Max Ostalsky; get him out of my life for good.

It had been bad in August. The whole month. It had been lousy hot. Real dog days. I couldn't sleep, not even out on the fire escape. I recalled that. I remembered people were cranky. Agitated. There had been bad news on the TV; people saying the Russkis were up to something in Cuba.

All I care about is passing the nights when I can't sleep. People are cranky. Fights break out on the sidewalk. I can hear the sound of breaking bottles and sometimes breaking heads. If I'm not in the mood for drinking, I haunt the bookshops and the stalls on Fourth Avenue where you can get second-hand paperbacks for a dime. I pick up crime novels, cop stuff. Ed McBain does it great. It's why I'm taking the writing class at NYU.

I know a lot of the insomniacs who haunt the stalls, junkies, old men, students.

One night around the time when the *Village Voice* article on Max comes out, I head for the Eighth Street Bookshop where I find Nancy sitting on the floor in a thin sleeveless yellow shift.

"Hi."

"Hi," she says and holds up the book. "You should read this. It's astonishing."

"What is it?"

"It's called *One Flew Over the Cuckoo's Nest*."

"I have a bone to pick with you."

"What's that, Pat?" She gets up off the floor, smooths out the shift and refastens a sandal, then takes the book to the front desk and buys it. "I just want to go home and finish my book, so what bone?"

"Who was the man I saw you with this morning?"

"Where?"

"At the Hip Bagel."

"What were you doing there? Why didn't you say hello? Jesus, Pat."

"I saw you with him through the window. You go there, right?"

"Sure. Frequently."

"He was in his forties, I'd have said, but that kind of silver hair only a vain man would wear like that. Lot of hair. Groomed. Gray hair that looked like it gets plenty of attention. He was wearing a dark blue blazer and light gray slacks."

"What about his shirt and tie? You want to tell me about that, too? You follow me, you watch me eat a bagel, you've lost your mind."

"Who was he?"

"What is this, an interrogation? You look terrible, Pat. Don't you ever sleep?

"Who was he?"

"Nobody. You saw you got a nice mention in the piece about Max, didn't you? I want a cigarette, please. Let's go outside."

So we stand in the street, and I light her cigarette. "I'm bored with Max Ostalsky."

"You do look awful," says Nancy. "Is it the case? It must be wearing you out." She touches my arm. "Come on, let's eat something. What about pizza?"

"I don't want pizza and I don't want to talk about the case."

"You're really down in the dumps."

"I'm tired. Fed up."

"With me, Pat?"

"Been seeing our friend Max a lot, then? Why don't you come clean with me."

"You just said you were bored with the subject. Come on, my treat, I'm taking you out to eat, and that's it. OK? Come on."

"Let's go to your place."

"Don't be silly, you have to eat something. You know I can't cook."

"Maybe you should learn, didn't your mother tell you the way to a man's heart is through his stomach?"

"Please, just spare me. We'll go to Waverly Place, they're open all night," and saying it, Nancy heads briskly for Sixth Avenue, and into the coffee shop on Waverly where we climb into a booth in the back, and the weary-looking waitress, a pencil in her tangle of dyed blonde hair, comes over. Smiles when she sees Nancy.

"Hello, Nancy, doll, what can I get you?"

Nancy greets her by name, and Mary, her name is Mary, goes for food. Without paying attention, I wolf down a hamburger and French fries, and coffee.

"Better?"

"Thank you. How come you're being so nice?"

"I'll always take care of you, you know that. We're friends, aren't we?"

I bite my tongue and shake out a fresh pack of smokes, and light up, lean on the table, look through the plate glass to my right, where I see a man in front of the apartment building opposite us. Nancy picks at her cherry pie; I ask for lemon meringue.

"What's up, darling?"

"There's a man across the street, I think he's watching us. The one in the blue denim jeans and a white T-shirt, you see, smokes are rolled up in the shirt sleeve?"

"Like he thinks he's Kerouac. Or Brando or something. Maybe he's just a jerk. You're paranoid, Pat. You are," she says, but she's nervous, she slides lower in her seat. "You need to get off this case. You need to just cool it."

The pie comes. The man across the street walks away, but he comes back, a newspaper in his hand.

"I don't think he's anything," says Nancy. "Too obvious."

"This is stuff you're familiar with?"

"You can bet on it. They've been following my family for a long time." She pushes her pie away. "People think the FBI resemble agents in a movie, you know? Crime fighters. G-Men. They think ever since McCarthy, that son-of-a-bitch, got what he deserved, lost his power, then died, it ended. Nobody scared of Reds. Nobody spooking students, or kids who go on peace marches, or old men who once went to a socialist gathering thirty years ago.

"It goes on and on, Pat. Somebody like you, you don't always see them, the good ones dress up just like regular people, they infiltrate NYU got up as college boys. Some of them *are* college boys. They go to class, they go to parties and dances and clubs with the other students. You think that I'm paranoid, don't you?"

"No."

"You know what I am?"

"What?"

"I'm scared, Pat. I'm scared all the time. At first when I met Max, I noticed an agent who was around a little bit. I knew any Soviet would be watched. But lately, it's been different. The dorky-looking fellow who dresses like a student, crew cut and all, stopped me at Chock Full O'Nuts and offered to buy me a donut, and asked about an assignment in my French history class, but I'm not taking a course on the French revolution, so I walked away. I know the game. I knew he wanted to pump me about Max, but I made sure he couldn't get to me."

"Nothing's up then, with Max. Nothing to tell the FBI?"

"Max is our friend. I thought we could all be friends together."

"Nice. The three of us, you, me and Max, like that French movie, is that what you thought, the one we saw last winter?"

"What's wrong with it?"

"I bet your pop likes him."

"He does like Max. Sure, why not?"

" Is he feeling better?"

"Who?"

"Your father."

"When did you see Daddy?"

"Didn't he tell you? I went by to ask him about a case involving Cubans."

"Oh God, yes, of course he did."

"I needed some information."

"About what?" She leans across the table "Just tell me, I won't get mad, not about this, but I need to know." She pushes her pie away.

"I went to see him about a Cuban connection on the case I'm working."

"Leave him alone, Pat. Please. Leave him be. Is your case that important? We've had enough from you and the FBI, enough of the terror."

"Can't you get over it? McCarthy's been dead five years."

"No. It's never over. Ever since McCarthy hauled Daddy in, it's never stopped. They watch him, they follow him, his wife is a Negro, my Uncle Nate was blacklisted. Did I ever tell you that Uncle Nate went on TV on 'The $64,000 Question', people really liked him, and then the FBI got in touch with the show and made him give the wrong answer to a question everybody knew." Nancy shakes out a pack of Kents, and lights her own. "It's like falling into a bottomless pit, it never stops. They've been doing it since I was in 7th grade. Didn't you guess?"

"I didn't think much about it."

"How naive you are."

"Go on."

"The fear destroyed my parents. My parents had another child, and my mother wanted to name her Rosa. My grandfather put his foot down. Rosa was a communistic name, he said, said it would hurt all of us."

"What happened?"

"Rose—they called her Rose, Rose was OK—she died from polio in 1948. I was eleven. She was only two. My mother couldn't handle any of it, and she died the year after, around the time the goddamn FBI started following Daddy. I would do anything to get the goddamn FBI off Daddy's back now."

"Why didn't you tell me?"

"You weren't the type to understand."

"Why now?"

"Because he's got some horrible lung cancer, and they can't do anything much, and I want him left in peace. You hear me? It's all I want. I want my father to die in some kind of peace." Silently, Nancy starts to cry, enormous tears—you wouldn't think anyone could produce such big tears—running down her cheeks in a flood.

"Do you think that's one of them, across the street, white T-shirt?"

"I don't know. I can't always tell, some of them look so normal, they even smile. They're the scariest ones."

For a while we sit without talking much, and she lets me hold her hand, until she's cried out. "It's like this,

Pat, sweetie, since you asked, Max is a comfort for Daddy, somebody he can shoot the breeze with, who admires him, tells him stories about the great revolutionaries Daddy admires, people Max's grandfather knew. He doesn't get in Daddy's face, like his crazy friends who are all Trots and stuff, never mind, you have no idea what I'm talking about."

Across the street, the man with his newspaper, the man in the white T-shirt has gone. I never saw him go.

"Are you sleeping with him?"

"Don't be such a prude. What difference does it make?"

"You're a fool. Max is married."

"He's separated."

"He has to go back. He's not going to defect for you, honey. He loves his damn country. He's a patriot. You know what, Nancy, if you go on like this, just screwing every man, you'll end up on the shelf."

"That's crude and it's cruel. What do you want? You want me to be a dopey character in *Father Knows Best*? I see the girls I went to Vassar with, with their nicey little husbands and their nicey babies, and most of them, all they do is cook and knit. It's not me. I'm going to be a great painter and a teacher. Max is a fine teacher. My father was a teacher."

"You are thinking about it. Marrying him. What, you'd go live over there? The Second Mrs Ostalsky?"

"I don't know."

"You can't marry some Commie spy."

"He's not a spy. He's a scholar." She looks out of the window. "God, it's hot this year. I can't wait to get to the beach."

"What beach?"

"Fire Island, we go every year, I told you once, the whole family."

"And Max? You're taking him on the family vacation?" I tossed a fiver on the table. "Nancy?"

"What?"

"I'm sorry. Let's not fight."

"I don't want to fight." She touches my hand. It makes me wonder if she'll invite me home with her, to that little apartment on West 4th Street, with some candles lit and music on her portable gramophone, and the rest of it. "I don't want to fight, and I know your case is driving you nuts. I want to help, Pat, darling. I want to make you feel better. OK?"

"How about I take you to dinner tomorrow, somewhere nice?"

"I'll think about it."

"I'll pick you up after your class, you finish at seven, right?"

"You know my schedule?"

"Yeah."

"You stalking me?"

"Only when I have to. Be a good girl and say yes."

"Not tomorrow."

"When?"

"Maybe the day after, I have to think about it. Why don't I give you a buzz, Pat? Let me call you."

"I'll wait for you outside your building."

"Like a proper suitor."

"Of course. Wear something special."

"I'm always special."

But it's three weeks until she calls me and says we can

meet, and on the night I dress up nice, new cream linen jacket, new dark blue shirt. I plan to take Nancy somewhere nice for dinner after her class finishes at 7, somewhere air conditioned, maybe even to Charles on Sixth Avenue, though it will cost a bundle.

In the park, even at dusk, people sit still, fanning themselves, having a cold soda or a languid smoke, the smell of the pot rising into the humid night.

For a while I sit on the steps of NYU, smoking and waiting for her. She never comes. It turns dark, and I know she's left, hasn't come to her class, or gone out another exit. I want to drink.

My car is parked on Waverly, and I head over to it. Nancy lied to me. She had no intention of meeting me. I'm a fool. A dope.

In the park nearby, somebody is playing classical music on a guitar, playing really well, so it catches my attention, and I turn and see them, Nancy and Max. She had left the NYU building by a back entrance, maybe to avoid me where I had been waiting.

Now they're sitting on a railing, their backs to me, eating Good Humor ice creams on a stick, unaware of anyone but each other. The jealousy that's been eating me for a lot of the summer punches me in the face now, whacks me so hard I lose my bearings.

Did she do it on purpose? Did Nancy agree to see me, and then change her mind?

Does she want me to see them? Does he? Did she whisper about me to him, and did they laugh about it? Right then, half subconsciously, I make up my mind to get something on Max Ostalsky. To nail him for something.

I look over at the park. Their heads are together and they're laughing like a couple, like people who just want to touch each other. She leans to him, puts her mouth to his ear. He touches her hair. He strokes it.

CHAPTER SEVEN

October 18, '62

THE FBI AGENT I had spotted near the High Line, the young guy with the butchered blond hair, was across the street from Ostalsky's building on 10th and University. I got there around five. All day, since I returned from Jersey, I'd been going at the case of the dead man on Pier 46, this Riccardo, working it in my mind, figuring similarities to Susana Reyes last July. Make the connections, I thought. But the connection I wanted was Max Ostalsky. I wanted evidence that he had been involved in both cases. I wanted to get him, to nail him. So I went to pay him a visit.

The agent glanced over at me. The Feds could never see what was in front of them; me, if I was running the show, I'd have two heavyweights parked regular outside Ostalsky's building. If I knew he had killed Riccardo on Pier 46, how come they were clueless?

Made me sick that J. Edgar Hoover, who had been a hero, who had run an FBI devoted to hunting down criminals, was now only obsessed with Commies. I'd heard there were ten times as many agents working the Reds as working crime. Hoover was nothing but a fat old man who, they said, wore ladies' dresses and lived with another man.

Nobody answered the bell for apartment 8D when I rang the intercom. I buzzed the super, who appeared suddenly, and opened the heavy door into the lobby for me.

"I'm looking for a Mr Ostalsky," I said. "He stays with the Millers in 8D, wonder if you've seen him." In my hand were two crisp bills.

"None of them's here," the man said. "The Millers gone out of town, the other fellow, that Max, the young Russian, you know? I saw him leave."

"When?"

"Don't know. Maybe yesterday morning."

Wednesday. The morning after he had murdered Riccardo, the morning I was lying in bed sick as a dog.

"You ever see a young lady visiting up here? Tall? Dark hair?"

"Saw somebody like that with the Russian coming up the street one time, arm in arm. Looked to me real cozy."

After I'd seen Nancy and Max in the park, I hadn't seen either one of them again. In September she went to Fire Island with her family. I didn't know if Max Ostalsky went with them.

The sickness I had been feeling since I saw them in the park together came over me again. "Anything else?"

"Not that I seen," said the super.

I held out some money.

"What's that for?" he said. "No thanks, man. This here is my job. You a cop or something, cause a few of them's been around lately. Some kind of cops, or something."

I slammed through the door of the station house, and into Murphy's office; nobody looked up. It was as if I was an outcast.

"What are you doing here, Wynne? I thought you were sick. I thought I told you to take some time off," said Murphy when I was in front of his desk.

"I'm getting to feel somebody's giving me the goddamn runaround. I been feeling this way all week since I caught the case on the pier. Matter of fact, I been getting some mixed signals from you, Murph, the last three, four months." I tried for a neutral tone. I didn't want to push too hard, but I was mad as hell.

My boss put his cigarette in a cracked green plastic, and unwrapped some candy. "Nothing beats a Chunky," he said, and stuffed the whole thick square of chocolate into his mouth. He was a greedy man. His drawer was always full of candy bars that he offered you if he felt you were deserving. He never offered me anything.

Murphy's suit jacket was over the back of his chair; his tie looked like it would choke him, he knotted it so tight. He left me standing in front of his desk. Never told me to sit down.

I said, "I know who the victims are, the girl on the High Line, the man out on Pier 46. I got the IDs."

"What are you doing here? Didn't I tell you to take some time off?"

"You want the case for yourself?"

Murphy was always up for a possible collar that would enlarge his reputation. My boss was a creature of the New

York Police Department, like his father, and his grandfather.

"Go home, Pat. We got Cheeks Farigno for the dead girl last summer, he killed her, and we'll get him on this one too. Same style. Same signature. You would know that if you damn well paid attention."

"Fill me in, then." I sat down and looked at the picture of Robert Kennedy on the wall. Murphy was pissed Bobby was his personal friend, he had often pointed out to anyone who would listen. I loved Bobby. He was the runt of that litter, but he had brass ones, and he was ferociously loyal to his big brother.

"Did you know Bobby used to go on patrol with us at night," Murphy said. "Great guy. We let him ride with us. Sometimes he came along when we questioned thugs, and he loved it, playing cops. Call me whenever you need something," he tells me, and I say, Bob, you ever want a change, you'd be a great cop. He loved that. And he took on the Mob, and the rackets, he had no goddman fear at all."

"So you're charging Farigno to please Bobby Kennedy?"

Murphy didn't like Italians. He didn't like the way they had taken over Greenwich Village. Like a lot of Irish who came to New York earlier, he thought they were all low-lifes.

"Listen to me, OK? I know who the victim is," I said. "He's Cuban like the girl last summer on the High Line. His name is Riccardo. He was her boyfriend. It's all connected up, Murph. I got it." I slapped the desk, expecting some kind of praise, which was stupid, so I helped myself to some Goobers from a bowl on the table, ate them, and lit a cigarette.

"I told you that you were out of line on the girl when it occurred, I told you to let it go. Now, this poor bastard dead as a dead fish on the pier, and we got it, right, you read me, Wynne? We're ready to indict Luca "Fat Cheeks" Farigno. Like I told you, his signature is that Spalding rubber ball, he likes to stick it in their mouths, shut them up, for Christ's fucking sake. But you just keep making trouble, and now you got Captain Logan all riled up."

"He calls the shots for you, this Logan? Who the hell is he?"

"Don't be so smart. Listen the fuck to what I'm telling you. You are not required on this case. It's under control. Go home."

"I have names. The girl is Susana Reyes, the guy is called Riccardo."

"We had her name back in August. You think you're the only cop that knows his way to Union City? We met Mrs Alicia Reyes after the girl's picture went into the paper, she was not helpful, but one of her sons, he was more forthcoming, more, what should I say, easy to persuade, so yeah, we know who the girl was. We also knew you tried to see her during the summer, and we know you were out there yesterday."

I lit a cigarette to hide my surprise.

"You didn't think she told us you'd been pestering her? She was uneasy about your connections with that Russki you hang out with, so she calls after you leave, and she says to me, is Detective Wynne on their side, and I say, no way, he's a good detective, he's a patriot, I give her the whole line of horseshit. I protected you, Wynne. Soon as I find out the dead fish of a guy on the pier has the tattoo, that worm, that motto Cuba Libre, I get somebody on to Mrs Reyes. You're a day late and a dollar short, so they say, Wynne. Leave it be."

"Why didn't she tell me you knew?"

"What is this, boo hoo, you got left out? We told her you were on vacation. I told her not to talk to you. It would only upset her. Now ease up, Pat." He tried his little tight smile on me to keep me calm. "You're wondering if she told us about the tattoo, about all that political crap? Sure, she did. You think I believed it? What crazy person is going to take a worm for a symbol, I ask you? It was a couple of crazy kids, maybe on dope. I humored the woman because she lost her girl, and you gotta feel for her. But these are both Farigno's, and I've been wanting him for a long long time. Captain Logan is with me. I would put it down to Vincent the Chin, but he's in the slammer, they got him for trafficking heroin, you remember, OK? You hear me?" Murphy rose to his full height, which even with lifts in his shoes was around five five. "Pat, listen to me," he said, and again he was surprisingly soft. "You're sick. You need rest. You look terrible. Do me this favor. Go home for a week or two. Why don't you see if you can borrow that shack you love in Montauk. Take your little friend, Tommy Perino, and get out of town."

"What's it got to do with Tommy? You threatening him?"

"I just don't want to see a kid get caught up in anything. Pat, I'll call it sick leave. We caught a couple of homicides with the same MO. It happens. This is New York City. People get killed. Why in God's name do you have to make it something bigger? Cubans. Russkis. You hanging out with that damn Ostalsky. Going with girls who love Cuba and hate America. Yeah, yeah, I know all about you and that Nancy Rudnick. Father's a real Red."

"Some things are bigger," I said. "You remember that spy ring, those people out in Brooklyn? They got caught because somebody burgled their house, and found the radio they used to send messages to Moscow. Sometimes it's like that."

"Not this time, you understand?" Murphy said. "I'm your friend, Pat, OK? You think too much. You read too much. If I let you work this, you'll be telling me next there's some kind of world conspiracy. You used to be a fine detective, you still are, but you're making me nervous. You make other people nervous."

"Like Logan?"

Murphy reached in his drawer for a Clark bar. "Listen to me, Homer Logan is a player. He has the ear of some important men, you grasp this? He was a war hero, he flew planes, he bombed the goddamn Japs in Tokyo, and after that he became a cop, and now he's connected big time. So when he says jump, you jump."

"You jump for him?"

"Logan doesn't like you. For whatever reason, he doesn't like the sight or the smell of you, maybe he noticed you don't take kindly to authority, but if you're smart, you'll take some time off and stay away from him, and from these two homicides, you hear me?"

"And if I don't?"

"Logan will put the word out so nobody will talk to you, you understand? He'll ask your buddies if you been seeming unstable. Jesus, Pat, can't you just go along for once? It's the Mob. It's Farigno. It's a done deal."

"What about Mrs Reyes and the Cubans?"

"It's baloney. Poor Mrs Reyes needs to think her

daughter died for something, that the tattoos stood for something. They didn't. They died for nothing at all. They were in the wrong place." He came around the desk and stood over me. "Detective, please give me your weapon, just for a few weeks, while you're off duty. You understand?"

I figured I had nothing left except to play his game. I got up. I gave him my gun.

"Good. That's good, Pat. Your badge too." He held out his hand. I did what he told me.

If Murphy and the Feds had known about Mrs Reyes all along, if they were going to indict Farigno and his Mafia pals no matter what they found out, I had no cards left.

"There's been some cops visiting Ostalsky's building, did you know that?" I said.

"You think he's maybe less than kosher, Murph?"

"I thought he was your pal."

"Let's just say I saw the light. He's a Red bastard like the others," I said. "Maybe worse."

It was done. Murphy would not forget. Then I called Seamus Brennan, my nebbish brother-in-law, who mostly does paperwork at the FBI. I asked for information on a Maxim Ostalsky. I put it out there in a way I could never take back.

Was I so jealous that I'd want Max accused of espionage, thrown out of the country? Sent back to the USSR in disgrace? Didn't they shoot you over there in Russia if you screwed up?

CHAPTER EIGHT

October 19, '62

NOBODY TOOK MY CALLS after Murphy told me to beat it. He must have phoned around as soon as I left his office. Thursday, the rest of that day and night, I called friends on the force, trying to find out what was going on. Max Ostalsky had been involved but nobody wanted to hear it. Not even my oldest friend or my cousin who worked at headquarters would talk. My own sister said Seamus was out, and I said where was he at one in the morning, she said, "You woke us up, Pat. I can't talk now. Come for Thanksgiving, Pat," and hung up. At best I got evasive; at worst, threatening.

Stay away from Wynne. The word got around fast. I had seen it happen before. The year after I joined the force, rumors went out that a certain captain midtown was unfit for duty. I knew the guy a little from around. He was a brilliant detective, a few years from retirement. Somebody—it was never revealed who—took against him. Said he had a copy of *Spartacus*, the novel Howard Fast wrote when he was in jail for being a Communist. That was it. The captain had a book.

Within a few days, everyone is talking about this fine cop, and saying he's some kind of Red, a corrupt policeman who uses local whores, and snorts horse, and privately the other cops say this is bull, he's a good guy, but they're scared to say it aloud. Somebody wants him out, somebody up high, and by the end of the week he's gone. Turned out, the book had been left on his desk by somebody else. I ran into him about a year later, and he looked bad, shriveled by the experience, and sad, and he begged me to go for a drink. He had no friends left.

Now it was me nobody was talking to, not even the sergeant in Chinatown who had taught me the ropes way back. I'd been cut off by my own boss, and probably by Logan who didn't like me the minute he saw me on the pier. I was out in the cold, except maybe for that kid I had met the night of the murder. What was his name? Joe? Jim? That was it, Jim, Jimmy Garrity. He had been pissed off at Logan using him for a chauffeur. I'd give him a call. See if I could make him mine. But when I reached him at home, he told me he had been transferred to the Bronx, and then he got off the phone as fast as he could.

Nobody believed me. Nobody believed Ostalsky had been involved in the homicide. He was not at his place on 10th street. Nobody else was home either. Nobody answered the phone. At NYU his professors said they had not seen him all week long. If I found him, I couldn't arrest him; I had no badge, no weapon. Where the hell was he? Was he with Nancy? Was he hiding at Saul Rudnick's house?

Late Thursday night, not Thursday, it was already Friday morning around three, when I looked out of my window, there was a car parked across the street I had never seen before. Nobody parked on Hudson Street at night, unless you lived here. Outsiders didn't trust it. Gangs sometimes wandered downtown, drunks too, and dopers. Most of the time I parked in a garage a few blocks away, if I had the dough.

After I shut off the lights, I stood for a while. A blue Impala looked out of place. Two-tone. Big. Times I did surveillance, I never went in the Corvette, a real pain of a car I bought second-hand off my Uncle Jack. It was sweet, though, and I took good care of it, but you didn't do surveillance in it. You got hold of a department car.

This, what was he, a cop, a Fed, on my tail?

It made me sweat. If they watched you, they could do anything. You'd come home and find they had planted something, a left-wing magazine, or a book about Civil Rights, or a letter from a friend with seditious material. A friend like Max Ostalsky. We didn't do black-bag jobs; but the Feds did them.

It wasn't fear that got me drinking that night; it was terror, a small potent dose of it, of something unknown, something about to happen that I couldn't control, but that I had set in motion. I had no friends, either.

The next morning at six, the phone woke me up. It was Nancy.

"Is he with you?"

"What? Who?"

"Max. I need help, Pat. Can I come over, please. I'll be there in ten minutes, please. Just let me in."

She was wearing denim overalls spattered with red paint, a rumpled pink blouse, and blue sneakers when she arrived at my place. "Oh, Pat, thank you," she said. "Thank you."

"Sit down. What is it?" I had slept in my clothes. I wanted a shower.

"Do you love me?"

"What?"

"Please, just say that you love me, and you can help me, Pat?" She leaned against my shoulder. I put my arm around her. "Do you?"

"Yes, I love you. OK? What's up?"

"I mean really, if I were pregnant, would you marry me?"

"Are you pregnant?"

"No."

"What is this?" I started to get up, and she put her hand on mine. "Sit down."

"Max is dead."

"How do you know?"

"I feel it. I can't find him. Monday night, we were at the Village Gate, we were having a good time, and then I see him, he's gone to the back of the room, and talking to some fellow who looks like a musician, I don't know, Brazilian, maybe, it was Latin night at the Gate, long black hair, green shirt, you know, with one of those big collars. Max says he has to talk to him, he's a friend from Moscow. He doesn't look Russian, but Max goes outside, at first I'm furious. Please, can I have a drink, Pat?"

"It's seven in the morning."

"Coffee, then."

I put the percolator on, and sat down again.

"What kind of friend?"

"How would I know?"

"Go on."

"The next day he calls me, and I tell him to take a short

walk off a long plank, you know? I was mad. He was calling from that damn drugstore where he uses the pay phone, and he was begging me to be patient, some damn thing, and then I hear him swearing to himself in Russian."

She wasn't petulant, not this time; she was worried. I bit my tongue, kept the sarcasm to myself. But I believed her.

"It began to make sense to me, that Max was dead, that somebody had had enough of his sticking up for his country and its system, you know? You remember when he gave that talk and that terrible idiot Sean Cleary punched him in the nose when he talked about the Berlin Wall, and how the Cubans have a right to decide what they want in their own country, remember? Sean was livid. Maybe Sean killed him. I should have seen it coming. I should have paid attention. All summer there were these feelings I had, that somebody wanted Max out of the way."

"Sean Cleary is a knuckle-dragger, but he's not insane."

"You don't understand. Max said we would be together this weekend."

"Let me ask you something."

Tears had welled up in her eyes, and one slipped down her cheek. "What?"

"Did Max ever talk to you about the High Line murder?"

She rubbed her face. "Yes. I think so. Everybody was talking about it; it was always in the papers. Yes. We were both interested, he had never really known about American criminal law. Sure, he was interested."

"In me? In the way I was working the case?"

"So what? Pat, he's not at home. He wasn't at home when I went over earlier. I left a note for him in his building. I buzzed the apartment. I was there Tuesday night, and

Wednesday, and yesterday. The people he has a room with are out of town, the super told me. They're gone, and he's gone. I left him a note. I said I wasn't mad. Why wouldn't he answer me, Pat? Everything was good, you know? Listen, I'm sorry to lay this on you, I am," said Nancy, crying. I had never heard her apologize. I had never seen her so frightened. It made her seem small and very young. Tears welled in her eyes. "Pat, I have such a bad feeling."

"What kind of bad feeling, honey?" I would help her. Whatever she needed. I took her hand, and she held on tight.

She leaned forward and lowered her voice, and it wasn't melodrama driving her; just fear. "I don't know. I just feel it."

"Just try to calm down. I want to help."

"Don't tell me to calm down," said Nancy. "I'm in love with him."

What a heartless girl she was. I loved her, but I could hear the determination. She always got what she wanted. Her desperation about Max carried a sense of entitlement, a feeling that he had crossed her by disappearing. I almost felt bad for him.

"Just, please, find him. Even if he's dead, I have to know. We have to tell his parents. Please, Pat. Here, I made a list of places we like to go." She took a list from her pocket. "When I talked to him on the phone, I got the feeling he was dreadfully frightened. Scared, you know. Like a naked man in the snow, trying to find shelter."

"Did you talk to your father?"

"Yes. He agrees that we have to try to find Max, even though I know if he's not dead, they will have spirited him away."

"Who?"

She looked at me, uncomprehending, shook her head. "You can't be that naive."

Her hand was on the table. Something missing. Nancy always wore her bracelet. I grabbed her hand.

"You're hurting me."

"Where's your bracelet with the silver charm your father gave you, his Marine insignia?"

"I don't know,"

"Go home, Nancy. Stay with your father. You won't be alone then. Max Ostalsky can take care of himself. He's not dead. Maybe he's a spy, and he just left, recalled on business, told to head for some other country."

"Daddy says Max can't be a spy. He says Max doesn't have enough treachery in his heart."

"Maybe he's a spy, too."

"You're a cold bastard," she said.

"Where's the charm? Did you lose it?"

Anger screwed up her face, and lines appeared on her forehead; I could see how Nancy would look as a mean dissatisfied old woman; it was a look that said she had smelled some stink she couldn't quite identify; that told you she expected to get what she wanted because she was a princess, her daddy's girl.

From the chair where she sat at my kitchen table, she rose slowly, stared at me, and before she turned away, said, "Are you sure you want to know? Don't push me on this, Pat, unless you're quite sure." Her face still wet from the tears, she put her hand up, as if I might hit her.

"Go on."

"Since you ask, I gave it to Max."

PART TWO

Part Two

October 19, '62

Moscow. June 2

In one week I leave for New York. From now, I will speak only English, read it, write it, dream, in English. Can you control the language of your dreams?

I worry that they will keep me from going. Even with Stalin gone, in our country things can turn 180 degrees in a second. This journey can be stopped. My fellowship can be cancelled. I will never see New York City. Strange, but it is my Uncle Fyodor Grigoryevich who reassures me. The General everyone calls him, even my father his own brother addresses him so.

But I call him by his name and kiss him on his birthday. The General's wife died when my cousin Sasha was born, and I blame his bitterness on it. Sasha, my best friend, says, "Don't be an ass, Max. He's bitter because Stalin is dead. This was the love of his life."

My uncle speaks of the United States' desire to sabotage socialism, of its imperialist ambitions. But he admired them as fighters in the Great Patriotic War.

He met President Roosevelt at Yalta, when he was still a young man. Only to me does he say these things.

Last week, when I say goodbye, he presents me with a fine Parker pen he received during the war from an American general he helped at Yalta. He says he will miss me. Nobody has ever heard him say such things.

One week. What will it be like, the United States? New York? Sasha has this idea I will drink rum cocktails in a penthouse and listen to live jazz music by Mr Duke Ellington in Harlem, and sit under the clock in the Biltmore Hotel as did Holden Caulfield. Sasha is nuts. I will miss him.

That Friday night, when I broke into Max Ostalsky's room, I set in motion something I couldn't stop. It was the worst thing I ever did. I went looking for something to hang on him, something more I could use to nail him. I already had the silver charm. Nancy had given it to him. He had dropped it on the pier when he killed the Cuban. He would be picked up for murder, or sent home. Somewhere, I had a faint sense I wasn't thinking straight. I didn't care. In a way, Nancy had made it easy for me.

At the drugstore downstairs in the building where Ostalsky lived, I drank a cup of coffee and got friendly with the counterman; in his white apron, he was a garrulous type of guy, though behind the cheerful fat red face, he was no dope.

Lucky for me, the article from the *Village Voice* with the photo of Ostalsky had been framed and hung on the wall behind the counter, next to a pile of pineapple Danish.

"Maxie, sure, that's him," he said squinting out of his

little blue eyes, sunken in the heavy flesh of his face. "Sure, I know him, he always comes in for tuna on rye, a black and white soda. Didn't see him now, what, three, four days? Nice fellow. Uses my phone. Heard him talking to that girl the other day, pleading, like, you know, a young fellow does, but he's OK. Lives with the Millers in 8D. I just seen them leaving for the country. Always get quart of butter pecan to take with them," said the counterman. "Fill you up?"

"What about Max Ostalsky?"

"Yeah, I saw Max leave, too, bag in his hand." It was what the building super had told me the day before.

"Were they going together?"

"Nah, no, I think he said Long Island."

I drank more coffee and ate a frosted cruller.

When did he hear Max pleading with his girl? Monday. Probably Monday. No, Tuesday morning. Nancy had said Max left her at the Village Gate on Monday.

To keep the guy sweet, I ordered a Coke, smoked a cigarette and told him I was a cop, checking out reports of a burglary earlier in the month. Yeah, he said, good to know you're on the case, and let me into the building through a door between the lobby and the drugstore. I walked up the back stairs. By the time I got to the eighth floor, I was winded, panting and coughing hard.

It only took me sixty seconds to pick the lock on Max's door. Sixty seconds, and I was in. That was it.

I was in Max's room, what he called his rabbit hole.

What I did was illegal. Worse. When I thought about it later, the way I broke into his room, the reason for it, made me sick. Over and over, I told myself he was a suspect, a possible killer and this was why I did it. He was a Commie, and if he was a brutal killer, he deserved anything I could serve up, and more. Deep down I knew I did it out of jealousy. It was like a worm that had burrowed deep inside, and was eating me alive. The way things went after that the whole business took on a life of its own.

The room was chilly. One window was open a few inches, odd if Max had been going out of town. I looked out before I shut it. A young man in a gray crew-neck was in the alley beneath the window, smashing a pink rubber Spalding ball against the wall; hitting it hard, as if he was bored, or angry. Weird, though while I watched I realized he wasn't looking at the wall. He was looking up at the window where I stood. A cheap alarm clock ticked loudly from the bedside table.

I checked the door to the Millers' apartment was locked. I knew how to toss a room fast and leave it looking like nobody had been there.

The room was too tidy, as if it had been evacuated quickly, no time to take much. The books, the records, were in place. In the closet were Ostalsky's new American clothes. On his desk, an essay on Melville he had started writing.

The desk drawers contained only pencils and blank yellow pads, but no notebook. He had often carried that damn notebook in his pocket, writing down everything he saw, words he heard. I had a hunch there was other stuff.

Where the hell was it?

In the bathroom, I flushed away my cigarette, and sat on the edge of the tub, elbows on my knees, staring at the wall, head pounding.

What made me think the damn notebook would tell me

anything at all? I lit up again. I was smoking three packs a day, and my mouth was like an ashtray.

Then I noticed a part of the radiator cover was askew. A noise from outside stopped me dead. Not the handball player. I thought: I should get the hell out of here before it's too late. I didn't. Somebody rattled the doorknob. A vacuum cleaner chugged into life. I hoped to hell it was the super.

On my hands and knees, cigarette still in my mouth, I yanked at the radiator cover; it came off, leaving paint like flaking skin on the bathroom floor. Nothing. I hauled myself to my feet. Then, I saw something, a light blue tile where the grout seemed new. I got out my pocket-knife. The tile came away. Behind it the wall had been gouged out. I stuck my hand in. I found a small package, two notebooks, held together with a rubber band, wrapped in a small blue towel. I felt as if I'd found a cache of forbidden books, like the fireman in *Fahrenheit 451*.

A photograph of Nancy slipped out and I flicked it away, and began to read at random. Who was this man? Was he a killer? Was he going to take Nancy away from me? I sat down on the floor, my back against the tub.

In the first notebook the entries were chronological, more or less, beginning in June before Ostalsky left Moscow.

Moscow. June 7
Out the window of our little flat, I watch my wife leave me. She walks away, growing smaller in her pretty yellow blouse and blue skirt with white flowers. She looks older now, heavier, than when we got married three years ago, as if there is no more joy to be had. Then she turns the corner and disappears. She says she will stay with her

parents while I am in the United States. She leaves. I still smell her cigarettes.

She saw, though I said nothing, how happy I am for the chance to go to the United States, to serve our country, but also, I think: New York City! I feel my head will split with excitement. In front of my superiors I pretend I am only glad because of the opportunity to serve.

I run up onto the roof like a ten-year-old boy and lie on my back, look up at Sputnik in the night sky. Sputnik 11. What a country that put up eleven of them! Going to New York, this is my chance to fly. Two more days, my heart is thumping like a crazy person. I think: I am not going into space, but much much further. I am a cosmonaut cut loose. Thoughts whizz in my head, like pieces from an asteroid that will collide. I have never been on a plane.

Max Ostalsky had written it all down: movies, places, record albums, radio stations, clothes, book lists for his classes—Hawthorne, Whitman, Poe, Fitzgerald, Saul Bellow, every American author I had ever heard of, and plenty I had only a vague idea about, but Ostalsky was a scholar, wasn't he? Isn't that what Nancy had said?

Sometimes he simply jotted words—beatnik, peacenik—or book titles; he commented on color television, which he had never seen, and girls attired in blue jeans; how he loved his "Privacy", and could lie in a bath full of hot water as long as he wanted, drinking a can of cold Rheingold beer, listening to Ella Fitzgerald, all by himself.

So many bad habits to change before I can go home, too
much chocolate cake, beer, hamburgers, I have become
a decadent man. I think too much about N.R.

Nancy, he meant Nancy.

The next entry was the draft of a letter to his grandmother. I remembered. The first day I met him, he had told
me about his grandma, the woman he called Sunny because
she did not like the idea of being an old lady grandmother
in a headscarf.

New York City. June 20
Darling Sunny, You would say to me: Write everything
down. If you write in English, tell jokes and dream in
English, you will be intimate with the language. Keep a
private diary. Savor everything, but keep your thoughts
to yourself. It is never safe to talk, but for your soul, never
acceptable to forget what you see, hear, think, feel. So I
have begun my writing things down, even before I leave.
And now I am on the plane in the sky, my seatmate is
asleep. He snores like a chained-up dancing bear.

His name is Bounine, he is perhaps thirty-five
years old, and he is a doctor on his way to Columbia
University on a research fellowship. "Such good fortune
we are seated together," he says, this very tall fellow who
folds himself in three, it seems, to get into the seat. He has
a yellow mop for hair, and thick spectacles, and a satchel
so full of books it has burst its lock. I do not think he sat
beside me by chance.

I introduce myself. Sunny, I am not born yesterday,
as the American saying goes. I know this type of fellow,

so charming, so casual, too forthcoming, the kind who may accept to keep an eye on his comrades. Do you say, "keep an eye on?"

But I am glad for company. We talk. His father, like my own, is a doctor, and a hero of the Great Patriotic War.

I have only my Belomorkanals but he offers me Winston cigarettes and his gold lighter. He says, his father travels frequently and gives him these cigarettes. "Winston tastes good like a cigarette should," he says and tells me this is the slogan the capitalists use to sell them, he has seen it in Life magazine. As soon as he falls asleep I write down the conversation—write everything you told me, Sunny.

"You get Life?"

"You would be surprised," Bounine says, smiling. "Maxim Stepanovich, I need some help. You see, my name I think will be a problem, I am Vyacheslav and what American can say this? You will be Max, of course."

I ask his patronymic. "Mikhailovich," he says, and I say, OK, you will be Mike. "So I am Mike Bounine," he says triumphantly. "We are Max and Mike. We will be good friends."

At Idlewild Airport, we part ways, and then I am on the bus. The bridge, the sight of the skyline, my heart seems to stop. New York shimmers in the bright light of a June afternoon, the buildings piled up on top of each other like an Aztec dream, the city surrounded by water. So brilliant is it, I shut my eyes for a minute not to be blinded. The bus stops. I have arrived.

At first, I stare at everything, like a country bumpkin, so to say, a redneck peasant villager who has arrived in the big city. The buildings: the Empire State; the Chrysler Building, and the others, and so forth, all gilded and silvered at the top; and private mansions, apartment buildings like castles, people emerging onto the street in evening clothes, is like entering a film.

Darling Sunny, those first few nights I never sleep, but I walk and I ride the Staten Island Ferry. When I see the city floating on water, I feel myself astonished by this city that is an archipelago, a place made of water, so different from Moscow five hundred miles from the sea.

New York is like a country to itself, the five boroughs floating on water, connected by bridges, tunnels, with the rivers and beaches. One evening I walked right up to Harlem, where I see the poverty and divisions between rich and poor, but also see people with little shops, people quite proud of themselves, the ladies and men dressed up and wearing hats. "People striving for something better," somebody says to me.

There was a club, and outside, men in very nifty suits, two-tone shoes, one very tall man in a purple suit, and a Cadillac car, and all the children dancing around him. I think he resembles a great African idol. He is a genius at basketball. They call him Wilt the Stilt.

I have a room in an apartment in Greenwich Village, which is like a small town, perhaps Moscow as you describe it in your childhood, with low buildings, some shabby, some of red brick, which is very elegant, along Washington Square Park where young people play guitars or declare poetry or Negroes blow jazz. Old men *play chess. Students lie with their books on the grass. Everything is very bright: the girls in pink, yellow, red blouses; the boys in plaid trousers. My classes will begin next week. Mr and Mrs Miller whose apartment I live in are very kind, but Mrs Miller provides more food than I have ever seen, and I think of the scarcity and starvation during the Great Patriotic War, but I am greedy. I will soon be fat. Mrs Miller tells me that the fridge—what she calls the refrigerator—is always full, and that I must raid it—raid it, I like that—any time I might feel hungry.*

Late at night, when the Millers are asleep, I open the door of this fridge, stare at the interior where there is an entire pink ham, a tray of yellow and white cheeses, a compartment for cold meats, roast beef, salami, there are peaches, melons, lemons, cherries, as much as you want, and chocolate cake, large bottles of milk, orange juice, Coca-Cola. There is a special section for frozen items, and always ice cream in chocolate, vanilla, strawberry. Help yourself, Max, Mrs Miller instructs me.

Sunny, I can only tell you this, but the awful thing is the first time I see her, she reminds me of Mrs Ethel Rosenberg, the little bow-shaped lips, the tight dark hair, and I feel ashamed, thinking of such a martyr as a plump housewife. She is so kind. I have a bad tooth and she escorts me to her dentist, and he gives me nice drugs, I feel nothing, but he says my teeth are not so hot. You can say that, not so hot. Muriel offers to pay for repairs. I cannot allow it.

In Washington Square Park, about four days ago, I met my first American friend. His name is Pat Wynne. He helps me to buy a hot dog. He is a police detective but quite educated, though working class—I should not say this about the workers, but it is true—and of the Roman Catholic faith.

I am not sure how to understand this man, who is so kind to me. He sees terrible things in his work. He is a homicide detective. There is melancholy. Surprised I have never seen a church. Shows me St Joseph's.

We visit the Cedar Tavern, a place for artists, and for the first time I drink whisky and I like it very much. He asks many questions about socialism and the Soviet Union. He allows me to ask him anything. People discuss nuclear war and build private fallout shelters.

I am a bit like a character in a comic film, they say a fish out of water. I think they are surprised that we Soviets—Commies, as they call us—smile, and love American literature, and enjoy music, and even do magic tricks, as I did for some little children in the park on my way to New York University. They called me Max the Magician.

Sunny, I can never admit it to the Americans—it would be unpatriotic to say—but after Moscow's gray deprivations, here it is as if somebody switched on the lights, and the world is all in bright colors.

If only I could know that you would read this, but you are no longer with us. It is nine years, 1953, since they sent you far away because you helped a friend, where you died in the cold, alone and sick. But I have never accepted this. I do not have to believe it. I pretend you are alive, and I write to you. I tell friends of this wonderful grandmother.

This man Ostalsky had been writing letters to his dead grandmother. I recalled suddenly that in the Cedar back in June, I had asked if his grandparents were alive. His grandfather was dead, he had told me. He had never answered my question about the woman he called Sunny. He had been writing to a dead woman.

I turned the pages of the notebook, tossed my cigarette butt into the toilet, and lit a fresh one. Some of the pages were filled with vocabulary and plenty of slang—Flipped out. Faked out. Get with it. On the make. Dope. Balling a chick. Jugs? Surfin'? Malarkey, Kvetch. Schlemiel. Gavone. Street names, notes for essays, food prices, magazines— he liked *Life*, *Look*, *Esquire*—flavors of ice cream, he liked toasted almond, and sandwiches, roast beef on a Kaiser roll with mayo. He had written down street names, and drawn little maps, cartoons really, of the area around his building, complete with stick figures.

Some of the entries were dated, but not all. His handwriting was very small, every line filled to the margins, as if he had been taught to save paper.

He had a knack for description, and he loved adjectives. The people he met were congenial, grumpy, humorous, wry, vain, pushy, arrogant, sometimes more than one, and no detail was too small, not even a girl with one brown eye and one blue, or one named Cherry with a big bust who wore a Woman's Strike for Peace button and invited him for square dancing at Judson Memorial Church. He had written:

Dose doe, nice dancing, sympathetic people, but I cannot help thinking of Comrade Khrushchev and his wife so dancing.

June
My FBI tail is very young. I see him as soon as I land at the airport, he comes to Washington Square Park, waits near the building where I live. Pretends to hide behind newspaper. No evasion skills. He sticks out like, what do they say, a sore thumb. I pretend not to notice. Privately, I call him Ed. For J. Edgar Hoover. I have an urge to wave. This would no doubt confuse Ed.

Long ago I put away my desire to tell jokes, do tricks, play pranks—except with the close family—for they said when I was little, Ostalsky has no discipline. Here it returns. Pranks, jokes, magic tricks. Perhaps if I make them laugh, they will not believe that it is better to be dead than Red.

Here everyone cares for fun, or excitement, happiness, of course. Killing time is considered OK. Everyone here is a kid, bud, buddy, kiddo, son, boy, they call me this though I am a grown man of almost thirty. I hope this will help me in learning the culture and language to make me able to contribute more to the future of my country.

What I was reading was an alternative version of Ostalsky's time in New York. His version. Restless, I hurried through more pages in the little book; I wanted something, some sign, something I could use on Max Ostalsky. Where was it?

June 23
Is rock and roll pornographic?

June 25

It is very hot. New clothes. Mrs Muriel Miller helps. My friend Pat Wynne always looks, as they say, sharp. Fine cotton chino trousers that are made in China and so are called chino, I think. Soft shirts with short sleeves for summer heat, blue, yellow, button-down collars. I shall become addicted to these clothes, though my mother thinks I am already vain. Window shopping is a pastime enjoyed by all New Yorkers.

I feel good, and like somebody else. In my new clothes, do I look like a clown? Like a man in a costume on a stage? My nice landlady, Mrs Muriel Miller, takes me shopping, and says I must call her Muriel. She feeds her Cocker Spaniel before we leave. His name is Cugi. "I just had to name the dog for him, I'm mad for Xavier Cugat, do they have the Cha Cha Cha in Russia, Max?

How colorful Muriel Miller's New York looks, so prosperous, shiny, like a book for children. We ride the Fifth Avenue double deck bus, and from the top, I look down at people going to work, women in summer dresses, men in suits.

The crowds on Fifth Avenue coming in and out of office buildings, department stores, tea rooms. In Moscow, we do without so many things, but I keep this to myself. Of course, we fought hard, and withstood the terrible sieges. Americans do not understand this or that we want justice and peace as much as material goods.

Mrs Miller chatters, she is quite interested in politics, and says she feels quite liberal, having voted for JFK. Confesses as a Jew, it did worry her a little that a

Catholic President might take orders from the Pope. Still respects Ike who won the war, though Mamie, his wife, was rumored to drink.

She asks many questions, about my family, my work, my hobbies, what I like to read. Sometimes in the evening I find sweets in my room. Mrs Miller leaves them for me. This is so she can examine my things, I imagine. These chocolate chip cookies she provides, the chocolates, like cheese in a mousetrap. I am the mouse.

Mr Stan Miller, her husband, is an advertising man on Madison Avenue, and asks if I would like to be a test subject. This means you go in a room with other people and say what you feel about a certain cigarette, or breakfast cereal or Old Spice, a deodorant product you put under your arms to conceal the odor of sweat. I think I must use this. American men smell of this, like ladies with a certain perfume. For this effort at the ad agency, you receive money. I spend it all on record albums, including Kind of Blue by Miles Davis.

Stan Miller seems a kind man. He inquires if I would care to drive his beloved Oldsmobile. He shows it to me, white, with a fold-down top—a convertible—and the interior in red leather. I say I can't drive. He looks at me as if he now believes in my country transportation is only by donkey cart.

The American President wears no hat, he is young, slim and handsome, he speaks to people directly; he jokes with reporters; he seems entirely alive when he plays with his little children; his young wife is beautiful *and speaks in her whispery seductive voice, and is very cultured. Everybody refers to him as JFK. They have charm. I watch them on TV. The English word is mesmerized. Enthralled, charmed, as if by a charm, a magic trick. Nikita Sergeyevich Khrushchev is a fine leader, but his wife looks a peasant woman with shoes that seem to hurt her feet. Many Russians were embarrassed the day NK bangs his shoe on the table at the United Nations, or when he speaks of squeezing JFK's balls over Berlin, as if he is telling dirty jokes in some village hall. NK is a good man, though. He has done wonderful things for our country. Without his desire for peace, I would not be in New York. Our men may not smell of perfume, but they are brave, and NK has been courageous, and I think of Yuri Gagarin, and how he just goes like a stroll in the park. When I am down in the dump—this means sad—I say to myself: "Poyekhali!!!"*

This was the kind of stuff he had written in his first weeks in New York, first true things about America or JFK, then this idiotic automatic political speak, the kind of thing we assumed of Reds, Russkis, Bolsheviks, of these brainwashed people who had been fed propaganda with their cereal.

Gradually, the robotic Commie-speak began to disappear, and I had a faint sense of a man gradually leaving his country behind, as if he had boarded a boat and, not quite sure how it happened, had now sailed beyond the three-mile limit.

July 4
Independence Day. Coney Island for swimming on the
beach, corn on the cob, pink cotton candy.

Rides. The Cyclone was a blast. Bounine accom-
panies me. I expected him, sooner or later. He remarks
on certain young men with beautiful clothing. He has a
taste for expensive things.

July 9
Pat Wynne, my friend who I see at university, or after
a class, has been named as the detective by the news-
papers in a terrible case of a young girl, last week, July,
Independence Day, tortured and killed on the High
Line, the freight railway near the Hudson River.

I ask about the case. He says little. We go to Minetta
Tavern. I meet Nancy Rudnick. Miss Rudnick. Nancy. I
want to look at her, and I know this is improper. I am a
married man. She has short hair like Shirley MacLuine,
my favorite American actress. She has blue eyes. Fine
skin.

The next day she waits for me at the library, she
says there is a party in Brooklyn Heights, gives me the
address. I meet her there that night.

Son of a bitch. Her, too. She gets me to drive her to Brooklyn,
doesn't want me at the party because she says I'll hate the
music, and invites him. Ostalsky. All the time I spent with
him. Christ.

Young people picket Woolworth store to protest for Civil
Rights of Negroes who are not allowed to eat in their

restaurants down south. Nancy invites me, but I only watch. They call out:

"Mary had a little lamb whose fleece was white as snow and everywhere that Mary went, the lamb was sure to go. But Mary had another lamb whose fleece was very black, and everywhere that Mary went her lamb was turned right back.

One, two, three, four, don't go into Woolworth's Store."

These young people are wonderful. I must learn some of their names.

July 29
Saul Rudnick and Nancy invite me for dinner for the second time. They are generous. Mr Rudnick—I must call him Saul—is ill, but a proud man, and he likes to hear my stories of my parents and grandparents, of the great days of the revolution, and the many characters involved. Pat has been there that afternoon. I know, but I keep it to myself. I saw Pat watching me from the coffee shop on the corner of Seventh Avenue and Charlton Street.

He knew. He saw everything. What was he?

I must try to find books for my uncle. He admires certain American military men such as General Patton and General Curtis LeMay, General MacArthur, men he admires, for he says they are, in their country, patriots.

August 5

The Village Voice *prints an interview about me. People congratulate me on the article. I worry that this may attract too much attention to me from Moscow.*

Even Mr Pugliese who cuts my hair on Sullivan Street hangs the picture on the wall. Next to Frank Sinatra, the Pope, JFK, Jesus. I am up there with Jesus. What would my superiors think? Mr Pugliese tells me his wife is an Italian socialist, and was a firebrand in her girlhood, sticking up for Sacco and Vanzetti in 1927. He says there is always a room for me at their place, over the barber shop, that I must eat Beatrice's veal one night.

Bounine visits me in the Village often in July, in August, too. He says we are real pals. I am not so sure of this. He knows many things about my family. He pretends he knew nothing of me before the flight. I know he has an obligation to watch me. He is a physicist. But I am sure he is also an agent. Bounine invites me to visit Columbia University. We meet at the statue of Alexander Hamilton. "The father of American capitalism," Bounine says. "Do you think he is pointing to the future?" In Bounine's room, I see he has very expensive tastes. His new phonograph, his record albums, his new suit, shoes, sweaters. Where does a medical researcher find so much money?

He tells me he finds my stories of Pat Wynne intriguing and would like to meet him.

We discuss Cuba. We discuss American jokes. Bounine questions me about my taste in films, and he

pretends this is simply casual conversation, but I know.
I know this is a cross-examination.

I tell him I will always prefer our films, which are
serious and important, or certain American films with
a correct social purpose, such as To Kill a Mockingbird,
or perhaps an older film I saw, Twelve Angry Men. *I*
tell him I read my Theodore Dreiser and Tom Paine in
my classes, when I prefer F.Scott Fitzgerald.

I do not tell him that. Oh, have I learned the culture!
I have become a man who prefers the films of Billy Wilder
to the films of Sergei Eisenstein. I love The Apartment,
and best Some Like It Hot. *I go to a film house where*
they show revivals, and watch it three times. The next
time somebody asks if we only have donkey carts in our
country, I say, "Nobody's perfect."

Museum of Modern Art, Guernica
Metropolitan Museum of Art
Guggenheim Museum I would like to run down and
down its galleries in a spiral.

Marilyn Monroe is dead, and people mourn her.

August 12
Mr Stan Miller invites me to dinner at the Luchow
Restaurant on 14th Street. It is all dark wood, and
German food, and very delicious. Sauerbraten. Heavy
beer. He is proud of his son, but more of his nephew
who is in the Air Force, and shows me the picture of this
young guy in uniform, so young he is like a chicken just
hatched, and tells me of the wonderful benefits of fighting

for the United States. I realize that Mr Miller is probing gently, like a doctor, to see if I might come over. I think he considers this as if I would give up my favorite Moscow team for his Yankees.

Does he mean for me to defect? He speaks of vigilance. Collusion. Informants. Hints a second time I can defect.

Did Mr Miller request for a Soviet exchange student to stay at the apartment? I feel uncomfortable here, but what can I do about it? Does he believe I will defect for a white Oldsmobile car?

He is naive. He feels I enjoy myself so much in New York, that I would betray my country, its system, its goals.

Dear Sunny,
I feel so homesick. Out of the blue, this comes on me. I want to write to my Nina, but I know she will not reply. She never writes.

I must know more about Pat's case. The young woman was Cuban, perhaps a counter-revolutionary. I know this from the tattoo. It was in all the papers last week. Bounine asks me to find out more about this case. The worm. The words: Cuba Libre. Pat shows me the warehouse where the girl hid out, above the railroad tracks. He is uneasy doing this, and leaves quickly. I continue to look around, though it is raining.

Village Vanguard.
Nancy. Slim red dress, a pearl necklace, high heels. Club crowded. Thick smoke. I tell her I will write it all down

to remember. She asks if I have a good memory, and I tell her yes, I have trained it to be so. She looks at me in a strange way, but then we are inside.

Miles Davis arrives. I feel the adoration in the crowd.

He plays. Even with his back to the audience, he has magic. Here, in person, I never heard anything so beautiful, long notes that go on and on, sweet, melancholy, almost unearthly in my ears. "So What?" "Summertime". The set ends.

Nancy knows Mr Gordon who owns the club. He introduces us to Miles. "So you're from Russia, man. Welcome anytime, man." He tells the other musicians "This cat must be a black Russian."

Never have I been so close before to a genius. Miles asks about Moscow. He asks about jazz music. I tell him I heard Benny Goodman in person.

Miles shakes my hand, climbs to the bandstand with his guys, and very soft, so nobody else hears it, blows some few bars of "Moscow Nights".

Did I dream this?

"What do you feel, Max?" Nancy says after.

I tell her I feel I am some sort of Neanderthal who arrived in this land of civilized Homo Sapiens, like The Inheritors, *this sad wonderful book by William Golding. This is how Miles's music makes me feel.*

August 15
Wherever I go, there is so much music. Music in clubs, bars, streets, radios in cafés, beaches, and building sites. Gerdes. Blue Note. Half Note. Five Spot. The Town Hall. Charles Mingus. "Eat that chicken." I like the folk

music, the singers such as Josh White, Joan Baez. Peter Paul and Mary, though Nancy says they are not quite authentic. I don't care. Gerde's Folk City.

Pat Wynne invites me to the Brooklyn Fox for a rock and roll show, and everyone dancing in the aisles to this music that makes them feel free. I am uneasy with Pat. I think that he likes Nancy very much, although I asked him once, and he said they were merely friends. But he is not the same. He drinks more. His conversation is more cynical.

I am under siege by music. Rock and roll. Alive. Wild. This music is changing me. Ray Charles. Little Richard. John Coltrane, Bill Evans, Thelonius Monk. And, oh, Ella Fitzgerald. I listen for hours and hours. Rock and roll people and jazz people do not like each other, but I love it all. My obedient Soviet soul is being sucked out by Ella, if there was a thing such as souls. This sucking noise is coming from me. How will I go back?

Mrs Miller invited me to ask some friends to dinner, and when Pat asked me who else was coming, I said only a friend from Moscow. I knew he was thinking of Nancy. I must put this to an end. I will write to Nina tomorrow.

I remembered that evening. The weather had been hot, still August, but cool at the Millers who had an air conditioner in the living-room window. By then, I was already pretty jealous of Max and Nancy, but I was curious to get a look at his room.

Mr Miller opens the door, and shows me into the living room where his wife is playing *Swan Lake* on the piano, and she does it well, with style and feeling, sitting straight on the piano bench in her green cocktail dress made of raw silk—it had been a present from Thailand, she had said—pearls around her neck, dark hair newly done, fingers flying across the keys, so her diamond rings flash.

In his late 40s, Miller, a well-built guy, he makes drinks, taking care not to allow the ice cubes to fall against glass so his wife's playing is not disturbed. In that living room, I get the impression of good taste, a sofa and chair covered in good pale green fabric, nice drapes that go with it, bookshelves, a fireplace with a fine old mantelpiece, the silver vase with yellow roses on it. There is art on the walls.

I'm glad I put on a new slim lightweight gray summer suit with a narrow black silk knit tie. Miller is in advertising, and he'll get the look, I figure.

From a settee, where he is sitting quietly beside another man, Max unfolds himself and greets me, accepts a highball from Mr Miller. His wife finishes playing.

"That was terrific," I tell her, and she takes both of my hands. "I know you must be Pat Wynne. Thank you, dear. But I must get dinner. Stan, tell them how much you admired the Russian Army."

"The Russians were some fighters," says Stan Miller. "They would fight in their bare feet if they had to. They fought until they died. You have to admire that.

"In this picture, you see, this is me, quite young, and this fellow is General Curtis LeMay. He was something. He did what nobody else would do. You ever hear of how he mined the Jap waterways? Practically finished the war, he looked after his own. Troops loved him. I was with him in England early, 305 Bomber, taught his men right. I knew him in Japan, too, where he really stuck it to them, I flew for him, we strafed all the waterways over there, flew so low you could see women on the river banks washing their clothes." A nostalgic smile crosses Miller's face. He loved his war, and I knew other men who felt that way. His war; not mine.

My war? It was shit. Korea was a dung heap. I keep my mouth shut except for drinking Mr Miller's Scotch—a very nice bottle of Chivas Regal—and wonder why this gung ho officer is housing a Commie like Max Ostalsky, but maybe he was asked to do it by NYU, where he went to school. He's a loyal sort of fellow, a follower, a little bit oafish but good-natured enough.

"It's nice to meet you, Pat," says the friend Max introduces as Mike Bounine. Seems his real name is Vyascheslav, and who in America could pronounce that? "We decide on the flight over that we shall be Max and Mike," he says, "you see my patronymic is Mikhailovich. My father's name is Mikhail. Max gives me a name. He becomes, you might say, my godfather."

"What's your work?"

"I'm a medical doctor, but for the most part I do research, this means I look into a microscope a lot. How do you do?" He is tall, with a mop of yellow hair, but wearing a Brooks Brothers summer suit I could never afford, with a white shirt that was laundered professionally, and a red silk tie, Italian. I remark on them and he is polite and pleased, and comments on the excellence of American clothing.

"That's a fine watch you have there," Mr Miller says to him, and Bounine holds up his wrist, very proud of the timepiece. "It is from Hamilton, and also self-winding, this is quite amazing, this new way to wind your watch," he says. Miller nods, and they exchange some more words about the best watches. Like Bounine, Miller is a bit of a dandy; attired in Daks summer slacks, and an expensive silky cream-colored sports shirt with French cuffs. His sports coat has narrow lapels, and around his neck he wears a blue silk ascot with cream-colored polka dots. On his left pinky finger is a heavy embossed gold ring, the kind you might see on some Englishman, a family crest or something. I ask about it, but he just smiles, and continues his chat with Bounine.

Mrs Miller has returned with a tray of canapés. "You know we had a very nice Russian family just across the street, 24 East 10th I think, or at least the father was Russian, two little boys, Paul and William. Such handsome little boys, it makes me furious to think of the way people regard Russians, what bad thing could these lovely people do? They left quite a few years ago and I wondered why. Now, drink up, and we'll have dinner. Stan dear, put that lovely recording of "Sleeping Beauty" on the stereo."

The music plays. We sit down. At the table, Muriel Miller presides like a dope pusher, urging more and more food on us, lamb chops, with mint jelly or mustard, baked potatoes with sour cream and butter, seconds of everything. In and out of the kitchen she teeters, in her high heels, the heels going tap tap tap on the kitchen floor.

They have a double act, she cooks too much food, plays the piano, hovers, chatty and wanting to please. He is the businessman who tells us about how the gears of business are greased by advertising. I help her take some dishes into the kitchen where she detains me. "Pat, ask Stan about his campaign, he is such a brilliant advertising man, but I want him to join that company, Doyle Dane Bernbach, you've seen those ads for Volkswagen, so witty, and they like Jews, some of them are Jews, I think, and I know Stan feels in a bit of a bind where he is, so anti-Semitic, he has to pretend. I know they talk behind his back. He's so sensitive about it. Sometimes I think he loved his pals in the army so much because they just accepted him. Before that he felt he was a little Jewish boy, and he couldn't belong, and then he goes into the military, expecting them to keep their distance, and they just make him one of them. His commanding officer was his biggest hero, still is. The only time he feels good is after those get togethers with his military buddies. He can't shake it that people called him a dirty little kike when he was a boy. I say to him, Stan, but so many lovely people are Jewish, look at Tony Curtis, do you know his real name is Bernie Schwartz? But I do love a nice mass, Pat. You know, I sometimes go to Old St Patrick's for the music."

We rejoin the others. Three kinds of cake follow, also apple strudel, and vanilla fudge ice cream.

"Max, dear, take the boys and show them your little hideaway while I just put the food away. Stan, make the boys one of your Rusty Nails, such a delicious drink."

It's the first time I see Max's room, the way it's connected to the Miller apartment by a door next to the kitchen; it has its own second door leading out to the back stairs.

We troop into his room. Stan Miller brings a tray with Scotch and Drambuie and glasses, mixes the drinks. He's eager to join us, be one of the boys. He takes the desk chair. Max sits on the bed. Bounine asks to use the bathroom, disappears behind a door that leads to it, then reappears and perches on the window sill, glancing out the window, down into the alley behind. He could have used the blue armchair.

Now I was in that room, same furniture, bookshelves, a portable phonograph, a black and white TV set. I remembered how Bounine sat on the window. Was he watching the boy with the handball? Something else? There was bad feeling somehow between him and Ostalsky, and I couldn't put my finger on it.

"Why don't you put a record on, Max, please?"

With a grin in my direction, Max puts James Brown on the turntable. "Such noise," says Bounine, and Max replaces it with folk songs by Paul Robeson. "Is that better for you, Mike?"

"Much better," Bounine says mildly. "Pat, I believe you're Catholic, and I would like to visit a church. Max mentioned something about Old St Patrick's Cathedral? Or Stan? Do you belong to a church, Stan? No, forgive me, that can't be, your wife mentioned you are Jewish.

"Did she? I didn't hear her," says Miller, and before Bounine answers he adds, "Well, yes, my wife is Jewish, I'm only half Jewish, in point of fact."

"Listen, you know what? I'll take you to meet my aunt and uncle," I tell Bounine. "They live opposite Old St Patrick's Cathedral. My Auntie Clara, she'll take you to her church and talk until your eyes bleed and probably talk you into converting. I'll fix it. Next week, if you like."

"Good, fine, that's helpful. Thank you," Bounine says, in a way that suggests it was on his agenda from the moment we met.

August
Visit to the aunt and uncle of Pat, Mr and Mrs Jack and Clara Kelly at their house on Mott Street. To Old St Patrick's Cathedral. Why is Bounine so interested? What does he care so much for what the young priest says?

August 29
Ice cream with Nancy Rudnick in the park. When Nancy Rudnick touches my hair, this is all I think of. My feelings are not proper.

I am married. I want somebody to talk to, but you do not talk to other men. Cultured men do not engage in talk of women, not like peasants or workers. But all I think of is her hand in my hair, she says to me, "You know, Max, darling, there are some people who think Communists have horns" and I put my head down, and she strokes it, pretending to look for horns, and after that this is all I want, for her to touch me.

Ditz. Going steady. Films: Dr No, Lawrence of Arabia.

September 1
Labor Day Party. The Rudnicks. Charlton Street. Nancy's friend, a Cuban, Jorge is there and speaks eloquently about Castro. Nancy's uncle Nathan escorts me into the garden, and he is quite tipsy, and he says to me, "I see the way you look at Nancy. You have no chance. She will eat you alive. You will never belong." He holds out his arm to include the house, the people, all of it. He says "If you want to understand Nancy, you

have to understand all this. This is much more than where she lives. This is who she is."

Nathan is right in some ways. Wrong about this idea she will eat me alive. Moody, yes. But she has a huge appetite for life, for everything, something I have never seen. Tender with her father and her step-mother, adorable with little cousins. Beautiful.

I am invited to the Rudnicks' summer home on a place called Fire Island for ten days.

Vacation. Swim in the sea, lie on the beach, dig clams with our feet, try out water-skiing. Being in the sea changes me. I feel I can never again live away from it. Nancy in her bikini, Saul, Virginia, we drink wine, eat, talk, argue all night, listen to music. I read and read.

Lolita, this book keeps me awake for three nights, I gorge on it, I am excited and horrified, I have never read something like this, and I would like to take it home to my mother, but I cannot. Catch 22 makes me laugh. Dr Zhivago. I enjoy this, but why was there so much fuss? I cannot say this; to discuss it with Americans it would be a betrayal of my system.

September
On television, terrible scenes of violence and hatred. James Meredith, a courageous Negro, tries to go to the Univ of Mississippi, they forbid it. Riots afterwards. One French journalist is killed. President Kennedy must send the Army. We would not show such things. Thankful we have nothing like this in our country.

My back is killing me. I get off the bathroom floor and move to a chair in the bedroom, then the desk. I begin to copy out what I will need. Hurry, I think. Hurry. I read as fast as I can. He went to the beach with Nancy. He lay on the beach with her. I was betting he did much more. Did Saul let his girl have boys in her bedroom in his house? Damn Commies. Free Love.

Fall Semester begins. Very good class in the literature of the nineteenth century, though some ideas that shock me, that Huck Finn has what they call a homoerotic strain, an essay by Leslie Fiedler titled "Come Back to the Raft Ag'in, Huck Honey!", I am confused. A classmate, Harry Amos, an Englishman, tries to explain. Is Harry a homosexual? I am perplexed and embarrassed.

I receive my first grade, my first formal paper, on Mark Twain. I have received an A.

All summer, friends are so hospitable, people invite me to concerts, films, dinners.

Hootenanny Carnegie Hall. Nancy's neighbor, Bob Dylan, makes his first big appearance. She says his real name is Robert Zimmerman. He plays a new song. "A Hard Rain's Gonna Fall". I have never heard anything like this. Haunting. Terrifying. Important.

We hear the Weavers who sing of miners, railroad men, workers. Joyous audience, shining faces raised towards the stage. I sing, too, or hum because I do not know most of the words to these songs: "Midnight Special". "Rock Island Line". "Pay Me My Money Down". Love songs, too, "Greensleeves", the audience sings and sings "Good Night Irene".

Pete Seeger, the others, everyone believes peace and good will truly prevail. Many shake my hand and say they know the Soviet Union believes in peace, too.

On the train downtown, Nancy holds my hand. I spend the night at her apartment. I must stop this.

Harry Amos, that exchange fellow from Cambridge University I have a class with sees me in front of NYU. He makes me laugh, but he is the most frivolous man I met ever. English. Pointed shoes. He says: silly things, hipster, flipster, finger popping daddio. He has great wads of cash in his wallet, and happy to treat his fellow students. He invites me to the Peppermint Lounge. This is, what you could call, CRAZY. He instructs me to practice the Twist with a towel. Also asks me if I know another Russian. Name of Mike, he says. I tell him Mike is not a Russian name. I know he means Bounine. Where did they meet?

Then a girl in a beehive—a high hairdo—and a short skirt pulls me onto the floor while the band plays. Joey Dee and the Starliters. Is that Mrs Kennedy? Is it possible?

I imagine my tutor, Comrade Kunityna, who is known to report on unseemly students and I would grab her, and sing, "Come on, Comrade, let's do the Twist, let's twist again, like we did last summer."

Harry has so many beautiful suits, pairs of slacks, a fine leather jacket, pointy toe boots, and he walks, as if, what did Pat say, light in his loafers? Is Harry homosexual? Not a subject we discuss at home. In class, where we discuss blackmail, our instructor says we must beware of homosexuals. Of all sexual entrapment, but

I have been entrapped, if that is the word, by Nancy.

I want things from her that are not proper, not even possible.

At the end of this entry he had scribbled something in Russian. Something he didn't want me to read?

What sort of class did they discuss sexual entrapment in? Wasn't Max an English teacher studying Mark Twain? My heart was beginning to race. I read as fast as I could, smoking, lighting one cigarette with the other.

I put the first notebook down, and picked up the second one. It was labeled October, 1962.

Parched, I got some water from the bathroom sink, and sat down again. Above me, pinned to the wall, was a photograph of a pretty young woman: Max's wife, Nina. I had not looked hard at it before. She was beautiful but sad.

October 1

Another new month. Autumn. I will miss my mother's mushroom soup, or so I say to people, for I do not miss anything, what I want is here. Nancy is here. Every night I sit up late, writing and writing. I feel tired, but I cannot sleep. I am confused. I believe as deeply as ever in my country, and my work. If I were a Roman Catholic like Pat's family, I would confess to a priest. To understand why I question my beliefs, to redeem myself. It is a crime?

Now I understood why Ostalsky wrote in English. He intended for me to find this diary. Instinctively I knew this. He wanted me for his priest. He was isolated, unsure, scared. He had nobody else.

Was it true? My fantasy?

October 2

This comes now, in October, like some whisper, like it is a feather on my skin, like fall blowing away the summer, this sense I have of New York as a wonderful place. But if this is true, they lied to me. They lied to us. They said America is evil, imperialist aggressor, pushing a capitalist propaganda for the rich.

New York is not evil. Americans are not evil. My country lied.

All systems have flaws.

October 3

Bounine is in trouble. He drinks too much.

I ask what's eating him. He asks, can he trust me? I say, sure.

He says he has to tell me something. He tells me he loves America. He loves that he can travel anywhere without permission. Loves jokes about politicians in public. Food. Clothes. Material things. He says, "They lied to us. They lied. The fuckers lied." He begins to cry. He says our country lied about America. He stinks of whisky and cigarettes, and says he loves our country, but not the lies. He says to me, "Isn't that what you feel? I can see you feel it, too. Don't you? Those fuckers just lied. I can tell you because you are my friend."

Is Bounine a true friend? Is this an effort to provoke me? I listen, but say nothing.

October 4
Muriel Miller gave me Ship of Fools, *a popular novel when I arrived, a bestseller about passengers adrift on a great ship. Sometimes I walk near the Hudson River, and I like to walk along the piers and gaze at the great ocean-going liners. I think I am on my own ship, the ship Manhattan, so many people, strange, new, interesting.*

I have boarded this ship for a long journey, these passengers are my friends now. Everyone has been kind. I do not want to think about future uses for Mrs Pugliese, or Nancy Rudnick, or Pat Wynne, though, unlike the others, I do not think he can ever be convinced of the value of socialism.

Things upset me more. I cannot tell if somebody has been in my room. Is it just Gladys, the maid. She wants to clean my room, change my sheets. There are things I must put away so she doesn't read them. I keep her waiting. I feel uneasy with servants, this making of the Negro race an underclass, but it is her job.

Do other agents have their plans threatened by laundry? Does it all come down to clean sheets, and buying hot dogs and girls who tempt you? Is there no grander agenda? What am I? Only a naive agent who worries that the maid will find me out, as if my secret job left stains on the sheets?

I re-read the last paragraph. Agents. Secret job? What did he mean? Was Max Ostalsky an agent? Was he KGB? Jesus. Of course he was. He had written about sexual entrapment. He had taken an interest in the names of Nancy's friends on the Woolworth's picket line.

I was sweating. I opened the window. The handball player had gone. I examined the notebook again.

Max Ostalsky was a trained KGB agent. Christ. Sweet Mother of God. He had lied, and lied again, even when I asked him if he was an agent, he said he was too clumsy, too inclined to tell jokes, wasn't that it? Something like that, the night on the High Line?

Before, when I had wondered if he was a spy, it was the kind of idle assumption you just make about a Russian. I had him figured for possibly small potatoes, a casual spy, the kind who passed on a little information; maybe he slipped titbits from US newspapers into his letters home.

This was different. He was a fully fledged agent; he was a spook like the bastards who brainwashed my pals in Korea, and tortured them. He had come to New York to spy on us. He had made me his friend. He made Nancy love him.

I kept reading, my brain working overtime, trying to figure out where he could have gone. Had he fled? Was he already on his way to the Soviet Union? Had they extracted him? Would they give him a medal? Execute him? If Nancy was right, he was already dead, and this, these notebooks, were his last will and testament.

I turned back to some earlier entries at random:

Greenwich Village Peace Center 133 west 3rd, first birthday:
   CORE, General Strike for Peace Julian Beck of the

Living Theater, so many new friends committed to our way, to world peace.

What shall we teach our children about Race? Wash Sq Methodist Church

    Ronnie Gilbert of the Weavers says, "we all thought people would be swept away, and say hey this is fun, this hope and peace and love, this cold war ain't no fun, let's sing instead."

I began to understand. Some entries were simply notes on what he had done, but others were relevant to this bastard's work. No wonder he went to peace meetings, went to make use of the people who attended them, use them as informants. It suddenly hit me like a blow from a baseball bat, this was exactly the same as the Feds who tried to get information on the same people, find out if they were Commies. God. Jesus wept.

October 12
Harry Amos invites me to a theater, a preview of a play with the title Who's Afraid of Virginia Woolf? *by Edward Albee. Broadway is all neon and lights and the man smoking a Camel cigarette, blowing real smoke. The play, to me, is ugly. People who hate one another. The audience claps and claps.*

October 13
Nancy. I left her one hour ago at her apartment. I never felt like this. I am losing control. I think about a life here, as an agent with a cover as correspondent for a Soviet

news service; or perhaps as a teacher. Perhaps I would be sent as a sleeper, burrowing into the local life, waiting and waiting to be called, to be awakened for my real job.

I would have a life in Greenwich Village, an apartment with a little garden outside. Entertain friends like Saul, and Pat, if he comes, I will play Marvin Gaye and Little Richard and James Brown. My kids will go to local schools.

The tree in my back yard will grow deep roots. I will name my daughter Sunny.

There are men like that who stay many decades in foreign places, who gradually adapt to the culture, almost changing shape.

For a dime, from a stall on Fourth Avenue, one day I buy a collection by Ray Bradbury including ' Dark They Were, and Golden-eyed'. I have always loved Ray Bradbury. I joined the Bradbury Club at my school in Moscow. I love him for he understands the fear caused by a possible nuclear war. He understands that science is both good and bad. In this tale, he tells of Americans who, stranded by war on another planet, stay so long, they begin to look like locals; their children forget all about America, and earth. But I will not stop being a Soviet man. I will always believe in the socialist way, in the workers, in equality and justice. I will teach my children Russian.

New York. It would be a life.

Stop it. Stop.

I can't stop. I flick the thoughts away, like a malarial mosquito that could suck all my blood. My life isn't my own. I have been trained to serve my country. This year was a gift, a chance to learn about the United States.

Every time I imagine a life here, I am stopped in my

tracks, for I cannot imagine Nina in it. She would not be happy, not in America, not with a husband lacking ambition who settled for this little life as a teacher, or a low level correspondent.

When I think about that life in Greenwich Village in an impossible future, I hit a wall. The girl in the picture isn't Nina. It is Nancy.

October 14
The Millers invite me for coffee, and spend time discussing with me my plans for studies, for possibly a visit home. I don't understand what it is they want. I eat a big slab of coffee cake with raisins. Tomorrow I will be with Nancy at the Village Gate.

October 15
Out of the blue, Rica Valdes, my old friend from Moscow, appears at the Village Gate. Latin Night, this evening. Charlie Byrd, Stan Getz playing Bossa Nova. Symphony Sid. Nancy with me. Then a voice. I am thinking of Brazil. Perhaps Brazil. Desifinado is the tune, it makes everyone sway, all the boys, and the girls in their big skirts, and flat shoes. In the room dense with smoke, filled with bodies swaying to the gorgeous music, I close my eyes. Hot and lush. Brazil. I would like to go to Brazil. Nancy's arm is around my waist.

"It is me, Maxim, it is Rica. Your old friend, Riccardo Valdes," a voice says, a ghost out of the dark, out of the past. "Come with me."

Valdes has not slept for days. Walking the street. Sleeping in parks. Says he arrived with Cuban President

Dorticos' delegation and heard Dorticos speak on October 8, says Cuba will not accept an invasion. Shows me a piece from the newspaper Revolucion: "Rockets will blast the United States if they invade Cuba." What rockets, I say. They are in Cuba. On the street, he says, "There will be an assassination."

"Who? Where?"

"I don't know. I need one more piece of intelligence." He seems distracted, seems almost out of his mind.

"How do you know?"

"I hear things. I am considered safe. I am a trusted member of the Revolution, they believe. I work as a translator. Russians speak carelessly in front of me."

"What Russians?"

"In Cuba. There are many Russians with the missiles."

There are no missiles in Cuba. No American newspaper has reported it. Rica has become crazy.

At first, I believe Rica is a triple. Faithful to the cause of the Cuban Revolution, but presenting himself as a "worm", a man who has turned, and now a man who tells me he is still loyal to Castro. I am uncertain.

In a deli on Bleecker Street, I buy Rica some food. I have not seen him since the spring, when I left Moscow. He had finished his second year of Russian studies, a young Cuban everybody loved. "Max, I will write everything down for you, in case I disappear."

Who sent him to me? He says Irina Rishkova. But she told me she was not planning any trips to Moscow.

Rica says he has more to report. He needs a place

to stay. *He wants to stay with me. I find some money, and accompany him on the subway to Harlem, to the Hotel Theresa in Harlem, where he has been with his delegation, the Cuban delegation he arrived with on October 6. "We must stop it, Max. We must stop this thing." What thing?*

War, he says, The end of the world.

October 16
You idiot, you damn fucking idiot bastard, You stupid deceitful useless prick, you spend time with Nancy, then you walk away, and for what, because Rica Valdes, that crazy febrile Cuban shows up, and tells you crazy stories about war that nobody would believe.

You listen to him because you're an inept, incompetent agent who's never done a job, and stumbles around like the fucking fool that you are. Sure, your English is good. Your English is great now. You can slip into your American shoes and your American slang, you can swim in the current, and nobody will take you for a patriotic Soviet citizen. I read these pages. I see how my English has improved. I will be a great teacher. The KGB can employ me to teach agents, moles, sleepers, so they go to the United States and subvert the enemy. I can teach them how to write in magazines that we run, where we make allegations against the right-wing, and the racists, provocations, but which the left believes are merely the expression of progressive ideas. I have come to hate this. This people of the left in New York are good people, decent, the best I have ever met. Saul Rudnick is a truly noble man. He never lies.

Before I began to ask all the questions. Before questions went off in my head like grenades planted somehow, sometime. Now, they can examine me for signs of ordinary mortal confusion, of moral ambiguity, and finding it, declare me a one-off, a freak. Americans like me because I am this freak. My own people will say, he has imbibed some terrible thing, he has been brainwashed by the Americans, he has fallen prey to the seductive ugly songs of capitalism. He has drunk American whisky, and learned their ways. The running dogs of imperialism have infected him with it, as if it were rabies.

Nothing prepared me for the reality. The United States for me was constructed of little pieces, snapshots, propaganda, novels, our newspapers, some films, many little bits brought back from the war by our fathers, such as American boots, binoculars, films such as Sun Valley Serenade. *I heard of a returning army officer, who plays Frank Sinatra while he shaves. "Come Fly With me." I would like to fly.*

Nothing prepares me for New York, for The United States. In the United States there are many bad and difficult things, and they do not have our passion for equal distribution for all, but also good. I read what I want. I do how I like. In Greenwich Village, people seem free. This shocks me first. Then I get used to it. I like it.

My only brief for New York, they tell me, is to study hard. Learn the culture. Perfect your English skills. Make friends who will be useful in the future.

Rica. Riccardo. Mrs Reyes had referred to her daughter's lover as Riccardo. Was this Ostalsky's friend from Moscow?

Feeling caged in that room, I walked in circles. Closed the window. Listened for noise from next door. Was this the Riccardo Mrs Reyes had mentioned? The second in the little brigade of "worms", she had said. Was there a third? Rica had told Max he had only part of the information. Susana had told her mother the same.

Things are happening too fast. Can I call? G.U. in D.C.?

What was it, this GU in Washington? Who?

Bounine calls me, orders me to meet him. This is not an invitation. We meet at the Carnegie Hall where Bounine must pick up concert tickets, and then to the Carnegie Deli. I am looking for any tail. Bounine seems unworried.

He eats a large pastrami sandwich, drinks Coca-Cola with his pinky finger raised in the air. Eat, Max, he says in Russian. I tell him in English I am not hungry. What do you want, I say. I have a class. He wipes his mouth carefully and tells me that Rica is against us. He talks too much. "Do you understand, Ostalsky?" Bounine says this. "Valdes must go away. You will take care of it. Tell him to meet you."

At first, I am confused, but Bounine, when we are in the street, explains. It is my job to make Valdes disappear.

Everything has changed. When the message comes from Bounine, I am no longer simply an exchange student. Nothing in my training prepared me for my old friend Rica, and what I was asked to do.

My superiors trust me with an important job. They ask me to eliminate a friend. I am scared. I am the greenest of agents now with plenty of craft and no experience at all.

Rica has said he must pass information to me. I contact him by phone at the Hotel Theresa in Harlem, I gave money for a room, I tell him to meet me at the old Pier, I give him precise instructions. We will be safe to talk there, I tell him.

October 17
I must get out of this room. When I returned from Pier, number 46, I didn't sleep at all, and this morning, I went out and saw Mr Miller was getting out of his Oldsmobile. He said there was business to be done in the city, and he had stopped by to collect some things for Muriel who is still in the country. But he is startled to see me, something is not right.

I hear him in the apartment's foyer. Later, there is a note under my door to say he has gone to the country, with a phone number in case I need anything.

They will come back. I have to go away. Where will I go?

Now Rica is dead. He was my good friend.

Ostalsky was a KGB agent. He had been on the pier the night the Cuban—Riccardo Valdes—was murdered. I had been right. Ostalsky had murdered him, his friend, Rica Valdes. He didn't kill the girl on the High Line though. Over and over I had wondered if he killed Susana. How badly I wanted to hang it on him, but I had been with him and Nancy at Minetta Tavern that evening, before I went to the

High Line. There was no way Ostalsky could have gone and murdered the girl and returned to the bar.

I would find Ostalsky and confront him, or kill him. They could fire me from the force, they could do what they wanted, but not until I got Ostalsky.

What I had on him—this vicious Red, this killer who had plied us all with his charm—was Nancy. I knew it was his soft spot. If he could consider a life in New York with her, he was vulnerable. This was how I would get to him. I should have called it by its right name: blackmail.

There was pain in my chest, my lungs, from the wracking cough and cigarettes, and because it felt like a hardball had been thrown at my heart.

In those little notebooks, there was plenty that would be of interest to the FBI.

Nancy would hate me. It would make her hate me. The FBI would want more. My betrayal of Max Ostalsky would make me their stooge.

Again, I flipped through the pages. On the inside of the back cover, he had written a list. Names. People he had met in New York. Nancy Rudnick. Saul Rudnick, CPUSA. Phone numbers. Addresses. In some cases, attitudes and tastes.

Saul Rudnick. True believer? Useful?
Nathan Brody. Angry at US government. Blacklisted by Senator McCarthy. Possible alcoholic. Vulnerable to attention.

Mrs Miller appears liberal? She sits with Gladys, the Negro maid, for lunch, coffee. They smoke cigarettes together. Mr Miller does not approve. Mr Miller, an ad

*man, with a previous life as military officer, more active
than it appears?*

This was why he was here. To make friends who would be
useful in the future. This was his brief.

Make friends.

And me. Even my license plate number.

*Pat Wynne. 32. Hudson Street. Second-hand red Corvette
car. Homicide Detective, New York Police Department.
Irish Catholic, possibly lapsed (or skeptic?) Parents devout
Catholic, anti-Communist. Korean veteran. Typical anti-
Soviet. But curious about USSR. Flexible?*

    *Secret desire to write police novels. Chesterfield
Cigarettes. Cedar Tavern. Prefers Rheingold beer. Italian
food. Meatballs. Obsessive at work. Favorite books—
Catch 22, detective Ed McBain. Ross Macdonald?
Close to family: sister, Colleen (married to S. Brennan,
FBI desk man); uncle, aunt, Jack and Clara Kelly.
Democrats. Union people.*

    *Wynne loves rock and roll Negro music. Is James
Brown fanatic. Fond of good clothing.*

    Visited Cuba on holiday.

    *Enjoys fishing, basketball, well-informed about
players. White Horse Tavern. Associates with radicals,
M. Harrington.*

The bastard knew everything about me, including the
goddamn meatballs and the cop novels. How the hell did
he know I had thought about writing a book? I never told
anybody. Except Nancy.

Ostalsky must have questioned Nancy to learn more about me. Sucked her dry on the subject. She was the only person I ever told about my idea of writing a cop novel. She told him. She betrayed me with the Commie bastard. I lit a cigarette and put it out. Got up, opened the window, breathed in some damp cold air. Sat down again and began to read.

This was his goal. To make friends. To use them. To turn them. Make me defect? Did he think he could buy me for the price of a few beers?

Make friends with Pat Wynne, the chump of chumps. I was now sure our meeting wasn't accidental. I had been the target.

I found some paper and began copying out Ostalsky's notebooks.

I would return them to their hiding place when I'd finished. He would come back for them. It gave me more power if he had no idea I'd read them. And I would find him. Wherever he was, I'd hunt him down. It would be much easier now. Now I knew he had killed Riccardo Valdes; now I knew who he was.

When I broke into Ostalsky's room, I had wanted something to hang on him, to nail him with, to make Nancy stop wanting him. In the notebooks, I had struck gold, the jackpot.

There were only a few more entries in the notebook, and a letter to Sasha, his cousin.

October 18
I need money. Muriel Miller keeps what she terms "pin" money in a cookie jar shaped like Minnie Mouse. I find almost thirty dollars. I take it.

175

Dear Sasha,

I know this will never reach you, so it is safe to say I feel trapped. I have barely finished training and I am in the middle of a trap, like a baby mouse I saw in a lab once: the fur was not yet gray, but only a little pale fuzz; the mouse it ran around, beating this tiny body against the steel springs of the mousetrap they put in the cage for some psychological experiment. I am straining against these springs. This Cold War is for nothing. It is to serve only the men who make war. I can say so since we will never see each other, and Sasha, my dear friend, my cousin, you will never read this, I think. Perhaps somebody will find it and send it to you, if I can't come home.

Are you on a ship on its way to Cuba? I hope not. Rica said there are Soviets in Cuba, and missiles. Can this be true? That we are sending missiles? If so, then you as a Naval missile engineer will surely be on a ship. I hope all this is untrue. I hope Rica Valdes had false information, I believe he had become so confused that he was mentally deranged when he said there were missiles on their way, warheads stashed in the hold of the ships. For, if there is a war, we will all be dead. I hope you are well. Be happy. Max.

October 19
This morning I came back to this room for the last time, my own "hideaway" as Muriel Miller called it. My last visit to this room where I was happy.

Of all my new friends, Pat concerns me. He is a detective. He sees around corners. He is a clever man.

Is he clever enough to see that it might not have been an accidental meeting when I sat down near him on that bench in Washington Square?

Pat loves Nancy too, I understand now.

If he finds me, will he help me, or will he betray me? But perhaps there will be war, as Rica said, and nothing will matter any more.

PART THREE

October 22, '62

"GOOD EVENING, MY FELLOW citizens.

"This Government, as promised, has maintained the closest surveillance of the Soviet military buildup on the island of Cuba. Within the past week, unmistakable evidence has established the fact that a series of offensive missile sites is now in preparation on that imprisoned island. The purpose of these bases can be none other than to provide a nuclear strike capability against the Western Hemisphere.

"The characteristics of these new missile sites indicate two distinct types of installations. Several of them include medium-range ballistic missiles, capable of carrying a nuclear warhead for a distance of more than 1,000 nautical miles. Each of these missiles, in short, is capable of striking Washington DC, the Panama Canal, Cape Canaveral, Mexico City, or any other city in the southeastern part of the United States, in Central America, or in the Caribbean area."

On my black and white television set, the President looked handsome but tired, deep gray shadows of fatigue seemingly carved out under his eyes.

Next to me on the couch sat Tommy Perino. His father was at work on the night shift, as usual. I had made Tommy a grilled cheese sandwich, but it lay, untouched and cold now, on the plate. When he asked for a smoke, I let him have it. I gave him some of my beer. If we were gonna die, the kid might as well smoke if he wanted. I had smoked at his age. Me and my pals. Some of them, those friends, had been drafted into the goddamn military like me, some died fighting the Commie bastards in Korea, or lost their toes to frostbite in that miserable country.

"Nuclear weapons are so destructive and ballistic missiles are so swift, that any substantially increased possibility of their use or any sudden change in their deployment may well be regarded as a definite threat to peace." JFK's voice was cool and sober. I turned the TV set up louder and told Tommy to eat his food.

"It shall be the policy of this nation to regard any nuclear missile launched from Cuba against any nation in the Western Hemisphere as an attack by the Soviet Union on the United States, requiring a full retaliatory response upon the Soviet Union."

Was it a provocation, these missile sites? The Russkis didn't need Cuba. They had rockets powerful enough to nuke us from Moscow. They wanted to make us sweat. They wanted a base ninety miles from our shores. If they got it, they would own a piece of us.

"To halt this offensive buildup, a strict quarantine on all offensive military equipment under shipment to Cuba is being initiated. All ships of any kind bound for Cuba from whatever nation or port will, if found to contain cargoes of offensive weapons, be turned back."

JFK knew what he was doing. He outlined his plans. He said he was calling for a blockade, an embargo, a quarantine. Whatever you called it, it meant trouble. Starting Wednesday, the day after tomorrow, Soviet ships on their way to Cuba would be boarded.

"What's that, Pat?"

"What?"

"You was talking about Cuba."

"Never mind," I said to Tommy, realizing I had been speaking out loud without meaning to. "I always thought they'd come for us over Berlin," I said, and we went back to watching the TV in silence.

This was worse than Berlin. This was our territory. Cuba had always been ours, more or less, at least until Castro and the Commies got hold of it.

Khrushchev I didn't trust. He was an animal, a short fat piggy-looking man who had treated our President with contempt in Vienna when they met.

The President said that the Russians had been planning the shipment of arms for months. The Soviets had promised him if there were weapons, they would be only for defensive purposes.

The Soviets had lied, and Americans would not stand for it, or at least our leaders would not. They were shipping their shit to Cuba, and Cuba wanted it, and we were all going to nuke each other. I didn't want to die yet. My stomach was in knots.

Kennedy announced that he had been shown photographs of the missile sites last Tuesday morning, October 16. Almost a week ago; the night Tommy had found the body on Pier 46.

"Pat?" Tommy said. "We gonna die, Pat?"

We stared at the photographs taken by U2 planes flying over Cuba. The planes go up. The camera cover, like an eyelid slides back. Like a naked eyeball, the camera peers down. It snaps the missile sites. Launch pads. Padlocked sheds.

I peeled the cellophane from a fresh pack of Chesterfields, removed it, put one in my mouth. The city outside was very quiet, a thick dense sort of silence, as if everyone had died, and only the television sets and radios left playing. It was Kennedy's determination to stop the Russians, his assertion that he would resist intimidation, that made me proud and also scared me good.

The President told the "captive" Cubans he was their friend against foreign domination. He would not allow them to be puppets and agents of an international conspiracy. Told them the new weapons were a lousy bet for them. That America was set on a dangerous effort to resist.

Looking into the camera with that steady gaze, JFK said, "The cost of freedom is always high, but Americans have always paid it. And one path we shall never choose, and that is the path of surrender or submission. Our goal is not the victory of might, but the vindication of right; not peace at the expense of freedom, but both peace and freedom, here in this hemisphere, and, we hope, around the world. God willing, that goal will be achieved.

"Thank you and good night."

After the speech, some of the commentators noted they had seen it coming, too; that last week, people had seen lights on all night at the White House, had seen wives of government officials solo at cocktail parties, and they knew something was up.

I put in a call to the Millers. Muriel answered. I could hear the TV in the background.

"Oh hello, Pat, dear. How are you? It's a very difficult time. I assume you're phoning to speak with Max, but he's not here. Are you watching the television? Terrible news. Terrible."

I said I was fine.

"Max left a note saying he was going to some friend on Long Island. Are you all right? This is quite a nerve-wracking time, and if you would like to drop by for some coffee, dear? Are you on your own? Or come for a glass of whisky, given the situation? You musn't be alone. Stan says it may be very bad, that we need to leave certain things to the generals who will know what's best for the country. I trust the President, of course. Stan says the military has it in hand. Says the generals will take care of things.

"But I'd actually like to talk with you, Pat. Let me be frank, do you imagine that Max would be capable of something improper?"

"What kind of thing?"

"Somebody took money from my Minnie Mouse cookie jar. And he left without leaving his phone number. Why would he do a thing like that?"

I told her I had no idea, and got off the phone, with a promise to drop by some time or other.

No surrender, no submission.

I was behind the President one thousand percent. I'd put on a uniform again if I had too. We could never let the bastards put nukes ninety miles off our shores. I felt for JFK. He was alone, it seemed, except for his brother. Thank

God for Bobby. But if the President stayed tough, we were all dead. If he backed down, we would live under the heel of the Red Menace. The thing we had been waiting for, all the Cold War fear, it was happening now. Tonight.

"You OK, Tommy?" The kid was on the edge of the couch.

"You know what, Pat? We should nuke 'em now," he said.

"Goddamn right, we should do it to them before they do it to us," said Tommy, who had seen too many movies. "Listen a me, Pat, I gotta go."

"Where? You're not wandering around the piers anymore? Tell me the truth."

"I'm not. No way. I just want to wait for my pop when he gets home. I gotta be there for him, so are you gonna be OK by your own, Pat?" He touched my arm as if to somehow reassure me, and left quietly, his shoulders squared in some imaginary military style, his stride sharper than usual, as if he was already practicing for his part in the coming conflict. Tommy was twelve. In five or six years, some lousy war would probably claim him.

I called my ma to make sure she was doing OK. She said she was praying. Said she was also eating most of the Whitman's Sampler, the chocolate I gave her for her birthday. Might as well, Paddy, cause you never know if there will be a tomorrow, and then I left all my gorgeous chocolates behind, which would be a crying shame.

My ma, in spite of being a crazy lady with her Sacred Heart pictures on the wall, always had a sense of the ridiculous. I called over to my sister Colleen, and woke her up. After that, my instinct was to phone Nancy; I dialed her number; I listened to the phone ring, and pictured her little pink Princess phone that lit up when you used it. Nobody answered. I lay down on the couch, and when I opened my eyes, it was midnight. I fried some eggs, and made coffee. I ate. Then I went out to get some papers and a fresh pack of smokes. The streets were empty and I had to walk all the way to Sixth Avenue to get the early editions.

U.S. IMPOSES ARMS BLOCKADE ON CUBA ON FINDING OFFENSIVE-MISSILE SITES; KENNEDY READY FOR SHOWDOWN.

The *New York Times*. All the News That's Fit to Print. I didn't usually read the *Times*, but when you looked at it, you knew it was for real.

After I got home, I scanned the other papers for any news of the homicide on the pier. It had been front page last week, especially in the *Daily News* and the *Journal*. Now it had been shoved inside all the newspapers. What was reported was that it was a Mob case. That it was a Mafia hit had been confirmed by sources inside the police department, one of the articles noted. Indictment pending. Same killers as the homicide on the High Line during the summer. Proof the cops were on the job, cleaning up the city. A ray of hope in a gloomy time.

Again and again I had wondered why the brass was determined to hang it on the Mob. This was why. This was the deal. This would make them look sweet to the politicians.

I read the lead piece in the *Times*, reporter name of Anthony Lewis. My stomach turned over. "Mr Kennedy treated Cuba and the Government of Premier Fidel Castro as a mere pawn in Moscow's hands and drew the issue as one with the Soviet Government." The Russians; it was always those bastards; of course it was.

Was Ostalsky reading the papers somewhere? Watching TV? Had he been in on this too, sent over here to wait for this event that must have been planned a long time ago? You didn't put together all those ships and men and hardware overnight. This would be a war between us and the Soviets. The Cubans were small potatoes. The Russians held the reins; even I had that figured out. I kept reading.

"The other aspect of the speech particularly noted by observers here was its flat commitment by the United States to act alone against the missile threat in Cuba."

There was such a heavy feeling in my gut, I couldn't sit still, and I went up on the roof for air. I could see all of Greenwich Village spread out, houses, little gardens, narrow streets; and I could see the skyline, still alight, and looking, for once, heartbreakingly fragile.

I had to find Ostalsky.

For a second, I felt almost sorry for him. Except for the business about Nancy, I had liked him. Now, he was running, on his own in a hostile country, thousands of miles away from his family, knowing if war came, he would never get home. If in some strange way I was a little sorry, I was also ready to hunt him down.

CHAPTER TWO

October 23, '62

SHIPS MUST STOP. BIG FORCE
MASSES TO BLOCKADE CUBA.

WHEN I PICKED UP a paper Tuesday morning the headlines were bad, and men I saw on the street were reading as they walked.

That morning, the city was too quiet. Everything was normal, except for this heavy silence. On their way to school at St Luke's, children who would otherwise be running and yelling clutched their parents tight; a pair of young women, one blonde, one with short black hair, both in slacks and car-coats, wheeled their babies to the playground, no chatter, no small talk; an old woman, a green shawl around her, sat on a stoop, intent on her rosaries, and you could hear the beads, click click click.

Like film at the wrong speed, the city moved by me, second by second, as if suspended in glue. What always seemed a vast unknowable city, made of steel and stone, huge and solid, seemed tiny now, and vulnerable. If they hit America, they would hit New York; no one would survive.

I didn't know what waited for me at the station house—I had told the boss I was going out of town—but I needed information about the Pier 46 case, on Ostalsky and on the dead Cubans. The President's speech had changed everything, and I had to figure even Murphy would see that.

It was brisk that morning. I buttoned my tweed jacket. Murphy liked his detectives well dressed. I was wearing a good blue and gray silk rep tie.

On my way to the precinct, I got coffee, same place I always went.

"Pat, mornin'," called out one of the elderly men who sat on stools at the counter. I had known most of them for years.

"How ya doin', Whitey?"

"It's quiet like Pearl Harbor time, I ain't heard nothing so quiet since then," said Whitey Clark, and bit into a jelly donut; purple jelly stuck to his gray mustache.

"It is that," I said, took my carton of coffee from Selma, who had been behind the counter forever, and went to work. It was 8.30 in the morning.

Tomorrow, Wednesday, the embargo would go into effect. I knew how the military thought. I had been in the army. They reacted. They would react now. Action, they understood. Waiting was not their game. I was scared of the crazier generals who were always pushing Kennedy to invade, to nuke Cuba, nuke Moscow, go for a pre-emptive strike on the Soviet Union. They leaned on JFK hard; there were congressional elections in two weeks and Republicans were saying the President was soft on Communism.

Tomorrow Americans were set to board Soviet vessels. The Soviets would resist. They only wanted an excuse to blast us to extinction. Already, they were slowing down traffic at the goddamn Berlin Wall. I remembered the airlift the year I finished high school. Last year they put up the wall, and for what? To fuck with people and keep them penned up like animals.

I tossed away the paper I had been reading. It was like the order of service for a funeral; and we were the dead.

"I was expecting you, Wynne," said Murphy when I reached his office. I knew he had put somebody on my tail, and whoever it was had told Murphy I was coming.

"Listen to me, Wynne. I got enough trouble." He gestured to the newspapers on his desk. "Nobody can get a call through any place, I got guys in the Reserves being called up. We're worried about riots. We don't have enough shelters, we got them in crazy places like the base of the Brooklyn Bridge. We're worried about a run on goods at the stores. In DC, they're buying up bottled water, even Seltzer and Coke. People are fucking buying appliances, like if they're going to die, they want a new washing machine, you believe that?

"Not to mention we got those Fair Play For Cuba idiots are out in front of the United Nations screaming and yelling. Not to mention if this thing heats up, how the hell do you think we can evacuate eight million people? We tell people it will be fine, orderly, it's horseshit, and you know, and I know. You can't move millions of people is the answer. We pretend we can take care of our own so people don't go nuts and panic and start exiting the city, jamming the bridges, the tunnels. You ever consider that? We would have to go into lockdown.

"Anyways, if we take a direct hit, you have any idea what the survival rate in downtown Manhattan? We're toast. So I'll be glad to put you back to work. I can put you on a Civil Defense detail right now. You can spend your days watching supermarkets in case of looting."

"And you're in charge of all this personally?"

"Sarcasm won't do you any good, kid." From his pocket he pulled a wallet, removed a snapshot of a young pilot in uniform. "My boy is in Key West. They're moving troops in fast. He says the whole town is military now. He's on the front line, man, he's a navy flier."

"I didn't know."

"Don't come here again, OK, Wynne. Don't keep calling up cops you got connections with, I know that's what you done last week after I told you to take some time. Get out of here. This is a crisis. People are busy, man, really busy. Nobody's going to take your damn calls."

CHAPTER THREE

October 23, '62

I T WAS A MISTAKE sitting down with Max Ostalsky's friend, Bounine, and I knew it the minute I saw him. It had taken me an hour to drive up to Columbia. Traffic was bad, radios blasting from every car. It looked like people were fleeing the city, up the west side, over the George Washington, or maybe they were just going home early, sit in front of the TV with their families, hold hands, pray, listen for death coming in overhead.

All the way uptown, I watched the city on my right, the river on my left, New Jersey across the water. When I was in sight of the George Washington Bridge, I could imagine how it would blow apart like matchsticks.

The bombs would turn the subways into a fiery hell, incinerating men, women and children trapped under-ground. More nukes would hit us, the Empire State Building, the Chrysler, all the skyscrapers that pierced the New York sky, all that gleaming steel, concrete, marble, wiped off the face of the earth as if the buildings were sandcastles caught in a stiff breeze. People, too, the flesh turned to poisonous dust and blown away.

It was coming.

You could see it in the faces on the street, in the cars; you could hear it in the voice of the newscasters.

The Cold War, the threat of nukes, had been the air we breathed for so long that we didn't consciously think about it all that much. Not after Korea. What could be worse, I used to think when the nightmares got me out of bed shaking and sweating? What could be worse than that hellhole on the other side of the world?

Some stuff had really got, though. There was that picture, *On the Beach*. Started with, what the hell was it? Soviet nukes dragged in? I couldn't remember the details, but I remembered the last people on earth huddled in Australia waiting for the radiation cloud to drift down, with their suicide pills.

Two weeks ago I had picked up a *Saturday Evening Post*; it contained the first installment of a book called *Fail Safe*, the story of an accidental nuclear war. The second part had appeared the last Saturday, two days before the President's speech. How did they time it like that? How did they know?

After I had read it, I couldn't sleep, and when I did, my dreams were soaked in radiation. Radiation would cover the earth, and your skin, if you survived the initial blast, would fall off like it had been flayed, like a wet suit.

The war coming wasn't a novel now; it was real. Cops, firefighters, medics, had been sent to lectures on civil defense. I knew the sound of the warnings. I knew where to lead groups of people underground; how to maintain order; how to organize them in these subterranean cells behind iron doors, with their lead-lined water cans, and portable toilet packs. We were on the front lines, the chief said. We were to consider ourselves soldiers in the line of duty, if the time came.

All those years, the little kids ducking under their desks, watching Bert the Turtle tell them to duck and cover, and it would be OK, it was horseshit. I knew people with bomb shelters who discussed what you did if strangers tried to get in.

Did you welcome them? Push them out into the howling gale because you didn't have enough food? In the basement of my building was a makeshift room marked with a nuclear symbol. All pointless. They had ICBMs pointing at us. We had more.

Limited war. Percentages. Collateral damage. All the theories were horseshit. Deep down people knew that once it began, there would be no hope.

Outside Columbia Presbyterian Hospital, a few patients, still attached to their IVs, or in wheelchairs, were smoking and taking the air, shooting the breeze. Maybe they had nothing to worry about anymore. Figured they'd be dead before the bombs hit.

I stuck my police ID in the front window and went looking for Mike Bounine. I had never liked him. I couldn't put my finger on it exactly, but I had him figured for the man who was running Ostalsky, and that was enough.

"This is a pleasant surprise," Bounine said when he saw me. "Can I help you, Pat?" he said, and shook my hand. He had a firm handshake, manly, and I didn't believe it for an instant. "I am glad for this visit, Pat. It's a difficult day for so many people, therefore so nice to see you, please, sit down, and welcome. Tell me how your aunt and uncle, Mr and Mrs Kelly are? They were so kind to show me their home, and their church."

I ignored the niceties. The confidence was palpable. This Russian who called himself Mike, though I could never get used to it, seemed to wear his self-assurance like an impenetrable garment. He was not at all unnerved by the arrival of a New York cop.

In his starched white coat over a good suit, Bounine rose from his chair and suggested coffee.

"You must be catching plenty of flak what with the Cuban thing, your country shipping over missiles, and wanting to nuke us."

"People are surprisingly tolerant," he said. "They consider me a guest. You Americans are wonderfully friendly."

The hospital corridors smelled of ammonia, and there was the squeak of rubber soles on linoleum as nurses hurried by with that air of self-importance, white caps perched on their hair like birds ready for flight. As they passed, they addressed him as Dr Bounine. He enjoyed the attention.

In the cafeteria, Bounine said, "Would you care for coffee, or would you enjoy tea? What can I help you with? What do you say to a slice of cake? I am a fan of coconut cake."

What did he mean, what do you say? It was something Ostalsky often said, as if inquiring about my opinion. I knew it was only a verbal tick, something translated from the Russian, but it always unnerved me.

"No cake," I said. "So you're getting on?"

"Oh, indeed yes, I like the people so much. I feel myself learning many things. I am enjoying my time at the College of Physicians and Surgeons, and I hope I am imparting some useful knowledge as well. Coffee?" He asked again.

"Black, no sugar."

At the cafeteria counter, Bounine got coffee for both of us, and cake for himself. He sat down again, long legs stretched out in an easy sprawl. A couple of younger doctors came by, but he stayed where he was and they were forced to lean down to speak to him. This was a man used to a certain status, comfortable in his own world.

He looked at his watch to let me know he was a busy man.

"You and Ostalsky, you told me how you traveled together from Moscow. But I don't remember if you said you had been friends back home? Colleagues? Ostalsky is an English teacher, you're a doctor, so I say to myself, how on earth could you be colleagues? But perhaps you were friends."

As soon as I mentioned Ostalsky's name, there was a faint flicker in Bounine's eyes. Something that shifted, darkened, turned inwards. He had burrowed inside for the appropriate response, or the right lies quick, like a prairie dog or a rat into a hole.

"Indeed, I flew over to the United States with Max. We met on the plane, as we told to you, and found we had been assigned seats next to each other, so much happens just by chance, don't you think? We stop in Stockholm. Excellent little fish sandwiches at the airport, I recall that, because Max eats many. We talk together, and discover both of us wish to have been cosmonauts. I think that was a bond. My good fortune to meet such an intelligent friend before even arriving," said Bounine. "Of course, I knew of his uncle. General Fyodor Grigoryevich Ostalsky, a hero of the Great Patriotic War. My father and the general served together as younger men. Now, how may I be of help?" He poured half a pitcher of cream into his coffee, and started on the coconut cake.

Bounine spoke very fast, as if to leave no room for your questions; like a brilliant suspect on the stand, he diverted the real question, and filled the space with details about cosmonauts and sandwiches. He was lying. I knew it. Ostalsky had known it. In his notebook, he had written that Bounine had been assigned to watch him.

Was Bounine really Ostalsky's—what the hell did they call them in spy novels—his operative? His operator? Like at a switchboard? In my head, I got the idea that Bounine plugged Max in whenever he wanted, or let him hang at the end of the phone, waiting for the connection. The Max Ostalsky I knew was no match for this cool customer across the table.

I kept my tone conversational and slurped my coffee as a distraction. It was hot and bitter, and I scalded my tongue. I lit up a cigarette and offered him the pack of Chesterfields.

"I prefer these," he said, produced his Tiparillos, and put one between his lips. With a handsome silver Dunhill, he lit it.

His voice remained amiable, amused, but something about his words gave me the creeps. I felt he could produce a knife, slit my throat, then claim I was one of his patients, all without missing a bite of his coconut cake.

"What's your specialty?"

Bounine looked up. "Medicine. I imagine you were hoping I'd said nuclear medicine. I'm sorry. No, as I have said, I am a geneticist, also with a sub-specialty in pathology. I spend most of my time looking through a microscope. Viral diseases, nothing very, how would you say it, glamorous. A bit boring, comparatively." He sipped his coffee. "It is quite a pleasure to see you, but is there something I can help you with because I have an appointment?"

"When's the last time you saw Ostalsky?"

"Let me see, last week, I think, or was it the week before?"

"Are you concerned about the Cuban situation?"

"We all believe in peace."

In his notebook Max had written about Bounine's sense of betrayal by his country and that they—Max, Bounine— had been lied to.

Sitting with him at the cafeteria table, I knew Bounine had handed Max a line of purest horseshit to try to provoke him. Come on, Comrade, confess your doubts, I could imagine him saying. Perhaps this was the Soviet version of the confessional.

"You and Max are still good friends?"

"Certainly."

"Then perhaps you are helping him?"

"But why does he need help? I don't understand?"

"He's disappeared. Gone. Vanished. Who knows, maybe he's dead?"

He hadn't known. Bounine didn't know. Pushing his plate away, he got up and said, "I really must go now."

"I wonder if you've seen the paper today?" I said.

"I've been quite busy. Not one moment to spare."

"Please don't go." I handed him a copy of the *Journal-*

American on the table, folded back to page 19 where there was a picture of the dead man on Pier 46. "This man was murdered last week on a pier in Greenwich Village. I was sure you would have seen it."

Bounine feigned surprise, and said, "No. Indeed, I rarely look at these sensationalist stories in your less savory newspapers. Who is this? Poor fellow."

I waited.

"It's possible, yes, you're right, perhaps. I think I saw something in the *Herald Tribune*, but the report was of a Mafia crime. I must say I feel lucky to live in a country with nothing of that kind. But why would I ever know the name of some poor dead Cuban?" He gathered up his coffee cup and cigarettes. "Poor man. Perhaps he was the victim of your country's hostility towards the Cuban people."

"I'll take that," I said. "My newspaper."

"Of course," said Bounine as he set off, and I followed. "If I can do anything to help with Maxim Ostalsky, let me know, please, I would worry if there is a problem. Apologies but I'm due at a lecture. Do you have any idea at all where Max is?"

"Do you? Why do you care?"

"As a fellow countryman, exactly as I would any of my comrades. Also, he is my friend."

"Is he?"

"Yes, of course."

"Just one more thing. The murder on Pier 46 is my case. I'm sure you understand how an investigation works. Questions, and more questions, no let-up until it's done."

"As I have understood, you were removed from the investigation, this means your visit to me is not official. You are now on your vacation. Isn't that correct?"

CHAPTER FOUR

October 23, '62

HOW IN THE NAME of Christ did Bounine know I was off the job? That Logan got me dumped. If I went to Bounine's office, would I find Captain Logan in his Rolodex? Or Murphy? Did they have a relationship with the Russians? Was it possible?

Mike Bounine was not a careless man. He might have ordered Rica Valdes' murder; Ostalsky might have done the killing. But they would have done it on orders. They were Soviet agents, not cowboy spooks. They had been trained; they would be disciplined, focused. They knew what they were doing; they did what they were told. Evil bastards, sure, but meticulous.

On the ground floor of the hospital, I put in a call to a friend who knew her way around the police archives, somebody who would always take my calls, I thought. I had been cut off, but for sure she would help, and I blurted it out, what I needed. It took her a while to answer. I thought to myself: even she's scared of doing business with me; and when I mentioned the name Homer Logan, there was a tiny sharp intake of breath. "Don't call me again, please," she said. "Don't use this number."

"Help me," I said.

"I'll try," was all she said. "I'll try. I'll call you," she added in a whisper. "If I can."

Smoking, furious at myself, I slammed my hand against the wall. I was sinking in my own mess; I was sunk; I was under water; I was as good as dead.

Nobody ever said I'd be a good secret agent; Jesus, no. But if I was going to hunt down Ostalsky in my own time, I'd have to stay under the radar, out of sight of Murphy and Logan, but also the Russkis. Shit, I thought, shit.

Distracted, I dropped my cigarette. The stink of burning fabric from my pants was acrid, vile. "Goddamn it to hell."

I ran out to the street, got rid of the burning butt, and by the time Bounine emerged from the hospital, I was in my car. He had obviously waited until I left. He walked with that confident swagger, a blue topcoat over his shoulders.

Just then, as if it had been choreographed, another man, a fat dapper fellow in a camel-hair coat and a gray fedora, got out of a taxicab that pulled up, and gestured for Bounine to join him. The coat was the kind I once saw on Bugsy Siegel when I was a kid, and my pa had taken me to the Lower East Side to buy a jacket cheap from some pal of his who was a Jew in the garment business.

To my surprise, Bounine obeyed. The two men sat down on a bench. The fat one did all the talking. Bounine seemed to ask permission to smoke, and as he took a cigarette from his silver case, stood up and turned away from the wind off the river to light it, saw me. He raised his hand and waved. "Hello," he called out. In his mind I was his escape route. The swagger was gone. He had a hunted look, like an animal in a trap.

The fat man smiled slightly and put his hand on Bouninc's arm. It might have looked friendly enough to most people, but I knew it was to stop him, detain him, warn him, the act of a cop who had collared a criminal.

The cliff of elegant apartment buildings on Riverside Drive was on my left as I drove downtown, the dark blue river to the right; and all the way I had the sense somebody was trailing me in a Chevvy Impala, the car I had seen the other night. I took a detour by NYU, hoping to spot Nancy, and not wanting to. I stopped a couple of her friends who said they had not seen her all week, and then went back to talking about the crisis. I had the feeling a lot of babies would get made that week. I don't want to die a virgin, I heard one of them say. God, I don't want that.

On the way to my building, I lost the Impala, parked a few blocks from home, walked over and went upstairs.

As I took my key out, from behind my door, I heard somebody on the prowl, somebody walking, the old floorboards creaking. Somebody had beat me home and was waiting for me.

CHAPTER FIVE

October 23, '62

"I ALMOST JUMPED OUT OF my skin when I heard somebody walking around in here, but I'm glad to see you, I really am, Uncle Jack."

"I was thinking you could use a friend." Jack Kelly got out of the chair where he had been watching TV. He had on his ancient Dodgers jacket with the number 42 on the back—for luck, he always said when he wore it. I hugged him, and kissed the top of his head, almost bald now, only a few wisps of white hair left.

"How are you, Paddy?"

"Is Auntie Clara OK?"

"Scared. She watches that damn set, and she runs to the church, and I say, 'Take it easy, the President is on this.'"

When I was a kid and my pop was on the rails looking for work, and my ma was doing domestic work where she lived in—rich family in Greenwich—Jack Kelly was the big man in my life, physically and in every other way, and I had learned to be a cop, and a human being, if I had managed it at all, from him.

"I said, Clara O'Mara Kelly, do you think I am going to allow them Reds to scare me, well, to hell with them." Jack was my ma's younger brother, a smart cop and an optimist, to him, like all the family, JFK was a prince among men, as Franklin Roosevelt had been. For Jack Kelly, a man who avoided church at all costs, these were secular saints.

"Did I ever tell you the time I got a glimpse of FDR during the war, passing by, in that car with Mayor LaGuardia, and he was smiling and smoking that cigarette, and he was a cripple, and he saved us, you know that, boyo? So I'm not afraid about some Commie bastards. Like Roosevelt said, it's the fear that's killing us."

I got out a bottle of the Old Bushmills I had been saving up for Jack, poured it into a pair of glasses, handed one to him.

"You OK?"

"I'm OK." He drank the whisky in two swallows. "But you're not, Patrick. You are not OK at all. I can see that."

"What are you talking about?"

Jack got up close enough to me that I could see the light brown eyes behind his spectacles. He put his hand on my arm, in a protective gesture.

"What is it, Uncle Jack?"

"You gotta get your nose out of this thing over on Pier 46, Patrick. You have to stop it. The homicide, it ain't your case, and you're making a lot of people very very angry, you see what I mean? I'm asking you to stop."

"The brass sent you to me?"

"I'm going to pretend you didn't say that. You don't believe it, but I got the message. Don't ask how. It doesn't matter. Stay away. It's the Russkis got you into this, that pal of yours, Max, whatsisname? I thought he was OK at first, even if he was a Bolshie, but his friend, the other one, Boney, what was that?"

"Mike Bounine."

"Yeah, Mike? What's his real name? That day you brought them to Old St Pat's for your Auntie Clara to show them over the place? August, right? Well, I'm sitting in the back of the church, watching, and I don't like it, I don't like Boney's damn face one bit. I say to myself, Jackie, this is a bad fellow, I mean not just some Bolshie like your Max, but a dirty Red. Dirty spy. Dirty tricks. Clara introducing Father Sean. Him showing those boys around, like they were interested in religion. You know I don't care for the church much, but I pretend for Clara's sake. This made me mad as hell and Father Sean dancing around with those long skirts like some fairy, showing those Reds everything, the chapels, the organ, the mortuary vaults, nobody never gets to see that. Probably thinking he can convert the Russkis; I bet he told the Monsignor all about it.

"And Boney keeps asking questions like who has the keys, when was it built, all that stuff, and saying he's an amateur student of architecture, and stuff, what's a fucking Red doing with so much interest in churches? They're all fucking atheists."

"You sound like my pop when he told me how evil the Reds are, and made me pray for the souls of little Commie children. I asked him how come we gotta pray for them if they're so evil. He slapped me with his open hand." I sat down opposite Jack, and poured more whisky.

"I'm not like your pop."

"I'm sorry. Go on," I said.

"Yeah, I keep my trap shut because my Clara is having the time of her life, and that Boney is playing her. Soon as he hears she worked for Rose Kennedy in Bronxville, he's all ears. You remember, we're at home and she's serving them tea and my best whisky?"

I remembered. We had gone from the church to the red-brick house on Mott Street. Clara's saying to Ostalsky and Bounine, "I helped out at Mrs Rose Kennedy's parties, I was a very comely girl, I worked relief for the nursery maid."

"She always likes talking about the Kennedys," I said.

"You remember?"

"Remind me." Jack wanted to get it out, and I sat and listened.

"You bet she does," said Uncle Jack. "And this Red is pumping her, and her saying how she loved Bobby best cause he was the runt of the litter, and how later he would sometimes drop by Old St Pat's, because it was the oldest in the city and he always lit a candle for his poor sister, well, I'm giving Clara a look, and finally she clears away the tea, and your friend, this Max, he gets the message, at least he has some manners, he brings Clara a nice little present, one of those wooden painted dollies, you know? He knows when it's time to go. But the other one, what's he so interested in the Kennedys for?"

"I don't know."

"Anyway, Paddy, stay away from them. From the case, like you were told. I'm not just talking about you getting canned from the Force, I'm talking much worse. You hear me? There's something going down, and it involves the Feds. I want you safe. I'm thinking of taking your ma and Clara up to the Adirondacks where she'll feel safe if this Cuban thing goes down bad. You remember Bumpy Heaney, my partner back when? He's got that place on Raquette Lake, why don't you come up. "

"What about my pa?"

"He doesn't want nothing to do with us, just sits in that chair. I think his brain went dead a long time ago. Your ma won't leave him." He got out of the chair. "You hear my knees creaking? I'm getting on."

"Uncle Jack?"

"What's that?"

"Who's Captain Logan? Homer Logan."

Jack took a step back. He looked frightened. "Is he involved?"

"He's the one who told me to stay away. He was at the pier when I found the dead man. Uncle Jack, you have to help me out, because there's nobody. Nobody is talking to me. Nobody will take my calls, including guys I been friends with for a long time. I have good information on the homicide but my boss just tells me, take a vacation. Everyone just shuts me out. Who the hell is Logan?"

"He's connected."

"You mean the Mob?"

"Bigger."

"Christ."

"You feeling that cold wind on your neck?"

"Yes."

"These boys push you out, they freeze you out. We used to say you was out in the cold for good, if it happened."

"You knew?"

"I felt it, sure. Your other homicide, way back last summer when the girl got murdered on the High Line, I got the feeling you were not flavor of the month, kiddo. Suddenly the brass starts dropping by, asking me about my nephew, Pat. Offering me a nice retirement package. I said, forget about it. I don't know what else you're up to, Pat, but I have to think you're not hanging with the KGB for nothing."

"Is that what they think? How do you know Max is KGB?"

"You're fucking kidding me. The fellow is a Red, they let him out of the country, they let him loose in New York, like he told me when you brought him to the house. Told me how much he likes going around in the City, listening to music, walking around. I'll bet he likes it. Never been free a day in his life before. You think that comes without strings? I'm going to assume that whatever you're onto with him, it's for our side. I'm assuming that, Patrick." Jack lowered his voice. "I'm assuming this is a delicate situation and you can't tell me certain things because you don't want to put me and your aunt in danger. Can I take it you won't go crazy, with one of your impetuous hare-brained schemes?"

"Yes."

"You are working for our side."

"Is that what they're saying? That I'm some kind of traitor?

"You always been different, you never put up with a lot of the shit that goes with being a cop in this city. Plus, you go around with that girl, Nancy, you introduced me one time, and she has some pretty radical ideas for a young lady, but now listen to me, no matter what you been doing, I'll take care of you, which is why I want you to come to the Adirondacks, where nobody gives a shit about anything except a good day of hunting." Jack's eyes were filling up. He held out his hand to me. He would take care of me even if I had betrayed everything he cared for, even if I had signed on with the KGB.

"Thank you."

"You're like my own kid, Paddy."

"It's OK, Uncle Jack. I'm working for our side. Of course I am." I had been tempted to tell him Max Ostalsky was the killer, that he had murdered the man on Pier 46, and possibly Susana, the girl on the High Line, but when I looked at him again, I saw how old he was now.

"Thank you. Now, what about you come up to the mountains with us? You can bring that boy, that Tommy, I know you treat him like a son, and if it helps make him safe, bring him too."

"I'll think about it, I promise."

"No, you won't. You'll do your job, like always. But you take care. Nothing matters more than your life, Pat. I wouldn't make it if anything happened to you. There's no goddamned politics that matters as much as life.

"I used to tell those Irish bastards in the IRA who wanted money for guns, and were always acting tough, you know, and pretty crazy, you'd run into them in some of the bars on Third Avenue, and they're saying, the cause comes first, the cause is the thing, and I'm saying, fuck the cause, I have family over there, and some of them married to Protestants, you touch one hair of somebody I love, and because you don't play their murderous game, you're ass is grass. You hear me? If you don't want to come upstate, go out to Montauk, get some fishing.

"If you need me, I'll do what I can, but once I get upstate, the only phone is at the hardware store, so mostly I'm out of touch. You got that number, Pat? OK, I love you," said my Uncle Jack, swallowed a couple of gulps more of the whisky and kissed me goodbye.

I had never felt lonelier, or more frightened than when Jack went out the door, and I heard his slow heavy steps on the stairs. But I was sure now that not only was Ostalsky the killer, but somebody—our people, his people—wanted to keep it a secret. Otherwise, why keep it going that this was the Mob? Why not pick up Ostalsky? Why freeze me out? Or was Ostalsky dead, after all?

I was lost. I almost ran after Uncle Jack, but instead I turned the TV on.

Later that night, Walter Cronkite, the new anchor on CBS, was reporting troop movements, the location of Soviet ships, the growing probability of an encounter with the Soviets.

That week, the people on the screen became characters in a real-life soap: JFK, Bobby Kennedy, Lyndon Johnson, Khrushchev, Castro, Adlai Stevenson. Cronkite was the everyman in this play. He looked weary.

Cronkite, with his little mustache and receding hairline, the heavy pouches beneath the sympathetic eyes, the broad Midwestern face, the voice was calm and straightforward. Tonight, for a split second, he rubbed his eyes and emotion ran across his face.

We got to know that look later. When the President was shot, he kept putting his glasses on and taking them off, as if he needed a prop to get through the terrible moment and to cover the damp naked eyes; when he told the country the truth about Vietnam; when Bobby Kennedy and Martin Luther King were murdered. Got to know that if Cronkite, his hair thinning and going first gray then white, if this modest man could not keep his feelings to himself, it was bad.

The Cuban Missile Crisis, even Cronkite let it show he was unsure of the future. I can't recall now if it was the Tuesday or Wednesday for sure, or if Cronkite wore his glasses. We didn't know how long it would go on. Fifty years later, thinking about it, my gut heaves.

Looking at the camera, Cronkite just said, "See you tomorrow if there is a tomorrow."

Then the phone rang.

CHAPTER SIX

October 23, '62

"PLEASE DEPOSIT TEN CENTS."

The world could end because you'd failed to stick your extra dime in the phone.

"Please deposit ten cents." The operator's voice came through on the phone. "Please deposit ten cents, sir," she said. "Sir, will you please deposit ten cents now," she said again and again.

"I already put in the dime, plus a nickel for extra time, please connect me." It took me a second or two to understand, because I had never talked to Max Ostalsky on the phone. His voice was soft, a faint but distinct accent noticeable; maybe it was fear.

It came through the phone like a shockwave. The cold black phone receiver in my hand seemed like a foreign object; I sat down hard on my bed, and tried to light a cigarette, and dropped the worn Zippo that my Uncle Jack had taken to war and had given me when I went to Korea. Like a silvery icon, it lay on the thick Hudson Bay red and black blanket I got up in Canada on vacation hunting with him years ago. My place stank of cigarettes. A green china ashtray I swiped from some pub in Ireland was piled high with butts.

I checked the time on the watch I had received for my high school graduation; it needed cleaning. All these souvenirs, all this stuff, these things I had carefully assembled, seemed somehow like evidence from a crime scene that was my own life. I was hallucinating.

"Hello?" said his voice.

I waited. Was this some kind of prank?

"Who is this?"

"I am so glad to hear your voice, my friend." He didn't say his name, or mine, probably in case somebody else was listening. "Is this my old friend I recently ate meatballs with?" His breathing sounded shallow.

It startled me again, hearing his voice, the sound muffled by the receiver, or by his own anxiety. This was not the easy-going student I had known around the Village. I had read his notebooks. I knew that he was an agent with the KGB, or whatever they called it. I was glad I had done it. I felt triumphant, because I also knew Max Ostalsky was a murderer and I had the evidence. The silver charm I had picked up from the pier, that Nancy had given him was in my pocket where I kept it like a talisman; I let my fingers run over it when I reached for some change.

There was a click on the line. Was somebody listening? I knew Hoover's people could bug you easy. If you had contact with a Red, they could get into your place and fix it easy enough, and you'd never know unless you had reason to look. I would look after I got off the phone. The phone in one hand, I began emptying the pack of Chesterfields onto the blanket, then lining them up like soldiers. It kept me calm, focused.

"Hello?" said the voice. "Please speak if you are able to hear me."

"Where are you?"

"It doesn't matter so much, but I need a favor from you. You must not look for me. You must tell this to our mutual friend. She should no longer call me and leave messages. People will think something is not normal. It will be harmful to her. I don't want to cause harm. I didn't hurt anyone. I don't want to hurt anyone. I beg you, don't search for me any more. Please."

"Are you still in the United States?"

"Nowhere," said Max, his voice low and sorrowful. "I feel very bad to make my good American friends worry about me. This is why I'm calling."

"Tell me where you are?" I was trying desperately to keep him on the phone, to hear anything in the background — traffic noise, subways, restaurant noise—any sound I could grab hold of. "Are you here in New York? I can help you." I said the words, the hollow stuff cops always say, but neither of us believed it.

"I apologize. When this is over, if you can, please take the remaining things from my room, I would be grateful. Please say to everyone I intended no harm. But don't look for me. Don't put yourself in harm's way. Can you agree?"

I was silent.

"I will be in touch."

"When?"

"One day," he said.

"Hello?" I called out to him. I could tell he was still on the phone, not wanting me to go. In some way I couldn't explain, he was hanging on as if to a life raft. "You knew I was looking for you."

"Yes. The Millers had left several phone messages last week, including two from you. It doesn't matter. Please, tell everybody I am away in vacation. Say hello to my friends." There was a kind of longing buried in the brisk voice. "Please."

"You should tell them yourself. You owe them that."

"Yes, I know."

"Who else is looking for you?"

He was silent.

"Your own people are looking for you, so are ours. I think you know. I think you know I'm the only one who can help you."

"I must go," he said. "I just want to say thank you for everything."

"What things?" By now, keeping myself steady, I had rearranged the cigarettes twice, reminding myself that this man with the soft voice and pleasant manner was a cold killer who had murdered a young Cuban, and maybe the girl too.

I made a bundle of the cigarettes and, only half aware of what I was doing, crushed them in my hand. Tobacco clung to my fingers.

"Everything. Thank you for your friendship."

"Where are you, goddamnit?"

Then I heard it. Just before Max hung up, I heard the announcement. He was at a train station. I played the phone call back again in my head, and I heard it, first a jumble of sounds, the low-level buzz of the city. It was the city. He was here. Then: a voice announcing a train.

Suddenly I recalled that I'd once told Max about the Mad Bomber case and how tough it had been evacuating Pennsylvania Station. "A good place to hide," I had said.

On my table were some notes I had made in Max's room. G.U. D.C. Who was G.U. Did he mean Washington DC? The trains to Washington came and went through Penn Station.

Who was in Washington? His embassy? Would they give him cover? Send him home? Smuggle him out and stick him in one of those camps? Kill him? Hang a medal on the new jacket that made him look like an American college boy?

I ran for my car.

When you work crime as a city detective, things eventually fit together, more or less; if not, you can tweak them, give them a little shove, reorder the circumstances, pray for a good DA to prosecute. You consider motivation, circumstance, opportunity, forensics; you apply logic, and then things fall in, more or less.

While I stuck the key in the ignition, it hit me hard. I was no spy. I had none of that kind of subtlety. Except for a few movies I had seen, I had no knowledge of burrowing deep and waiting for people to reveal their flaws so you could expose them, no understanding of saboteurs or provocateurs, of double agents, or moles or sleepers or cut-outs, or whatever the hell they called it all.

With this business of Ostalsky, a KGB agent murdering a Cuban, I was in over my head, unable to even work through the evidence. Before I had left my apartment, I had called my boss and told him I was going fishing like he wanted.

"God bless you. God bless us all, if we make it through this week." Murphy had a sentimental streak.

How could I have misjudged the Russian? But everyone had liked him. He had been a good actor; his likeability was a role, a cover, something he had been taught. He had been taught well.

When I parked and ran into Pennsylvania Station, it was mobbed. People surged from the tracks underground. They circulated and sat, and read, and slept, in the immense lobby, with its pink marble and columns, like too many extras in a period movie, ancient Rome in the middle of Manhattan.

For a split second, I felt terror. This was the kind of place you could hide a bomb. It had happened before when the Mad Bomber was terrorizing the city; it could happen again—would happen.

In Penn Station, a killer could hide, in the toilets, in some of the out-of-use waiting rooms, under tarps at the building sites. It was huge and there were also warrens of offices and storage rooms where old luggage went when nobody claimed it. This was a place for an assassination, if you used the right weapon; use a knife, use a wire for strangling, then stash the body in a hundred abandoned places.

Every time a departing train was announced, the crowd surged forward. Where was Ostalsky? Was he dead? Why had he called me? Why did this murderous Russki want me to know where he was?

Suddenly, it came to me. The word—assassination. I had read it in Ostalsky's notebook. Not for a long time, not since Lincoln, had we done this kind of thing; Lincoln or the other president, what the hell was his name?

We didn't do that kind of thing any more, did we? The Russians did it; maybe those Banana Republics in South America—not us, not the Americans.

Ostalsky knew what was coming, he knew, and he needed help. He was scared.

CHAPTER SEVEN

October 23, '62

T HE HANDS ON MY watch seemed to move too fast, as if out of control, speeding ahead, making me crazy while I tried to search the immense station. Some of it was already under tarps, ready for the boneyard, as they planned on tearing it all down. I knew I was too late to find Ostalsky, but I searched the place anyway, running in and out of the shops, crashing into waiting rooms, people cursing me, knowing that he would not have stayed long enough for me to get him. He was on the run, and he would have moved on to Washington, or Moscow, or gone to ground, God knew where. He had been calling me to say goodbye, but why? What reason did he have to stop and call? I didn't believe all his words of friendship and thanks, not again, not anymore.

"Watch out." I had bumped into a woman who dropped her shopping bags from Orbach's. She yelled at me some more, and I ran again.

On the lower level of the station, the trains departed and arrived, sucking people in, and pushing them out of the glass and steel train sheds. Even at this hour, the station filled and emptied constantly, wave after wave of passengers coming and going. Everybody instinctively looked up at the big clock—it was 9.21— as the hands moved the minutes forward.

"It's getting late," said a voice. The fat man I had seen with Bounine outside the hospital was standing next to me.

He wore the same expensive camel-hair coat, his stomach straining against the belt. He could have been a banker or a lawyer, and like many large guys, he moved lightly. He raised his *Wall Street Journal* to his face, as if to inspect the closing prices on his stocks.

When he put the paper down, I saw he was relatively young, about forty, not more, but with jowls that, in a few years, would grow fat as his stomach, and drop like a basset hound's. He wore horn-rimmed glasses.

He caught my eye. "May I help you with something?" he said, tipping his hat. "Are you perhaps lost? It's quite easy to get lost here, would you not agree?" he said. "It's happened to me quite a few times."

"I'm good."

"Are you coming or going?" he said.

I played the game. "Waiting for a friend. You?"

"It's sad that they will soon tear down this wonderful train station, don't you think so? I have heard the waiting room upstairs was compared to the Roman Baths of Caracalla."

"Very sad."

"Are you interested in architecture, then, in the preservation of old cities? I understand your lovely first lady, Mrs Jacqueline Kennedy, is quite a force in this area."

He examined his gold watch. He removed his fine brown leather gloves, extracted a pack of foreign cigarettes, opened it and offered it to me. "These are quite tasty," he said. Two of his fingers were missing.

"The Great Patriotic War," he said. "We all lost something."

Had he somehow followed me from Columbia? I accepted a cigarette, and let him light it.

"The weather has changed suddenly, don't you think? Such lovely Indian summer, and now it's quite chill. Chilly." He corrected himself. "What do you say? Is that usual?"

"What do I say about what?"

"This weather."

"Do you visit New York often?" Only clichés fell out of my mouth. I wanted him to make a move first.

"Yes. Sure. It is normal. I come here as often as possible for you have very fine theatre and concerts. On some occasions my wife accompanies me as well. In fact, I have been here to see the ballet. My wife is a musician," he added, maybe to let me know it wasn't a pick-up, that he wasn't queer. "She plays the cello."

"Where are you from?"

"Washington DC," he said, and, glancing at the clock, added, "I have only five minutes before my train departs."

"But have you got something to tell me? This isn't an accident, is it? Our meeting?" I was impatient. "I saw you with Bounine outside Columbia."

"Yes." He put out his hand. "If you come to Washington, please look for me. Here is my telephone number," he said, reaching into his pocket for a little blue leather case. From it, he removed a card and handed it to me. I examined it. In elegant script, it read Mr Gennadi Ustinov. It was engraved.

"As you see, my name is Gennadi Mikhailovich Ustinov. I work at the Soviet Embassy," he said.

"Pat Wynne."

"Yes," he said.

"You knew my name, didn't you?"

"Yes. It's written on the return address of the envelope in your pocket." He was right. There was an envelope sticking out of my jacket pocket that I'd meant to mail to my cousin in Liverpool for her birthday and had forgotten. "Please, shall we sit down?" He gestured for me to follow him to a bench in the waiting area. He sat. I sat next to him. A group of suburban women took the rest of the space. Ustinov then looked around the cavernous hall, got up again, and led me to an empty corner, where his back was against the wall.

This was a man who always preferred his back against the wall. You could see that. From his black leather attaché case he removed a copy of the *Journal-American*. He folded it so I could see the story about the dead man on the pier, with a photograph.

"You knew I was coming?"

Ustinov lowered his voice. "Our mutual friend mentioned he had telephoned you, and thought you might make your way here."

"Enough games," I said.

"But this is a sort of game, is it not? Or call it magic. Things appear. They disappear. People as well."

"Look, I'm just a dumb New York policeman, just tell me what's going on, and where Max Ostalsky is."

"Who?"

"Stop." I got up. I was furious now. I felt in my pocket for the gun. "Stop fucking around, man. You know who I mean and you know where he is."

He looked across the hall and removed his hat and put it back.

"Do you want to say why you were standing on the sidewalk with Mike Bounine up at Columbia?" I asked him. "It didn't look all that friendly to me."

He grinned now. "Is that what he calls himself here? Mike? Very, what would you say, charming? Mike, this is quite a piece of news."

"Is it? Why? It's what he told me. Don't you people have nicknames over there? Is it against the law?"

"It is not. Certainly, we have many. This Mike, he, too, comes from the Soviet Union, like me, you know that, of course. We are compatriots. I stopped to say hello."

"Outside a hospital on 168th Street? Really?"

"As I have said, I work in Washington where I have a job at the embassy. Cultural attaché," he said. "If you will ask why I was in New York, for the truth, I tell you I was here to attend to something for our famous Bolshoi Ballet Company. Several of our dancers left their slippers behind, and I must send them off to Chicago. Now I am waiting for my return train."

"Come on, you're telling me it's about ballet shoes? You think I was born yesterday?"

"I do not imagine this. But it is true. Our ballet company has gone on tour, and the ladies cannot dance without their pink satin shoes. This was important. I have been on 39th Street at the Metropolitan Opera House to arrange for these shoes to be sent."

"Ballet shoes." I was looking for answers to a homicide, and this joker gives me ballet. "Listen, I'm going."

"Please sit down again."

Shifting closer to Ustinov, I let him know I had a gun. I was carrying my personal weapon, the one I kept at home, though it would not have pleased my boss.

Ustinov seemed not to notice, or to care. He was a secure man. "The ballet shoes were a cover." Then he turned to look at me. "Wait, please." He looked out into the crowd again, and as he did, I saw that he was looking at a man with a thick neck in a tan raincoat and a checkered flat cap standing under the clock.

"What did Ostalsky tell you?"

"He says he needs help."

"So you just stepped up."

"Our families are close. This is a difficult time. We go for a ride on the Circle Line boat, a nice quiet place to talk in the middle of a cold day. Poor Max, he looks out at Manhattan passing across the water and I see how much he likes this city, and he tells me he is in trouble, that the Americans think he killed a man on the piers. Somebody told the police. He even leans out over the railing of the boat and, to tell the truth, for a moment I think he's going to jump into the river. I grab him as tight as I can, but he just points to a pier and I see in his face how melancholy he has become. 'They are hunting me,' he says. I have known Maxim Stepanovich since he was a child. He didn't do it, Detective Wynne."

"Oh, please. You're going to tell me you baby-sat for him, that you taught him his first little magic tricks, to pull money out of people's ears."

He looked surprised. "How did you know? Yes, all this is true."

"Why would I believe you? Why are your own people on his tail? Is this about Cuba?"

"Yes. And other things."

"What other things."

Ustinov lowered his voice. "There are people in my country who want a nuclear war, and the same is true of people in your country, I know this."

"Yeah, so? How do you know? Your job is ballet slippers, isn't it?"

"There are other, more informal jobs, too. I frequently meet with many officials of the United States, but not formally. Just, so to say, friends who might have a cigarette together on a park bench, or a bite to eat in a restaurant they both like, perhaps an accidental meeting on the steps of the Lincoln Monument."

"But not accidental?"

"Not quite. You probably understand that by telling you these things it is a risk for me."

"I don't know anything about Washington politics. Who is it you have these meetings with?"

"That I cannot tell you. Just understand there are good people on both sides, who do not want war, but also the others."

"Military guys."

"You know?"

"I read *Fail-Safe* last week, for Christ's sake."

"This book tells the truth. I can't say any more. But I think that Max has found himself involved with all of this by accident."

"Somebody is using him. Framing him."

"It's possible," said Ustinov. "May I give you some advice?"

"Sure." I was angry, and I was on edge. Where was Max? If he had killed before and somebody got in his way, he would do it again. I had no idea what to make of this fat man with the soft voice and mild manner.

"Stay away from Bounine," said Ustinov. "I think he has, how would you say, gone off the rails, Detective. I'm afraid he has, how do they say, problems that he cannot solve. Personal problems, do you understand what this means? I have a feeling he will not be welcome here in the United States very much longer."

"Or in your country?"

"Perhaps."

"Is that why you went to see him?"

"You could say this."

"What kind of problems. Women? Money?"

Ustinov smiled sadly. "No ideology can protect from certain desires, I'm afraid. But no, not women or money."

"Spell it out for me." I guessed Ustinov was a lot more senior than he had said. In some way he was Bounine's superior. I smoked, and followed his gaze as he looked at the departure board overhead.

"My train leaves for Washington in several minutes, so I must board now." Ustinov rose, and put out his hand. "Be careful, Detective, please. I know you have been kind to my friend." He turned just slightly, and I saw the man with the checkered cap. His shoes looked like a cop's; rubber-soled, they were heavy and had been repaired more than once.

"Yours?"

"I'm sorry? What was that, Detective?"

"How did you know I was a detective?"

"The envelope in your pocket."

"It only has my name. No title."

He didn't answer. Again, Ustinov looked around. Again, he lowered his voice; he spoke so softly this time, I could barely hear. "Your friend needs your help. He needs it very much. He is not a bad man. Help him if you can. Please. You have my telephone number."

"Who the hell are you really?" I thought about grabbing Ustinov's lapels, but I held back. "Tell me what the hell is going on, and where Ostalsky is. You know, don't you? Where is he? Did you know I'd be here? You knew, you were with him when he called me. Weren't you?"

"I will miss my train."

I put my face into Ustninov's. "Tell me."

"I must go."

I caught his sleeve, but he extracted it from my grasp. "You're a foreign agent, I could get you arrested."

"I am an official cultural attaché. I have the protection of my country. I didn't tail you, as you put it."

"Where is Ostalsky?"

The goon in the cap and tan coat edged closer. His face was hard and expressionless, like Russians in a bad movie. Maybe they hired these Ivans because they would scare you with their looks alone. He looked like the kind of man—I had met a few of ours—who would kill you if there was a reason, and sometimes if there was none. Sometimes, these men did it from boredom.

Ivan moved closer to us, within reach of Ustinov. From where he stood now, he could hear us talking.

Ustinov straightened up, bowed slightly, a courtly

228

old-fashioned bow, and replaced his hat.

"My friend needs you, please help him, he is a good man," he said. "He wouldn't tell me where he has gone, for my own protection, but he said you would know. You would know because the two of you had been there before. He phones you, says goodbye only in case somebody is listening," says Ustinov. "Detective?"

"Yeah?"

He lowered his voice, glancing around as if to see who might be listening. "If you can avoid a certain Captain Logan, it would be quite a good idea."

"How do you know Logan?"

But Ustinov only offered me his hand, and I shook it and then, as he buttoned his coat, he felt in his pocket for his ticket. He walked steadily towards his train, with the man in the raincoat following him. He never looked back, just went calmly towards the tracks and the train that he believed would take him home, his camel hair overcoat billowing behind him.

CHAPTER EIGHT

October 23, '62

"HELLO, PAT."

"What goddamn assassination?" I said.

I found Max Ostalsky in the warehouse near the High Line, sitting on an empty chicken crate in the dark, a gun in his hand. It was eleven, Tuesday night, about an hour after I'd left Penn Station. The place was bare and cold. The concrete walls dripped. It was the place the Cuban girl, Susana Reyes, had camped out before she was slaughtered, and it still stank of rotting fowl—chicken or turkey—and piss.

"Some kind of warehouse," Ustinov had said, when I asked where Ostalsky was, and I had driven from Penn Station like a crazy man, soon as it hit me: the High Line.

The street-side door to the warehouse was missing. The cops must have yanked the door off when we were searching for clues to Susana's murder. All that was left were some yellow strips of police tape and cigarette butts the detectives would have tossed onto the floor.

Max knew the place; I had shown it to him. All the questions he had asked me about the High Line case, all the pestering.

I went up the stairs. Most of the doors were bolted and nailed shut except on the fourth floor where I had found Susana's little encampment, the faulty heater, a nest of newspaper. The door had been removed. For a moment, I listened, but all I heard was the wind, and the rats. I took a breath and went in.

A couple of empties rolled under my feet, glass clinking on the concrete floor. Used needles. Dope addicts came here to shoot up, drunks to sleep it off.

I didn't see the rat until it ran over my foot, looking for food. I never got used to rats. Cockroaches you could smash, you could even enjoy the cracking of the shells. They say cockroaches can survive nuclear war. Rats, I hated; hated the teeth, the paws.

During the war, I had seen a Navy poster that showed a rat who looked like Emperor Hirohito, and he was nibbling cheese out of a trap labeled Army, Navy, Civilian with the words: ALASKA: DEATH TRAP FOR THE JAP. I was eight. I asked my pop what it meant. "It means them Japs are dirty rats, kiddo. You understand?"

Feeling the animal getting at the flesh of my leg, I shook it off. A match struck.

It was then, in the light from the match, that I saw him. Ostalsky was sitting on that crate, near the rusted heater. A snub-nose nickel-plated .38 special, same as most cops used, same as me, was in his hand. He held it like a man who understood guns. The fact that he had used a .22 on the dead man didn't mean much. This was the kind of killer who knew his way around every weapon. He had been trained.

Yeah, sure, maybe Ostalsky spoke good English. He laughed a lot. He liked the movies, and good American shoes. He had willingly played a fool, a clown, grinning and laughing at himself trying to learn the local customs: how to buy a hot dog; how to do the Twist; how to drink whisky. He had not been sent to America just to learn about *Moby-Dick*, or listen to Gerry Mulligan, or make friends in the park with a gullible cop who loved James Brown. The encounter in Washington Square had not been accidental. I had read this in Ostalsky's diary. Max Ostalsky had been sent to use us.

The dark was playing tricks on me. I had trouble judging distance and, fumbling forward, I tripped over a paint can. When he struck a second match, I realized Ostalsky was only a few feet away, sitting on the wooden crate, back against the wall, elbows on his knees, the gun aimed at my heart.

Through the broken window behind him, I could now just see the tracks along the High Line, thirty feet above the street. He must have ditched his FBI tail, climbed up the ladder to the viaduct, stumbled along the tracks, onto the loading dock, into the warehouse through the window.

The only light came from the moon; distant, cold, half obscured by a reef of clouds over the river. Fall. Winter soon.

"I'm so sorry, Pat," Ostalsky said. "But would you mind giving me your weapon? I'd like not to have to ask, but I must do this. Please." A rueful smile crossed his face. "I didn't mean for a thing like this to happen, not at all. Forgive me. Can you tell me anything of what's happening?

Cuba?" His right hand was bandaged with an old rag, and bloodstained.

"Your killing hand?"

Max looked at it. "I cut it. When I broke the window to get in. I was left-handed as a child, they tried to cure me of this, so I can use both."

"Very handy." I was scared, but I was mad as hell. I wanted to punch out his lights and throw him in a holding cell for a long long time, and then watch him fry in the electric chair. But he had the weapon, and I understood he would have no scruples about using it.

"Right now, please, Pat. Your pistol."

He had changed. All that soft charm, the humor, the exuberance, was gone. He was quiet and polite, but behind the glasses, his eyes were focused and hard. He had shot the man on the pier—a man who had been his friend—had stuck a pistol in his ear and pulled the trigger. He had ripped his tongue out, wrapped his head in duct tape, maybe while he was still alive. He had stuffed the body in a black bag and dumped him on the pier. I had put my hand on the corpse, I had felt inside the wound, felt the flesh, the shattered bone.

I took my gun out of the holster, and slid it across the floor. Without looking down, he picked it up. "There's another empty box just there, that one that says Purdue Broiler Chickens? Won't you sit down?" He gestured to a wooden crate a few feet from where he sat. "You'll be more comfortable, though it's damp like hell in here. The smell is quite bad." He shifted his weight, and buttoned his jacket with one hand. "I'm sorry it's so cold."

"Yeah? That suit looks warm enough."

He was wearing the heavy gray suit I had first seen him in. He had left his new clothes behind—I had seen them in the closet on 10th Street—as if shedding a skin, leaving behind his American self. Only the loafers remained. Maybe he had forgotten. Maybe he couldn't give them up.

With one hand he got a cigarette out of his pocket. Examining it, he said, "My last Lucky Strike. Please tell me the news."

"We're probably going to war. Your people have been shipping nukes to Cuba," I said. "I brought you a couple of packs." I reached for my pocket.

"Don't do that. I'm sorry, Pat. Keep your hands, if you won't mind, out of your pockets, would you?"

Even in the dim warehouse I could see how tired he looked. Maybe if I could get him talking, it would change things. The more time passed, the less likely he was to shoot me. Talk, you bastard. Talk to me.

"You knew I'd come, didn't you?" I said. "Isn't that why you chose this place? Didn't you send me a message? Did you think I'd help you, or I'd go easier on you than the FBI?"

He was silent.

"Are you planning to kill me?"

"I hope not," he said.

Could I jump him? He was tired. I got up off the box and stretched.

"Sit down, please."

If he didn't kill me now, I'd get a better sense of his intentions. I stayed standing. Stretched again. I heard him cock the gun. I sat down. A rat ran across the space between us.

"You got in the way. You told the police I killed this man you found on the pier last Tuesday night. It seems so long

234

ago, a week and a day already." He rubbed his eyes. "Yes, it's Tuesday now, isn't it?" He seemed uncertain. "I'm just a bit tired. Yes. You should have let it be, Pat."

"How did you get the gun?"

"In your country it is quite easy. No problem, as you say."

"But you didn't buy it yourself?"

"What difference does it make?"

"I assume you know how to use that thing."

A rueful smile passed over his face. "Actually, I was on the Soviet shooting team."

"Yeah, so what?"

"We were very good. Sadly I was not at the competition this year in Cairo. I would like to have seen Egypt, Pat. The Pyramids, the temples at Luxor, the tomb of Tutankhamen, these were things I dream of seeing from the time I was a boy. I came here instead."

"What kind of pistol did you shoot?"

"Similar to a .22. Easy enough to make it look like I shot Valdes for somebody who knew about my sporting achievements in the USSR. You know what? I wish I could have seen more of America. New Orleans. San Francisco. Chicago. Well, it was never possible."

"Your bosses wouldn't allow it."

"You're right."

"Who are you going to assassinate?"

"What? Nobody. Nobody."

"Is it Bounine, then? Does he run you, are you his creature?"

"Although I would like to have seen the Wild West, as they call it. Perhaps I could have been a gunslinger of old western style?"

I was under no delusion about Ostalsky, who was a cold-blooded killer, and I wasn't laughing.

"You think this is funny? Does it make you laugh? You think this is one of those quaint American ideas that you can turn into one of your little ironic jokes?" I said.

"I am not ironic."

"No? What are you, then? A trained murderer? A killing machine? What else did they teach you?"

"Do you want to know?"

"I'm not in any goddamn hurry, am I, Max? I know you killed Rica Valdes on Pier 46. I told my boss, and he'll have his men on your case, the FBI too, and as for your own goons, how come you're hiding from them? How come you don't go to your bosses and say, I need help. This makes me feel they're not one bit goddamn happy with you, isn't that so?" I was bluffing, but it was all I had. "So entertain me."

The large rat scampered across the floor between us, and began to run around in frantic circles.

"We are in the rat race now, don't you think, Pat?" said Max, laughing. He aimed his pistol and shot the rat, but it didn't die. Max shot it again. Now it was dead.

The action startled me.

Max stared at the dead rat, stretched out his foot and kicked it away. "They taught us everything you would imagine," he said. "Languages. How to behave in a foreign country, to find your way around, to elude a tail, to see quickly who might be following you, their tactics. How to adapt to the culture, even which type of telephone might be used. We had a great deal of physical training, of course, and we were taught the use of weapons. Technical stuff, too, such as how to use radios, code, all that you would think. Did you know we make the world's very best pen for invisible writing? It's true. I should have procured one for you as a gift."

"Adapting to the culture didn't turn out the way you thought, did it? America wasn't what you had been taught."

"You're right."

"Propaganda. Brainwashing. Blackmail?"

"Sure. The brainwashing, as you call it, is more specialized. It's more to the Chinese tastes. Propaganda, naturally, how to detect what is real and what is not in foreign propaganda, although I suppose you could say propaganda depends on who is looking at it. But, yes, we are taught this, and also how to provoke, if necessary."

"But in your country nothing is real, is it?"

"It is more complicated."

"Christ, Ostalsky. You still believe. Jesus."

"Yes, I believe in socialism, of course. I love my country very much. Even though I have learned many other things here."

"You still sound like a fucking robot. It's horseshit, and I'm guessing you know it. You know better now. I guess they hired you because you had the brains for it. For the propaganda, and the lying, and, of course, your talent with guns. And for using people."

Max shifted his weight. "You misunderstand, Pat. We only want people to see that our system is directed towards social justice and against imperialism and the enslavement of the less able."

"You think we enslave people? The United States? You sound like a brainless Bolshie when you talk like that."

"Perhaps no more than when your own people talk of America as the greatest nation on earth, and say their Pledge of Allegiance, and tell the world that peace and goodness depends on your system of capitalism, even when there are hungry people, and Negro people hanging from trees." He looked at me. "As if making money is essential to these things. Do you believe money can buy peace or that capitalism will purchase equality for your Negroes?"

"Can it, Max. Just give me a break, OK? You don't have to impress me with how you con people with your Marxist horseshit, OK? I know it by heart. Your country's idea of peace is to ship a bunch of nukes across the world to Cuba, right next door to us, ninety miles away. There's probably going to be a war because of your people."

"Cuba has a right to self-determination."

"It was all a fucking game, wasn't it? You, and NYU, and Greenwich Village, and Nancy Rudnick, and me, Pat Wynne, the easy touch." I saw that he looked nervous. I kept talking. I would talk until I dropped. I didn't want to die in that warehouse.

"You imagined because I love Greenwich Village, and baseball, and the Half Note, and John Coltrane, even your rock and roll, and fried clams at Howard Johnsons, and espresso coffee at Café Figaro, and *Some Like It Hot*, and I do, I do like them a very lot, you didn't see that this could be true, my sincere delight in all this, but that I could also love my country, and that learning about these things could be part of my job. I was good at it, too. They didn't have to teach me much, it came to me, naturally."

"What about Nancy? Was she part of the plan?"

"Nancy was not in any plan, or you. You were not in a plan." He was bitter now, and in his voice was despair, and then he yawned, like a man desperate for oxygen to keep him going. He saw my face and laughed. "Oh, yes, we are also human beings. We yawn, we cry. We laugh. All of it."

"So what? I've collared killers who loved their children and ran home to them right after they strangled some poor bastard and watched him die. They're all human, even the maniacs. That gun you're holding isn't a .22. Where's the gun you used on your friend, Valdes, the friend you slaughtered at the end of Pier 46? What kind of man shoots an unarmed friend?"

"I didn't kill anyone."

He was lying. *They ask me to eliminate a friend.* Ostalsky had written it in the notebook.

"You can believe me or not believe me, but Riccardo Valdes was my good friend and I would never hurt him."

"When forensics finishes with this case, your prints will be all over him. We already know there were prints on him. Not too smart, Ostalsky. They must have left something out of your training, or is it the soft life in Greenwich Village that got to you? Too many songs about brotherhood peace?"

"I didn't kill Rica, or his girlfriend, Susana Reyes. They were wrong because they betrayed their revolution, but why would I kill him?"

"One of your bosses ordered it."

"You already know I could not have killed Susana, because I was with you that evening at Minetta Tavern, and later I was with Nancy. It's not what you want to hear, but you can ask her."

"What the hell were you doing on the pier the night Valdes was murdered?"

"How can you be so sure I was at the pier?"

From my pocket I took the silver charm that had belonged to Nancy, and held it up to him.

Ostalsky moved closer, peering into the dark at the silver object. "I see, yes," he said.

"Do you think Nancy also knows that you're a killer? Right now, she just thinks you're dead. Just as well, if you ask me."

Saul Rudnick had said Ostalsky didn't have what it took to be an agent; didn't have the right kind of treachery in his heart. How wrong Rudnick had been. How much Saul, with all his righteous decent misguided ideas about the workers, about equality and justice, lived in a fantasy of socialism. He had no damn idea. He had no idea there were Cuban spies everywhere, no idea that people like Ostalsky were part of a network of spies who killed, even their own friends if necessary.

Deceit, lies, treachery, it was all part of the game. My game, too, of course. You lied to solve a case. If you went undercover, you lied. If you collared a suspect and wanted to push him over the edge, you bent a few rules, but in the end, you did it to catch a killer. Everyone knew this; we just didn't talk about it.

Max Ostalsky was in a different league. He had deceived everyone. He had made up stories. He had worn his charm, the curiosity, his smile, his love of the city and its music, like a costume. He had written it in his notebook:

In my new clothes, do I look like a clown? Like a man in a costume on a stage?

He was a clown all right; he was the murderer in the mask who came up behind you and slit your throat. Max the magician.

Even after he had butchered a man in the most brutal way I had ever seen, Ostalsky had remained composed enough to make his way back to his apartment, to keep out of sight for almost a week, to summon a friend from Washington, to get here, to this warehouse. That same evening before he had committed murder, he had been cool enough to pass the time at the Village Gate listening to Stan Getz with Nancy.

He stayed silent.

"What are you going to do after you kill me? Your Mr Ustinov said you needed a friend. Things can't be all that good."

"Did he say that to you?"

"Give me the gun, Max."

"I can't."

"Fuck you. You want to kill me because I know who you are and what you did. So you got your fat pal to say you needed me, tell me where you were hiding. You knew I'd find you. I'd find you and you could kill me and you figured you'd be OK, because some of my people want me off the job. There are others on it." I was bluffing, it was all bravado; I was scared as hell. "Just out of curiosity, now you've killed one friend and you've got me in your sights, how does it feel? Or maybe you've done it so often you don't feel anything."

Max got up from the box where he sat. The gun still aimed at my heart, he took a few steps towards me and sweat began to ooze down my back. I was more terrified than I had ever been at the prospect of this man getting ready to murder me.

Slowly, I got up from the chicken crate where I had been sitting. For some insane reason, I didn't want to die sitting down. Maybe I read about somebody in a battle who said he wouldn't die sitting down. Or was it with his boots off? Who the hell knew? In one hand, I had a pack of Chesterfields and a box of matches.

"Can I smoke?"

Max nodded, watching carefully while I lit up, and the seconds ticked away.

Through the cracked window I saw the moon slide behind the clouds. A tug on the river hooted mournfully, and I tried to judge the distance between us. Somewhere in that vast concrete space, water dripped down the walls. Max Ostalsky was three feet away from me, gun steady.

And then he said, "Pat, please, just go now. Just walk away from this thing, which is not normal, not good at all. This is not a good place for you. Go away. Go to your life."

"So you can shoot me in the back?"

"Tell my friends I am sorry, get my clothes from 10th Street, if there is anything you like, please take it, or ask Mrs Miller to give these to her nice charities, and say to everyone how much I enjoyed New York. Just go away."

"Is it because you're too much of a coward to shoot somebody who was a friend in the face? Is that it? You want me to turn my back?"

He took another step towards me.

"There's nowhere for you to go, Max," I said. "You won't make it."

"I know this," he said. "But even more sad than this makes me, it makes me so sad because I know now that I am very bad at my job."

"What the hell does that mean?"

"Finally, I was asked to serve my country, according to how I was trained, to do, how do you say, the real thing?"

"How?"

"By eliminating my friend, Rica Valdes. This was my task. And I failed. You ask how I feel? Do you still want to know?"

"Sure."

"Filled with fear. Scared. Unhappy. I'm not going to shoot you, Pat." He dropped the gun to his side, but kept a tight grip on it.

"Then give me my weapon back."

"I can't do that. But I didn't kill anyone and you will understand that if I could not kill one good friend, I won't kill another. I won't kill you if you just leave. If you leave, I can say I never saw you."

"Somebody wants me dead."

"Yes."

"Who?"

"Not now."

"Is it your friend in the camel-hair coat?"

"No. I asked Ustinov to send you here because I need your help. You asked me about an assassination. I need your help to try to stop it."

"Yeah?" I didn't believe he'd let me go. He'd shoot me, and I didn't care for the idea.

"There will be an assassination," he said. "Ustinov agrees this is possible and he is close to things."

"Where? Who? Why? Is it an American?"

"I think so. All I know now is Rica Valdes was trying to stop it, in his own way, and of course he had no power, and I was ordered to kill him."

"Your people are planning this assassination."

"Or yours," Max said, and I was so enraged by his crazy talk now, that almost without thinking about it, I kicked an empty bottle I spotted. Kicked it hard. Ostalsky was distracted for an instant. I lunged.

I grabbed at his arms, dragging him down onto the concrete floor and clawing at his eyes. If you could make somebody blind even for an instant, you could change the odds. My fingers were in his left eye; I felt the eyeball, the liquid, the soft tissue.

Close to where I was, something else—not the bottle, but something light—shattered and there was glass on the ground. Then the gun went off.

CHAPTER NINE

October 24, '62

MAX OSTALSKY WAS ON the cold cement ground. I kept hold of his gun. He opened his eyes and struggled to get up, reaching for the wall to steady himself, but it was too far, and he fell back and lay on the floor. There was blood on his hands, where he had tried to break the fall and some on his face. Instinctively he reached for his face, but his glasses were gone. I had heard them shatter.

I said. "Get off the floor and sit down."

The gun had gone off by mistake when I grabbed for him. Even before I had a chance to hit him, the force had knocked him back.

"Get up off the floor and sit down on that box, goddamn it, and keep your hands where I can see them," I said, and Max crawled to the crate where he had been earlier, a blind man feeling his way forward. I'd have cuffed him if I had a set. Maybe I could find some wire later. Ostalsky looked defeated. He reached down, trying to find his glasses.

I picked them up, what was left of them, and tossed them over. He put them on. One lens was completely gone, the other was cracked, and Ostalsky peered through it, squinting. From my pocket I grabbed a handkerchief and tossed it to him. "Wipe the blood off."

"A one-eyed man, this is what I am now," he said. "Maybe I was always half-blind."

"You got me here, now what the hell do you really want from me, because I'm tired."

"I want you to trust me."

"Yeah? Why? What I can't work out is the way you did it. I can imagine you killing a man, but the rest of it, the brutality, the cutting out of his tongue."

"I didn't do it." He leaned back against the rough wall.

"If you want my trust, give me something back, man. If you want to get out of here alive, you pretty much have to kill me, which is no longer an option, or tell me what's going on. You say you have to stop some assassination, save the world, which is crap."

"You're wrong."

"You tell me you failed to do your job, then your people will show up sooner or later, isn't that right? I assume that they do not like their agents to fail?"

He nodded.

"Your fat friend told me Bounine had gone off the rails."

"Bounine was only the messenger."

"For who?"

"I don't know yet. It's cold in here. I have a sweater in that green bag. Can I get it? You said you had time to listen." He looked around the empty space.

I kept the gun on him. I got the sweater and tossed it

over. I sat back down and lit another cigarette. Max jammed the green sweater over his head and pulled it down. "Thank you."

"Sit down."

He sat on the crate again. "What I had no idea of at first was that Bounine knew everything about my life, where I was living, where I liked to eat, who were my friends," said Max. "It was so easy. I had made it easy for him, letting him into my life, but why not, I thought? We were comrades. Bounine is nothing. He is, what do you say, like stool pigeon? He will do anybody's work for a little advancement. He will do as he's told. But it took me a while to understand this. His father is high up in the government, but he's spoiled and stupid. He had no idea about Rica Valdes, who was good person with a good heart."

"You spent time with him here, in New York, when he was still alive?"

"Yes."

"You went to kill him, you didn't kill him, you ran away—what is this, one of those Russki puzzles, like those stupid painted dolls you pull out of each other? I'd say you're plenty capable of murder. It's your business, isn't it?"

"Not in New York, no," he said and began speaking Russian, half to himself.

"In English."

"I was not sent to do this sort of thing, certainly no wet jobs."

"But they changed their minds."

"Things change. Perhaps it became a necessity. Maybe a plan I didn't know of was activated."

"Did they know Valdes was your friend?"

Max grimaced. "They usually know these things. Right now, everybody believes they know something about me. Your police think I murdered a man on your soil, because you told them I did."

"Goddamn right."

"The FBI already knows I am a KGB officer because they consider every Soviet an agent, or at least an informant, and in the last weeks I noticed there were different agents, my regular came and went and then returned—did I tell you that I called him Ed?"

"Very funny."

"He returned with a second agent, so they must have been taking a more serious look at me. In my case they were right. Their suspicions were true."

"Then someone will get you, one way or the other."

"Do you hate me so much, Pat? My real crime was that I am a fool. I thought I could have this life in New York. A clown. To myself I pretended it would serve my work. I became indulgent. For a little while, at least," he said. "I was very foolish. They were right, you see, my teachers at home would say Ostalsky asks too many questions. He reads the wrong books. He is always kidding around. But I wanted to serve, so I pretended I had changed, and I took this road."

"You become a KGB agent to help your country? Give me a break."

"Yes, I did, of course, as a young man here might join the CIA. Naturally I wanted to help protect my country. I missed the war. It was a time of such exciting change, Pat, after Stalin, I don't know if you can understand, but we felt patriotic about our country, and the future."

"Why'd they let you into the KGB if you were such a joker?"

"I think my uncle looked out for me for an opportunity."

"He can do that?"

"He's a powerful man, or he was, he was a great general. Perhaps he put in a good word so I was able to enter the course. Also, language skills are considered valuable."

"That's how you got here?"

"By chance the exchange fellowship comes up, and it is at NYU and to study American literature and this is considered a good fit for me, and I find myself in Greenwich Village, the most wonderful, lovely place I have ever been, among such good and decent and funny people. When I left Moscow, I assumed simply that my superiors felt it would help me with my English language skills, and in learning something of American culture, and I would eventually be assigned to teaching these things to young spies, and living at home with Nina, my wife.

"But then I had to ask myself if it was just because of my good English that I got the place, or was there more? Was I set up for something else even before I got on the airplane?"

"Set up? You think they intended framing you for something. What?"

"I don't know. Tell me, Pat, is it about Nancy, that you stopped being my friend? Because you imagined that I am fond of her?"

"Imagined?"

"I am fond of her. Truly, in the beginning, I believed her when she said you were simply her friend, like a brother. Of course I wanted to believe, even after I knew it wasn't true. I am sorry."

"Does Nancy know you're a KGB agent?"

"No. But you knew. You read my notebooks."

"When did you find out?"

"I went back to get my notebooks on Saturday morning. I had changed my mind about leaving them. Somebody had been there. I'm a, how would you say it, Pat, a fucking spy. Did you think I wouldn't notice? I could smell your Chesterfield cigarettes," said Max, who burst into a stream of furious Russian, the first time I'd heard him speak his language this way. I knew he was using words so bad he didn't know the English; or else he wouldn't say it out loud. "I apologize, Pat."

"For what?"

"My language."

"I don't understand your damn language."

"Did you find what you wanted? Were you looking for something to, as you would say, to nail me with. You have quite a bit now."

"Does Nancy work for you?"

"What?" It startled him.

"You heard me. Her father is a true believer, why not her?"

"They have no idea."

"About you?"

"About many things. But they are such decent people."

"You would think so. Christ."

"Not because they are socialists, or even belong to the Communist Party, or did once. They are patriots who want to make their country better. Most of them simply believe in the Constitution, in the true meaning of democracy, and in equality. These people want to make a good world. They love the United States, and many have been willing to suffer for their ideals. There are also others not on the left, who care. Like you, Pat. How lucky I was to meet such people. Or unlucky, because I was so tempted."

"To stay? Like all the romantic nonsense in the notebooks?"

"Yes."

"Let's get back to this Valdes. If you didn't kill him, what the hell were you doing over at the pier?"

"At first, I told myself I could carry out my orders. Deep down, I think I knew I was simply going to warn him off. There wasn't time for him. They sent somebody else."

"What for?"

"They didn't trust me to do the job, so they sent back-up. When I got to the pier, Rica was already dead. I knew it was over for me. They never trusted me at all. I'm so tired." Max Ostalsky leaned back against the wall, and waited.

Somewhere in the huge hollow space, a faucet was dripping. Drip. Drip. Drip.

"Do you know this tale of Ray Bradbury? Of the young couple on the last night of the world, and there is a dripping tap. The wife gets up to turn it off, even though what does it matter? This is how my life is now, I think. Pat, you can shoot me if you want, it would be better," said Max. "There's nowhere left for me to go."

CHAPTER TEN

October 24, '62

"Get up."

Max hauled himself to his feet. I forced him to move to the opposite corner of the warehouse where I had a better view of the tracks outside. If somebody showed up, a second cop, a railway worker, if I got some help, I might be able to take Ostalsky—punch him out, tie him up—instead of killing him. I told myself I was happy to kill him, but he might have information. There was still a chance this assassination thing had some truth to it.

"How did you meet him?"

"I was asked to look after Rica when he came to Moscow. I knew some Spanish from high school."

"Who asked you?"

"It doesn't matter."

"Who?"

"My cousin Sasha. I guess he met Valdes somewhere and he asks me because I speak a little Spanish, so why not? But, then, nothing happens by chance with foreigners in my country."

"When?"

"About two years ago."

"Were you already an agent?"

"I was doing my training. It was snowing in Moscow," said Ostalsky. "Can I sit down, please? Can I smoke?"

"On that box. There. Away from the window, and keep talking."

"I had told Sasha to say to this man to meet me in Red Square, and I would show him around the city. The snow is piled up high, and here comes this young man in line for the tomb of Lenin, and he is wearing a thin red nylon jacket and white shoes that appeared to be made from cardboard. But he waits patiently. I greet him and we make conversation, he speaks terrible Russian, and I say we can speak in Spanish. He says, 'This is so beautiful. I never saw snow.' He is in Moscow to study Russian, to be of service to his country. I help to find him a coat and boots. I bring him to my family for dinner, because people are so curious about Cuba, and we admire so much these people, we, how should I say, imagine them as brave revolutionaries but also from an exotic and beautiful place. We play their music. We examine all pictures of the tropical island. Rica teaches my mother the Rumba, and says this is the dance of the working people. Rica tells us how he was raised in an orphanage where every child was named Valdes for the founder of the institution. He would tell tales of how he was noticed for his languages, and sent to the Jesuit Fathers in Tampa, Florida, for English. He said he was known as El Papagayo, the Little Parrot, for his skill. You don't want to hear all of this, do you, Pat?"

I told him to keep talking; you never knew when a detail would give you some clue, and I needed clues bad.

"I remember clearly that Rica was a bus-boy at the Hotel Nacional. He tells us he barely got crumbs from American gangsters. Once he serves cake, and one says, 'this boy did not give me a good slice' and Rica is fired from his job. So the Revolution makes of Valdes a patriot, and he is sent to Russia for his education in the language, and he learns well. He works as a translator for Cuban officials. He left Moscow last summer to return to Cuba." Ostalsky shifted his weight on the box. "Can I walk a little?" he said. "My legs have, what do you call them, pins and needles."

"When did Valdes contact you?"

"You know already. You read my notebook. Last Monday night at the Village Gate."

"Valdes knew how to find you," I said. "A woman called Irina Rishkova at the United Nations probably gave Valdes my address, and family photographs from my parents."

"Who is Irina Rishkova, or whatever she's called."

"She's what we call a letter carrier."

"What? I thought she worked at the United Nations."

"She brought mail from my family. For other people, too, letters other things."

"Orders for agents?"

"I think so. Encoded usually. This is why we call them letter carrier, or mailmen. These sound small, but they are big jobs, important jobs. Pat, please, can we talk about the assassination? I feel there isn't much time."

"Then who is it? Who's the target. Do you have some idea? You said an American."

"Yes."

"Then you better damn well convince me you're not just a murderous Commie, who's been killing people, and suckering everybody you come across. Persuade me."

"Yes, of course. We have been good friends, Pat, don't you agree?"

"You're very sentimental, aren't you, for some old Commie con?"

Max smiled sadly. "I am quite sentimental, yes. But not so old."

"What kind of mail did this woman send you?"

"Valdes had some photographs from my family. He says my mother asks him to bring these photographs to me from Moscow. As soon as I saw the pictures, I knew something was wrong. The photographs had been taken quite recently when it was already autumn. There was snow on the ground. My father was wearing his heavy jacket, and a scarf. Nina was in a sweater that I gave her. Anyway, my mother always put the date on these snapshots. She had previously written to me of Valdes' departure from Moscow months before the pictures could have been taken, and there's no letter. My mother would always include a letter. It was an obvious ploy. Somebody, and I think it must have been Rishkova—she had said she had not been back to Moscow when I saw her, but she could easily have lied—because she's the only one who would have pictures of my family. She probably told Valdes to look for me at NYU, even what time my classes finished. He got there too late, and someone said I liked music clubs."

"They knew your class schedule?"

"They knew plenty of things."

"Who you know, who you talk to?"

"No doubt."

"Including me?"

"Perhaps. Yes. Almost certainly. Are you thinking it is possible that these people also somehow know your bosses?" Max asked.

"Don't be an imbecile," I said, but I had thought about it before, and now it threw me off-balance, this idea that there were cops—cops like Logan—so corrupt they were doing business with the Reds. My stomach turned.

"What happened between the time he arrived and the time you got the message to kill him?"

Max looked at me, a man already lost to his own life; he had trusted me, would trust me, because he had no option now, or maybe because he was bitter about the system he had signed up for. As if he understood, he said, quietly, "You must believe that I love my country. Pat, please permit me to stand for a few minutes. I have no sensation in my legs."

I waved the gun. "Get up. Over here." I let Ostalsky walk the few feet to where I sat, and I got up and grabbed his arm. "Walk," I said.

Our steps rang out, hollow on the old concrete floor. "You can keep talking," I added. "So you signed up for socialism, but not for murdering a friend."

"I was given no more choice than an officer in a war. That's what I signed up for, Pat. And I failed."

"When did Bounine tell you to kill him?"

"I saw Valdes Monday night, I took him to Harlem. Bounine calls me at the Millers, and says to meet him, Bounine, I mean to say. This will make you laugh, he invites me for a pastrami sandwich. Afterwards, we stroll along 57th Street, and Bounine says, 'Max, you must help your country. Valdes is a loose canon. He has a big mouth. He goes everywhere speaking crazy things against Cuba, and nobody knows what he is now, with us, against us, double, triple. This is no good.' I knew Bounine was right. I had seen the tattoo on Rica's arm when he changed his shirt at the hotel. The worm. The words: Cuba Libre. He had gone over to the other side.

"'Who ordered this?'" I said to Bounine.

"'It's not your business. Valdes is a danger now. It would be very good if Valdes were gone by perhaps next Tuesday night,' he says. I understood what he meant. I was to do a job, and it would also be a test."

"Show you were a viable agent."

"The joke was if I didn't kill him, they would send me home. Or worse. I would have failed. If I killed him, or the cops thought I did, they can arrest me, lock me up, electrocute me, or hand me over to our people."

"So they wanted him dead because he might have changed sides?"

"Or because he knew about an assassination. Either way, he was trouble."

"After you left him dead on the pier, if that's what happened, where did you go?"

"I found a sailor's hotel, what you call a flop house, near the river. For two nights, it's all the money I have. On Saturday, I have no idea where to go, so I walk, I walk to Hudson Street, I am thinking of ringing your doorbell, asking for help, but I know it's the crazy idea of a desperate man.

"Bounine must have guessed my thinking, he had been looking for me, and he just shows up in the Village to tell me I failed at my job. I have no idea what Moscow knows."

He stopped, and looked around suddenly, as if he had heard something, and I said, "What is it?"

"I thought I heard something."

"There's nothing. Go on."

"I never quite believed Bounine was my friend, but even so I had probably said too much about my feelings." Max laughed bitterly. "Must I tell you the whole story?"

"Yes." I didn't believe his story would reveal much that mattered but it would give me time to figure out my next move. The brass already had it in for me. Where could we go, where could I take him in a city that was reeling from terror and wondering if there would be a nuclear war? JFK had announced the quarantine for Wednesday. It was Wednesday morning now. Ostalsky kept talking.

"That morning, Saturday, Bounine insists on going to Caffe Reggio, he is a connoisseur, he pretends, and this is the best coffee in New York City, and he is not quite himself without the right coffee, so we must walk to MacDougal Street, and I look for ways to escape him, but where would I go? Bounine is, you would say, Pat, a jerk. A horse's ass. Me? I am a dope. My slang is improving, don't you think? We arrive at the café, he seats himself in the window and I know, as I have known all the time we are walking—this is why I can't escape—he is not by himself. Somebody in a car is close by. A black car, and I see it quite quickly. For a moment, I wonder if I can run over to the Rifle Club you pointed out to me, where they practice shooting in the basement and there are many so-called Mafia men. Perhaps they would help me. You understand, Pat, that by now I am feeling a little crazy, because I am so out in the cold, I'm shivering, running from everyone, from my people, from your people, yes, perhaps the Mafia would be better.

"I know Bounine's friends, so to say, are across the street, because he would not otherwise choose the window, but he pretends this is only a social occasion. 'I am so taken with this place,' he says to me in Russian, and points out the old espresso machine, and the tin ceilings, and marble tops of the tables, and the dark Italian paintings on the wall. He relates to me that many poets and writers have spent time here, and he insists we have cappuccino. 'This is the very best in New York, Maxim, you see, and you must join me in a cannoli pastry. My treat, of course,' and then he calls for the waiter in Italian. He is, Pat, an ass, a spoiled man, what might be called a deviationist in my country."

Ostalsky was a good storyteller. I had noticed it before, this ability to remember details—he could say what kind of silk fabric was in a certain window he passed, or what the guy on a stool beside him was eating—for the way people talked. He played his part and all the others. Now I understood he had been trained for all this, a way to blend in, a way as he had put it when we were friends and he was telling me how he wanted to "swim" in American life. He had achieved it all, had fooled me with his sometimes bumbling efforts to learn the lingo and his laughing at himself; with them he had won over Nancy, and used her and her family.

"So I am trapped in Caffe Reggio with Bounine, while he drinks several little cups of coffee."

"How did you get out?"

"Bounine's vanity. I have a small camera. I say I would like a photograph to send home, and I suggest Washington

Square, where I make him pose under the arch, he removes his tweed jacket, and tosses it over his shoulder like a photograph of Frank Sinatra he has seen. Then he stops a woman passing and asks her to take a picture of the two of us. 'We will always remember. We will be Max and Mike in Greenwich Village. I will be sure to make a copy for you,' he says. I have no idea what the hell he wants, but we're out of doors, and I get Bounine to walk to the university with me, and when he's distracted, I slip into the building, and out of the side, into the next building on Washington Street, and then out onto Broadway among the crowds of people."

As he told his story, Max kept looking at the window, and around the warehouse, his face now covered with the pale clammy sweat of fear. It gave me the impression he was looking for a way out, but only in a theoretical sense, because he sat, almost passive, smoking one Lucky after the other, as if his life depended on them, tossing the butts onto the concrete floor and the matches into an empty pail.

"Go on."

Max told me then that he kept walking down Broadway, passing 3rd Street, Bleecker, Houston, and on and on, not looking back, assuming the look of a busy man in a hurry, occasionally glancing up as if to locate the number on a door, or a particular loft building, a tool and dye company, a print shop, a fabric store with bolts of brightly colored material—gold, red, pink, yellow—cramming the window, he kept going, feeling in his pockets for change, for crumpled bills, wondering if he had enough to keep going. His green canvas book bag in his hand, he was glad he had put in a sweater, and heavy socks, the temperature was dropping.

The further downtown he got, the easier it was to disappear into the crowd of workers coming out of the sweat-shops, small factories, machine shops. Slipping through the crowds, he replayed all he'd been taught about losing himself in a foreign city. And he had wandered here before, and always liked the feel of this part of the city where things were made—garments, buttons, machine tools, printed matter. He liked the way there are Italian signs, and then Chinese signs. A few blocks from the University, it's a different city.

He didn't look back, only sideways in the large glass windows of the fabric stores, to see if anyone was following him, his reflection full of the dread that comes from not knowing who's behind you, or where to go.

I'm with Ostalsky as he flees, I can feel his terror. He makes the story real. Is this how they teach them, how they instruct the agents—tell a good story, make your interrogator sympathetic?

"I don't look back at all, Pat. I just keep going, but I'm looking sideways, in the windows where there are bolts of brocaded cloth, gold cloth, silver cloth. In Chinatown, nobody looks at me, people in a hurry surge this way and that, in and out of restaurants, those pork buns in the window, the bronzed ducks hanging upside down. Old ladies are poking vegetables. I try not to run, Pat, I try. But I am scared."

Max kept talking to me, as if possessed.

"It's getting dark," said Max. "I think where can I hide? Who will hide me? I can try Brooklyn, but I do not know Brooklyn, except for a story I have read by your Thomas Wolfe, it is titled 'Only the Dead Know Brooklyn'. But I am already dead in Manhattan. I feel they are watching.

Queens? The Bronx? These remain mysterious to me, Pat."

"Did you consider going to Nancy?"

"It would be so harmful for her, and her family. I felt like a fugitive."

"What about coming to me?"

He smiled. "Oh, Pat, that would not have been an option. For you. Or me."

"Your FBI tail was around?"

"He had disappeared. 'Ed', my young tail, the one with the bad suit and the Bermuda shorts, he had gone."

"But there was somebody in his place."

"Yes, a squat thin man with eyes set low in the face, the whole face as if the features had to be set low, and he resembles some sea creature. A checkered flat cap."

"Car?"

"Black."

"He was at Penn Station tailing Ustinov."

"My God."

"God?"

"I eat a hamburger at Dave's coffee shop on the southeast corner of Canal and Broadway. The thin guy with the red socks is on the street when I left Dave's. Pat, if you should walk on a rubber floor in the middle of an earthquake, this is how I was feeling. I begin to run, into Chinatown, towards the river, through the Fish Market, and I see a man who's keeping a few paces behind me, and now he is looking into the window of a shop selling eye-glasses."

"Your FBI tail?"

"No. Stan Miller. Mr Miller, I'm absolutely sure, and he is wearing his tan raincoat, belted like a military man, and I think, perhaps he is only in Chinatown to buy something, an embroidered satin jacket for Muriel, or a pair of fancy rhinestone sunglasses."

"You were sure?"

"Do you know once I saw him wearing his uniform that he keeps in a plastic bag in the hall closet. He was examining himself in the hall mirror, and I am, right then, opening my door to the apartment, the door between my room and the main apartment, I am intending to get myself a Coke from Mrs Miller's refrigerator. When I see him, I retreat to my room. I didn't want him to know I have watched him looking at himself. Watched him salute himself in the hall mirror."

"Christ, you think Miller is in this?"

"Yes. Once I passed him on the 11th Street and he was using a pay phone, I could see him through the glass, bent over, as if it were something quite, you know, hush hush, and he saw me. Why would he do it, when he was a block from where he lives? "

"Maybe he has a girlfriend."

"I don't think so."

"You had wondered why he had offered you the room, why he tried to get you to defect?"

"Yes. I'm pretty sure he was watching me in Chinatown. He saw me, and stared for a moment, and turned into a doorway. I went the other way after that. It was getting cold. I left Chinatown, and I walked again, all the way to Greenwich Avenue where I went to a movie house. I must have fallen asleep because I stayed for two entire shows and I can't remember what film I saw.

"When I woke up it was very late, and the theatre was empty. Somebody was picking up empty popcorn cartons.

I spent the rest of the night at the automat and a couple of bars. I learned to drink beer very slowly, I didn't have much money left. By the morning I had a kind of plan."

"Go on."

"I walk to the Port Authority bus terminal, and I simply call the Embassy of the USSR in Washington DC and ask for the cultural attaché's office. It didn't take me long to discover that an old friend of mine would be in New York on Monday, to make some arrangements for the Bolshoi Ballet at the Metropolitan Opera house."

"Ustinov."

"Yes. He took the train to meet me. He knew enough to confirm my suspicions. To make me believe what Valdes hinted at might be true. He tells me to lie low for a few days, while he tries to make some calls, and then we go to the train station where he asks me if I have got a friend in New York I trust. I tell him about you. He says it might be worth a dime to telephone you."

"So he said. You should have rung my doorbell Saturday."

"Oh dear, my good friend, Pat," said Max, and then he began to laugh. It was the crazy laugh of a man without any hope left. In the old warehouse, the laughter boomeranged off the walls and came back hollow. "How could I? You believed I murdered a man in this city. You would have to turn me in. But this is the irony, you see, you could not report it because nobody listens to you. Don't you think I know that you are, what do they say, out of the loop? Cut off. Suspended. Bounine knew. Ustinov knows. You are, as they say, out in the cold. Like I am."

"How the hell do you know about it?"

"I'm a spy."

"You bugged my phone?"

"Does it matter? No. I didn't. I would have, but I had no way to do this. I, too, was cut off."

What scared me wasn't that he had bugged my phone—I didn't see how he could have put the bug in, or when—but that somebody I knew had done it. I had thought about it before. I had forgotten to check the phone. Did somebody set me up? Ostalsky was still laughing.

"You think that it's comic?"

"It is comic. It is terrible and comic. You find a murderer, or so you believe, but nobody will listen to you.

"Pat, I believe Rica knew he was in danger, that he understood who the man was who would kill him. He always loved melodrama, but this was real. Now you know where I have been these days, you know everything I can tell you, that I myself know. I feel myself almost worn out." He rubbed his face. "Now, I am wondering if you are going to kill me?"

CHAPTER ELEVEN

October 24, '62

OUTSIDE, A SMUDGE OF gray light smeared the sky. In the distance, a rumble—a train, thunder, trucks in the Meat Market—I couldn't tell.

"What's that? In the street? Pat, what's the noise?" Max leaned forward, a crouch, a runner ready to move. He mumbled something in Russian, looked up at me, terrified now. "What is that?"

In the street below, the noise came closer, sirens screamed through the early morning, ripping up the silence. Cops, or an alert that the war had begun, that they were going to drop the bomb. Again I listened.

"It's the cops," I said.

"Are they coming for you or me," said Max.

"We have to get out of here."

I kept the gun on him and yanked at his arm. He picked up the dark green book bag and I pushed him in front of me.

"Now."

"How do we go?"

I gestured to the street side door of the warehouse. He stumbled after me, grabbing my arm because he could barely see. We went down the four flights, the old boards creaking loud.

I had parked in front of the warehouse. I opened the passenger side door, kept the gun on Max, pushed him in, then went around to the other side, cursing the bucket seats in the sports car. Thank God I had left the top up.

"Close the goddamn door."

With one hand, I reach for the key. I fumbled with the gun. I was twisted like a pretzel. I knew I was losing control. The sirens were screaming closer.

A pair of workers on their way to the docks, lunch pails in hand, stared at us. I could see them whispering, discussing if they should act. I had been yelling. They knew something was wrong. I fumbled with the handbrake.

Then I lost it. I still had his gun, but my grip was loose. When I looked sideways at Max in the seat next to me, he also held a weapon.

"You forget there were two guns," said Max. "Yours and mine. You forgot that, Pat. I think it would be better if we go now." He looked out the rear window.

I stepped on the gas hard.

"Why didn't you use it?"

He took the gun from my hand, where it dangled uselessly, and tossed both weapons in the back seat.

"The assassination."

"I don't believe it. It's too crazy, man."

"I believe it. Please, can you go faster? There's a car following us."

In the rearview was the two-tone Impala I had seen before, and a second car, a large black Plymouth, shined up like glass, with a driver in a checkered cap. It was the man who had been following Ustinov in Penn Station.

"The Impala, I think it's our people, my tail."

"The black car is ours." Max slid further down in the seat, out of sight. "I think it's the agent who followed me in Chinatown."

"You're scared of your own people? They are yours, aren't they?" I put my foot on the gas, not knowing where to go, not thinking about anything except losing the cars behind us.

"Where are the police? The sirens?"

"I'd bet they're searching the warehouse."

"Somebody knew we were there?"

"Maybe a lot of people."

"Yes. I am scared of my people," said Max. "Pat, do you think we can get to Harlem? Rica said he would leave something for me if there was trouble—he meant if he was dead, I think. I think he left a letter."

"He knew he was finished."

"I think, yes."

"We'll go as soon as it gets dark. We have to lose these goons behind us. I'll try. I have to make a phone call. Where was he?"

"The Hotel Theresa. He knew of it because his delegation stayed there. Cubans love it because Fidel had stayed."

"Jesus Christ." I kept my eye on the rearview while I went through the tunnel. I couldn't go home. I couldn't go anywhere at least until I lost the cops and the Russkis, and maybe after dark, I could find a way to get us to Harlem, but not now.

"Are they still behind us?" said Max as we got close to the tunnel.

"Stay down," I said, ran out of the car, and picked up the newspaper. By time we got to Jersey, and I had turned off the main road, I had lost them. Near a building site where the countryside was being dug up to make new roads, I found a ramshackle gas station attached to a crummy-looking motel. I handed over six bucks for a room, told Max to go clean himself up, locked him in the room—I knew he could get out if he wanted to but where the hell would he go?—filled up the car, went next door to a diner. I ordered sandwiches and coffee, and looked at the papers.

SOVIET CHALLENGES U.S. RIGHT TO BLOCKADE; INTERCEPTION OF 25 RUSSIAN SHIPS ORDERED; CUBA QUARANTINE BACKED BY UNITED O.A.S.

It would begin at 10 a.m. Surface-to-surface missiles, bombers, bombs, air-to-surface rockets, guided missiles, all these had been authorized by the Defense Secretary. JFK had pictures of Soviet ships heading for Cuba with Ilyushin-28 bombers in crates. It was coming.

On the counter was a small black and white TV. A few customers watched and ate breakfast. The line JFK had marked was five hundred miles off Cuba. American ships were to turn back any Soviet vessel suspected of carrying missiles to Cuba. Somebody leaked it to reporters that there was a Soviet submarine in the area.

We were dead. The politicians would screw up, or those gung-ho generals would take charge, or there would be an accident. A meeting had been called at the United Nations for the next day, but it would be a joke, a lot of diplomatic fussing, while the bombers were already in the air.

For a while I watched, staring at the screen where there were blurry photographs of the missile sites and maps depicting the position of the ships—ours, the Russians—out in the Atlantic. I drank some coffee.

A shot fired across the bow of one of their ships goes unanswered, maybe we board, maybe one of their sailors, a young kid, misreads all the signals or, encountering Americans, waves his pistol around. He doesn't speak English. Worse, he thinks he knows some words and gets it wrong. His hand shakes. He's shitting himself from fear. He fires too soon.

Or it would be us. How many naval guys spoke Russian? How many wanted to take a potshot at the Reds? There were a million possibilities, and I had seen it all in Korea where mistakes had meant a hundred dead boys lying in the mud. This time it would be everyone, all of us, dead.

Who said that it only took one sailor or a civilian translator, or a low-level spy, to start it, to push the trigger?

Finally, incredibly, we were on the brink of a nuclear war, the thing we had all dreaded for most of our lives, that drove everything in my life from the time I finished high school and the Cold War began. Everything. The way my ma and pa looked at the world, their hatred for the Reds, the certainty if you didn't live a decent family life, you were playing into the hands of the Communists, me going to Korea, my interest in the whole Commie thing.

Before the Cold War, nobody had ever threatened the American mainland, unless you counted some crazy old Brits in red coats once upon a time. This was what we had been taught by Mr Roth, the history teacher—and the only Jew—at the parochial school I had attended, and the single teacher who had ever taught anything true about current affairs. "Red coats, Reds," he used to say. "Maybe we have to watch out for this color, boys, what do you think about that? Anyone here want to venture a thought on the meaning of this? Could it be that by now red has become the color of fear? Why would that be?"

Mr Roth brought us books to read, he tried to teach us; hardly anyone paid attention, except me, and another kid who became a Jesuit priest later, but in '48, the year I graduated high school, the Cold War was heating up, and by 1950, Joe McCarthy had begun the witch-hunts. I heard later that Mr Roth was accused of lefty tendencies, and possible subversion, and had been fired. I ran into him only once after that, at the Strand on Broadway where he sold me a couple of second-hand books, *The Naked and the Dead*, and *Animal Farm*. Mr Roth never gave up on trying to teach us.

Subversion my ass, I had thought even then, but in my narrow little world, teaching the truth to Catholic boys was seditious, or worse. My ma had believed only Joe McCarthy could save us. Her favorite book was *Is This Tomorrow? America Under Communism*. She kept it beside her bed; the cover showed flames consuming the flag and evil men—cartoon-like characters—attacking ordinary Americans.

"He will get rid of the Red devil," she would say. "We will be safe."

I remembered McCarthy. I remembered my ma calling me in to watch the TV. She's ironing my pop's shirts. In her green housedress, her feet stuck in some pink slippers, she stands at the ironing board, a cigarette burning in an ashtray, spitting on the iron to make sure it was hot.

"That senator, he's a good decent man, keeping us safe from them godless Communists."

My mother's life—all of our lives—was driven by this terror of Communism, but also, even if we wanted to destroy them, nuclear war was the thing, no matter how much we were scared to death by it, we never really believed would happen. This was where we lived, in an atmosphere of dread, of tension between it happening and not happening. The bomb was always a big topic, even with little kids who had grown up crawling under their desks, or hugging the wall during air raid drills, eyes closed. Anxiety. Tension. I even knew a cop who got so screwed up worrying about it, he whispered to me about visiting a headshrinker. Still, and yet, life had seemed pretty good until now; for all those years, nuclear war had had the feel of a movie being made just over the horizon.

I went to the phone and called Jimmy Garrity, the young cop from the pier.

"They want you bad, Wynne. They got you down as more than a pain in the ass, they'd like to make you for something much bigger. They think you're in bed with the Reds, and right now, when we're about to go to war with the Russians, nailing somebody, anybody, for collusion, or subversion, or whatever the hell it is, you've got a target on your back."

"I'm in Montauk. Fishing."

"Nobody believes that; they been questioning me as to your whereabouts. Stay safe. I have to go. Don't call me anymore."

Cowardly little shit, I thought. I was enraged by him, but I was scared too. "Fuck you," I said, before he hung up on me.

In the motel, Max Ostalsky was asleep on one of the beds. In the bathroom I stripped off all my clothes and climbed into the shower. My foot, where the rat had bitten, was covered in sores and dried blood. The water was tepid but I stood there for a while, thinking if they indicted Farigno, in the chaos of the Cuban crisis, nobody would ask any questions. If I said anything, they'd pick me up. Garrity had said so. They wanted me out of the way. When I dried off and got dressed, I looked into the mirror and saw an older man, a version of myself I had not expected for years.

Max was already awake and sitting on the edge of the bed. I gave him a sandwich and he ate hungrily.

"Let's go back to this assassination fantasy," I said to him once we were in the car. It was almost dark.

"We need the letter Rica Valdes left for me."

"You believed him?"

"Yes."

"You think it's somebody high up?"

"Yes, and Pat?"

"What is it?"

Peering out through his cracked glasses, Max looked out at the trees, leaves falling, the ramshackle roadhouses and small bungalows along the old country highway. I only took backroads. I drove them towards the city until I found my way to the George Washington Bridge.

The other side of the bridge, once we were in Manhattan, the big black Plymouth appeared. It was close on the rear of my car. They must have had Spotters, as the Feds sometimes called them, maybe even in goddamn Jersey. In the red Corvette, I was a sitting duck, and so was Ostalsky. I had to get rid of the car.

"Is it connected with the missile crisis, this assassination?"

"It's possible."

"But who, goddamn it, who is it?" Even as I whispered, I felt my flesh prickle. "Not the President."

"I don't think so."

"Goddamn it, thinking isn't enough. Is it? Do you know? Are you keeping this from me, man, cause you better come clean."

"No. It's to be in New York City."

"You keep saying you don't know who, so how the hell can we stop it? If Valdes didn't know who or where, how did he expect to stop it? Him or that girl, Susana? You have an idea when it's planned?"

"Soon."

"Listen to me, Max, if it's fucking soon, you must know something. Is this just stuff your pal Rica told you? Isn't he a loose canon?"

"I heard mention of this elsewhere. I have heard some whispers."

"Where?"

"At the United Nations. I know people there. I heard

some whispers in a hallway, I didn't think it meant anything at all. Maybe it doesn't."

"You have people at the UN, right? Some of your people there are spooks?"

"You're a bit naïve, excuse me, Pat. All of the Soviets stationed there are what you would call spooks."

Christ. We were two guys swinging in the wind, out in the cold, the Russian spy who steps off a cliff, falls into New York where everything changes for him, everything up for grabs, a girl he's desperate for, and music that possesses him. He could not go back; all there was for him was to move forward.

The Plymouth on my tail, me stuck with Ostalsky, me a cop temporarily off the job because I didn't play by the rules, nobody taking my calls, people saying I'd gone over to the other side because I knew this Russki.

The brass had never liked me. I never wanted into the racket that was part of police life, I never wanted any, the drugs or the whores on offer, and I liked the wrong music and the wrong girl who was Jewish and a pinko and said whatever came into her head. This was no spy story like the kind I had read that were full of dark places and strange landscapes: this was New York City. Maybe an assassination coming up. Maybe not. And me and him, the Russki, chained together like those escapees in that movie, what was it? *The Defiant Ones*?

"Let me ask you something. You picked me out in the park, didn't you? It wasn't an accident."

"Yes," said Max. "You read it in my diary?"

"Right. Why me?"

"Somebody mentioned to me the first week I arrived

in New York that it would be good to get to know a cop, it would be quite useful to have such a friend. I didn't ask why."

"Jesus, they knew who I was?"

"You were described to me. I was told you were a cop and an adult student at NYU. An intelligent man curious about the world. I'm sorry, Pat. At least they mentioned that you were good-looking and always very well dressed."

"What if I didn't fall for the hot dog thing? What if I didn't offer to help you out?"

"I don't know," says Ostalsky. "Maybe I would have asked you about your hat."

It made me feel sick that I had been such a patsy. But for the first time I believed Ostalsky, because he had, for once, told me the truth.

"I'm worried," he said. "Can you get us to Harlem, Pat? Soon?"

"Yeah," I said, and stepped on the gas.

PART FOUR

CHAPTER ONE

October 24, '62

"ARE YOU READY FOR Star Time?" yelled out the MC, Lucas "Fats" Gonder, from the stage of the Apollo. "Thank you and thank you very kindly. It's indeed a great pleasure to present to you at this particular time, nationally and internationally known as the Hardest-Working Man in Show Business ..."

The crowd, about 1200, maybe 1500, I couldn't count exactly, they yelled out yes, yes yes in agreement, yes, they were saying, we are ready, and I figure they've been waiting for James Brown, they've already seen the other acts, and they're worked up, and I'm backstage with Ostalsky, but it was Clay Briscoe, the detective I knew from the academy, who had fixed it up at the Apollo.

By the time we had found our way to Harlem, and the Hotel Theresa, it was dark, and on 125th Street I was feeling like a fish out of water; with Max, we were two white men in a Negro neighborhood. Inside the hotel, packed with people heading for the bar and the ballroom, mingling in the lobby, the clerk was wary; who the hell were we, his expression said. I had no badge. Max no ID he could show without them making him for a Russian. Finally, after a few bucks changed hands, the clerk turned over a large brown envelope addressed simply to MAX.

"We can't stay here," I said, but when I looked at the street, I saw a uniformed doorman watching everyone, and on the street two cars—the black Plymouth; the two-toned blue and white Impala. This was not a good time for us to be out of doors, so I ducked into a hotel phone to call Briscoe. I wasn't sure he'd answer; I was out in the cold, and no cop wanted business with me. I didn't want to hurt Briscoe's career; he was a Negro, and that meant he was automatically under some kind of suspicion. I was desperate. I had nowhere else to turn.

A few minutes later Briscoe appeared; maybe he hadn't heard I was a pariah; maybe he didn't care.

Clayton Briscoe was a tall lanky fellow with a loping stride like the basketball player he had been in college, and he was medium brown, sharply dressed and had a neat mustache. He had lived his whole life in Harlem and everybody knew him. Briscoe shook hands with everyone he passed. Smiled. Inquired about families. Nobody asked him any questions about the white men he was with, and he got us out of the hotel's back door where kitchen workers were smoking and shooting the breeze.

"Bad times, Pat," said Clay, then turned to Ostalsky, who couldn't see much with the cracked glasses and had stumbled and fallen onto his knees. Clay put out his hand. "You OK, man?" Max nodded, then climbed to his feet. "What do you need? I know the word is out not to talk to you, but what the hell, we're friends, right?"

"Thanks, Clay. Yeah, I could use a friend." When I told him we needed to get off the street for a while, he gave me a triumphant little smile, stroked his trim mustache, pushed us into his maroon Buick Electra, and drove us around for a while, making sure nobody was on our tail. He never asked me what was going on, just did the favor. He was a decent man and a good cop; he knew the favor would be repaid but he never asked for anything. Eventually, we pulled up on 126th Street.

"This your car, or official?"

"Mine," said Briscoe.

"Good. Less of a target," I mumbled, and when Briscoe said, "What the hell?" I just said, "Nothing, forget it. Where are we going? You look like the cat who ate the cream, man, in spite of us probably being at war over Cuba any minute."

"In there, that door." It turned out to be the Apollo Theater's stage door. From the stage came the sound of the band, horns, voices; an audience in ecstasy.

"He's not on yet, you haven't missed much," said Briscoe. "Look, I'll hang around best I can," he added. "But there's some stuff going down, and I have a nervous partner, young cop, only in a couple years, who's sure the Reds are going to invade the city, and I best keep him from hiding under his desk, so to speak. You'll be OK here until I get done. Try not to make yourselves too obvious, especially you, Max." He lowered his voice. "If anybody asks, Pat does the talking. Say you're with a record label; you came by to check out the show. They're recording an album tonight, it will be chaos, so nobody will pay attention, just watch out for Mr Brown's bodyguard."

"I'll watch for him."

"It's a her," said Briscoe. "Only James Brown would get himself a lady bodyguard. Stay this side of the stage, near the door. There's dressing rooms upstairs, you can always take your pal into one of them that's empty. Right? I won't be long." He shook hands with both of us. "Enjoy the show, man. Didn't I tell you I'd fix for you to get in?" Grinning to himself at the idea, Briscoe opened the heavy stage door and left, and I could hear his car as he drove away.

Already, I can hear an instrumental of 'Mashed Potatoes USA'. I'm holding my breath, in the moment, and somehow the thought of nuclear war and the whole damn case is falling off my back, and Max Ostalsky, clutching his brown envelope and in that heavy old gray suit, looks like he's entered an unknown planet.

For the first few minutes, I don't care. This is a crazy thought, but it's true. I'm living in this theater, cream paint, gold decoration, red seats, murals of the old burlesque house the Apollo once was, and hundreds of faces, expectant, urgent, ready for it all, music, entertainment, redemption, and all of them colored, all the way up to the second balcony. And Fats Gonder going for broke with his intro.

"The man who sings 'I'll Go Crazy'! 'Try Me'! 'You've Got the Power'! 'Think'! 'If You Want Me'! 'I Don't Mind'! 'Bewildered'! Million-dollar seller, 'Lost Someone'! The very latest release, 'Night Train'! Let's everybody shout and shimmy! Mr Dynamite, the amazing Mr Please Please himself, the star of the show, James Brown and the Famous Flames!"

The horns are beginning the fanfare. The band is on a riser at the back of the stage in two tiers. Horn section, trumpeters, trombonist; I knew about Dicky Wells from

Count Basie's band. Of all the jazz musicians I had always loved Basie. The Flames are singing tight.

Then he appears. James Brown's big black hair shining, perfectly coiffed, tight three-piece suit, his feet have a life of their own as if they have wheels implanted. He slithers across the floor, no sound, no friction at all, the feet carrying the body as it dips and bends, and the voice, and the audience is hollering in ecstasy.

You've got the power of love in your hands …

The microphone is like a woman for him, pulling it, caressing it, purring into it, screaming out like a man possessed; James Brown is twenty-nine, same age as Ostalsky.

You've got the power of love
To make me understand …

This, all of it, Brown himself, the band on the two-tier riser at the back of the stage, the musicians themselves, and the singers, this is all happening while Max Ostalsky is trying to open the envelope from Valdes and read the letter inside, and I'm trying to find a better place to watch, and worried about some of the people backstage staring at us.

If you leave me, I'll go crazy,
cause I love you, if you quit me, if you forget me …

Afterwards I can't remember what order the songs came in. For those minutes, I didn't care if the nukes fell on us. The noises Brown makes, the apocalyptic feel, the abandon—

frenzied, feverish—as he implores the audience, he's a preacher, they're his congregation, he works the stage with those crazy small inhumanly fast steps. I never again saw anything like it, not even the last time I had been here. People in the audience get out of their seats, they shriek, and he sings, body twisting, hair dripping with sweat now, the music, James Brown and his music is what makes it worth being alive.

Through his one-eyed glasses, Ostalsky, on a chair and half hidden behind a pile of stuff—recording equipment, trunks, props, girls in feathered bikinis coming and going—is frowning at the letter from Rica Valdes.

Brown moves, he implores, "Don't leave me ..."

I'm practically on the stage, practically standing by the Flames. Ostalsky reaches over and pulls me back, but all I hear is the music coming at my face, from under my feet, the whole place shaking.

"Pat, please, you must hear this." On Ostalsky's face was a look of panic, of desperation. I pointed at the stairs and pushed him up a flight to an empty dressing room and locked the door. A metal rack of suits stood to one side, and on a dressing table was make-up, a pile of rhinestone earrings and a pink feather boa. I could still hear the music. The dressing room stank of heavy perfume and hair oil.

"What?"

"I've read Rica's letter," said Max. "It's in Russian."

"Then read it to me."

"My Dear friend, Maxim, I am writing to you just before we are to meet at the pier near the Hudson River. I feel that I may not have time to tell you everything or if you will believe me, because I know you are loyal to your country, and to the Cuban revolution, which now depends on the Soviet Union. I no longer feel this way. Our revolution has betrayed the people."

"Just tell me, Max. Come on, man, just tell me the important stuff. I don't care how he feels about some revolution." From below, the horn section was shaking the building.

"He writes that on October 7, Osvaldo Dorticós, the President of Cuba—Rica came in the delegation, spoke at the United Nations—and he said, let me read this, 'If...we are attacked, we will defend ourselves, I repeat, we have sufficient means with which to defend ourselves; we have indeed our inevitable weapons, the weapons which we would have preferred not to acquire, and which we do not wish to employ.'"

"Jesus. It obviously means nukes. Where the hell were our people?"

"Nowhere, according to Rica, not paying attention, thinking of most Cubans as just people who brag a lot, but have no brains, and then Rica says, after they got to New York, some Russian at the UN asks him to deliver family photographs to me."

"The Rishkova woman? The what you call, Letter Carrier?"

"Yes."

"Let me finish," said Ostalsky, who read out loud in Russian. "Hold on, please, Pat. I'm just translating," he added.

"What about the nukes?"

"He talks about Moscow, and how he learned Russian and was asked to help with translations for delegations from Cuba and other errands. They trust him, they promote him, send him home to work as a pretty high-level translator, mostly at the main newspaper in Havana because he also knows English. But he's been away for two years. He sees things have changed, he says. He fell for Susana Reyes, an upper-class girl who returned from America, and found, he says, 'her beloved brother disappeared because he was a homosexual'. Old friends who disagreed with the government were executed.

"'The worm began to burrow inside my brain. I played the game, and I waited. They saw me as possible bait, as *carnada*, a "dangle" they call it, to offer me to the CIA who would hire me, and I would be a double agent, burrowing deep into the United States. Many CIA in Cuba are so stupid. They do not see what's in front of their eyes, including Soviet troops arriving. They cannot believe that Cuba has a brilliant intelligence service; they assume we are a silly little people, lazy, macho and useless. But people, even including Che Guevara, a man I idolized, had become possessed. When I heard my hero say he would gladly destroy America with nuclear weapons, even if it meant destroying his own country it changed me.'"

And James Brown sang "Hold me hold me, and your love we won't hide."

"Rica and Susana, and her cousin, somebody named Jorge, joined a small group. They decided, 'If Castro called dissenters worms, then we were glad to be worms.'"

The cigarette had burned my fingers, and I tossed it in an ashtray. "What else?"

"Let me finish the letter. He says he's enclosing snapshots, here, look at them," said Max and passed me four small black and white photographs. "Rica says shipments have been arriving from the Soviet Union for quite a while, and that on October 4, when the *Indigirka* docked at Mariel, which is Rica's hometown, it was easy for him to visit home, and find out what was going on. Forbidden to most, but Rica had become a Party member and was trusted. Listen to this, Pat.

"He says there are thousands of troops, Soviets, even some others, who have been arriving since August. Cuba is a Soviet military camp, he reports. 'Missiles are taken by truck across country, through little towns, and because I have worked as a journalist, many people know me, and I go where I like.' It is hard to hide trucks with huge metal tubes. Also, the Soviet soldiers are miserable, it's hot, they're sick, they would like to drink, and though the officers are quite correct, some of the men, so homesick and unwell, will tell you anything for a glass of rum, or an introduction to a nice lady, you can take a look at anything. You can give a Russian soldier a cigarette, and he says, 'Take a photograph, if you want. So I took these pictures.'"

"These pictures don't look like anything to me," I said.

Max got up from where he had been sitting and smoking, and looked over my shoulder. "The one you're holding is interior of some sort of bunker, with a stack of what look like rockets. This next one, look, you see, this trailer-truck has a missile launcher, with the missile, the warhead in place. It looks like a MIG, a fighter plane, you see, attached to a little hump-backed car?"

When he pointed out the details, I could see it clearly. The missile was set in a clearing, with scrubby tropical foliage around the edges. In it was a man in a checkered shirt, his right arm cut off by a photographer who was either incompetent or in a big hurry.

"Cuba?" I said.

"Yes. A missile."

"How the hell do you know?" I said, holding the photograph close to his face.

"I have seen similar missiles on parade in Red Square," said Max. "Funny, as a younger man, I often admired these ranks of missiles. I was so proud of our power. I loved the great long-range intercontinental ballistic missiles. This vision of such military might gave me goose bumps. My cousin Sasha, I think he became a missile engineer because of what we used to see. They have missiles on Cuba, Pat, and aircraft that can carry them."

"But there aren't any warheads, the nukes, the things that blow up the world. The President already said so; we know that. We know this."

"Not according to Rica."

"I don't believe it."

"Rica is sure. It's in one of these pictures, if you know what you're looking at."

"I don't think so."

"According to Valdes, these here are Ilyushin 28 planes, already uncrated and ready to go. Each one can carry a single warhead. I told Rica it was nothing without the warhead. He told me there were warheads, already targeted." From my hand, Max took the final two snaps. "Officially only a Soviet officer on direct command by Khrushchev can fire a nuclear weapon. Valdes says there may be officers who ignore this order, all it takes is one rogue officer, or Cubans who work with them. These here, you see, the Americans

288

call them Cruise Missiles. They can do great damage, they spray radioactive material everywhere. This means they can reach fifteen or twenty miles."

"Guantanamo?"

"You guess correctly. You don't need ICBMs to start a war. I had already guessed at some of this, I had time in that warehouse, that what the Cubans want is a provocation. Some of them, a few with power."

"And your people?"

"I'm sure there are some in my country, as well, of course. But Rica Valdes writes that the Cubans are tired of feeling like little brothers, as they were once tired of American oppression, very nice that Khrushchev hugs them like he is a papa bear, but they want weapons, and so he sends them, and now a few of them want an excuse to fire these weapons."

"How much more is there?" I felt impatient and impotent; what could I do if the nukes were coming? I could go back and listen to James Brown.

"He goes on to say there are people who want to provoke an invasion," says Max.

"What is it?" I can hear screams from the audience downstairs that punctuate Ostalsky's news of Armageddon.

"The provocation will be this assassination. A powerful American will be killed, the United States will retaliate, do you see, Pat, to provoke the Americans to invade Cuba, and then to fight back, it is perfect. This means everyone then starts throwing nuclear missiles around. This means, as you might say, Pat, Boom!"

"Who's the target?"

"Rica says it is scheduled for October 28, the day when

Columbus discovered Cuba in 1492, and not as Americans believe, the United States. It sounds idiotic, but this is what he says. It will be in New York, for this is the great symbol. Susana knew the possible target, and another man may know the location."

"Susana is dead. Who? We have four days."

Max looked at his watch. "It's after midnight. It is the 25th, so three days. Three."

"Why now? What the hell point is there anyway? We're about to go to war, why not lie back and wait if you want war. Are they connected, this so-called assassination and the missile crisis?"

"I don't know. I really don't know, and I've been thinking and studying, what this means, trying to understand. I think the crisis is an opportunity, or a deadline. Perhaps this even, this idea for provocation was put in place years ago, to be activated when the time is, can you say, ripe?"

"At least we know something, we have a date, we know about the Cubans."

"We know something. If Valdes is telling the truth," said Ostalsky. "Perhaps he is a triple," he added, half to himself.

"What?"

"Nothing. Our problem is just who will believe us?"

"Please please please ..."

Backstage was jammed, singers, stagehands, someone hauling props, and I was looking for a way out, when I could have sworn James Brown turned in our direction, and saw me.

The band played, the crowd surged forward, moving, ecstatic, like people in a holy-roller church I'd once seen in a newsreel. All I see is James Brown, who on the beat falls to his knees.

> *"Honey, please don't I love you so*
> *Please please please please ..."*

A man puts a cape on Brown's shoulders. Is he sick? Is Brown having a heart attack? No, he rises, Jesus from the tomb, or a cardinal, the pope, playing with the microphone like it's a crucifix, or a weapon, and all the time I'm thinking about nukes raining down on us, and an assassination that will take place in three days, and when I look out towards the audience, all I see are black faces, people worked up in some kind of frenzied swoon, probably thinking they're gong to die as the nukes fall, and deciding this was their only escape, this music, this ecstasy. "Please please please please." Brown works the stage, he steps towards the wings, returns. "Honey, please don't ..."

Everybody in the theater was moving around, audience on their feet, seeming ready to storm the stage, recording engineers, dancers, all pressing against us backstage, and we were trapped, stuck with no way to get in or out, no way to move, just us, me and the Russian spy.

Who will believe us?

CHAPTER TWO

October 25, '62

THANK GOD FOR CLAY Briscoe's old Buick. I had offered him a temporary trade when I told him the truth. I told him somebody was watching me; I laid it out for him because Briscoe had done me plenty of favors and I trusted him.

"No trouble, Patrick. I always loved your little car," he said. "Also, man, I am taking my new lady away for a few days, and she will be so down with that Corvette. You just let me know when you want it back. Also, figuring the Russkis might be going to drop that bomb on us all, I might as well enjoy myself, you know? But, listen, Sam Cooke's coming to the Apollo in a couple weeks, I'll get you some tickets if you want."

Even in Briscoe's car, I was uneasy about parking in front of my building, so I let Ostalsky off, told him to get upstairs, watched him duck into the door, and drove a couple of blocks in case somebody was following me, to make sure I had lost the tail.

It was already early morning, around 3 a.m., and I needed sleep bad. I didn't like it that Ostalsky was at my place, but where else could I stash him for now? I was so tired, I was hallucinating, figured there were agents on my back, theirs, ours; I parked a few blocks from home, near the White Horse. All I could think about was getting home, getting a few hours sleep, see if there was anything to wake up to, or if we'd been blown to hell, and get out of there and find out what was happening. Christ. Nukes on Cuba, already targeted. Jesus Christ. I was plenty scared, and having Max Ostalsky at my place made it worse. Fatigue and fear made me cold. I had started coughing again.

Standing near the White Horse I could see a few die-hards still inside the bar, including a man in a snappy tan raincoat who peeled away, came out to the street and approached me. He doffed his hat as if by way of a friendly gesture, put out his hand and said "Rush O'Neill". At first I thought he was just a well-dressed drunk.

"No kidding, what's Rush stand for, you in a hurry?"

"Ha ha, very nice, but no, it's for Rushton, it's a family name." He took out his FBI badge. Rushton P. O'Neill. "Don't ask about the P." He was very pleasant except for the cold gray eyes, very round, very cold, like marbles set in his eye sockets that, when he talked, he fixed on my face, without blinking.

"Then I have to ask, don't I?"

"It's for Providence." He laughed, and fumbled in his pocket for a pipe and a leather pouch of tobacco.

Then it came to me. The Hip Bagel, I had seen him wearing a natty blue blazer, talking to Nancy one morning while she got her breakfast; the minute I saw him I had recalled the face, the silvery hair worn in a modified pompadour, the look of a vain man.

He was forty-five, possibly fifty, but trim; good bearing, square shoulders, that English raincoat was belted, the collar turned up like an officer in the movies—David Niven, that kind of guy.

Now I saw O'Neill close up, I made him for possibly ex-military, a man who had led other men and let you know it with his big firm handshake and the way he looked you in the eyes. His nails had been manicured. The only men I knew who were vain enough for manicures were mobsters and politicians.

"Pat Wynne," I said. "But you know that, don't you? Glad to know you."

"Would you care to join me in a drink?"

"Agent O'Neill, you weren't waiting here for me so we could pass the time. Why don't you tell me what you need."

"Shall we take a little ride? I've got my car nearby."

"I'd rather walk. If you don't mind." I was polite as could be, thinking it would get me away faster, and out of the line of fire if O'Neill had anyone else tailing me.

"Of course. I phoned your apartment, I went by, but there was no answer when I rang the buzzer." He had no accent, the kind of man who has been raised on military bases. He turned to look at the few people on the street, out late, walking off the tension, one man whistling tunelessly as he went.

"Cuba," said Rush O'Neill. "People are scared out of their wits. We may soon be under attack. The Soviets are completely capable of a first strike."

I lit a fresh smoke, and walked alongside O'Neill. Normally, I would have told him to shove it and gone home, but, given I was supposed to be off the job, and also with the war coming, it was not a good time to cross the FBI unless you had to. Also, he had my phone number and my address.

"Unless we take immediate action, it will get worse, you know that. We've got to make damn sure the Reds understand that we will never permit them to install nuclear weapons so close to us. In my view, we ought to strike now, hit their ships, take out the goddamn lot, while public opinion is on our side. We must never ever allow Soviet nukes ninety miles off our shores." For an instant, his face tightened in anger, but then he relaxed and produced the genial smile. "I apologize for the lecture. I'm a bit worked up."

"You're telling me you want a pre-emptive strike?"

"I think our country will do whatever's right," he said, and set off towards the river. I was sure we were heading to Pier 46. "Detective Wynne, I have a favor to ask. I know you're a patriot, you served in Korea, it was rough, not much glory, plenty of guts. I got lucky. Everybody wanted to fight the damn Nazis. Me, I flew those B-17s with the 305th out of England. Terrific commander, a fellow we would have died for, he was tough, but he took care of his own. Called him 'Old Iron Pants'. The kind of man we need in charge right now."

"I thought Bobby Kennedy was your boss now, isn't that right, he's Attorney General. Isn't he tough enough for you?"

"He was. He does only the President's bidding now."

I was sick of the rhetoric. "How can I help you?"

"You know this pier, of course, just across the West Side Highway. You had a case out here, isn't that right?"

O'Neill stopped, fussed with his pipe, loaded it up with tobacco, lit it, blew out smoke, looked at me. "I need your help, Wynne."

"I'm always happy to do your august organization a favor, Agent O'Neill. But I've had a long day." I was on edge. "I'm happy to go to the pier, if you want, but it's cold and if you tell me what you need, we can save some time." My willingness worked. He said, "Forget it." Abruptly he turned, and started back downtown.

I didn't want this man, whoever he was, anywhere near my building, or me. He was slick. His warm, clear, sharp voice—like a radio announcer—was intended to seduce if he wanted your help, or induce fear if he failed to get it. I was betting he didn't often fail.

"Could you use some coffee? We could grab a cup of Joe and then you could go home," he said. "It is cold tonight, it seems to me, so early too, still October."

At the corner of Christopher Street, he gestured to a coffee shop, and I knew he had already picked it out. Everything had been planned; I knew this could easily be a trap. Did he have his men waiting, their weapons hidden behind the cistern in the bathroom?

The place was almost empty, except for a tall thin man in a cheap dark suit, crouched on one of the stools, dunking a donut in his coffee. He didn't look up, not at me, or O'Neill; Rush O'Neill never looked at him. I knew they were both Feds. A waitress in a hairnet was wiping down the counter with a dirty rag, a cigarette in her mouth.

O'Neill slid into a booth at the back. I sat opposite him, put my smoke out in the ashtray and stretched my arms back along the back of the green leatherette booth, and tried to get the attention of the waitress. O'Neill was waiting for me to make the first move, I realized. Show my hand. A large clock on the wall ticked loud. The man with the donut put a nickel into the jukebox on the counter. "Green Onions" played.

"I might as well ask this, but you've had someone on my tail, isn't that right? Somebody with a big flashy Impala, not your usual FBI vehicle?"

He looked at me straight on. "Yes."

"Your fellow over there is on his second donut."

"Very sharp of you. We have a liberal budget for donuts."

"Do you think he's hungry?"

"I wouldn't know."

"Maybe he comes here for the music."

"I have no idea."

"Do you want to tell me why you're following me? Aren't we on the same side, Agent O'Neill. That's Irish, isn't it? Makes you a Mick just like the rest of us, so why don't we stop the horse shit."

"On my father's side."

"What, you're saying your ma's descended from the Mayflower?"

"Something like that. It's for your protection, Detective. The tail."

"Why would I need protection?" I called out, fed up now, "Can I get a cup of coffee here?"

The waitress in the hairnet trudged over to where we sat and I asked for coffee and a tuna sandwich.

"Why would I need protection?" I said again.

"You're friends with a Maxim Ostalsky?"

"Yeah, so what? I know him a little from around, is that a problem?"

"We think he's dangerous."

"Why didn't you talk to me in the first place, instead of wasting some poor slob of an agent?"

He looked pissed off, possibly at the way I had described one of his men, but I didn't care. I ate my sandwich when it came and gulped down the black coffee, followed by a Coke.

When I made to get up, O'Neill said, "I think you should hear me out. Some of our younger agents are not subtle, and I apologize, but one of them had this idea that he could find Ostalsky by following you. Where were you coming from?"

"Jesus, Rush, the Impala was on me, he must have known where I was. Just stop blowing smoke up my ass. I'm going to level with you, because I admire you people."

"Good."

"I was working on finding Ostalsky myself. I had intended to pass on anything I learned to your people. In fact, maybe you heard, I already called my brother-in-law who works at your New York Office. Brennan? Seamus Brennan. I knew exactly what Ostalsky was from the beginning. He wanted a friend in New York, and made friends, it seemed a good idea since I was attending NYU."

"You spent a lot of time with him."

"What does that mean? I fought those dirty Reds in Korea, you think I don't want to stop them? Jesus Christ, man. I got a purple heart, and my best friend was blown to pieces. Do you think I could really be friends with one of them? Dammit, Rush."

O'Neill was confused because I had grown testy; after all, I was a cop, a vet, a patriot.

"I understand," he said. "I'll let the bureau know they can leave you in peace. By the way, have you seen Ostalsky lately? Probably not because, as I heard it, you're on leave, isn't that right?"

Slowly, he put away the pipe and opened a box of Viceroys, a fussy sliding box made for women.

What did he want? What was he waiting for? When I looked over at the counter the other agent had gone; the waitress was nowhere in sight; the big clock on the wall ticked the minutes. Tick. Tick. Tick. From next to the clock, the President smiled, handsome, strong, assured. O'Neill followed my gaze.

"Thank God for JFK," I said.

O'Neill was silent. "Excuse me a moment, won't you?" he said finally. "I have to use the head."

"Sure." I thought about leaving. It would make O'Neill suspicious. He might put a car on me again. The first place any agent would show up was my apartment where Max Ostalsky was waiting. I hoped to God he was waiting.

Outside the city was dead quiet. At five minutes past three, O'Neill emerged from the bathroom.

I got up and put a dollar on the table. "What do you want?"

"I want to believe you'll contact me the next time you see Ostalsky." He handed me my dollar. "This is on me. We're at war, Wynne. We've been at war with the Reds a long time now."

"You don't need to say it. Just one question. In your law enforcement career, I'm wondering if you've come across a Captain Homer Logan?"

O'Neill's expression remained exactly the same. Only a tiny, almost invisible muscle twitched at the edge of his mouth, a womanly mouth with heavy, pinkish lips.

"Can't say I have. Sorry about that, Pat, shall we go?"

I picked up a matchbook. Inside was an ad for an art school. Maybe I should learn to draw. I could quit being a cop and go in for art. I tossed it down again.

"Why don't you walk with me to my car," said O'Neill, as he put on the English raincoat, buttoned and belted it, replaced his hat, and went out to the street. I followed him.

"Where?"

"What?"

"Where did you leave your car?"

"Charles Street."

Near my precinct, I thought. Had he been talking to Murphy? The streets were empty, silent, dark, as we walked east on Christopher and across Bleecker Street.

"Pat, there's a girl I believe you know, name of Nancy Rudnick. Father's a committed Communist, a Party member, did time for it."

I inserted a toothpick between my teeth. Easy does it, I said to myself; Nancy was in trouble, and me getting riled up at some Fed wasn't going to help. "Sure, I know Nancy. She's a grad student at NYU. Nice enough girl."

"We worry about the likes of Rudnick. It threatens our country when these so-called peace-loving radicals are in every Communist-front organization. My God, they have Pete Seeger at their house, they support Fidel Castro and give money to Martin Luther King. We have files on him you wouldn't believe. The boss has a bug up his ass about King."

"I'm listening."

"Some people think we keep files on people out of malice, but we're only protecting the American way of life."

"I thought Rudnick did time when he refused to testify."

"It didn't change the bastard one bit."

"Rush, is Ostalsky your real focus, because I can give you a list, places he likes to go, people he meets, Café Figaro, Gerdes Folk City, he talks with writers there, he plays chess in the park, he attends meetings, and square dances at Judson Memorial Church."

"I've never cottoned on to the idea that the revolution would take place during square dancing, between you and me," said McNeill with his idea of a chuckle.

"You see, Rush, I've been on this," I said.

From his back pocket McNeill removed a notebook and pencil. "Any specific names?"

"Rush, you've been pretty frank with me, so let me repay the favor, what you may have thought about me is not exactly what it seems. You catch my drift? If you need to know more about Max Ostalsky and pals, I'm always willing to help. But I'd like to keep it quiet, at least for now. For instance, did you know that he has developed quite a liking for American whisky?"

"That so? Are you saying what I think? You've been working this from another angle? I parked across the street." O'Neill groped in his coat pocket for his car keys. "I'm glad. I really am."

"Nobody knows, not even my boss," I said. "I report only

to, well, you can imagine, I'm not even talking about the New York office."

If he bought it, it would give me a day or two. Chances were we'd be in a war, and then dead; suddenly, I felt released from the creeping fear I'd felt when the FBI started tailing me. I began to embroider. "So to put your mind at rest, I haven't been hanging out with the Russki for the hell of it." I said. "Why don't you give me your private number, Rush, I'll keep you in the loop best I can, but if word gets out, I'll lose my sources. You know how useful those damn student radicals can be."

"You've been able to mix easily with the students at NYU, is that right?"

"Jesus, I must have been to more damn peace meetings, and the lectures, and the fights about Trotsky, and Stalin. Look, when I get the goods, you'll be the first to know. You can pick him up. Take the kudos," I said. "You mentioned Nancy Rudnick?"

"What about her?" said O'Neill. "It's the father we want, like I said."

"I see." Even now, I worried about her. Even now I wanted to take care of Nancy, to protect her from this slimy bastard O'Neill.

"You're Nancy's friend, isn't that right?"

"I see her in the park. Sometimes I give her a lift."

"I'm glad, she needs a real friend, not those pinkos she seems to be chummy with."

Seems? *Seems?*

"She mentioned you to me, so I'm going to share something with you. Nancy is a fine young lady, and a true patriot. I'm telling you because I'd like you to help make sure she's OK. She is vigilant, and helpful to us, but I feel in my heart Nancy needs the right fellow to look after her. These girls are too easy, too free with themselves. I was worried at first that she might fall for Ostalsky, you know? With some of our young ladies, we run the risk of them romanticizing the subject."

Vigilant? Helpful? My heart was pumping so erratically, I thought I was having a heart attack; I had begun counting the blocks to St Vincent's.

"Take good care of her, Pat. She is one of our best sources. She's bright. She has an excellent memory. She knows what's needed. The way she's involved in the Peace Movement and Civil Rights, she has real access. Half the Reds in New York show up at her father's parties, as you may know. I wanted to share this with you because I know you're her friend."

He took his card from a pocket, handed it to me, put his key in the door of his car, which turned out to be a two-tone Chevrolet '59 Impala, blue and white with modified fins. "I'm afraid it's my car," he said. "I'm sorry I was on your back, you won't see this car again any time soon. And don't worry, my wife hates the damn thing," O'Neill added, and left me on the sidewalk not knowing if I should laugh or cry. Nancy was working for the FBI. She had been using Max Ostalsky. She didn't love him, after all.

Poor Saul Rudnick, I thought suddenly. I hated a lot of his views, but he said what he thought, and he loved his daughter. God help him now she was working for the FBI.

CHAPTER THREE

October 25, '62

I N MY APARTMENT, OSTALSKY sat on the couch beside Tommy, gently mopping the blood on his face. Tommy's eyes were closed. He had been badly beaten, face and hands bruised, eyelids black.

"What happened?"

Tommy tried to push Max away, failed and slumped back onto the couch. "He's a Russki, Pat."

"He's a friend." I took the cloth from Max and sat next to the kid, whose front teeth were missing.

Something occurred to me. I lowered my voice and said, "Is he the man you saw on the pier?"

"The devil man, you mean. I don't know. I can't say for sure, but I seen him in the papers. He's a Red. He's a dirty friggin' Red, get rid of him." Tommy's words were blurred as he forced himself to sit up.

"Lie down and stop talking, kiddo. I'm calling an ambulance."

He didn't protest, and I knew it was bad.

The lines were all tied up. I said to Tommy, "What happened, can you tell me?"

Breathing hard, he said that a big guy he never saw before banged on his door. His father had been at work; Tommy let the man in.

"When?"

"I don't know. Few hours, maybe."

"Did you pass out?"

"I dunno. Maybe."

"Anything else you remember? Don't talk if it hurts too much, but if you tell me, Tommy, I'll get the prick."

"Pat, he asks me questions about you. Stupid stuff I don't understand, but I won't tell him, he punches me in the face. Pat, I can't see you right. Like everything's blurry. Am I blind? I don't wanna be blind."

"OK, that's enough talking."

There was blood in Tommy's mouth. I couldn't wait for an ambulance. I couldn't risk being seen with Ostalsky and I got him into the kitchen, told him where to meet me, figured he was smart enough to make his way—he's a goddamn agent, I told myself. "You'll do it?"

"Yes," he said.

"Help me down the stairs with Tommy, then go through cellar door, it leads out into the backyard, and from there you can get into the next building and out that way. Nobody will be watching for you there."

"I'll do it," said Ostalsky.

By some miracle, we got Tommy into the car. I was grateful I was still driving Clay Briscoe's Buick, which had a backseat big as a bed.

"Pat?"

"Stay quiet, kiddo," I said, but I couldn't stop him talking as I drove to St Vincent's.

305

"I have to tell you this, Pat, this creep, he hits me, he says, 'You're Wynne's kid, we know he's a fucking Red, so you better talk.' And I'm so mad, I say, 'Yeah, I'm Wynne's kid, whadya gonna make of it, he's no fucking spy,' and they keep shaking me, and then one of them picks up my baseball bat, the one you got me at Joe DiMaggio Day at the stadium, geez, he almost killed me. He just kept whacking me with the bat."

"Was he a Mob guy? Did he look like one of them?"

"No." More blood was seeping out of Tommy's mouth and nose. "I don't know what he was. Fucking Commie, you know, or something, I can't remember, maybe he was talking some stupid foreign lingo, or maybe he was just cursing, I'm not sure," he said, and then he was silent.

By the time we got to St Vincent's, Tommy was unconscious. He had suffered concussion and lost a lot of blood and I waited until they took him upstairs from emergency. One of the sisters on his floor gave me her name and a phone number. I tried to reach Tommy's father, who wasn't at work, or at home. I called his sister in the Bronx and gave her the message to call St Vincent's.

I couldn't leave Tommy. I couldn't do it. What difference did it make if some damn spies blew each other's brains out; who cared. I thought, fuck everything, I'm staying, and so I smoked a pack and drank four cups of coffee and sat, looking like a bum, not having slept all night, in the waiting room.

I must have dozed, and around ten in the morning a young doctor touched my shoulder, woke me up and told me Tommy was dead. His father had phoned to say he was on his way.

The concussion meant a blood clot had developed; it went to his brain. Too much damage to his skinny body, too many internal injuries.

Tommy was just twelve. He had been wearing the sweater I had given him; it was so drenched in blood the nurses had to throw it away. I waited for Tommy's old man, and then I left.

In my car, I started thinking about Tommy, how he told the bastards he was my kid, and I started to cry.

CHAPTER FOUR

October 25, '62

"OSTALSKY? YOU THERE?"

He wasn't there, wasn't at Uncle Jack's house on Mott Street when I got there from the hospital. It was noon. He wasn't there. I had told him where to find a key.

So far no blue and white Impala had appeared. Maybe Rush O'Neill had believed me. The TV played news, the crisis, the ships, the necessity for civil defense drills, how to stock our fallout shelters with canned goods.

I thought about people I loved, and some I liked, and I knew, by the next day or the day after, I'd never see them again. Even if the Russkis turned the damn ships around, there were still the nukes already in Cuba. If I knew about it, if Rica Valdes had known, for sure our government would see this—see there were nukes aimed at Guantanamo.

"I'm sorry I just got here, Pat." Ostalsky had entered the house without me hearing him, and he was standing now in the doorway to the parlor, wearing a black overcoat and a gray hat. They were mine. Max looked like a priest.

"I apologize for borrowing your clothes, but my own had probably been noted. I went back to your apartment to get them, forgive me, Pat." He removed the hat and coat, and put them neatly on a chair near the door, along with a paper bag that contained his own clothes. "How is young Tommy?"

"He's dead. The bastards banged his brains out with a baseball bat."

"I am very sorry," said Max, and I saw his eyes fill, although maybe he was just weary.

"Where were you?"

"Do you think your aunt would mind if I ate something?"

"Help yourself."

He returned from the kitchen with bread and cheese, salami and cookies, and a bottle of Coke.

"You're addicted. I have to make a call." In the bedroom I called Jimmy Garrity on Aunt Clara's powder blue telephone.

"Anything?" I said.

"I can't talk."

"Talk to me."

"I'm on my way out, I'm going to meet up with my brother who's a firefighter. He's saying the Commissioner is asking for almost fifty thousand volunteers to register, in case of an 'attack'. We have to get ready. I'll call if there's anything."

"Jimmy?"

"I can't talk now." He hung up in a hurry.

"Don't you think we should be doing something instead of watching TV," I said to Max who was in front of the TV, finishing his bread and cheese.

"What kind of thing?"

"Finding the goddamn assassins. You people must know about that. Didn't they train you?"

"Where would we begin?" Max smiled. "Can I turn the TV louder?

"How did you get into the house?"

"You told me where the key would be."

"Christ, it's in three goddamn days, if Valdes was right. I need some kind of weapon."

"You have your gun."

"I meant something a little more effective."

"This means, you would like a surface to air missile? What kind of weapon can help us, Pat? By the way, I removed the bug from your telephone. I hope that's all right."

"What damn Russian put that in?"

"I'm sorry to say, but it was an American wire."

It's what I had thought. It scared me more because it was our people; it meant you couldn't trust even your own.

"Pat, look at the TV."

Placid, balding, decent Adlai Stevenson had always been considered overly cautious, even a bit of an old lady. I'm a Democrat; I voted for Adlai; I still had a Stevenson campaign badge, a shoe with a hole in the sole. He wasn't JFK, though. "He's not going to get anything done, he's a decent man but he's weak. What can he do?"

"He is a good person," said Max. "Watch the goddamn TV," he barked. "Maybe something will come of this."

At his desk at the United Nations, Stevenson sat, hands folded, face growing tighter and angrier. The Russians stared back.

"I don't take orders from you, man."

"Sorry. I thought I saw somebody. Forget it." Max reached for a can of Planters peanuts my uncle had left on a side table. He took a fistful and put them in his mouth. "I like these nuts." He chewed them slowly, swallowed and lit a cigarette.

I went to the window again. The big Plymouth was outside. The Russians again, I thought.

But Max Ostalsky was on his feet. He hurried to the television, and squatted up close. His eyes were not good, and his glasses half-broken, and it made him squint and put his face almost on the screen. "My God," he whispered.

On the TV, in the blurry black and white of a live broadcast, Adlai Stevenson is leaning forward now, angry, scowling at Zorin, the Soviet Ambassador, and he asks him point blank if his country is installing missiles in Cuba.

There is a lot of fussing around with paper, and the translators are holding tight to their earpieces as if they would otherwise fly off. Zorin fails to answer. His people look around, fool some more with paper, they whisper to their underlings and consultants, and tap their headphones, as if the translators had gone silent. And then Stevenson, with his icy patrician manner, gets furious. He says, very intense, very grand, "Don't wait for the translation, answer 'yes' or 'no'!" Zorin refuses. Stevenson comes back at him: "I am prepared to wait for my answer until Hell freezes over." He shows Zorin some photographs of the missile sites in Cuba. No pussy that day: Adlai was tough, a man who accepts no horse shit. "Yes or no!"

"Zorin is, what would you say, a jerk, and I've heard the rumor that he is off his rocker," said Max.

311

"Where did you hear it?"

Max had his face flat against the TV, intent on the screen.

I jumped up. "Listen, you tell me there's an assassination in three days, and now you want me to sit down and watch television. For Christ's sake, just tell me what the hell you're looking at."

Max turned. "It's Ambassador Stevenson."

"I can see that."

"Please, enough sarcasm. I'm trying to tell you something important. The target is Ambassador Stevenson. Look at the row of men behind Stevenson."

"So? A bunch of diplomatic big shots, what else?"

"Yes. What would you say, Pat? That they are diplomats? People from the State Department, is that right? A translator? A military envoy?"

"Right."

"Can you imagine that there would be an ordinary citizen right there in the Security Council when the fate of the world is in the hands of these men, our people, your people, Stevenson, Zorin?"

"I guess not. Why, for Christ's sake?"

"You see that man, just at the edge of the screen, behind Stevenson and to his right? Thinning hair. Small head. Big, black-rimmed glasses that are very large for his face, don't you think so? Big and square, as if for him to hide behind." Max reached for the cigarettes.

"You have one lit already."

"I've met that man." The cigarette hanging from his lips, Max removed his broken glasses and started cleaning the remaining good lens. "I met him in Moscow, at the American Exhibition, that was three years ago, Pat. I met him demonstrating large American refrigerators." Then suddenly, Max burst into Russian. He looked at me. "Sorry. He told me he was a businessman. He gave me a card. He said he was from Florida. He said he sold refrigerators, and other appliances."

Max said he had never met a real businessman, a true capitalist, and this one asked such good questions. He was a small man, with a pale pudgy face and heavy glasses. He wore a gray suit and white shirt, with a button-down shirt. But he wore a red silk tie, which Max, in his naivety, took to be a pleasant gesture towards his hosts. He had approached Max and, in a quiet voice, asked him many questions. Max was impressed with his curiosity, his interest in Moscow and the Soviet Union.

"What is your business?" Max asked.

"Ah," said the man. "Nothing exciting, I'm afraid. You saw the kitchen where Vice President Nixon gave his talk? The refrigerator is from my company. I'm afraid that I sell refrigerators. They are useful things, but perhaps not too exciting."

"Yes," said Max.

"Excuse me, I can see my translator waving at me. Very nice to meet you," he said and shook Max's hand.

Later, when he saw the man standing with Vice President Nixon, Khrushchev and the American ambassador, Max realized this was somebody important. "Then I made my report."

"What report. Jesus, they're still talking. Maybe we should go to the UN and warn Stevenson."

"No. They won't believe us, not yet. I want to see what happens at the session. Let's just watch."

"What report. You said you made your report, on what, on refrigerators?"

"In a way. My superior officer asked me, 'Did you find it appealing?' I said I did. I told him the American guides were excellent and open to questions and spoke correct Russian. He asked if we should do something like it. I say I think it is good for people to talk to each other. I announce—I was quite pompous in those days—that cementing international relations is an excellent thing, if it furthers the progress of the USSR. I say all these things, and because I am a good Soviet boy at the time, I also allow that I think it is shameful to see our own people lining up for plastic bags and small cups of Coca-Cola, which everyone knows is made of shoe polish. This makes an impression."

"They'd be more surprised now you love the stuff."

"But Pat, what astonishes me is that they never asked about the American who sold refrigerators."

"The KGB?" I said.

"Yes. Six months later it was made known to me I could apply for KGB training." Max crushed the cigarette, and got up and paced around the room, distracted, examining some of my aunt's paintings and the little blue glass objects she collected. "What do you say to this, Pat? What can it mean, a refrigerator salesman from the southern area of the state of Florida is at the United Nations next to Adlai Stevenson?"

"Is it Stevenson? Is he the target? Is that what Valdes told you? Christ."

"I felt it must be somebody in the American administration. Rica thought so. He had heard there were hard-line Cubans who hated Stevenson because he was so soft, that he would never make a confrontation. He was a man of peace. It would be useful to get rid of him, and also use him to provoke a confrontation. At first, I went up a stupid garden path, is that the right expression? I thought this whole business was only about the Cubans. It was also about us. There are Soviets who do not love peace, who dislike Khrushchev.

"My refrigerator man you see on television here goes back and forth between the Soviet Union and Florida. He tells me he is an unofficial ambassador.

"I remember, I remember. Everything about this man comes back to me now, he even tells me to visit him if ever I come to New York, which seems so improbable, so crazy, that it will ever happen, but such a delightful fantasy that I even keep his business card. He tells me he lives in Greenwich Village, and this sounds so magical, I think about it quite a bit."

"But you don't call him when you get here?"

"It seemed complicated. I wasn't sure who this man really was, and I knew my FBI fellow, Ed, you remember, with the bad crew cut, was watching, and I wasn't so interested by a refrigerator man. But I kept the card. It was the first one I had ever been given."

"And you have it."

From his pocket, Max pulled an engraved business card with a flourish, as if it were a sleight of hand. "Like magic, I still have this card. Mr Edward Forrester. 12th Street. Teddy. I heard somebody call him Teddy. He told me his wife teaches at the New School. This is the same man who whispers in the ear of Ambassador Stevenson, who also meets with our leaders so regularly, and so intimately."

"You're saying that this Forrester is a Communist spy?"

"Who can say? All I know is that I met him in Moscow and now he sits with Ambassador Stevenson, whispering into his ear, and it would make sense for an assassin to be so close to his target."

I got up.

"Where are you going?"

"I'm going to see him, this Mr Forrester. It's a very slim lead, barely a lead; it's nothing except a hunch you have, but we have less than nothing, so I'm going to find out how close he is to Stevenson, how close they are, where he was the Tuesday night when Valdes was murdered. I'm no spy, but I'm a pretty damn good cop, so sit down, Max, You'll get us both killed. What time is it? As soon as he's off TV, I'm going," I said. "While I'm out, you'll stay here, won't you, Ostalsky? Take a shower. Get a little sleep." In a bag I always kept in the car, I had some jeans and a gray sweatshirt with a hood I got working construction one summer long ago. "Here, take these," I said, throwing Ostalsky the clothes. "Somebody might recognize that old suit of yours, and I'll need my coat and hat back from you."

"I don't want to impose on your aunt and uncle for the shower."

"You know we have plenty of hot water, you've been here long enough. This is America, man."

"Then thank you. Perhaps it will help wash away the stink."

I looked at him.

"This moral stink, Pat. The horseshit."

"Wait." I went into the kitchen and got us a couple of beers. "Listen, Max, we're probably going down together, so you want to confess to anything? Us Catholics, we got confession, so you get to offload stuff. What do the Russkis do?"

"Also, we confess. We admit our mistakes to our comrades. For some of us, there is also what the Greeks call catharsis."

"You ever do anything you feel really bad about, I mean, personal stuff?"

He didn't laugh or make a crack about Catholics, just smoked silently for a while. "I did, yes, I did more than one bad thing. I had heard how the KGB conducted interviews from my friend; his name was Vassily. We were in our third year at university when he is summoned to a hotel room somewhere. I was nervous for him. I knew what this meant. Others had been interviewed. He has a willful streak, he says what he thinks, and likes to do things his own way." Max gulped some beer. "I said, 'Vasya, please, be careful,' but he is as cocksure as always, and later he tells me he went along, gave his name to the man outside the hotel room, and was told to go up. Afterwards, he told me, which was so dangerous for him, but he wanted to warn me. He was such a good friend.

"Two men were inside. One says he is KGB, and shows his pass, the little pass with the red cover and the KGB insignia, and introduces his superior, then locks the door. Vassily says later he recalls only the musty smell and the cigarettes, and the odor of men who have not washed, and his own fear. The senior man asks if Vassily wants to help his country by reporting to them on his co-students and friends. They tell him if they know what's going on, it is better for everyone. Vasya says to me he was so frightened he becomes contentious. He says to them, 'But I'm a biologist.'

"'Oh,' says the senior man, 'So you're not a patriot?'

'Can't I be a biologist and a patriot?' replies Vasya who is irritated now, as well as scared. In the end, Vassily refuses, but they want him to sign a piece of paper saying he would never tell anyone about the meeting. 'What will you do if I don't, put me in jail?' he says.

"'You'll wish you were in jail,' says the other agent in a way that terrifies Vassily.

"He never told me about this until many years later, when I ran into him. He was no longer a top biologist. He was working in a lab somewhere in the Urals, and was in Moscow only because his father had died."

"What about you?" I said.

"They left me alone, until after I finished my degree, and my MA and had begun work on my doctorate. With me they were polite, perhaps because my father is well connected. They proposed I should go on with my studies, and just occasionally tell them what was going on among the students I knew, but, more importantly, with foreigners in Moscow. By this they meant Americans. They told me I would be invited to events—concerts, lectures and exhibitions—like the one I told you about—even parties at the American embassy. If I would tell them who I saw and met, it would be a patriotic gesture. So I did. I told them I would do it. I was recruited for training, and then offered the graduate fellowship in New York."

"Lucky for you."

"You could say so. Shall I tell you what I did, the worst thing I did? You asked. I lied to get a better job, to get ahead, as you would say. I lied when I was interviewed," said Max. "I told them what they wanted to hear. I learned it was the thing you had to do."

"Are you looking for expiation? Absolution?"

"Those are Catholic ideas, I like to read the novels of Graham Greene, because I admire his writing and his stories, but I wish this thing he believes could be true. I can't believe in a God I don't understand. I can't believe in God at all. Perhaps God would have saved me from what I did.

"I lied about a friend. I colluded. I schemed, and I did it in a way no one quite saw what I was up to. I was some bastard. For instance, this means I always knew how to ask a friend for a favor and make him believe I was doing one for him. I pretended I was only good at telling jokes, and having fun, but my superiors knew I was quite sharp and my superior said, 'Max is the best, he can see around corners, he can fit in, he has the chameleon character of the best agents. Max can get what he wants, and that can be most useful.'

"Did I tell you how I got my fellowship to New York? Did I say another man dropped out because he had a skiing accident and fell in love with some girl on the slopes? I didn't? Well, Igor Petricov was much more talented than me, a much better candidate who spoke better English and already had his doctorate, and he was not so badly injured, or led by some girl, of course, but I made it seem as if he was unreliable, and I was from a better family and my father knew important people. There were many other students, more serious, I didn't care. I lied and they considered Petricov undisciplined for chasing women, and he got a minor posting far away from Moscow and no real possibility of advancement. I got the fellowship to New York. They believed me. I fabricated just enough. I was a magician. I could easily conspire in my own interest. I told my uncle, the general, that I would so like to have this job, and he was happy to help, and I was charming to him. As my friends, my cousin Sasha most of all, said, Max gets what he wants. I think I even took Nancy from you, Pat. I am sorry. I will take a shower now."

Max came out of the bathroom, wearing my jeans and sweatshirt with the hood up.

I laughed. "You look like a two-bit gangster."

"What else am I, Pat? This is what I am, wouldn't you say so? Just a two-bit gangster, a hoodlum, what else is a spy? What I've discovered is that to be a good agent, you have to be without human feeling in order to do your job. We celebrate spies as daring men who will do anything, and we pretend it is about patriotism, and this might be true, Pat, for some, for some who do it for idealistic reasons. They also consider themselves in a sort of brotherhood, as priests, somehow ordained to do the unspeakable in the name of country, instead of God. We used to talk of the great undertakings of the great agents with such envy.

"This is what they enjoy. I enjoyed this. Men together, bound by all the rules of their game—subversion, sabo-tage, spying—convinced like little boys these games are for the good of all. Did you know we have sports teams at the KGB? We have a house band? We are often bound together by families, because it seems safer to rely on somebody with good family connections. Some are cynical about it, of course. But all of us have a sense of entitlement. We convinced each other that this is for socialism, or capitalism, or freedom, or democracy. And it is all, all of it, as you say so often, Pat, horseshit. Crap.

Farce. Malarkey. Isn't that a term your uncle uses? We have much worse words in Russian."

"So do we."

"This is not the same as being a cosmonaut, or a great soldier in a patriotic war, like our fathers, or perhaps those girls in France who went behind enemy lines. They were different; they had an idea of what was proper. Professional agents are arrogant, but we are nothing. Just gullible, fallible men, like others, except that we are a little less human.

"In that warehouse I was scared to death, cold, wishing I had, I don't know, all kinds of ordinary things, even a cup of hot coffee and a roast beef sandwich, and a paperback book. I discovered that I am a terrible agent, and I was relieved. It seemed to me I might have a shot at being human. I was probably wrong. It's probably too late, and you'll understand when I tell you something about Bounine. In case you have to finish this case by yourself."

"Fuck off."

Contemplating the can, Max finished the peanuts. "Let me talk. Bounine is in trouble. I failed at the job he ordered me to do. This means he failed. They will go after him. He might take chances to prove himself loyal. He's, what do you say, a creep, but he is shrewd, and he may come looking for you. "

"Is he the assassin?"

"He has a defect."

"Is he retarded or something? But he's a doctor. He seemed pretty smart to me."

"His soft spot is my insurance policy. Everybody has a soft spot. Greed. Money. Women. Ideology."

"He was your friend."

"He made himself my friend. But it was to provoke me to talk freely so he can make, what you call brownie points. What he didn't know was that two of us could play at the same game, and that I am better at it. But his job was always to watch me."

"Christ."

"Do you know what my cousin Sasha always said about me? He says, 'We always knew this about you, Max. You could get anything out of us even as little children. You could always press the right buttons; you are like the magician with your silk scarves and disappearing coins, you are an actor. We used to whisper about you. Max is going to be a spy. Maxim is a spy. One of the girls even called you Felix.'"

"Who?"

"For the founder of our Secret Service. It doesn't matter. When I was with Bounine at Caffe Reggio, and I see how intimately he speaks with the young man making coffee, I said nothing, but I let him know I saw, that I understood. He had been quite eager once in the summer to show me a new watch he had been given, and after he had enough to drink, he told me it was a young doctor who had presented it to him."

"You mean Bounine is homosexual."

"If you need help, you can use this."

"You're a cold bastard," I said.

Max nodded. "Oh, yes, sure. Cold. Arrogant. Stupid, treacherous. I now understand that spies are the lowest form of all human life because we think we're invulnerable, and we think we can do anything and say it's for our country, for honor, for the motherland. Anyway, if Bounine intends to kill me, or you, I will use whatever this takes."

He picked up a letter he had left on an antique desk against the wall. I had seen it. It was addressed to Nancy.

"Did you read my letter?"

"No," I said. "I have to go now. Do you love Nancy?"

"Yes," said Max. "I still do. I can let you, would it be right to say, off the hook?" He smiled slightly, sadly. "I know that Nancy gives information to the FBI. I believe she does this so they will leave her father alone. He is very ill. Or perhaps she does it because she believes it is the right thing. What came to me in that warehouse is that I love her anyway."

CHAPTER FIVE

October 26, '62

I MADE THE CALL I never wanted to make. From the hospital, when I had seen Bounine, I had phoned up the only friend who might still help me. She had said not to call. Said she would be in touch. Then, nothing. It was a chance I had to take. I had been asking friends for help, friends like Clay Briscoe, now this: I hated it. I hated putting them in jeopardy, but what else could I do?

On my way to see Edward Forrester, I saw the fear on people's faces, fear reflected in their eyes. I walked to Sixth Avenue where I saw a familiar figure. "Hello Pat," said Muriel Miller; for some crazy reason I wondered if it was accidental. In shop windows, in bars, and cafés, every television was on, and people watched, speechless; a reporter said that the Pentagon had assessed the space in fallout shelters, and concluded that in the whole country there was space for 60 million people. For the rest of us, there was nothing.

The gaslights were already on in Patchin' Place off Sixth Avenue, as I arrived at the tiny house where Shirley Cowan lived.

Shirley was past ninety, spry, an elegant woman with short white hair who had all her marbles; more than most. Her father had worked in Teddy Roosevelt's department when he was Police Commissioner of New York in the 1890s; the first woman journalist to cover both world wars, she had known everyone who mattered, and had been pursued by many of them, though she never married. She had gone into the department as its archivist. In that room at the Centre Street headquarters, she kept files on every cop who had mattered, and some of them she had taken home with her when she retired to this doll's house with poets down the lane for neighbors. She had had enough of cops, she once told me; but she never had enough; her files were her obsession.

"I'm sorry, Shirley. I couldn't wait any more. I'm sorry to come here like this."

"Just come inside quickly," she said, closed the door and put the chain on.

"I'm sorry."

"Enough, Patrick. Enough. Your uncle was my friend. You're my friend. You're the one who always comes when I fall down, or make a fool of myself, and you always make me feel it's your pleasure."

"It is."

When I entered the little parlor, she kissed my cheek and said simply, "You're in terrible trouble, Patrick. When you telephoned me on Tuesday, I went through my files, and I made a few phone calls, and if you are somehow involved with Homer Logan, if you've got up his nose, and you have, it's much much worse than you can imagine. Would you like a drink, dear? You'll need one." She asked me to pour out the whisky from an old glass decanter on an upright piano. Near the decanter were pictures of her—she had been a great beauty—with Douglas Fairbanks, FDR, Caruso, even old Joe Kennedy.

"Thank you."

She cleared a pile of papers from a small armchair. "Sit. You are in very bad trouble, my sweetheart. I called you at home, but there was no answer." She sipped her whisky. "Have you talked to your Uncle Jack?"

"He's upstate."

"Why don't you join him? It would be a very good idea."

"I can't. I'm so sorry, Shirley, but I'm in a hurry."

From the pile of papers, she extracted a brown file marked Homer Logan in her neat cursive script. "Logan has a reputation as a man hungry for power, but you knew that. He has been obsessed with getting the Mafia since the 1940s, when he came back from the war, and was only a young cop." She turned the yellowing pages. "He thinks of every Mafia collar as a notch on his belt, so to speak, and he'll do anything to make it, even if he has to bend the rules or corrupt the information. I do mean anything, Patrick. He takes risks. He puts himself in harm's way. You see he idolizes Bobby Kennedy for what he did on the racketeering cases, and most of all on that union thug, Jimmy Hoffa. To make a Mob case, he feels, is to please Bobby. It's his life."

I told her about the case on Pier 46. I told her how Logan had pushed me off it, and my own boss, Murphy, had gone along with him. "They threatened me."

"I'm not surprised. There are a few reporters who eat out of his hand, and write whatever he tells them, and of course, these make good stories. It's never the whole truth. Logan has made certain gangsters disappear so he can claim his victories. I wouldn't be surprised if a few cops who knew too much also found themselves off the force, or worse."

"What about the case on the pier, the dead Cuban? I heard they're going to indict Cheeks Farigno.

"It was set, then Farigno came up with an alibi. He says he was in Chicago at the time of the murder, and one of the locals, one of Sam Giancana's men, confirmed it."

"Sweet Jesus. But I guess Logan will say, who can believe anything Giancana's Mob say?"

"Exactly. In fact, I think this will add fuel to Logan's fire, because if he can get to Giancana himself ... do you recall during the racketeering trial, when Bobby Kennedy said to Giancana, 'I thought only little girls giggled, Mr Giancana?' Homer Logan keeps that news clipping on his wall, framed."

"What about the young woman who was murdered last summer on the High Line?"

"It was dreadful. I looked it up, the best I could, but some of the files were missing, and I can only get access to the archives on weekends, when there's no one around. I made a copy of the key." Shirley asked for a cigarette, and I gave her one and lit it. "As far as I can tell, her murder was just possibly a real Mafia hit," she said. "There are some reliable people who believe this.

"Easy, then, to insist that the hit on the pier last week was the same perp, or a copy-cat." I said.

"Thank you. Shirley, I should go."

"I'm sorry if that's not much help. I have a few more things on Logan. He's a brutal man. When he was in the air force during the war, he was greedy for missions, and he bragged about people he had killed in Dresden. He flew the fire bombing of Tokyo, and was part of the mission to poison Japanese waterways. Of course, plenty of fliers took these missions, but they say that Logan begged for them, and talked about them, and kept photographs, the cities, the people, on fire; he has said we should do the same to the Cubans. The department had to shut him up," said Shirley. "Have you heard of General Curtis LeMay?"

"Sure. He's crazy. He wants to nuke everyone."

"He was Logan's commanding officer."

I got up. "Thanks, Shirley. Will you be OK?"

"Of course," said Shirley. "And be careful. I don't want to hear they picked you up as some kind of rogue cop, or worse. Pat, just switch on the overhead light on your way out, would you? And don't worry about me. Homer Logan can't intimidate me, because I'm an old lady and people consider the old incapable and next door to senile. So I'm quite safe. And I know all about him."

"Thank you. Is there any more?"

"His wives. The other women. The fact that he changed his name. He's Italian. Peasant stock. Logan was his mother's name; his real name is Enrico Pazzo. Where he got the Homer is hard to say, but he went into the military, he was very keen on becoming an officer, and Italians were not entirely popular during the war. So Enrico Pazzo become Homer Logan. He was raised on Mulberry Street. His father was a butcher who beat him up, and before he became an Episcopalian and attended services on Fifth Avenue, Logan went to Old St Pat's where he was in the same confirmation class as your Uncle Jack. He hates everything to do with Little Italy, with his family, the Church, which is probably why he is so obsessed with stamping out the Mafia. Thinks it's responsible for giving Italians a bad name."

"Jack was pretty upset when I mentioned Logan."

"No wonder. Logan is certainly aware that Jack's been onto him for a long time. Did you catch Adlai Stevenson on TV today? I thought he was marvelous, the way he stood up to Zorin was very brave, and he will opt for a peaceful solution to this wretched crisis, if they let him." said Shirley. "I was always a great fan of Adlai's."

CHAPTER SIX

October 26, '62

"**W**HO DO YOU WANT?"

"Mr Forrester. E. A. Forrester."

"And is he expecting you?"

"Yes." I had been to the building the night before. Forrester was out. I had gone up to his apartment and banged on the door; nobody had answered. A neighbor looked out and said they were away. "Back tomorrow. Now stop that racket." She waited like a guard dog in the doorway until I left.

Under the canopy of the apartment building on 12th Street, stood the sullen doorman in a shabby blue uniform, cigarette hanging from his lower lip, looking me over with the disdain of the underpaid, nothing except this tiny piece of turf to protect and the power that went with it. It took me a fiver to change his attitude. I didn't like it. But the bastards were going to murder Adlai Stevenson, and I needed some kind of proof. If Forrester had been whispering in Stevenson's ear, maybe he would help, if he could, if—and I remembered Ostalsky's theory that he might be working both sides—he wanted to help. The 28th was coming fast; Sunday would be the 28th. It was Friday.

"What name shall I say?"

"Maxim Ostalsky."

The doorman tossed his cigarette butt into the gutter, and buzzed the Forrester apartment. After a few seconds, he turned to me. "He says you can go right up. 7C."

I could have saved the dough.

On the way up, with the elevator operator, a dwarfish man who never said a word, I considered what the hell I was going to say. Unlike Max Ostalsky I had no spy tricks, nothing up my sleeve; I was no magician. All I knew was Adlai Stevenson was in danger. This was a long shot, but it gave me a focus; then the elevator door opened and I was standing in front of the door to apartment 7C.

"Coming. Just please wait. I'm coming." A woman's voice trilled out from behind the door to 7C. I removed my sunglasses. Turned my coat collar down. Smile, I thought. The door opened a crack.

"Yes?" A middle-aged woman in a pink housedress peered through the crack in the door. "Is that Mr Ostalsky?"

"Yes. Hello. How do you do?"

She removed the chain from the door and let me inside. "I'm Mrs Forrester. Please, my husband said you're to go right to his study."

The walls were tan, the furniture, the rugs, all old and expensive, were brown; in the faint sunlight that crept between the slats of Venetian blinds swam motes of dust and anxiety.

I followed her along a corridor hung with watercolors

and framed diplomas. The study door was open, and behind a large partner's desk with a green leather top, was the little man I had seen on television.

He rose slightly. "Sit down," he said, removing the thick-rimmed glasses. He wore an open-necked white shirt with a button-down collar, a woolen tie, a dark brown cardigan that you might see on some English professor. The whole apartment had an unused feel, an air of drab melancholy, as if it was an occasional stopping-off place, nothing more.

"I wondered why Maxim Ostalsky would be here," he said, pleasantly enough. "What's your real name? You must know Max, then, isn't that right? Is he still studying for his advanced degree in Moscow? What news of him? You are not Ostalsky, obviously. The news is not good," he said, glancing at the TV where a reporter droned on about ships in the Atlantic, possibly carrying warheads to Cuba. There were already nuclear weapons on the island, I knew. Who will believe us? Max had said. Nobody, I thought; nobody at all.

"My name is Patrick Wynne." I remained standing. It made him very small. "I'm not, as you can see, Max Ostalsky."

"But you do know him."

"Sure."

"Is he well?"

"Well enough."

"Please sit down," Forrester said. "You were here yesterday."

"Yes."

"I'm sorry. My wife and I spent the night with friends on Sutton Place after a long dinner."

"Was Mr Stevenson there?"

"Yes, as it happens. Why?"

He gestured at a chair. So I sat. I was taller than him anyhow. As he reached for a fancy cigar box, his long hands, the fingers slim and graceful, were out of proportion with his small body. "Cigar?" he said.

"No. Thanks."

He held the match and puffed to get it lit, and smiled. "Cuban," he said. "Lovely."

"Good for you."

"If you're a friend of Maxim's, I'm happy to meet you. Did you know I met him in Moscow? He was very helpful; he was an excellent guide. In fact, he gave me a whole new sense of what our Soviet friends were like.

"You were there for what reason?"

"Didn't Max tell you? I sell refrigerators and other appliances and we were showing these wonderful American items to the Soviet Union. It was quite an event. Vice President Nixon, was there, I'm sure you recall."

"They liked it all, did they, the Russians?"

"Of course. Mr Khrushchev is a practical man. I believe he would like all his people to have such modern wonders, and has promised them for everyone in twenty years." He smiled. "Over the years, I've been lucky enough to see that vast country, I really got to know its people, to understand their culture, even to help them, and I was also able to report to Mr Khrushchev on the economic advances in the USA. And I admired the Soviets, they knew I did, and they appreciated it. After the war, I often thought that only the Soviets understand, only they had suffered enough and knew what it was to fight, in their bare feet, with their bare hands, without food if necessary. You know, I met a few young Soviet officers when I went to Yalta."

"Fine, and you intend to cash in this big new market with your refrigerators? What about washing machines?"

"Certainly. But I was simply there to help our country, as you might imagine. I've been of at least a little help in other places, I think."

"What kind of places?"

"Indochina, for example. Shall we get down to business, Mr Wynne?"

I gestured to the apartment. "This doesn't look like the place a refrigerator salesman would live."

"It belonged to my wife's aunt and uncle. When she first came to New York, she lived with them, and they were like parents to her. She finds it hard to give up."

"But you prefer Florida."

"This apartment permits me to spend some days in New York City from time to time."

"At the United Nations, for example?"

"Yes, certainly, it's a very important organization. Don't you think so?"

"I saw you on TV. I saw you sitting behind Adlai Stevenson."

"Maxim would have spotted that. I'm so sorry he hasn't called by to see me in all this time."

"Then you knew he was in New York. What were you doing at the UN?"

Forrester, looked at his watch, then removed his cufflinks, polished them on a tissue, put them on the desk, turned his cuffs back, like a man getting ready for action. I tensed up. Was there a weapon in that big mahogany desk? What was he, this little man who knew so much. "I sometimes act in an unofficial capacity as an advisor," he said.

"Who to?"

"Excuse me one moment, Mr Wynne," he said, and left the room. In the distance, I heard him talking to his wife, but I couldn't make out the words. I rummaged in the green leather wastepaper basket, grabbed what I could, and shoved the bits of paper into my pockets. I noticed the gold cufflinks were engraved with a military insignia.

On the wall, diplomas revealed that Forrester had gone to Princeton and then to Columbia Law School. I had met his kind once or twice, the men with such certainty about everything, so much charming passion for their country, and the assumption of intimate knowledge of many others. He was CIA, clear as day, and Ostalsky must have spotted it; or maybe back in Moscow, he had been too naive.

Propped on top of a bookcase were photographs from Indochina and Chile, Algeria and the Soviet Union, all meant to look like tourist snaps, but you would ask, why the hell was he in these places, and how did he know so many officials? In Moscow, he had posed with Khrushchev; in Vietnam with one of those dragon ladies who ran the show; in Cuba, he stood alongside Battista, the bastard who ran it before Castro took it over, and Forrester had a picture of a very young Fidel Castro too. I thought about Mrs Reyes' description of the man who came up with the idea of the worm. I recalled her words: "Somebody quite silly, an American official in Washington DC, one of those, what do you say, gung-ho ex military men who feels he is a diplomat and understands a country after a few months ..."

There were family photographs, too, and snaps from Forrester's college years when he had played football at Princeton. There were pictures of the young Forrester in uniform, on an airfield with three other young men. In the background was what looked like a B-17 Flying Fortress.

I was looking at a picture of Bobby Kennedy, when Forrester returned.

"I admire Bob," he said. "I saw quite a bit of him when I worked in Washington. He has stood up for the few good men who returned from the Bay of Pigs. By the way, I asked my wife if she would make some coffee for us."

"I don't need coffee. I need to know what the hell you were doing at the United Nations with Adlai Stevenson?"

"I told you. I advise."

"On what?"

"I try to act as an informal mediator. I happened to be at the United Nations. I saw that Mr Stevenson and Mr Zorin were not in any way ready to reach a satisfactory conclusion. We are very close to a terrible confrontation. I had an idea or two. I know Ambassador Stevenson quite well."

"What is your idea of a satisfactory conclusion?"

"Peace, of course."

"At any price?"

"Look, Detective, I think there is some misunderstanding. Why don't you tell me where Maxim Ostalsky is? I'd so like to see him, and to help him."

"Help him with what?"

"I know that he's in trouble."

"How do you know?"

"Actually, I tried to reach him. I wasn't entirely straight with you, but I was a little thrown when you said you were Max Ostalsky. I had heard he was studying in New York, and I wanted to meet him again. I made inquiries at the University, and they gave me a phone number. I reached the apartment where he was staying only Monday, in fact. I was concerned. I thought it might be difficult if he was here and the crisis had begun, and I didn't want him to feel everyone was hostile to him. I talked to a Mr Miller, very helpful, and he told me he'd give Max Ostalsky a message when he returned. He was out of town, Miller said. In fact, I have a letter for Max."

"From his family, no doubt."

"From one of his teachers in Moscow, in fact."

"Why don't I get it to him?"

Forrester ignored my offer. "I think I told you, I sell appliances," he said. "Look, our government sees my job as a way to break through the deadlock between us, as a more personal kind of communication. I do it because I love this country. I do what I can."

"Selling refrigerators?"

"Sure."

"And advising our diplomats on the side? You're CIA, aren't you?"

From the way he turned to avoid me, I knew I was right. I was itching to get a look at more of his paperwork.

"Where's that coffee?" he said. "You know, of course, that I can't directly answer those kind of questions, Detective Wynne. Let me just say you're quite wrong about things."

"What's going to happen on Sunday, October 28th?"

Again, he failed to answer, but this time because he

was startled. He knew. I recognized Edward Forrester's surprise, the brief flash of, what, of fear?

He hurriedly reclaimed his placid expression. "I have no idea what you mean at all. On Sundays, I attend church with my wife. She's rather a devout Roman Catholic."

"I have one more question."

"Of course."

"Do you think Adlai Stevenson is getting in the way of what you might call negotiations?"

"Of course not. I'm personally very fond of Adlai. We're old friends. We were both at Milton Academy, at different times of course, and I was at his son's wedding out at Big Sur."

"You know him that well?"

"Yes, indeed. I worked in Chicago when he was Governor of Illinois. I helped on his '56 Presidential campaign. I'm close to many politicians. In fact, Bobby Kennedy worked on that same campaign; there were quite a lot of us young fellows. Does that help you?"

"I heard Bobby didn't like Adlai. I heard he didn't even vote for him afterwards, he voted for Eisenhower."

"Is that right?"

"You think Stevenson goes to church?"

"Not during this sort of crisis, no, I don't see Adlai as particularly devout."

"You think he's soft? You think Bobby Kennedy's soft?"

"I'm not sure what you mean."

Something occurred to me. "Your wife, she has a slight accent?"

"Yes, I suppose she does."

"Is she Russian?"

"She left as a young woman. She was so happy to be in New York, we met then, my goodness, it must be more than thirty years." He had a relentless manner of recounting the details of his life. "I met her on a student trip to Moscow, then she came here, I was at Columbia Law School, she was a student at Barnard College." He smiled. "She loved New York. America. Her uncle was a professor, you see, and this was his apartment, and when they passed on, my wife Katherine inherited it."

"You got her out? Of Russia?"

"I may have helped."

"Will you be staying in New York for a while?"

"Until Sunday, or Monday perhaps," he said. "I'll be here as long as I'm useful. Please tell Maxim Ostalsky to stop by, would you? We have so much to catch up on."

"I'll see what I can do. By the way, I was looking at some of your photographs. The picture from the war, is that you? My older cousin flew a B-17."

"Did he? Yes, it is."

"And your pals in the picture? Who are they?"

Forrester went to the door, opened it and called out, "Katherine? Where is that coffee, dear?"

The wife hurried into the study. "I did what you asked, dear. I hope that's all right."

But there was no coffee.

"Well, then, thanks again for coming, Detective. Of course, I was expecting you."

"How's that?"

"Our mutual friend, of course. He telephoned me to say that you were on your way, but you knew that, I'm sure."

Before I could respond, sirens sounded in the street. I thought at first it was an air raid. It was the cops. I was betting Forrester had told his wife to call the police.

Edward Forrester was getting ready to turn me in, which meant he knew I was in trouble with the brass. They would arrest me, fire me, push me out into the cold, and Forrester knew it. He knew I had been coming to see him; Max Ostalsky had called him. One more time, I'd been taken in.

CHAPTER SEVEN

October 26, '62

OSTALSKY HAD PLAYED ME yet again. This had been a double-cross all along. Ostalsky had phoned Forrester, told him that I was my way to see him. Together they had planned it. Both of them knew if the cops got me, they'd take me in, fire me, put me out to pasture; or else they'd get it out of me, what I knew. Either way it was a bad deal.

When Tommy got beat up with the baseball bat, I had found Ostalsky with him, Tommy saying, "Get rid of the friggin' Red," and I had ignored it. The kid must have recognized him from the pier. He had said a man with white hair, but in those lights on the river, you couldn't tell, not really. Max Ostalsky had double-crossed me and I had fallen for it like a ton of bricks, as my Uncle Jack used to say.

Somebody was going to murder Adlai Stevenson on Sunday, Ostalsky had said; but why would I trust him now? Forrester would be leaving town on Sunday. He had made a point of telling me his travel plans.

*

Somehow, in that study, Forrester and the wife still there, I got my gun out of my pocket, waved it at them and ran, crashing down the long hall, into the kitchen and through the backdoor. I had figured there would be a backdoor for the garbage, and from there I could make my way to the basement.

The light in the stairwell was dim. The paint was cracked. I had dreams like this, running down the stairs, using the railing to hoist myself up and cover a flight in two or three long jumps.

In the basement, I ran past the laundry room, into a storage area, and hid behind the bicycles and baby carriages, discarded furniture, cartons marked "coats" and "toys", crates of wine, and a stack of dusty books with fancy gold cardboard covers, all the stuff of the prosperous middle-class lives lived in the building upstairs, stuff that had been saved for a different season or because somebody could not bear to toss it out.

Forrester would tell the cops I had been bothering him, or pestering his wife. Maybe he was already on the phone to somebody he knew, Logan, the Police Commissioner, Mayor Wagner, Richard Nixon. Tell them that I had been asking improper questions during a national crisis.

In the basement wall high up were small barred windows. Somewhere in the street I heard people yelling, screaming, and I wondered if it had all started. If the nukes were coming, I didn't much want to die in that basement. I sure wasn't going to die for Ostalsky, or Forrester, whoever they were working with; it didn't matter; they were mirror images of each other.

All the deception, the falsehoods, the bullshit, the half-truths, the bare-faced lies on both sides, it was a world of intelligence that led nowhere, and the more you gathered, good stuff, bad stuff, lies about suspects when lies were required, no matter if the wrong person went to prison or fried—Homer Logan's game—it was a world that existed to service itself. Even Ostalsky's speeches about how duplicitous his world was were lies. Apart from fear, I felt nothing but fury, and disdain.

From somewhere in the cavernous basement, I heard the heavy steps of cops on the move. I knew they'd get to the basement at some point. Edward Forrester was no fool, and he was a pro. He would notice I had run through the kitchen—footprints, smell—and down the back stairs. Only a pro would have asked his wife to call the police the way he had done. He was CIA, but I guessed that he was playing both sides. Max Ostalsky had spoken of Bounine's weakness for handsome men. I wondered what Forrester's was.

Forrester and Ostalsky had buried themselves in so many layers of lies, it was hard to unravel, and for all I knew they had been working together. If Forrester intended killing Adlai Stevenson, who was going to stop him?

Forrester apparently went back and forth to the USSR like people take the Staten Island ferry. He knew all the players. Still, the little man with big glasses didn't seem the kind to get blood on his hands, though he wasn't some kind of pussy either—in the war he had flown those B-17s.

Two days.

"Where the hell is he?" A voice boomed loud into the basement.

The voices of city cops—loud, impatient and irritable—were in some idiotic way comforting. At least I knew how they worked. At least, they were not Commie spies. I ran into what I thought was a supply closet. Instead I found myself in a room without windows. Cots were stacked on the floor. On the door I saw the notice. I was in the building's fallout shelter.

I put my ear to the door.

"He's gone," one of the cops yelled. "Who was stupid enough to miss him. Christ. Come on. Let's go."

For the next hour, I waited around the corner from the Forresters' building and when the couple emerged, I followed them west on 12th Street, and down Sixth Avenue. She wore a black and white houndstooth checked coat, a black beret, matching gloves and she carried a large black leather handbag. Over his suit, Edward Forrester wore a tweed topcoat and a matching cap. They walked arm in arm until they reached Jefferson Market, a fancy grocery store where the windows were filled with good-looking fruit. I crept after them, making my way inside, keeping as close behind them as I could. The store was full. People shopping, kids in tow, stocking up. Maybe they were stocking up for the end of the world, if it came. Carts full of milk, bread, juice; lines had formed in front of the butcher's counter. I hid among them, all these desperate people buying groceries for the apocalypse; pushing my own shopping cart, I managed to stay out of sight of the Forresters.

They took a cart. Together, they wheeled it up one aisle and down the other, chatting as if it were a social outing, discussing various items on the shelves, heads always together. Neither one of them looked up much, except to pick a box of fancy crackers off a shelf or a bag of cookies. On Mrs Forrester's wrist was a gold charm bracelet that jangled every time she moved. I followed the noise, when I could. I couldn't hear much of what they said. Then the wife began to cry. I took a chance. I rolled my cart into the next aisle, stopped, pushed aside loaves of bread so I could see them standing in the cracker aisle. A knot of shoppers stood behind them, inpatient. The scene in the fancy store was chaotic. The Forresters never noticed me.

"Speak English for heaven's sake, please," Forrester said.

"I want to go home, Teddy, please," she said. "I do not want to die here in this awful country. Teddy, darling, I know we're all going to die. This crisis is getting worse, there will be nuclear war."

"This is your home." He was as patient now as if she was a child. "Dearest Katya, please, you like our evenings out. Soon we will meet our friends for dinner, and then a film at the Fifth Avenue Cinema, what do you say? And when this is all over we'll go for a visit to your lovely dacha and have time together?" His voice was beguiling. The wife stopped crying, and said she felt better. "Are you all right now?" he said, and she said "Yes, darling, I'm fine."

Then, without warning, he looked in my direction, sharp, alert, as if he knew I was there. I turned my back.

Somewhere I had read that certain spies used grocery stores as a drop. They might meet and greet their connection as if unexpectedly encountering friends over their trolleys. Maybe they put information in a pack of frozen peas. Later, Max Ostalsky told me that it was true. It seemed very funny, no, crappy and small, that the fate of nations could be hidden in a package of frozen vegetables.

I crept to the next aisle and waited. If this was the life of a spy, you had to take on the humiliation as the lowest of all human life forms, with your time spent gazing at a box of Tutti Fruitti Twinkles with an elephant on the side. I tried not to sneeze. I wanted to sneeze. But the Forresters were caught up in their purchases. Conferring, they finally procured a large box of chocolate cherries. They paid, and put the cherries into a shopping bag.

Arm in arm, her charm bracelet clanking, their steps ringing out on the hard supermarket floor, they went through the door and I followed as best I could back to Fifth Avenue and 12th Street, where they waited in front of Longchamps Restaurant. Then they were waving and calling out, making a point to greet a friend who had just climbed out of a taxi. The three of them started into the restaurant, as if they were merely a trio of friends on a night out. The man was Mike Bounine.

"Match?"

"What?"

A man passing stopped and asked if I had a match, a light, and I said, "Sure", and tossed him a pack of matches. I could see he wanted to chat. He stood there lighting his smoke. Made small talk about the weather, and finally I had to tell him to push off. He seemed offended.

Then I waited. I waited for almost an hour, on edge, nervous, unsure if I could do this, knowing I had to. No choice. No choice, I said to myself, over and over; I have to do this. And suddenly, after another twenty minutes, adrenalin coursed through my body, and I was ready. This is what always happened on a regular job. When there was nothing left to lose, I was OK. The whole week behind me, the sense that I was out of my depth, out in the cold, on a limb, all of it went. In the window of the restaurant, I saw my face. The color that had drained away was back. I tossed my smoke into the gutter.

When the Forresters emerged, Bounine in tow—or the other way around—I edged as close as I could. With the chocolates under his arm, Bounine shook Forrester's hand and kissed the wife on the cheek and turned to head uptown. The Forresters crossed Fifth Avenue, presumably on their way to the movies.

Bounine walked as fast as he could, trying hard not to run, but after a block, he broke into a trot. He moved forward; I kept behind. I couldn't tell if he saw me or not; I was guessing he had been trained to see whatever was behind him, but this was a frightened man.

He started west on 14th Street, then seemed to change his mind, and turned towards Union Square. It came to me that, for the first time on this case, I was taking some pleasure; that I was glad he was scared; I was pleased I had him cornered, especially as he entered the Union Square subway station. He fumbled for his token; I hid myself as best I could, but he was so intent on entering the station, he didn't turn around.

After Bounine disappeared down a tunnel to the platform, I put my token in the slot and followed him. No way out for you, I said to myself, as I nodded to a beat cop on the platform, letting the cop know I was one of them.

The platform was almost empty. Bouine walked to the

far end of it, and then I let him see me. There was nothing for him to do, no way out.

"Sit down," I said, indicating the worn wooden bench. "Sit."

He looked around like a scared animal, a deer in the headlights.

"I have a gun. Just sit," I said.

"What do you want?" Bounine put his hands in his pockets. He was shivering. It was cold in the subway station; cold and dank.

"Take your hands out. Where I can see them."

He followed my orders, but he held onto the chocolates.

"What's in the box?"

"Chocolates."

"Give it to me."

"Why not?" He passed it over.

With one hand I opened the box, and found only candy.

"I like your American cherry chocolates."

A young couple, arms linked, appeared on the platform, but they turned away from us, walking to the end where they could make out in private.

"What do you want?" Bounine's voice shook.

"I want you to tell me everything you know."

"There is not so much."

"Look, I went to see Edward Forrester. I talked to him. I saw the wife. The Russian wife. If you want, you can talk to me, or I can call the FBI."

"This is a joke," he said, but he wasn't laughing. Bounine looked worn out, a man who had given up, who had lost whatever power he had. Still, when he spotted a man in a tweed coat, he rose.

"Sit down. Who is he? Is he one of yours?"

"Nobody."

"Sit the fuck down, man. If he's nobody, why were you getting up."

The tweed coat came closer. I got my ID from my pocket and showed it to him. "Please, walk away," I said. "Do it now."

"I don't know more than you know, please, let me go, I want to get my suitcase, and I will return to Moscow, you will never know of me." Bounine had begun to panic. "I must get to my apartment."

"Why?"

"I have some work to complete."

"Listen to me, man, I'm not in the mood to take any crap now, I keep telling you and you don't believe me, but in about two minutes, I'm going to call the cop you probably saw on your way down here, and he will put cuffs on you, and together we will take you to the FBI."

Bounine looked at me. "I don't think so. This is not so easy for you. You are not welcome by your own people, I think. You are, what do they say, out in the cold?"

"Who killed Rica Valdes?"

"It was not me."

"Then who? I'm ready to let you off the hook, if you tell me who killed Valdes."

"Your Mafia. Mr Luca Farigno."

"Wrong," I said. "Don't look at the train," I said as it came into the station. "You're not going anywhere, you hear?"

"Please."

"Why was your pal Forrester whispering in Adlai

Stevenson's ear at the United Nations? Why were you out to dinner with the Forresters?"

The half dozen people on the platform had boarded the train, and after it left, the station was empty.

"I can help you."

"What kind of help?" he asked, sweating now, a man in a vise, a man trapped in a place he had no one to call.

"Come on, Mike, I know about your little problem. I know your tastes. I *know*. You want your secret between us?"

"I didn't murder Valdes."

"Come on, man, who will believe it? You set it up. You were the messenger between this Rishkova woman—the Letter Carrier, right? They call her the Letter Carrier, who provided photographs to Valdes to show Ostalsky. You watched Ostalsky from the time he arrived in New York."

"Yes. Sure. OK. Let me go now," he said and got up from the bench.

I grabbed his sleeve. "Listen to me. What's going to happen on Sunday. What's going down? You have no diplomatic immunity as an exchange student, isn't that right? You're not attached to a news bureau, or a consulate. If you're not a student, you're illegal here, and nobody at all will care about you. Nobody here, nobody in your country will even think of an exchange for you. You're nothing much."

"You're wrong," he said, but the conviction had gone.

"I'm trying to help you, man. I could have saved you from your thick-necked goons, I could still help you out, maybe, or maybe they'll just send you home. Be good to go home, don't you think? Except for your preference for, what should I say, nice-looking boys?"

"Yes, it would be OK to go home. Yes, that would be good," he said, frightened, a beaten man. I got the feeling he actually thought he'd make it all the way back to the USSR, at least at first.

"Listen to me, somebody is going to die, I want you to tell me who it is. Is it somebody important, an American?"

"Yes."

"So you know. You do know, don't you? Does Forrester know?"

"Yes."

"And his Soviet friends, his contacts?"

"You're looking in the wrong place," said Bounine. "It's not his Soviet contacts."

"I don't think either your people or ours would feel good about who some of your friends are. You know our mayor, the mayor of New York City that is, does not show much sympathy for, how shall I say, homos right now. You know what I mean. Isn't that right? Isn't that your thing, Bounine? You like boys."

"Let me go. Please." He was begging.

"Is Ambassador Stevenson the target? Is there an assassination?"

"Yes."

"Stevenson is the target?"

"No."

"But Sunday?"

"I think yes."

"Listen to me, why don't you make it easy? We're all going to die in this war probably, so, meantime, let me help you. Come with me."

"Where?"

I had no idea at all; if I took him in, I'd be on the line. I needed more.

"Which side is Edward Forrester on?"

"I think both sides. No sides. His own side. He does this for money, also for his wife, who loves her old country, but also, I think, for respect."

"What?"

"There is somebody he, what do you say, reveres? Someone he has worked for. For this man he does anything."

I looked down the platform and saw the cop I had seen earlier. A young, big-shouldered, tough New York cop in his dark summer blues, gun on his hip.

"Officer," I called out.

"Don't," said Bounine. "My train is coming. Let me take my train." I could hear the train coming. I could hear the noise.

Somehow, just before the train appeared, Bounine, gathering his strength, went to the edge of the platform, propelled, and jumped onto the tracks.

The train screeched to a halt. The beat cop ran to the edge of the platform, radio in hand. I couldn't risk it. I couldn't take the chance the cop would ask me too many questions, that he might have seen me with Bounine. So I hurried away. I hurried up the stairs into Union Square. I didn't wait to find out if Bounine was dead.

October 26, '62

THE DRAPES AT UNCLE Jack's were drawn tight, even though it was late, after ten, and Ostalsky was sitting in living room in the dark. In a rage, I said, "Listen, you son-of-a-bitch, you called Forrester before I got to him. You set me up."

He switched on the lamp with a green glass shade on the table next to him, and looked up. "It's not true," he said. "Forrester was playing you." His eyes were swollen, purple circles around them.

"What happened to you?"

"It's nothing."

"Where are your glasses?"

"Gone." He tried to smile and it made him wince. "So this means I am, as you say, blind as a bat."

"Edward Forrester told me you called to let him know I was coming. It makes everything you've said a lie. So I don't really give a good goddamn how bad you got beaten up, or if you can see."

"Isn't it possible that Forrester lied? Think about it. Did

you mention me before he said I had called? This means you must have used my name to get in? Pat?"

"So what?"

"It was a game. My God, I've revealed everything to you, what I do, who I am, details for which, if it was known I told you, I would be sentenced to death. Do you really think I would double-cross you now? Even if I wanted to."

"What makes you think I give a good goddamn what happens to you? You once you told me you couldn't possibly be a spy because you were such a joker, or was it a loser."

"Both," said Max. "I am both."

"Then tell me, what kind of spies exchange secrets in a box of chocolate cherries. What kind of creeps?"

"Every kind, Pat. Spies can be very silly people. Little people who would never get a proper job; nobodies all puffed up with importance. So they put secrets in chocolates. Do you know what Klaus Fuchs, the Englishman who handed us your atomic secrets at Los Alamos, did in his spare time? He was a babysitter for the children of American scientists. Truly. Or you try to blow off Castro's beard with an exploding cigar. Spies are just damaged people who hide behind this idea of national purpose, they lie to their own governments when it is convenient, and they make up exploding cigars. What's the expression? Small potatoes."

He had a good line in bullshit, a witty way of putting things, self-effacing charm, but he had screwed me over once too often. I turned my back and went to the kitchen for a beer because otherwise I would have socked him good and hard, punched him in his already bruised face; I would have made sure it hurt plenty. In the kitchen, I gulped a beer, ate a couple of aspirin, and realized what was really eating me: I couldn't do this on my own; I needed Max Ostalsky.

"Is Forrester CIA?" I said to him when I got back to the living room.

"From what you tell me, yes, and possibly working with our people as well. You say he had dinner with Bounine?"

"Yeah, and Forrester's Russian wife, who apparently dislikes this country plenty, was also there. I saw your pal Bounine. He told me it isn't Adlai Stevenson."

"At dinner?"

"Jesus, Max, you losing your mind? Afterwards. I followed him after. He told me before he jumped. Who in the name of God beat you up? I told you to stay put."

"Jumped?"

"In front of a subway train. I've learned plenty from you, I hinted to Bounine that I knew what his soft spot was, said I knew he preferred men. I wasn't exactly subtle. He gets the message. Before I can stop him, he jumps."

"Is he dead?"

"I didn't wait to find out. I took the chocolates off him. I couldn't find any damn thing. Mrs Forrester passed them to him."

"Give them to me."

"Why?"

"Pat, give me the box," he said. I handed it over to him. Inside two minutes, he had unpeeled an extra layer off the bottom of the box.

"What's there?"

He snorted, a dry laugh without any humor. "A letter for his family." He began to read in Russian.

"What is it?"

"You were supposing there would be great state secrets? Can you please look out of the window, Pat?"

"What for?"

"Please, see if the Plymouth car has returned."

Taking off my coat, I went to the window. "They're back. How did you know?"

"I saw them earlier when I went out," he said and I realized he had put on his heavy gray Russian suit.

"Where the hell did you go? Did they get to you?"

"It could have been a simple mugging. I took a little walk near the East River, I tried to lose my tail but they came up behind me. What you call goons. Thugs. Can you believe me about Forrester? I don't know how this can work if you don't believe me."

"What fucking choice do I have? What were you doing by the East River?"

"I went to the United Nations."

"You really are crazy."

Ostalsky leaned back in the chair and closed his eyes—he was obviously in pain—then sat up, found his pack of smokes, and told me he had gone to Irina Rishkova. He found her in the delegates' lounge having cocktails with some Swedes. "We're in a room with hundreds of people, what can she do to me?"

"Listen, if this assassination is some kind of provocation, a way to stir things up, provoke a war, why now? We're probably going to kill each other anyway. Did your Rishkova tell you that?"

"That's what I've been trying to, would you say, figure out, Pat? If it's true, or if the rumor itself is the provocation, this means a kind of fable-making, a story to tell that makes people react. This may have been planned long ago and activated when it seemed the right time. It can be flexible. It can be conceived with a variety of alternative aspects. I'm not a politician. I'm not much of a strategist. There might have been opportunities that came up at the last minute. There could be mistakes. Miscommunication. I have always privately believed that a war would begin almost by mistake."

"So is it real or a story?"

"You're so literal-minded, you Americans. It can be either, or both."

"Like those idiotic little wooden dolls you gave for gifts, is that it?"

"Yes."

"What's in it?"

"It's for his family, and his wife. He tells them farewell. He says he hopes they survive, and to remember he loves them, no matter what they will hear about him."

"He knew I'd give you the box. He knew you'd find the letter."

"I think he knew there was no hope left for him, so yes. There is also something written in the margin that is addressed to me."

"Go on."

"It says 'On Sunday morning at 10 o'clock, pray for my soul.' "

"What, he believes in God now? Did he get religion or something?"

"I think he means the assassination could take place in a church. What church?"

There were more than a thousand churches in New York, and all I could do was focus on Manhattan, though there was no reason except how would I manage the boroughs, and also if the point of this assassination was a public statement, you wouldn't do it at some storefront, tin-pot church in the Bronx or Brooklyn. Churches. Pray for my soul. This was Bounine, the Communist who had never been in a church, who had been so keen on seeing one. Was he planning to convert? Was he so disgusted with his own system?

Max Ostalsky started for the door.

"Where are you going now?"

"I would like to take a little sleep, and to think about some things."

"I don't believe you."

"I'm sorry."

"No way you're going to sleep now."

Ostalsky ignored me. "There are two cars now, if you look outside, Pat—black Plymouth with somebody from the KGB. They feel they have me trapped now. I am their prey, and no way out."

"Who's in the other car?"

"My old friend, Ed, and a new agent, also FBI, I guess, in an Oldsmobile. Gray. New," said Max. "I should be all right. I'm good at disappearing. You know that. Don't worry."

"Can't your Mr Ustinov help you?"

"I called Washington. Ustinov has been recalled to Moscow."

"How the hell could he have gone to Moscow so fast?"

"I ask myself. I've been watching the television. There have been too many changes in the negotiations, Kennedy and Khrushchev may work for peace but the others, too many who oppose them. Too much insanity and too much pride, and too many opportunities for mistakes. We have to move on the assassination, even if it's only a rumor. We must assume an attempt will be made."

"Sunday. Forrester said something about leaving town by Sunday night."

"I must sleep a little," said Ostalsky again. I didn't believe him. I knew he would find his way out of the house, but he knew what he was doing. I had to believe it; I had to believe him; there was nothing else.

"Use the guest room if you want to sleep. It's one flight up. Go ahead."

"Thank you. I am so tired. I have one favor to ask." From his pocket he produced three airmail letters, on thin greasy blue paper, carefully folded, names written in English and Russian. "Can you be kind and mail my letters for me, please, if things go wrong? If something happens to me."

"Sure."

"Did you see the newspaper this evening? On the table. I left it for you."

What I read froze my bones.

NEW INTELLIGENCE REPORT RELEASED BY U.S. DEMONSTRATING THAT SOVIET MISSILE BASES IN CUBA ARE PROCEEDING AT A RAPID RATE, WITH THE APPARENT INTENTION OF "ACHIEVING FULL OPERATIONAL CAPABILITY AS SOON AS POSSIBLE."

"What does it mean?" I said.

"I think full operational capability means nuclear warheads. That these warheads will be ready. This has not been mentioned before," he said, and then took the newspaper and left, and I heard him going up the stairs.

For a while I sat in the living room. I turned on the television. The news was very bad.

Above the TV Aunt Clara kept framed color portraits of the President and his brother. Handsome, smiling, confident men. If I was going to pray, if I went to church to pray, it would be for these two guys, but I knew too much to believe in anything now. Even JFK couldn't fix this. No even with Bobby's help. We were going to war.

CHAPTER NINE

October 27, '62

<hr>

CUBA SPEEDING BUILD-UP
OF BASES, WARNS OF
FURTHER ACTION

<hr>

O N SATURDAY, THE PAPER reported that 14,214 air force reservists had been called up for active duty. Adlai Stevenson told the Western Allies the US would take military action "in a brief space of time unless action is halted in Cuba". Black Saturday, they were calling it.

Ostalsky was gone. Sometime after he had claimed he was going for a nap, he slipped from the house, down to the vacant basement apartment, and then out, and I could only hope he had evaded the spooks who were tailing him. He left the green canvas book bag behind, as a sign he'd be back, or for me to keep.

Friday night, after Ostalsky had gone, I suddenly thought: Jorge. Jorge, the Cuban guy who worked at the optician's on 8th Street. Nancy's friend. The name in Rica's letter!

Saturday, I went over. The owner, a large bulldog of a man with a goatee and tiny wire-rim glasses said Jorge had not come to work, not yesterday, not this morning. I asked if he had ever met Jorge's friends, a girl named Nancy. He knew Nancy all right; he knew Saul; he made spectacles for Saul. I asked him to give Jorge a message to contact me at home, but I wasn't optimistic.

In the street, people seemed to drag themselves as if their feet were stuck in cement. Tomorrow was the 28th. If we went to war, I wouldn't have to worry about this so far elusive assassination that would take place. I didn't know who the victim was or the assassin. I didn't know anything, and I was exhausted and desperate; my stomach tightened at the idea of it, who, where, when God help me, there were no cops I could ask for help. Anyway, even the cops would go home to sit with their families in useless fallout shelters or in bed, thinking about how to survive or how to die.

Still, for now, the Saturday crowds were out shopping; tourists were buying Mexican wedding dresses at Fred Leighton; teenagers considered a visit to the pictures at the 8th Street Playhouse; a young couple, newlyweds maybe, stood in front of the entrance to Bon Soir, maybe wondering if they should spend their last night on earth listening to music. For a second it buoyed me up.

I got a hot dog and an orange drink at the corner because I was hungry, and then I went home to rethink this damn assassination, no point in planning a night out at a club, or a movie anyway; I was alone.

Wearing gray slacks, a heavy white sweater, a red scarf around her dark hair, Nancy was sitting on my couch.

I wanted to grab her and drive away, up to the Adirondacks, away from the city, from the coming war, from this whole goddamn mess I was in, that Ostalsky was in, that Nancy was in. What was it that Yuri Gagarin had said? "Let's go!"

"What are you doing here?"

"Hi, Pat," she said.

"What do you want? How did you get in?"

"You loaned me a key once, a while back, a night I was going to meet you here, I think."

"Where's your friend, Jorge Dias, the Cuban. Do you know where he is?"

She began to cry, not making a sound, and I had never seen anyone weep that way except when she had told me her father was sick; tears coursed down her face without cease. I handed her some Kleenex, and she wiped her eyes, but the tears kept coming. Nancy removed the red scarf from her hair and wound it nervously around her arm, and then unwound it, and wiped her tears again, this time with the back of her hand.

"Jorge is dead."

"My God. What happened?"

"Rush O'Neill shot him. Just took out his gun and shot him. It's my fault. Jorge never hurt anyone. He was just a nice kid who was trying to save the world. I take it you've met Rush."

"Yes. You told him you knew me."

"He saw us together."

"So he followed me. Very nice. What happened?"

"Please, Pat, please sit down here. Please, can you just sit beside me for a minute and I'll tell you. I can't stop shaking. I saw him do it."

So I sat, and I put my arm around her and we stayed like that for a few minutes, until she sat up straight, wiped her face and began to talk. She stopped crying as if what she had to tell me was too terrible for tears.

"I met Jorge ages ago, I can't even remember, when I went to pick up Daddy's glasses on 8th Street, and he was a sweet kid and I was interested in Cuba. I thought he was for the revolution, for Fidel, he was so passionate about it when he came to the Labor Day party at Daddy's house. He was sweet and eager to please, and a little bit lost, I felt that."

"You found out that he had changed his mind. He had fallen out of love with Castro."

"How did you know that?"

"Did he show you his tattoo?"

Nancy nodded. "He didn't show it to me exactly, but I came into the shop once when he was alone there, and he hurried to put his sweater on. I got a glimpse of something, and I asked him what it was. I said something idiotic like, 'pretty please with Ketchup on it', and you know, Pat, when I want something."

"You can be a bitch."

"Yes."

"So you saw it."

"The worm and the words Cuba Libre and I put it together with the terrible murder of the girl on the High Line; I remembered they published a picture of the tattoo. I asked Jorge if he knew her and he said he didn't, but I knew he was lying, and I thought, well, I'll get it out of him."

"Just for the hell of it, because you can get any man to tell you anything?"

"Not just that. He told me a few days ago that he did know her, and that he knew this man who was murdered out on the pier. They were his friends, he said, and he seemed desperate. I said I would try to help him."

"So you introduced him to your close chum, Rush O'Neill."

"Rush knew I had a Cuban friend, so I told him about Jorge, and he says, I'd like to meet him. Says we can help him. He's on our side, after all, and I introduced them, and everything was fine, we had dinner at Seville, that old Spanish place, and we talked, and Rush orders a lot of red wine and he promises to help Jorge. Rush calms him down, he has a certain manner, he makes Jorge believe that they were on the same side and of course, in a way they were—Jorge wanted Castro out, and so does Rush."

"A match made in heaven."

"I thought so. Jorge certainly thought so. He confided to us that he had some important information, that something is going to happen, and his friends, both murdered, had the rest of it. Rush says, of course, I see, for the sake of security. Very wise. Why don't you tell me? Rush says. Maybe I can help. To be honest, I think Jorge got cold feet. The next day, he came to my apartment by himself."

"What? Then why? Why in the name of Jesus, did you do this? Christ, Nancy, it would kill your father."

"Let me finish."

"Go on."

"I had a bad feeling about all of it. Rush had been pretty edgy lately, and I knew Jorge was just a pawn for him. I got Jorge to tell me when and where they were to meet, it was set for Thursday night. Jorge said they were meeting at Hector's, it's a diner in the meatpacking area, and Rush likes it because nobody you know ever goes there, it's on Little West 12th, near the High Line. God, Pat, I'd never been around there but once in my life when Daddy wanted to show me the meat-packers, and talk to me about working men. Anyhow, I managed to wait until they came out, and Rush says goodnight to Jorge and gets into that ridiculous boat of a car."

"The Impala."

"I always hated it."

"Not a cool car. You wouldn't want anyone giving you a lift in it, would you? Not like mine."

"No," she said, clutching her wad of wet Kleenex. "Hard to believe I ever cared about that kind of thing. It was like a movie. I saw the car slow down, I heard Rush call out Jorge's name, Jorge walked over to the car, and Rush shot him and drove away."

"What did you do?"

"I crossed the street. When I felt Jorge's pulse, it was too late. I've never even seen a dead body before. I thought he was dead. I went to a payphone and called the operator and I told her. I told her to send an ambulance or the police, I couldn't leave that poor kid like that, so I waited in a doorway until I saw the ambulance and some cops."

I reached for the phone. "I better call somebody and tell them who did it. You don't want O'Neill running around shooting people."

"Please, Pat. Please don't do that right now. If he finds

out somebody has reported him, he'll know it's me, and I'll be next. Oh, God, I'm so sorry for everything. I'm guilty of Jorge's death."

"Don't be so melodramatic. You're guilty of much more than that."

"Before you do anything, maybe we should talk to Max."

"Max is gone."

"No."

"Where is he?"

"He's safe. He's at my place, he showed up last night."

"I'm surprised you didn't give him up."

"I'm not going to give Max up."

"You knew he was a KGB agent all along?"

"No. Not all along."

"When?"

"I'll tell you. I promise."

"Your place can't be safe."

"It is. Nobody's going to look for him there, because if they thought about it, they'd ask Rush, or his buddy Captain Logan, and Rush thinks I'm a good girl, I'm one of his girls, I'm a patriotic little American. I'm fucking red white and blue. Sorry. He thinks I only ever used Max for information."

"Didn't you?"

"No. But you don't have to believe me."

CHAPTER TEN

October 27, '62

IN HER APARTMENT THAT night, Nancy held the pink Princess phone in both hands, staring at it, willing it to ring. The TV was on, the sound low. She had called Rush O'Neill, told him she was frightened and alone, and asked if he would take her out for a drink.

How convincing she had been, imploring O'Neill in her husky low voice, her sweetest, most seductive manner. He said he'd call her back. In her little apartment on West 4th Street, where you could always smell the rancid stink of pizza from the store downstairs, we sat and waited.

Max was asleep in the bedroom.

"There's only a tiny window on the airshaft, you know, so I put him there. But I put a sheet up over it in case," Nancy said. "I don't think anyone saw him come in. He said he got away from your Uncle Jack's house without anyone following him. Said he thought he had dumped his tail, or both of them. He needed sleep. He could hardly keep his eyes open, and he can't see without his glasses."

"Too bad Jorge's dead, or he could fix it, the eye-glasses, I mean."

"You're right to be cynical, God knows. I'm sorry, God, I'm sorry. I've been a fool, and I'm sorry. I'll always be sorry. I was a dope, really a naive idiot. I thought I could get them to leave my father alone, or maybe there was more, and I let myself get sucked in because I was flattered."

"What are you talking about?"

"You remember you saw me that morning with Rush at the Hip Bagel? I had seen him around, maybe starting a year ago, and then he just kept running into me and saying he was a professor, and after I agreed to have lunch with him, he takes me to a really fancy lunch at Charles' and he tells me he's FBI. Says to me, while we are drinking Martinis, all very cool and sophisticated, says if I help them they would let Daddy alone. It was bad last year, the agents hanging around outside the house. Daddy was deeply involved with civil rights, he was sure the FBI did at least one black bag job on him, you know? They planted stuff in my dad's study, make him look seditious, like he didn't believe in non-violence, which of course he does, he knows Dr King, he believes. They made him look like some crazy man with pamphlets on making bombs. By then he was sick, too."

"How is he?"

"Dying," said Nancy. "Rush told me he would get the agents off my father's back, he was high enough up to do that. He just kept after me, and he was charming. Your dad is sick, he would say, and we can be compassionate. When Virginia—Daddy is so lucky to have her—she told me how sick he was, I thought OK, I'll make a deal, I'll do it. Rush kept his part. Daddy told me he felt much better that the

FBI seemed to be leaving him alone. He was suspicious, but he felt maybe they had given up on him, and turned their attention purely to Cuba, or something. He didn't like it, either way, but he was tired. He was too sick to do much of anything."

"What did you think, for God's sake?"

"I thought the FBI had kept their word. I was too much of an imbecile to realize they didn't care about their word, they have no honor, and that they would want more from me. More and more. My God, I was such a fool. Do you know what COINTELPRO is?"

"More or less."

"Well, to Rush, it's sacred. He never told me in so many words, he never trusted me completely, but I was useful to him, because his big game, much much bigger than my father, was surveying, infiltrating, discrediting and disrupting domestic political organizations. All of it. He would say it like that. He would list the things he could do, he'd take me to some swell restaurant, and order martinis or whisky sours, and tell me what he wanted. And I had access to them all. Students. Teachers. Writers."

"Your friends in Brooklyn Heights?"

"Yes. Then Max comes to New York. Rush is thrilled. Says I should make friends with Max. Good friends."

"A real Red. Like you caught the big fish. So you just pulled him into your web, and told the FBI what you found out."

"I told them stuff I thought they probably knew like that I went to the Vanguard with Max, or his talks to students at NYU about the Soviet Union. Rush wanted to know who was in the audience. I told him. Probably I slipped and said other things. I was careless. I started feeling queasy about it when Rush showed up at our Labor Day party. We always keep the door open, people come and go, and when I saw Rush, I was terrified."

"When's he going to call, for Christ's sake?"

"He'll call."

"Because no man can resist you."

"I'll call him again."

"Wait a few minutes. I don't want you to seem too anxious. What did Rush tell you about Jorge?"

"I haven't talked to him since he did it."

"Killed him. Point blank."

"Yes. God, Pat, Rush shot Jorge just out of the blue, in front of me. Like it was nothing. I had never even seen a gun, except yours. I hate guns."

"Some little revolutionary you'd have made. Anything else?"

"I didn't know."

"Didn't know what?"

"They would kill people like Jorge. In New York."

"So it was OK in the Soviet Union, or anywhere you couldn't see it. Is that it? You wanted to join the revolution so long as you could get me to drive you around?"

"I don't know. I'm sorry, Pat. I am so sorry. Recently Rush started acting crazy. After the President spoke Monday night, I was at Daddy's for it, so I met Rush at a bar over on Seventh Avenue. I saw him get out of his car and he looked awful. He was furious at JFK. He said the President was a pussy. I had no idea what he meant. I said what's the matter? He said he couldn't tell me yet, then he kissed my cheek and left." Nancy wiped her face. "What should I do?"

"We need Max. When did you know he was KGB?"

"Not for sure until I saw him last night, and he told me everything. I swear to you. Rush told me he was sure about it, of course,but they think every Soviet is an agent. You're a Red, you even speak the damn Russian language, you're KGB."

"But Max is KGB."

"Yes. Please, Pat, go wake him up. Can you make coffee? And turn up the TV."

I got Max up. Then the three of us sat drinking coffee in Nancy's little living room.

A report on the news showed empty streets in New York, Washington DC, Miami. The other channels went on with regular programming, as if nothing had happened. When the bombs fell, the TV would still be playing—Hitchcock, or the *Tonight Show*, that new guy Johnny Carson in a funny hat, Clint Eastwood would ride the range in *Rawhide*. It was my fantasy that night, this idea that nobody would be left, but the TV would play on and on; even after we were all dead, even after the bombs had wiped us out. Rosemary Clooney would be singing, and Lucy would be there, in re-runs, or her new show without Desi, just Lucy and Ethel wacky and comforting; and on it would go. Somewhere I read Lucy had been a member of the Communist Party, way back, once upon a time, but I didn't know if it was true, or care.

All that day and into the night, between the sitcoms and the variety shows, there were reports of different versions of negotiations: letters between Kennedy and Khrushchev; rumors of Soviet nuclear subs off the coast; Cuba demanding the USSR move on America. On WINS radio, when I couldn't stand the news anymore, I listened to Murray the K. He played the Ronettes. He introduced a single by that group I saw in the Liverpool basement, not out in the USA yet, said Murray, but gonna change the world. Rumors on the air of people fleeing New York; the bridges and tunnels jammed with refugees, just like my boss Murphy had told me. People had purchased inflatable boats and were intending to take to the rivers. The banks had seen a run on cash on Friday. Now, the banks were closed for the weekend, and there was no way to get at your money.

Nancy sat down. Silently, Max tried to fix his eye-glasses. We waited. I got up, smoked; I was like a caged animal in that little apartment where I had always wanted to be, with Nancy.

The phone rang.

"Nancy?"

"I've got it." She ran back into the living room and picked it up.

For a while Nancy spoke into the phone, then hung up and said, "He'll meet me in an hour. I asked him to meet me at a restaurant on Greenwich Avenue. Nobody I know ever goes there. What do you want me to ask him."

"Get the coffee. And tell me which restaurant."

"Yes." Nancy went to the kitchen and brought out a tray with the pot and some cups, and a bottle of brandy.

"And put on a nice dress, and heels."

By now I was sure it was Rush O'Neill who was the assassin, and I was ready to push Nancy into his arms if necessary; heartless of me, but what else could I do, and maybe she could save her soul. O'Neill was FBI; he knew his way around; he had silver hair, and it seemed to me he was certainly the man Tommy described, the devil as he called him, a man with bright white hair he had seen under the streetlight.

Sunday. A few hours left.

"Does he trust you?" I said to Nancy.

"Yes."

"He's in love with you?"

"Oh, Pat, darling, not every man is in love with me."

"But you played the part."

"When I had to."

"I need to know where O'Neill is going to be tomorrow. I need you to find out. It might be a church. Max? You listening? I also want to ask you to keep Max here with you tomorrow."

"Yes."

"You're sure?"

"I'm sure. Would you like some brandy with your coffee? I have a bottle of cherry brandy."

"Yes."

Max drank the brandy steadily without speaking.

"Go change," I said to Nancy.

"Do you mind if I do something?" said Ostalsky.

"Like what?"

"Just so we know if Nancy is returning alone or with O'Neill."

"Sure."

After Nancy had changed into her red dress and pearls, Ostalsky explained the alarm system he was going to set up with some string and a bicycle bell he had removed from Nancy's bike, parked in the hallway.

"It's very primitive," said Max. "But at least there's a chance. Nancy, when you get to the front door downstairs, can you find a way to pull this string? I'll make it as invisible as I can. I'll attach it inside to the lock, so your key, when you will turn it, will connect with it. If you pull it once, you're alone. Twice, O'Neill is with you. Does that sound all right?"

"It sounds like a cheap spy novel," she said.

"I am a cheap spy."

"I should go."

After she left, we sat waiting, me and Max, in the dark, listening to every noise in the old tenement building, the sound of a guitar, the sound of some cats shrieking, the radiator banging. We waited for the sound of steps on the stairs, and the bicycle bell. We sat with the lights off in the dark, drinking the brandy, and when the bell rang once, a brief, barely audible sound, we jumped, both of us.

I took my gun out of my pocket and crept down the stairs, though there wasn't much point in the creeping. Every step on the old loose boards produced a kind of wooden scream. It was Nancy.

"I don't have long," she said. "I told Rush I had to go home because I got my period suddenly, and he was embarrassed, he called it my time of the month, so he drove me here. He's downstairs, Pat. Go on up, I'll follow you. Can you turn the lights on when you get upstairs, he'll think it's odd if I don't put on some lights."

Ahead of Nancy I went to the apartment, told Max to stay low, and put on the lights. Nancy arrived, and said, very softly, "I think Rush has pretty much lost his mind, and he just talked and talked, going around and around, telling me he had to save America from the Red curse, that unless he did what he had to, we would be overtaken by the Communists, and how God would not forgive him if he failed. He says only General Curtis LeMay ever understood the right way. That LeMay should be in charge. Might be in charge. This is a man, LeMay I mean, who wants to blow up the world. My God, Pat, I never realized that Rush was quite insane. I'm just going to change." She ran into the bedroom and put on the sweater and slacks she had worn earlier. "What on earth have I done? He made me promise I'd spend the night with him. He's staying in town. He's never done that before, not with me, at least; he's very paranoid about his wife who's somewhere in Westchester, but he said this was so important and it meant so much to him, so I said I'd think about it, but he insisted. I told him I knew something big was on, and I wanted to be part of it, I implied it was the price of my spending the night with him, and he said fine but I'd have to go to mass with him tomorrow morning, and I said, darling, I'm Jewish. He just laughed. I have to go now. By the way, if this matters, he says we're going to Old St Patrick's, isn't that where your Aunt and Uncle go, Pat? Didn't you take me to hear Christmas carols there once?"

"Yes."

"Well, so long, Pat. Bye, Max. Take care of yourselves," Nancy said, and without looking back, she went out the door and down the stairs.

"Do you trust her?"

"I don't know," Max said.

"Could she be telling us a story? Could she be whatever the hell you call it, a double agent or some garbage? I'm going to Old St Pat's."

"I'll go with you."

"You can't. I looked outside, they're back."

"All of them?"

"Just yours. Your friends in the black Plymouth."

"Get rid of them."

"How?"

"Call the police, not your own station, but a different one, and tell them the KGB is parked on West 4th Street," said Max.

"Do you think they'll believe it?"

"Perhaps not. But they may send a police car to check."

He was right. I muffled the phone with a handkerchief, and by some miracle I got hold of a guy in the First Precinct. Said he'd send someone by for a look.

"Wait," Max said. "Give them half an hour." From his pocket he took a photograph and said, "Would you like to see a picture of my family? I don't suppose I will ever see them again in my life." He stared at the black and white snapshot, as if he could see his lost Russian life come alive. "This was my last visit to the dacha."

"Before Nina left you."

"Yes. Look, here is my mother and my aunt Sveta, Sasha's mother, dancing together in their summer dresses and white sandals. My mother is the one with the short dark hair. My father is reading his newspapers. Here is Nina, with Sasha, on the grass playing cards. He always cheats."

A tall, dark, willowy woman in shorts, her long legs stretched out on the grass, Nina was laughing into the camera. Under his breath Max said, "I can smell the grass. Sasha's wife and little boy are inside sleeping."

"You're taking the picture?"

"Yes.

377

"It's hot for May, the countryside is green, and we think, who knows when we will see each other? Sasha has been my best friend always. He has been called back to his naval unit where he is a missile engineer. So we are a little drunk; and we drink and sing and pretend to weep, Russian-style, but also we laugh at our stupid jokes. When we are little, we had a reputation for fooling around. Why am I telling you this?

"Then Sasha tells me something I've been thinking about. He tells me his father, my uncle, the General, is out for some kind of revenge. Revenge for my mother's sister, my aunt Sveta, Sasha's mother, they split up right after Sasha was born. It was his fault, but this means it has been eating him up ever since that time.

"I've been trying to recall exactly what else Sasha said about his father, that this is a hate-filled man who wants to return to the way of Stalin when he was important and happy and had a beautiful wife. But then Khrushchev came in, and he lost some of his power. His wife was already gone a long time, but he picks this like a, do you say, scab? It made him very bitter, except for me."

"Except for you."

"I was his favorite, he told everybody. Only Maxim Stepanovich pays attention, he says, and I've been think-ing about this, Pat, about how easy it was for me to enter the KGB program, and how I got the fellowship to come to America. I knew my uncle always had, how would you say, put in a good word for me, but now I think it is much more. I would be his personal spy? He knew many men in the KGB, of course. I would be his for whatever he wanted."

I didn't know what to say.

"You see, my uncle believed we should strike at America first. Strike at Cuba, so the Americans would hit back."

According to the news on TV, the bombing would begin overnight, and I knew that if there were nukes, not much more than five percent of lower Manhattan would survive.

The black Plymouth remained outside. I got ready to go. I had a gun, and in the little kitchen Max found a knife.

"A knife, Pat. A knife with a dull blade, this is crazy."

"You're not coming."

"Listen to me. I told you I went to the United Nations on Thursday, and I insist to Irina Rishkova we go to her office so I can take a look at some Soviet newspapers, and I make like I'm a little bit tipsy, so in her office, in front of many reporters, I kiss her on both cheeks and I say, 'I hear you have some letters from my Aunt Sveta.' "

"Did she know anything?"

"She gets flustered in her pretty blue American suit. She's worried. I say, 'Have you seen your friend, Edward Forrester lately? Did you see him yesterday? He was here, wasn't he?' She's nervous, and I ask where is her friend Bounine. She doesn't want to answer. People are turning away from their TV sets to look at us. She knows I am desperate enough to expose her. I was very charming."

"I'll just bet."

"I thank her for the photographs she had given to Rica Valdes, and for helping me stay in touch with my family at home. I make her understand that I know she instructed Bounine to order me to eliminate Rica Valdes. I ask if she also sent Bounine to the pier that night, as back-up, in case I fail."

She says can we speak somewhere quiet, and I say no, the office is fine, but I keep my voice lower, and she whispers to me, yes—not in so many words, but she did this. I failed to kill Rica. Bounine has failed to do his job, also he has his personal problems. So Rishkova has also failed. She's scared. She doesn't know who I'm working for now."

"You're telling me this is all about, I don't know, some bureaucracy, some order of command?"

"Of course. I also ask if Rishkova knows about a certain plan."

"The assassination."

"Yes."

"She knows."

"What did she tell you."

"She only knows there is a plan. She can't, or won't say anything else, and then I make a, can you say, happy discovery. On her desk is a little box, very expensive, very old, a painted Russian box. As soon as I reach for it, she pushes me away and tries to grab it."

"'What a beautiful object,' I say. 'I must look at it.'

"'It's nothing. Just a gift.'

"I pick it up. When I remove the lid, I see there is a little silver plaque inside, and I know I have her."

"Her soft spot. Can we just move on?"

"Sure. Yes. It was a very personal inscription to her, engraved in silver, the kind you send to a lover, and it is from my uncle, the General, Fyodor Grigoryevich. I say to her, 'I thought you were friends with my Aunt Sveta, I thought she was your old good friend who asks you to post letters to me.' She says, yes, of course, but also with Fyodor Grigoryevich, and so I know. She is his mistress. My aunt and uncle never speak. They hate each other. You can't be friends with both. I tell her I know they are lovers. And she blushes. Such a simple thing. Rishkova is not a woman who blushes. In some way, she is proud of their love affair.

"They will take her lovely job away. It will be like dominoes. One, two, three, all fall down. My uncle can't protect her."

"Why not?"

"If she has failed, he won't risk anything for her. Where are the police, do you think?"

I looked out of the window. Only the black Plymouth stood at the curb.

"I've been writing to my father. Also Nina and my mother, in case, you understand, this means if I never..."

"I understand."

"My father told me that writing helps him to remember."

"He's a spy, too?"

Max laughed. "He's a doctor. But he's smart, and he pays more attention to politics than I do, what happens in and out of the Kremlin. He used to talk to me when we were at our dacha in the countryside."

"He can only talk politics in the country?"

"Easier," said Max. "Less people are paying attention when you're at your dacha. Cottage."

"Jesus, man, that's some country. So what did your pa say to you?"

"He tried to tell me there are men who were determined to return to the times of Stalin."

"Get rid of Khrushchev."

"You could be a good spy, Pat."

"Thanks, man, it's a big compliment coming from you.

But if we're all dead, how will that help our enemies, since they'll be dead, too."

"Politicians never quite think that way."

"You want to give your pop a call? I know it's expensive, but go ahead, it will be OK with Nancy."

"I don't think I can just pick up the phone and say, hello, Dad, my pal Pat, who's an American cop, he and I think there's an assassin loose, and can you tell me if my uncle, the general, put this into place, and got me sent me to the United States. Dear father, would you have any ideas about it? I can't call him at all, with people listening. This would put my family at risk. And Nancy."

My mind wandered to all the unfinished business in my life. The city was dead quiet, a fearful deep strange quiet I never heard again until the days after the planes hit the Twin Towers. "A pre-emptive strike," I said.

"Like your General Curtis LeMay."

"I told you about the photograph Forrester has, with LeMay when he was a young soldier. There were others with him, Rush O'Neill and Captain Logan, who wanted me off the job, or dead if necessary. Max, wasn't your uncle a soldier at the Yalta Conference?"

"Yes. He received a Parker pen from an American. He gave it to me before I left Moscow."

"Forrester was there. He told me."

"I don't think he's the killer. He's too valuable."

"Who to?"

"Both sides."

"There are four of them in that photograph of Forrester's take of the 305 Bomb Squad, with Curtis LeMay."

"Who was the fourth?"

The fourth man's face had been obscured by the wing of a B-17, and two mechanics, young, looking like kids, with crew cuts, grinning. "I don't know. It's O'Neill. It's him. He told Nancy it's Old St Pat's. We have nothing else."

"Who is the target?"

From outside I suddenly heard police sirens. "Good," said Max.

"I have to go," I said. "In case O'Neill is looking for me, in case he has someone in front of my building. I have to go home, I have to make them think I'm home with all the lights on. I need to put on the lights."

"You're not safe in the streets."

"I'll be fine." I looked out of the window. "There's a couple of uniforms out there, they're talking to somebody in the black Plymouth. I'll go now."

"Just wait until they all go away. Let's have another drink," he said.

So we sat in the dark, trapped in that apartment, somebody in the building playing a pretty version of "Autumn in New York". We finished the brandy and waited for the ring of a bicycle bell, in case Nancy had come back a second time, but she didn't, and I thought about all the things I had never done and would probably never do. There was nothing else to do except wait for the bombs. We drank, and again the TV droned on with news of the end of the world.

PART FIVE

CHAPTER 1

October 28, '62

U.S. AND SOVIET REACH ACCORD ON CUBA; KENNEDY ACCEPTS KHRUSHCHEV PLEDGE TO REMOVE MISSILES UNDER U.N. WATCH

THE NEWSPAPERS DIDN'T HAVE the story until Monday morning, but by Sunday everyone knew. Crowds gathered in front of the *Post* and the *Times*; the news was on TV. It was out, so that by Sunday morning at Old St Pat's, people were streaming into church. Everyone was smiling, and waving to friends, and crossing themselves. Thank God. Thank the Lord.

Almost everyone at the church was local: the Italian ladies in black and the husbands they dragged with them; the few remaining Irish parishoners like my aunt and uncle who still came to what they had considered their church back in the day when the Italians were nobody and were made to attend a separate mass downstairs; even artists from their lofts on the Bowery in spattered paint work pants and wrinkled shirts, a two-dollar tie thrown on to show respect.

The bells rang out like crazy at Old St Pat's. All morning they had been ringing from all over the Village, from St Anthony's and Our Lady of Pompeii, and maybe those stuck-up Episcopalian places on Fifth Avenue and over on Broadway. Bells ringing; people hugging, laughing, crying in relief. We did it. We faced down the Russkis.

Just outside the main church door on Mott Street, I stood and watched the faces of the men removing their hats. Teenagers, uncomfortable in their good shoes, eyed each other and figured out how to sit together, thigh to thigh in the back pews.

For the first time in a week, everyone felt safe, the relief was palpable, the threat of nuclear war had receded, time had stopped dragging itself from hour to hour and had speeded up to a normal pace.

"He did it. Our President. He won. We won." I could hear the voices as they repeated what they had heard on the television and read in the morning papers. Kennedy and Khrushchev had made a deal on Cuba; Khrushchev had agreed to turn back the ships; there was to be no war. No war, they said. It was over.

Miraculously the world had spun back on its axis; miraculously, our beloved President had done it, he had saved the world. The President had stared them down. Our President. Our Jack Kennedy. JFK belonged to everyone, but he was a Catholic, and an Irishman; and didn't he visit

Old St Pat's once, when he was a senator? Yes, at least once. Didn't he say how much he admired our church?

It had become a legend among the faithful at Old St Pat's, and there were photographs of Kennedy near the entrance. Pictures of all of them—the parents, Bobby, the others. All the Kennedys had come by, one time or another. Glancing at them, Bobby Kennedy caught my eye. He was a tough bird, but in the photograph with Ethel his wife, he was smiling. He seemed to catch my eye, seemed to understand something about me. One day, he would be President.

"Oh yes, he knows we were first, the first cathedral in New York," said a woman holding a tiny baby in a blue knitted blanket. "Of course," said somebody else. Sure. St Patrick's uptown was too gaudy, an upstart, one of the ladies in a homemade hat—this one with bright yellow flowers on it—said to another, then crossed herself hastily in case it was some kind of blasphemy.

Almost lulled into lethargy, exhausted by lack of sleep, I nearly missed Homer Logan when he strolled into the church, shaking hands, removing his navy blue alpaca overcoat.

I stayed out of sight, behind a crowd of people. Shirley Cowan had told me Logan attended an Episcopalian church. Had left St Pat's long ago.

What was he doing here? I watched him, and a woman with a grey mink stole over her pink suit, a pillbox hat on her head. A cop in uniform saluted as Logan passed him and went to the front row.

For a while, I was caught in the crowd; friends of my uncle and aunt who had known me from childhood stopped to shake my hand. "Paddy, dear, how are you? Married yet?

You know Terry Sullivan's daughter is very nice, single, a college graduate."

People couldn't stop chatting. The President, God bless him, had succeeded; he had won. Russian missiles were being crated up and shipped home, announced one of the men, a plump fellow in a navy blue suit. He had his morning newspaper with him and was reading out bits of it. "Turned back," he said. "Incredible. God bless him."

"And God bless Bobby, too," said his wife, adjusting her red hat and then crossing herself. "Without him, the President would not have made it. God bless Bobby."

My head was tight, pulse racing, sweat dribbling down my back, under my suit and my overcoat. Was Nancy coming to mass with O'Neill? Was she safe? Did Ostalsky stay at her place?

I remembered that day in Washington Square when I helped Max Ostalsky buy his first hot dog. I remembered how he had reminded me of a new convert faced with communion wafers and thinking: do I chew? Bite? Swallow?

The crowd streamed into the church. Women in their going to church hats, men in their Sunday suits. I watched everyone closely as they jammed the pews. It was cold inside the cavernous old cathedral but nobody seemed to mind. I saw myself looking—for what? For something, someone, a clue, a familiar face, an assassin, for Rush O'Neill. Or for a Russian? Why not Rishkova? A woman can use a gun. This is what Russians do; they kill people. Why not her? Why not Max Ostalsky? Bounine had been interested in seeing Old St Pat's, but didn't Ostalsky ask first? Didn't he pester me about never having been inside a church from the day we met in the park?

I moved into the church and found a place on the aisle where I could get up easily. I pushed up the collar of my coat, though I knew it made me look like an undertaker. Christ, was it Homer Logan? Was he the killer? No, he wouldn't risk it. It had to be Rush O'Neill. Didn't it?

The altar was banked with bronze and yellow chrysanthemums that somebody had splashed out on; this was no longer a rich church.

I had been here since very early in the morning, after I left Nancy's, went home briefly, put on a dark suit, and now I sat, looking for a possible target. But who was the target?

Nobody is at the church when I arrive in the dark.

In those pre-dawn early morning hours, I work my way around it. Either side of the vestibule are staircases to the organ loft. The doors to the loft are open. From it, I can look out over the church itself. Is this where the killer would hide?

Downstairs, in the body of the church itself, behind the altar is the sacristy room, but this door has locks. Do the priests lock up when they change into their vestments? I can't remember. I was never an altar boy. As a teenager I hated church, and when I kidded around with the other kids, I embarrassed my Auntie Clara.

All this time, I think about the day ahead, about the masses, about the crowds of people, and I think about the killer. Who is he? Who is his target?

And then, just as it gets light outside, when the ladies come in to arrange the flowers, the terror I feel rises. It pushes me out of the church onto Mott Street. There are lights on at Uncle Jack's house. Why is he back? I don't want him and Auntie Clara coming to church. From the corner phone, I call and Jack answers.

"How did you know we were back? What time is it? Jesus, Paddy, it's too early for calling on a Sunday. We drove half the night to get here. Well, it's good to hear you, boyo. It's a fine day. Looks like the world is going to survive a while longer."

"I want you to do something. Uncle Jack, are you listening?"

"Sure, sure, Paddy."

"I want you to keep Auntie Clara from going to church. And you. Tell her you don't feel good, or whatever the hell you tell her when you want something, OK? You're good at all that blarney."

"I am that. But why?"

"I can't say right now. You have to trust me. You told me you would always trust me."

"What is this? It won't be easy. She made me drive all the way from the Adirondacks because Father Sean told her somebody important would be attending mass today."

"Who is it?"

"She says the priest didn't know, but she has her own ideas. I say, 'So, you're telling me President Kennedy is coming to church?' but she's not that crazy. But I placate her, you know, kiddo? I figure it's the Archbishop, something like that, Clara once told me he was a lovely man. It will be hard to keep her from going to mass."

"Just keep her home. Just do it. Please," I say. "Tell her there's no way on earth the Archbishop is coming. Everyone will be at St Pat's uptown. Take her there if you have to, Uncle Jack. Tell her I said so. Tell her I heard it from my sources. Jesus, Jack, if you have to lie, just tell her I said Father Sean told me there's trouble brewing, keep the ladies home. Figure something out, but do it."

CHAPTER TWO

October 28, '62

T HE MASS SEEMED TO go on for hours, the lulling rise and fall of Latin, familiar, reassuring, mysterious, and for me now, meaningless. The words I'd been forced to learn by heart every Saturday morning at Catechism class when I was nine. *Credo in unum Deum, Patrem omnipoténtem, Factorem caeli et terrae.*—I believe in God the Father Almighty, Maker of heaven and earth—I wasn't sure what I believed any more, I hadn't been in a church for a long time except for weddings and funerals. Something in me stirred, though, as the great organ played the first notes of "Jesu Joy of Man's Desiring," a piece my grandmother loved to play on a battered old harmonium.

From where I was sitting, I could survey the whole congregation, but it was Homer Logan who had my attention. I could just see him, up at the front, rising, sitting, kneeling, but also glancing backward from time to time as if looking for somebody in the crowd.

As the priest concluded the offertory, I watched the trickle of people stepping from their pews turn to a river as they moved up the main aisle to take communion, including some guys from the Gambino crew. Logan was on his feet and then he was behind Gambino's men. Maybe it was this he had come for. Maybe he was after these men whose social club was around the corner on Sullivan Street. Logan was obsessed with the Mob.

I pushed forward. An old woman in black gave me a dirty look for pushing in, but I kept moving. I gave her a deeply pious look, and genuflected, making the sign of the cross. She had a sour expression when everybody else was expressing joy.

At the front of the communion line, a young redhead in a frilly pink, blue and white polka dot blouse smiled at me, and let me in front of her as if she thought I was desperate, and I needed the communion. Maybe I did.

The crisis was over. The world was safe. No bombs would fall. But if Ostalsky was right, and I believed him, by the end of the day there would be an event so terrible, it would all heat up again. There was no safe place.

Anxious, I kept my hand on the gun in my pocket, trying to look at faces in the crowd. Nobody here would make a worthwhile target for an assassin.

I waited until the priest came and took a host from the chalice and held it up. It was years since I'd done this. I barely looked at the host, as I took it in my mouth.

Adlai Stevenson was off the list. After I had called Uncle Jack from the corner, I phoned a cop I knew who worked for the United Nations. He said he had seen Ambassador Stevenson enter the building earlier. I told him to make sure Stevenson stayed inside, and I hung up; I didn't know if he would do it; I couldn't know.

"*Corpus Christi*," said the priest and I saw Homer Logan leave with his wife in the gray mink stole.

I said, "*Amen.*"

A man I hadn't seen earlier appeared, a man in a dark gray coat, collar up, holding his hat near his face. As soon as he saw me looking, he hurried to the Mulberry Street exit. When I ran after him, into the narrow corridor, out of the door, there was nobody around. The street was empty.

In the church again, I heard the words: *Ite, missa est*, 'The mass is ended'. As people began to leave, the organ played familiar, haunting arpeggios and a little boy, not more than ten, got up and sang Gounod's "Ave Maria" in that kind of clear pure voice that, on any other day, would have put tears in my eyes. Instead, I was sweating. My hands were cold.

Ostalsky. It had to be Ostalsky. He was a Red. He was a survivor. He followed orders. There were people over there who wanted us dead, who wanted a war. Ostalsky been willing to kill me in the warehouse; he had been waiting for me; I had walked into a trap. He had taken Nancy away from me. He was a Communist who loved Fidel Castro and hated the young Cubans who fought against the bastard.

I would get Ostalsky. I would stop him. I would make up for the Cubans who had been murdered, for Susana Reyes and Rica Valdes, and Jorge Dias. I would make up for the sucker I had been. I would kill the bastard by myself. If there is a God, I said to myself, help me. God help me.

Trouble was, I didn't believe any more. Maybe I had never believed. Max Ostalsky had been right when he told me he wished he understood about God. He knew there was no God to help him; and I knew it.

The organ loft had been empty earlier, but an assassin could have climbed up during the mass. It was where I would have concealed myself. A sniper's rifle would do it, one you had stashed in the loft, up under the high vaulted ceiling. A trained sniper could pick off anybody in the church. Wasn't Ostalsky trained? Wasn't he a crack shot with a pistol? Why not a sniper rifle?

Between masses, I crept up to the loft, but I knew I only had a few minutes. It was a busy day, people were everywhere, two priests hearing confessions, a group of little children in their white suits and frilly dresses making their first communion. In my mind, I saw the massacre. I saw the killer with his rifle aiming at his target, not caring who he picked off; I saw the little kids with blood on their white dresses, and tiny suits, the white shoes and little veils.

Looking down, I could see the whole of the church, the length of it stretching from Mott Street to the backdoor that led onto Mulberry. A city block. Near the Mulberry Street door was some scaffolding and large canvas tarps.

From up here, a rifle would do it. Had somebody stashed the rifle beforehand? I crawled all over the organ loft. Nothing.

Who was the victim? Someone important. Someone whose murder would provoke trouble, even a war. My gut turned over. Something had begun to form in the darkest part of me; something impossible, unbearable, too terrible to put into words. The name, the victim, I couldn't bring myself to acknowledge. Paranoia washed over me.

"Detective, can I help?" It was one of the church ladies I knew from when I was a kid. She saw me come down from the loft. I made an excuse and hurried away.

All day, and into the evening, I sat through the services. What surprised me most was that at the 7 p.m. mass, a woman I recognized but could not place right away came in just before the service began and sat towards the back of the church. She seemed middle-aged and was nicely dressed in a green coat and a matching hat, the brim covering part of her face. She sat quietly, no beads in her gloved hands, no missal either. This is what struck me about her, and then, at some point, as if startled by a noise, she looked up and I saw her face.

It was Muriel Miller. Mrs Miller, Ostalsky's host, the woman who had taken him shopping to show him capitalism at its most delightful and played *Swan Lake* and invited his friends for dinner. She was Jewish. What the hell was Muriel Miller doing in a Catholic church? I remembered then what she had said to me in her kitchen. "I do love a nice mass, Pat. You know, I sometimes go to Old St Patrick's for the music."

Mass over, I looked around the church one more time. Under the tarps near the Mulberry Street door, beneath the scaffolding I had seen from the organ loft, was some broken statuary. Nobody there. By then Muriel Miller had gone.

It was getting late, and October 28th—the day the assassination was to have taken place—was coming to an end.

CHAPTER THREE

October 28, '62

THE STEPS DOWN TO the mortuary vaults were outside the front door of the church. I lifted the metal cover, and hurried down, pulling the cover back into place.

Inside it was cold with a musty smell of death, water somewhere dripping onto old stones. A single bulb burned. This part of the church had been here since 1809, stone from the original church before it burned down and was rebuilt sixty years later. All that history that had been jammed into our heads as kids, along with the religious stuff, I knew it by heart, but I had only been down here into the vaults a half dozen times, when somebody important, some priest or bishop the family knew, was interred.

I had a small flashlight and I flicked it around the walls, the light making shadows. Sounds seemed to come from inside the vaults, like the dead whimpering. The dead calling out for me to save them.

The place had always scared me. It was the silence, and the smell. It was as if I was three years old again, terrified of the dark, wanting somebody to hold my hand.

I took off my suit jacket, patted the pockets for a cigarette, and realized I couldn't smoke here. Somebody would smell it. Somebody would come running, a priest, one of the parishioners, or the killer.

I stopped in front of one of the massive vaults. Thomas Eckert's red-brick vault had heavy iron doors that were surprisingly easy to open. I went inside; it was like a small apartment with its elegant electric lamps and the desk and a chair, all as if Mr Eckert had intended to continue working in the afterlife. You could hide here. You could stay here. Plenty of air came through the cracks in the ancient walls.

After that I covered the rest of the underground, and found nothing at all except the dead. I went back upstairs.

A high wall that bordered Prince Street surrounded the cemetery. It was cold. I put on my jacket and felt in the pocket. I was half dead with fatigue and I found a couple of Benzedrine I had stolen from Nancy's medicine cabinet. There was a water fountain near the side of the cemetery.

In the early days of the nineteenth century, when the church was built, this had been a graveyard for bishops and for the nobs and social elite; later it was a burial ground for immigrant families. I tried to sit against a headstone, but it didn't provide much cover.

Panicky now, I began to wonder if I'd got it wrong. If Rush O'Neill had lied to Nancy, or Nancy to me. Maybe it was St Patrick's on Fifth Avenue that was the location for this assassination. Maybe it was another church. Or no church at all. I kept myself alert as best I could, jogging in place, at least until the drugs kicked in.

Who will believe us? Max had been right. I couldn't name a victim. Even if I called my uncle and asked for help, and he called somebody he trusted, and while they heard my story—if they believed it at all—and discussed it with other officers, the assassin would get into the church and kill his target.

The drugs took hold. I was wired. My brain started doing overtime. It had been planned like this, planned for the day after the missile crisis had ended, and nobody was paying attention anymore. Already there were fewer cops on the street. Maybe the assassination had been scheduled for the 28th, maybe it had. But what was to keep them, whoever they were, from changing the date? October 28th was only some cockamamie date when Columbus apparently discovered Cuba, but these people, these Commies, or whoever they were, they were smart and they were good. Why not change it? Why not guess somebody might find out and change the date? Why not wait until nobody was paying attention at all? Maybe it was us. Maybe we had the date figured wrong, the wrong day. I had to hold on. I had to stick around another day, two more. It was all I knew.

What an imbecilic dope I had been. I went into the church and sat on a pew at the very back.

Maybe it was a decision fuelled by the drugs that had me wired, but suddenly I felt invincible. From where I sat I could see everything, except the organ loft, which was over my head. Still, I could see the stairs that led to it. There was no other way up.

I checked my gun. I had a knife too, but I was lousy with knives.

It was the longest night I had ever known. I tried to sleep. All the time, snapshots flipped through my head, and they were all of Nancy. I took the last pill I had and swallowed it dry.

CHAPTER FOUR

October 29, '62

DARK GRAY OVERCOAT HANGING loose, the man who had left earlier through the Mulberry Street door reappeared. Medium height, dark hair, upright bearing. Something familiar. Who was he? He was in a pew near the altar, and then he rose and started in my direction.

I ducked into a confessional and held the door ajar. Through the narrow slit, I could just make out what he was wearing under his coat. I thought he saw me because he hurriedly buttoned it, maybe to hide the uniform.

When he started towards the stairs for the organ loft, I crept out of the confessional and stayed low to the ground. I saw his face clearly. Stanley Miller was moving through the church quietly, swiftly, one hand in his pocket, feeling for a gun, or a knife, I thought.

Muriel Miller had been in the church the day before. Had she been preparing for this? Did she know? My God, I remembered, I remembered. In Edward Forrester's photograph, he had been the fourth man, a young soldier posing with Forrester, Rush O'Neill and Homer Logan. All of them devoted to their commander, Curtis LeMay.

I had met Miller only once, that night at dinner at his apartment on 10th Street. I had not made the connection when I saw Forrester's snapshots.

Stan Miller, the meekest of them all: the advertising man who went to Yankees games and washed his white Olds on weekends was the killer. *The only time he feels good is after those get togethers with his military buddies.* Muriel had said it to me that night.

It was Miller who had invited a Soviet student to stay with him. Not any student. Max Ostalsky. Ostalsky, whose uncle was a general, disaffected, furious with the current leaders, wanting war, wanting confrontation. And Forrester, who ferried back and forth between the US and the Soviet Union, was the messenger. Was it possible? That this provocation had been put in place by both sides? Was this the thing Ostalsky had tried to tell me?

Suddenly, Miller seemed to change his mind. He did not climb to the organ loft. He turned sharply and went back towards the altar, slid into a pew and onto his knees.

Intent on his prayers, for a Jew Miller seemed to know exactly what he was doing in a church. Anyone coming in would take him for a local who had stopped by before work.

I waited. I needed proof. I had to know what he was planning. So I waited. I waited while Miller prayed and the sunlight coming in grew brighter, and at 7.30 a.m., I saw somebody prop open the front door to the church, Mott Street side.

Crab-like, unwilling to stand up and make myself a target, I got as close to it as I could manage. From outside came the sound of cars. Cars arriving. Voices. Again I moved closer. At the curb were two black limousines. Beside one of them was Father Sean. With him was the Monsignor.

Father Sean opened the back door. A handsome woman in a bright blue hat emerged. She was familiar, of course. The photographs I had seen flooded my brain. It was Mrs Kennedy. Rose Kennedy. The President's mother. And then, quickly, a grin on his face, her son Bobby popped out of the car and put his arm around her.

"Thank you," he said to the bishop. "This is nice, having this time alone. My mother had planned it for so long, and it seems we were unable to keep the original date, which as you know was yesterday," added Bobby in that particular familiar Boston accent. "You know I've always liked this church. Shall we go in?"

CHAPTER FIVE

October 29, '62

BOBBY KENNEDY.

For a second I was paralyzed. If I went outside to stop the Kennedys coming in, Miller would be free to come up behind us, to shoot me, and to shoot Bobby. Bobby was the target.

My head cleared, but he was already inside the church, making his way down the aisle with his mother, the priests keeping pace with them. The only way I could stop it was to get Miller. Get to him fast. Do what I could. Shoot him. Kill him. Strangle him. Anything to stop this. Stop it, I thought. Stop.

I saw Miller when he slipped behind the canvas tarps, under the scaffolding. He was trapped. Could I take him there? Quietly as I could, but fast, I moved along the church wall, staying flat against it, feeling the cold stone, making my way towards the scaffolding where Miller was hidden.

Mrs Kennedy was seated towards the back with the the Monsignor. But Bobby was walking, looking up at the vaulted ceiling, inspecting the old church, humming to himself. I heard him humming. I thought I heard it. Christ. If they got Bobby... I didn't think any more. When he was halfway down the church Bobby genuflected and slipped into a pew and knelt down to pray.

How much time did I have?

Sweat poured off me. I was high on the Benzedrine now; high and very sharp. And I made it to the scaffolding, yanked back the canvas tarp, and crawled under it. Bobby Kennedy's head had been down. Praying. He had not seen me.

Miller wasn't there. Where the hell was he? He had slipped away. Christ, I thought, where is he? Is he in the organ loft after all? The sacristy? Had I missed a sniper rifle he had hidden?

The noise came from close by. Gunfire? A car backfiring? Nobody in the church seemed to have heard it. I turned around and I knew. The sound had come from somewhere near the Mulberry Street exit.

In the narrow corridor between the church and the exit door, Stanley Miller lay on the floor, gun in his hand. I lunged at him, I began punching him, I was losing it when I heard a familiar voice. "He's dead, Pat. It's over," said Max, kneeling down next to me. "It's over."

CHAPTER SIX

October 30, '62

WHEN I WOKE UP at Uncle Jack's the next morning, I felt rotten. My Auntie Clara brought some breakfast and said I had passed out the night before. The Benzedrine, the lack of sleep, had done for me. "There was a letter through the door for you," she said, and I knew that Max Ostalsky must have slipped the letter through the mailbox at the house on Mott Street.

Dear Pat,

I think I knew it would be Robert Kennedy for a while. I think I had guessed. People had said he was without Secret Service protection, and I found that alarming, but it was a clue that seemed to point to him as an easy target.

I am glad he is well. I saw an item on a local program showing him and his mother leaving Old St Pat's.

Don't ask too many more questions, my dear friend, Pat. I did what was necessary. There are times when the end justifies the means. Sometimes we do what we must.

I lay in bed and tried to understand.

Pat, all of this goes back a long time, a year and a half perhaps, even more. What I had understood finally was something my father would have known much sooner. In my country, there are people who hate Khrushchev, but how they hate him. Such hatred. The old Soviet leadership absolutely hates Khrushchev because of the de-Stalinization he initiated. They tried to take him down before, in 1957—but this is perhaps too much detail—these men who were Molotov, Malenkov and Kaganovich—and they failed. He kicked them out. My uncle was one of them. During Stalin he was an important general, he was happy, he had power, and a beautiful wife. Then he was nothing.

These guys are chess players, right? So they begin to plan. They want Stalin back, and if they can't have him, they'll put one of their own in place. They must have seen that to eliminate Khrushchev in normal ways, in other words by assassination, would not work. The people like this leader. Khrushchev adores Castro and calls him a little brother.

The men like my uncle, they say something like "So, Comrade, why don't we propose that you send some weapons to our little brother, Castro, and that will show the United States we mean business. They will stop bullying us in Berlin. They will stop showing off. We will put missiles on their doorstep, and we will do it in secret, and then you, Comrade, will go to Havana and ride in a parade and announce that you are the great protector of little Cuba."

Of course, Castro and the others were thrilled at the offer. They must have jumped up and down. But it was necessary that the Americans not spot the missile sites before this great parade.

But the men like my uncle, something the Americans did not know, and neither did most of the Politburo have, what would you say, a further plan in mind. They would provoke a war. The nuclear weapons would be in Cuba. The Americans would find out. A war would begin. These Soviets, who now had the biggest bomb, the Tsar Bomb, were deluded into thinking they had more power than the Americans, when in truth we had much less. What we had was propaganda. We had some operatives like Bounine who turned out to be useless, and Irina Rishkova at the United Nations who delivered messages between the Soviets and some of your people. Our four friends who revered General LeMay.

You see, the Stalinists had a great ally in the USA. There were generals who shared their views in a sense. Generals like Curtis LeMay. Edward Forrester was the liaison, for he knew his way around several intelligence agencies. Rushton O'Neill was his comrade from the war, and would do anything for him. Captain Logan's job was to cover up Rica Valdes' murder. Also, his hero, Bobby Kennedy had betrayed him.

I imagine each side thought it worth cooperating up to the moment for the pre-emptive strike, and each felt their side would get to it first. Poor little Cuba. We armed Cuba. We told them to stand up for themselves. They were like the first little ship in a convoy, where the weapons would be tested.

As for Stanley Miller, he was, I think, quite crazy. I knew there was something about him that was wrong. This day the assassination was planned, I went to the Millers. I waited, I followed them to the church.

I think that Muriel helped. She loved Miller and pitied him. Me? I just was handy. My uncle, the General, had urged certain of my superiors to send me to New York when that scholarship became available. There was no plan for me then, not at all. My uncle simply considered it useful to have a member of the family in place in the United States, and his contacts in the US suggested the Millers would be the right kind of hosts for a university exchange student.

Please let the police know they will find a body in the mortuary crypts below the church in the tomb of Thomas Eckhert. Say anything you like. Say he is a bum. A drunk. A dope fiend. He will be identified properly soon enough.

Please say goodbye to my friends. Anything in my room that you would like to keep, you're welcome to. Take care of Nancy. I hope some day to come back to New York, and to Greenwich Village, the most wonderful place I have ever been. Goodbye to you, too, Pat, my friend.

I put down the letter. I never saw Max Ostalsky again. I never knew what had happened to him. I made sure that young Jim Garrity received the call about a body in Old St Pat's mortuary crypt. They found a man with his throat neatly cut. It was noted by forensics that it was a very professional job. There was no identification on him.

Not long after the body was discovered at Old St Pat's, it was reported that Stanley Miller was missing. I knew the cops who put it together—the missing man, the body in the mortuary crypt. But nobody could identify the killer. A nephew claimed the body and buried it. Eventually Miller's file went over to Cold Cases; his wife Muriel left New York for France, and I was pretty sure she had been involved. That she had done it for Stanley, as Max had said.

The next year, JFK was murdered, and five years later, his younger brother. Whatever Bobby knew about that day or about the young Soviet who had saved his life died with him. There were no records of the incident in the church on Mott Street.

New York City, 2012

AFTER NANCY PASSED, I found copies of Max Ostalsky's notebooks and his unsent letters among her things. They were photocopies in a locked light-blue Samsonite train case, the kind girls used back in the day, hidden in a closet on Hudson Street where Nancy had kept her paints. I never knew if she had taken those from his room, or if he had given them to her.

We had moved to Sag Harbor; I got a law degree and became a small-town lawyer. Nancy, who had become a pretty good painter, sometimes worked at my old apartment when she was in town teaching her course on art at NYU. I never gave the place up.

When she died, I decided to clean it out, maybe spend some time there now that I was on my own and while I could still get around pretty good. I'd maybe hang around the Village, and watch football with the other old guys on Sunday at the White Horse.

It was one of the few old places left, now that even the West Village, Hudson Street, Greenwich Street, where the tenements and warehouses had been, were inhabited by rich people and movie stars, and brats from NYU. Most everything was gone.

The old waterfront was full of high-rise apartments and yuppies on thousand-dollar bikes. All fixed up now, Pier 46 was populated by people who read the *New York Times*. The High Line has become the fanciest damn park you ever saw. Nice, though. I go up and hang around some of the time.

Nancy and me, after we got married in '63, we didn't mention Max Ostalsky much. When her father Saul died of cancer the following year, she told me everything about the FBI.

"I made a deal with the devil," she said.

She had tried to spare her father when he was dying, to make his time easy. Anyway, I loved her. I always remembered Max telling me it didn't matter to him if Nancy had worked for the FBI. He loved her. That was all that mattered. We had a good life.

Some time in the early 90s, I think, I got a call from Jim Garrity who had become an enterprising detective and had, from time to time, taken up the case of Stanley Miller's murder. He contacted me. Something had been on my mind, on and off, and I offered Jim a deal if he agreed to keep mum about it. Sure, he said. Surely, Pat. I told him some of what I knew about Miller, although I left out the business about Bobby Kennedy; the information would have changed history and there was no reason, not now. In return, I asked him to get hold of Rica Valdes' stuff; his clothes had been stored in a plastic bag somewhere downtown. DNA matches had been perfected. I gave Jim those Russian puzzle dolls Max had given me, and asked him if he could match the DNA on it with that on Valdes' clothes and a cross that had been found around his neck.

There was a match, of course. There was more than one. The prints on the dolls belonged to the man who shot and killed Valdes; the other prints on the cross, the clothes, to somebody who cut out his tongue and sliced up his face. I was relieved it wasn't Max who had butchered him. Probably Bounine, I figured.

I guess I had always known that Max had killed Valdes; if he had not followed orders, they would have eliminated him, and he would never have been allowed to go home to Moscow. He was a good man, but he was loyal to his country; I would have done the same thing.

And that was it. Nancy and me, we never talked about it much at all. I never told how some of her actions almost caused the murder of Bobby Kennedy, whom she later came to believe would redeem America. In 1968, she sold Saul's house on Charlton Street, gave the money to Bobby's campaign, and worked her heart out for his election. When he was murdered, she was inconsolable.

On my own, I tried to find out what had happened to Max, but the Soviet Consulate had nothing to say. I always wondered. When the USSR went out of business in '91, I made a few inquiries, I read what I could, but, even in the tsunami of information and memoirs and articles that surged out of that now disappeared country: nothing at all. Everything passes.

Fifty years. And then, just around the anniversary of the missile crisis, when every damn station was showing old news reports, I got a call. A detective, who introduced himself as Artie Cohen, asked if we could meet. I said I'd be at the White Horse.

When he walked through the door, the minute I saw him, I knew he was Max Ostalsky's son. Although he was older than Max when I had known him, he was a dead ringer for his dad: tall, dark-haired, with the same blue eyes as his father, the same handsome, humorous face.

"Artie Cohen," he said, and shook my hand. "My Russian name was Artemy Ostalsky." He said he had received photocopies of his father's notebooks. A Russian official had given them to him, a guy name of Bounine, he said.

"Bounine?"

"Yes. In America he called himself Mike."

"He's alive?"

"Until last year, yes. He had a long career with the KGB."

"Tell me about Max."

"In the notebooks, my pop mentions a detective called Pat, but the officials have blacked out the last name with a felt-tip pen, and much else. I couldn't read it," said Cohen. "There were too many Pats on the force to figure it out, that's why I never got in touch before. Then I saw your wife's obituary, her name, your name, and it came together. You were friends."

"Yes," I said, and ordered some beers. "Is your mother named Nina?"

"Yes."

"How is she?"

"Very old. And sick. She doesn't even know who I am."

I took a deep breath and asked. "And Max? Your dad?"

I guess I had been hoping that somehow we could get together, two old guys shooting the breeze about another time, and things only we knew and understood. Until I saw his boy, Artie, I had never realized how deep the longing was.

"He died in Israel after we emigrated from Russia," said Artie. "He got on the wrong bus, and somebody set off a bomb. A long time ago."

"I'm sorry."

"I used to ask him about his time in New York. I knew he loved it, but he never talked about it. All he ever told me was that he had had a friend in New York, and when he returned to Moscow a few months before I was born, he had decided to name me for him. You see, I couldn't find anyone called Arthur or Artie or Art. In your wife's obituary it had your name as Patrick Arthur Wynne."

"My second name. My ma loved Artie Shaw."

"I see."

"Did you know your pop loved jazz? He loved it when he heard it played live in the little clubs around the Village, he said it changed him. Funny, I used to try to get him into rock 'n roll, and he was always willing, to please me, I think. He said music made him better, and that Greenwich Village made him better, too."

"I know," said Cohen.

"I never even knew if he made it back to Moscow. You say he went back because he got a letter your mother was pregnant?"

"Yes, and for his career. He was always a loyal man. He loved his country."

"How long have you been in New York," I asked.

"Almost thirty years," said Cohen.

My eyes filled with tears for so many years lost. "Is there more? About your dad?"

"It's a long story," he said.

"I have plenty of time."

Acknowledgments

Manhattan '62 is mostly a work of fiction, but there are a few books that I have drawn on for historical information and cultural insights, and I would like to mention them here:

Michael Dobbs' *One Minute to Midnight* is simply the best book I've ever read on the Cuban Missile Crisis, immensely informative, wonderfully detailed, historically revealing, a gripping read and beautifully written.

The First Directorate: My 32 Years in Intelligence and Espionage Against the West by Oleg Kalugin.

Parting with Illusions by Vladimir Pozner

'Collector's Item', an essay by Joseph Brodsky in the collection *Grief and Reason*.

On the 1960s:

Days of Hope Days of Rage by Todd Gitlin.
Awaiting Armageddon by Alice L. George.
331/3 Live at the Apollo by Douglas Wolk.

For their recollections of those years in Greenwich Village and New York, thanks to: Jane Doyle, Tom Doyle, Marty and Lynne Hectman, Alan Herman, Helena Kennedy, Paul Solman and Steven Zwerling; and for his memories of the Apollo and James Brown, Billy Mitchell, the Apollo Theater historian.

A few friends have provided company on trips to and great insights into the USSR, missiles to music: Artemy Troitsky, Svetlana Kunetsina, Leslie Woodhead and the late Jo Durden-Smith.

And for support of so many kinds, personal and professional: Barbara Edelstein, James Weichert, Salman Rushdie and Frank Wynne.